Saving Grace

J. M. Hill

Saving Grace
Book One of
The Grace Series

ISBN-10: 1480102482
ISBN-13: 978-1480102484

Dedication

For my husband, who after twenty-one years of marriage continues to be the voice of encouragement, and more often than not, the voice of reason. You still make my heart flutter.

And for my mom. Any amount of writing ability I possess comes from you. You are the wisest, most talented woman I know.

Acknowledgments

An enormous amount of thanks and love goes to:

Mom and Dad for a lifetime of love and sacrifice.

My amazing kids, Taylor, Connor, Madison, Hayden and Chase, for constantly saying: "You go, Mom! You can do it!"

My brothers, Rodger, Russell and Joe David, whose many wonderful and funny qualities are reflected in each of the Anderson brothers. Joe David, I miss you every day.

My dear friends, Ruth Tesh and Beth Driscoll, who became my very own personal cheerleaders. Your energetic support of Grace, Kate and the Andersons, means more than you'll ever know. I love you both, and your friendship is valued beyond words.

The Bill Bray Writers Group of Winston-Salem, especially Anderson, Sue, Bill, and Dan, who patiently assisted in honing my writing skills with kind words and encouragement. C.J. Graves, Super-Writing-Ninja, and Moderator Extraordinaire. Your wisdom in all things literary has been a gift, and your friendship an unexpected blessing. Thank you for all your help, even when I whined.

A HEAP of thanks to Sarah Hansen with Okay Creations for the gorgeous cover. I'm so thankful for you and your creativity. You make me laugh. I heart you big. That is all.
okaycreations.net

Lori Sabin, your kind heart and lovely spirit has been a light. Your help with the fine-tuning of this book is so greatly appreciated. Tarryn Fisher, because of you, I met Lori, and for this I am truly thankful. You're both beautiful and I couldn't adore you more.

Danielle Van Zyl, my beautiful, South African friend. Grace, Michael, Garrett, Miles and Kate brought us together. Your kindness and generosity blesses my heart on a daily basis. One day, we will meet in person and I can hardly wait to hug your neck.

Sweet Melissa Dunn. Your thoughtfulness surpasses most. You're amazing, and I love you.

And finally, my husband, for the nights the light of my laptop woke you while I worked on this project in the wee-hours, but you never complained. Not even once.

Prologue

My hands shook as I opened the door. Cold air hit me like a brick wall, stinging my skin through my sweats and tee shirt. The wind whistled loudly through the trees, and sharp rocks dug into my bare feet as I made my way across the gravel drive. My legs felt heavy as I climbed the steps of the Anderson's front porch.

When I reached the door my eyes blurred. I rubbed them roughly with the palms of my hands and pushed the door all the way open.

"Garrett?" I slowly made my way through the entry and cleared my throat before calling his name again. "Are you okay?"

The house was eerily quiet. A single lamp lit the living room, the rest of the house dark. I looked around, feeling a little dizzy, alight sheen of sweat forming on my forehead.

My voice shook with fear. "It's-it's Gracie." A sob pushed against my throat because something was wrong. I could feel it.

A light came on in Garrett's bedroom, shining dimly in the darkened hallway, and my breath hitched.

"Garrett?"

Nausea and panic took over as I walked slowly toward the bedroom, dreading painfully what I was going to find. I wrung my hands together anxiously as I looked around the door into his room.

Garrett was asleep. Sprawled across the bed on his stomach, the blankets in a tangle around his legs. The wide, dimpled grin on his face made me sigh in relief. I walked to his nightstand to turn off the lamp, when I felt something cold and damp beneath my feet.

Confused, I looked closely. Garrett's arm was draped off the side of the bed and something dripped from his hand. I reached out to touch him. His fingers were cold, but his palms were warm and wet.

Trembling, I turned his hand over. His palm was covered with blood. Then I noticed his face.

Even with the grin, his lips were a sickly shade of blue, his face an icy gray. I reached up to touch him with my fingertips, and he was so cold.

Tears came. "Please, Garrett. Please don't do this. Open your eyes. Please."

My heart raced as I quickly pulled the covers away from his hulking figure. The sheets were nothing more than a pool of Garrett's blood. It felt like something heavy pressed on my chest as I backed out of his room slowly, my breaths short and shallow.

I knew he was dead.

And I knew she had killed him.

"When the cloud in the sky starts to pour and your life is just a storm you're braving.
Well, don't tell yourself you can't lean on someone else, 'cause we all need saving sometimes."

~ Jon McLaughlin

Chapter One

I felt ridiculous, but this didn't keep me from watching the house across the street. Through the slant of the wooden blinds at our front window I peered, hoping to see someone. Usually I'm not the nosey type, but the excitement and anticipation of new neighbors had me so curious, I was spying through the blinds like Lucy or Ethel.

This morning a huge moving truck parked in the middle of our semi-private drive for over five hours, while a crew of six burly men in ugly gray jumpsuits unloaded furniture for the new residents. Residents I had yet to see. On the bright side, however, I was able to take inventory of some rather impressive furnishings. This satiated my newly discovered voyeuristic tendencies, to some extent.

My cousin, Kate, and I lived here our entire lives and shared the private drive with only one other house. The old Jenkins' place. It stood empty for over ten years, until about four months ago. A construction crew appeared one day and began working non-stop, refurbishing the dilapidated house that was somewhat of an eyesore. The once sad, depressing, two-story, red brick dwelling was transformed into a much more pleasant sight. A new porch with a black, wrought iron railing stretched across the front, black shutters framed tall, paned windows, and a massive garage extended from the right side of the house big enough to contain several vehicles.

We're a little pessimistic about new neighbors and very curious.

The shrill ring of the phone made me jump, and I sprinted to the kitchen, knowing it would be Kate.

"Hey, Gracie!" Kate's voice chirped on the other end of the line, barely stopping to take a breath. "I'm on my way home, are you ready to watch the game? Are you hungry? I've got Mario's."

"The game's on, and I'm starving."

"Anything new going on across the street, Ethel?"

"Nothing whatsoever, Lucy," I replied. "And why am *I* Ethel?"

She sniggered. "See you in a minute."

Shamelessly, I returned to the front window to peek through the blinds again. Still nothing. I'd been disgracefully lazy all day, so I went to the laundry room to start a load of dirty clothes, then to the kitchen to get plates and drinks on the table. When Kate came through the front door, she balanced a pizza box with one hand, and a container of salad with the other. We sat down and I dished the salad while Kate opened her soda, eyeing me expectantly.

"So what did you do today?" she asked, knowing exactly what I'd done.

"Nothing really. Although, I did just put a load of laundry in the washer, so I guess that's something."

"Mm-hmm," she hummed. "And you did surveillance on the house across the street." She took a sip of her soda and attempted casual, but she was just as eager to see who was moving into that house as I was, and I knew it. She tapped a steady rhythm against her plate with the fork, but I pretended to be oblivious. When dinner was finished, we retreated to the sofa to watch the Yankees game—already in the bottom of the fifth—and after a moment Kate heaved an exasperated sigh.

"So?"

"What?" I asked innocently, and she glared at me with irritation.

"So…you haven't told me what you observed today." Her head tilted in the direction of the house I'd been watching for most of the day. "Come on, I need details!" She was whining now. "What kind of furniture do they have?"

Deciding to end her torture, I began my surveillance briefing. "Typical bachelor furnishings. Lots of leather and dark wood. Pretty expensive stuff. Oh, a drafting table and a couple of desks. I figure they're setting up a home office."

"I heard they run their own design firm," Kate interjected. "But you haven't seen anyone?"

"Nope."

"Well, whoever they are, I hope they're friendly."She'd barely finished her sentence when we heard the low rumble of a car engine come up the drive. Kate's eyes widened with excitement, and I'm sure I mirrored her expression. In a flash, we were both off the couch, peeking through the blinds. Lucy and Ethel.

Three vehicles pulled single file into the over-sized driveway and parked inside the garage, side by side. Kate and I know little about cars. We bought a new Jeep last year, and the only reason we chose that particular vehicle was because we'd seen one in a movie and thought it was cool. Kate insisted it be red because according to her, we both looked great in red. Car aficionados we're not. However, these cars were easily identified. The first: a colossal, silver Hummer. The second: a shiny, black Yukon Denali. The third: a deep, blue Audi.

We watched with anticipation as two men exited the Hummer and the Audi, strolled to the middle of the driveway and scanned the area. It was obvious they were brothers. They were also quite good-looking. Kate and I looked at each other with shocked expressions and turned back to the window again.

The driver of the Hummer was huge. I mean, professional-wrestler-scary huge. At *least* six-foot-six, at *least*. His dark hair was wavy and hung in short, loose curls. I noticed he laughed a lot—a loud, booming laugh that made his whole body shake. There were also dimples embedded on both sides of his mouth, so big they made me grin. The faded John Elway jersey he wore caught my eye. I had an identical jersey in my closet, waiting for football season.

"A Broncos fan," I said, voicing my approval.

Kate giggled. "Excellent."

The driver of the Audi was nearly as tall as the Broncos fan, but probably more like six-four and dressed impeccably in a snug, black pullover that displayed a nice physique. He resembled the big guy in an amazing way. Same dimples, but his dark curls were cropped much shorter.

"Twins?" I wondered aloud.

"Possibly," Kate responded thoughtfully. "He's adorable."

I laughed. "Which one?"

"I'm referring to black-pullover-guy."

"No argument there," I said.

The third man emerged from the Yukon then, one hand shoved inside the pocket of his faded jeans, the other raked through his hair as he joined the other two at the center of their driveway.

A strange knot formed in the pit of my stomach.

Not as tall as the first two, he stood about six-two, his hair a rich shade of brown with no curl or wave at all. It was tousled and messy, with a small section that kept falling over his forehead just to be pushed back with another rake of his hand. He resembled a model from the glossy pages of *GQ*, exuding sexiness and something else I couldn't quite pinpoint.

The three continued their discussion, then in a synchronized motion turned to face our house. The big guy said something that made the other two laugh. After a moment they stopped laughing and focused intently on our window.

"Crap!" Kate threw herself against the side wall in an effort to hide. "Do they see us?"

I didn't care. I couldn't take my eyes off the third one, who shrugged out of a black leather jacket revealing a lean, muscular build. He was truly stunning.

"Get away from the window!" Kate whispered frantically as if they could hear. "I think they see us!"

I ignored her and watched them walk single-file into their house. Kate slid down the wall to the floor, grasping at her chest dramatically as if having a heart attack. Once their front door closed, I stepped away from the window and stood over her holding out my hand.

"These guys must be models, or actors, or something," she said, taking my hand and pulling herself upright.

I only shrugged, still a little stunned. Kate hooked her arm with mine, and we walked to the couch, flopping down next to each other. We sat in silence for a short moment, then at the same time looked at each other and laughed giddily.

Once we caught our breath, I tried to be serious. "Well, we have to be realistic here. There's no way these guys aren't attached to someone. I mean, they're just too…pretty."

"You're probably right," Kate agreed with a sigh. "But if nothing else, they'll give us something nice to look at every day, right?"

I definitely couldn't argue that point.

* * *

My alarm went off at seven o'clock as usual, and as usual, I cursed it to eternal damnation as I reached over to turn it off. I hated running on Sundays but made myself do it anyway. I rolled out of bed and went into my bathroom to wash my face and brush my teeth. I dressed in my running gear, smoothed my hair into a ponytail and grabbed my running shoes and iPod.

While I sat on the front porch and pulled on my shoes, I couldn't help but glance at the neighbor's house, curious about the new occupants. As I made my way to the gravel drive, I chose the playlist for my run and started a slow jog.

Though Kate and I are alike in many ways, running is where the similarities end. I've always loved running, while Kate thinks of the activity as a slow kind of torture. Of course, Kate doesn't need to run either. She burns enough calories just being Kate. Most of the time, she reminds me of a hummingbird trapped in a shoebox—always doing everything at a high-rate of speed, with endless amounts of energy.

"So What" blared in my ears, and I sang and danced, louder and with much more enthusiasm than was necessary, while I ran. I could never help myself when I heard this song, it always made me smile and dance, even while running. Solitary runs seemed to bring out my inner dancing-diva.

When I turned at my three-mile marker, I spotted him. Navy running pants, gray "NYU" sweatshirt, hair in a sexy state of frenzy, an amused grin on his face, less than twenty feet away, jogging toward me. I felt all the color drain from my face as I realized he'd been running behind me for the last three miles, witnessing my overly energetic love for all things musical.

I stopped singing. I may never sing again.

He got closer, not changing his pace. The closer he got, the wider his grin became and the more nervous I became. With effort, I managed to put a large amount of space between us, nodding politely as we passed each other, and before I could help myself, I glanced over my shoulder at his retreating figure. At that moment he did the same. I snapped my head around so quickly I think I gave myself whiplash. Ouch.

Now, on top of everything else, I was just caught ogling and my neck hurt.

When I walked into the house, Kate was at the kitchen table sipping coffee, reading the newspaper in her fluffy pink robe and fuzzy pink slippers that made her feet look much larger than they were. I poured my coffee, adding the necessary sweetener and cream and sat across from her. She slid the sports page across the table for me, and I opened it up right away, looking for MLB scores.

"Pettitte is pitching today, two o'clock," she informed me, preoccupied with some article she was reading. "We have time to get breakfast and do our grocery shopping."

I took a long sip of coffee. "You'll never guess what happened on my run today."

"Did you save Muffin again?" she asked, sounding bored.

Our elderly neighbor, Miss Whitt, lived two miles down the

main road and owned approximately twenty cats, including Muffin. Of all those cats, Muffin was the only one who managed to constantly get stuck in trees, and I managed to be the one to constantly save him. I don't even like cats that much. I also think his name is stupid.

"One of these days, you're going to fall out of a tree and break your neck," she continued without looking up from the paper.

"No, I didn't save Muffin again," I said. "But I did see one of the new neighbors. You know, the good-looking one?"

She snorted a laugh. "They're all good-looking."

"Okay, good point," I said. "But, I'm referring to the one with the brown hair."

"Did he talk to you?"

"No. I didn't really give him a chance." I felt my cheeks redden as I thought about what happened.

Intuition flashed in her eyes, and she giggled. "Dancing again, were you?"

I nodded.

"It was P!nk, right?" she asked.

This time she nodded with me.

"Yep, that song gets you every time," she said. "But, 'So what? I'm still a rock star, I've got my rock moves, and I don't need you'!" She bounced in her chair as she sang the stupid song that was the cause of all my trouble.

"Very funny," I said, irritated. "I just made a total idiot of myself in front of our new neighbor!"

"Relax. It's not a big deal," she said dismissively.

Kate and I had been together our entire lives, and I learned at an early age that very few things rattled her. When we were four years old, our mothers began teaching us piano. After they died, Uncle David arranged to continue our lessons with a teacher from the University, and we excelled at a rapid pace. We loved playing. We played our first recital when we were eight, in the gymnasium at the local high school. Kate had already performed flawlessly, but I cried in the corner of the girls bathroom, terrified of all the people who were going to be watching. She found me and spent ten minutes trying to calm me down by quoting our favorite lines from I Love Lucy, "Hello, Friends, I'm your Vitameatavegamin girl! Do you pop-out at parties? Are you un-poopular?" Because of Kate, I was able to take the stage that night, though she sat on the piano bench beside me while I performed. At twenty-four, not much had changed. She was as unshakable as ever.

"When do you think we should introduce ourselves?" Kate asked, unfazed by my humiliating event.

"I think we'd better wait a while," I replied. "I'm so embarrassed."

"Oh, big deal." Kate said, exasperated. "So he saw you shaking your booty. He probably would've seen it eventually anyway. You dance all the time when you run."

She was right, but it didn't make me feel better. At all.

* * *

Less than seventy-two hours after our neighbors moved in, Kate made an announcement.

"I think we should go over and introduce ourselves. You know, a welcome to the neighborhood type thing?"

Frankly, I was surprised it had taken so long.

"Sure," I agreed. "Or maybe a welcome-to-the-neighborhood-you're-all-incredibly-gorgeous-and-we're-your-incredibly-single-totally-non-stalkerish-neighbors type thing. I wonder if we could fit all of that on a cake?"

She laughed. "No, but we should introduce ourselves and take some kind of housewarming present. You could make some of your homemade bread," she said eagerly. "You can never go wrong with homemade bread."

Truthfully, I didn't need much convincing. I wanted to meet them, too, despite my recent humiliation. I went into the kitchen and pulled an apron over my head. I did make good bread.

Kate clapped happily, strode to the stereo to turn on music, and we got busy. While the dough was rising, we decided to mix together a batch of Kate's chocolate chip cookies. After discussing the size of the big guy, we figured bread by itself wouldn't be enough.

I brushed the warm, golden brown loaves with melted butter and set them in a basket lined with a white tea towel. We put Kate's cookies on a plate, covered them with plastic wrap and placed them inside the basket. I also whipped up some cinnamon butter—a necessary accompaniment for homemade bread—while Kate slid a gift card for our shop between the cookies and bread. We went to my bathroom to check our hair and wipe any remnants of bread and cookie dough from our face. Kate grabbed the basket; we took a deep breath and walked across the drive to meet the new neighbors.

Chapter Two

We climbed the steps slowly to the Anderson's front door. Well, *I* climbed slowly, Kate kind of skipped. She pulled me next to her and smiled encouragingly as she rang the doorbell. The door opened, and the big guy stood there with a huge grin on his face—dimples and all—as he looked at Kate first, then me.

"Hey there, neighbors!" His voice was loud, and I know my eyes widened when I saw how huge he actually was, because he was…*huge*.

"Hi. I'm Kate Donovan." Kate stretched out her hand, and he shook it enthusiastically. "This is my cousin, Grace Burke."

"Hi there, Grace." His giant hand shook mine gently, but with the same enthusiasm. "I'm Garrett Anderson. Do I smell bread?"

Kate and I both stifled a laugh. You can never go wrong with homemade bread.

"Yes, actually you do." Kate held the basket out in front of her. Garrett took it and brought it closer to his face, inhaling the aroma wafting from the bread. Just when I thought his smile couldn't get any bigger, it did.

"Homemade? Are you kidding me?" His eyes widened with what I recognized as food-elation. Kate and I often had a very similar reaction over Haagen-Dazs or cheesecake.

"Gracie makes excellent bread, and she does it from scratch," Kate bragged. I nudged her with my elbow, but she continued. "We don't want to intrude, we just wanted to introduce ourselves."

"You're not intruding at all. C'mon in." He stepped to the side, and Kate pulled me through the doorway.

"Hey, Miles! Michael! We have company!" Garrett hollered from behind me, making me flinch. I turned to look at him, and he winked as he shoved an entire cookie in his mouth. I had to laugh. This guy was massive and surprisingly un-scary. I liked him already.

We followed Garrett inside, and I was impressed at how orderly their house seemed to be, especially for three guys. There was a staircase in the foyer to the right of the front door, leading to a loft that opened to the living room below. The layout of the main level was very similar to ours. The modern kitchen opened to the living room, with a large breakfast bar surrounded by sturdy leather barstools. Tall windows made up most of the wall in the kitchen and eating area. To the right of the kitchen a hallway ran along the back of the house, which I assumed led to the bedrooms.

The walls were white with dark stained crown molding that matched the hardwood floors. Their furniture was rich, dark brown leathers and woods, and thick rugs in neutral colors accented areas of the floor. There were several, large black and white framed pictures of land and seascapes that decorated the walls, as well as built-in shelves full of books, CDs, a very intimidating stereo system and family photographs. A plasma television was mounted over the fire-place. There were hardly any accessories. Everything simple, clean and masculine.

As Garrett led us into the living room, we were met by the 'adorable one', and I was pretty sure that should be his name.

"Miles, this is Kate and Grace," Garrett said, as he pushed yet another cookie into his mouth. "And they brought food."

Miles shook his head at his brother and then smiled kindly at us. "It's wonderful to meet you both." He put his hand out to me, and then to Kate. His gaze fixed on her as they shook hands, and she smiled her sparkly-Kate-smile at him.

"And how did you know to bring food for him?" Miles tilted his head toward Garrett, who sat on the sofa studying the gift card with his mouth full.

"Lucky guess?" Kate said with a giggle, and Miles watched her intently for a moment and then motioned for us to sit on the sofa.

"The Open Book Café?" Garrett asked, turning the gift card over.

"That's our shop in town," Kate explained. "It's a bookstore and coffee shop."

"Excellent." Garrett said excitedly. Clearly, he was easily pleased.

"I've actually been in there," Miles said to Kate. "You two own that place?"

Kate nodded with a smile.

"You have great coffee," he said.

I couldn't help looking around for the 'stunning one', but he was nowhere to be found. Part of me was relieved—the embarrassment from that morning still fresh in my mind. Garrett pulled the small dish of cinnamon butter from the basket and brought it to his nose.

"What's this?" His nose wrinkled.

"It's cinnamon butter for the bread," I told him. "It's really good when the bread is warm."

He looked at me apprehensively.

"Haven't you ever had cinnamon butter before?" I asked.

He shrugged, and I stood from the couch.

"Shall we?" I asked him, gesturing toward the kitchen. He smiled widely as he picked up the basket, and we walked to the kitchen together, leaving Miles and Kate deep in their own conversation.

"Do you have a breadboard?" I asked.

Garrett scanned the kitchen for a moment, his lips pursed together as if concentrating, then looked down at me with a nonplussed expression. "Okay, I don't even know what that is."

I bit the side of my mouth trying not to laugh. "May I?"

Garrett nodded and watched me with his arms folded across his massive chest. I searched the kitchen for the necessary equipment, finding an unused breadboard and a knife. I spread some of the cinnamon butter onto a warm slice of bread and set it on a plate, sliding it in front of him. Without hesitation, he shoved half of the piece into his mouth and chewed. I waited, anxious for his reaction and wasn't disappointed. His eyes rolled into his head as he slid slowly into one of the barstools, shaking his head.

"Good?" I asked.

"This is the best bread I've ever had. You made this?"

I nodded. "You want another piece?"

"Hell, yeah," he said excitedly and then cleared his throat. "I mean, yeah."

I laughed and fixed him another piece, as he pushed the rest of the slice into his mouth.

"Tomorrow morning, toast the bread and then put on the cinnamon butter. You'll like that even more."

"Okay, I'll trust you." He winked as he finished his second piece. "Thanks."

"You're welcome." I walked back into the living room. Garrett followed, carrying the plate of chocolate chip cookies, sitting next to me on the sofa. Kate and Miles were still deep in conversation as Garrett turned on the TV. Monday Night Football was getting started, and Hank Williams Jr. asked if we were ready for some football. I loved that. The Raiders were taking the field against the Chargers.

"I hope the Chargers kick their tails," I muttered.

Garrett chortled and turned to me with a raised eyebrow. "You like football?"

"Yes, I like football." I'd always felt a little insulted when guys presumed I didn't like sports just because I was female. Garrett seemed entertained by the idea.

He chuckled. "Sorry. Didn't mean to offend you, I just don't know many girls that like sports."

"Well, you know at least two now," I informed him. "Kate and I love football."

"Really?" His tone was dubious, and he grinned smugly. "NFL or college?"

"Both."

"So who do you like?"

"NFL or college?"

He snorted a laugh. "Well, let's start with college and move on from there." His voice was thick with sarcasm, though he tried to look serious. I knew he was challenging me, but I was okay with it. Thanks to Uncle David, Kate and I were able to hold our own in any football discussion.

"Pac-Ten or the SEC?" I asked, settling in for the challenge.

He cocked an eyebrow at me in surprise and shrugged, no longer amused.

"Okay, how about if I start with the Pac-Ten, and...*move on from there*." I raised an eyebrow as I repeated his words. Garrett's eyes narrowed as I began.

"Our family had four generations of USC grads, including our parents, so devotion to the team is in our blood. People say their division is weak, but did you know SC has the most BCS Bowl wins and appearances in their conference? In the past ten years, they've had fifty-six players selected in the NFL draft, thirteen of those players going in the first round? In the last three years alone, an average of nine SC players are chosen per season." I focused my attention on the television casually, as I continued. "As far as the SEC is concerned, I've always liked University of Florida. They look great this season, and I love watching them kick Georgia's tail. Oh, and for the NFL, it's the Broncos, all the way. Win or lose." I smiled in conclusion while Garrett processed everything I'd said. Slowly, a huge grin spread across his face.

"Very nice." His voice was appreciative as he nodded.

"I think you just got told, big brother."

Garrett guffawed as I turned to see the 'stunning one' standing near the sofa in blue jeans and a black t-shirt. His eyes were green, and they held mine as he smiled a crooked, beautiful smile so sexy it was difficult to look away.

I decided 'stunning one' should definitely be his name. Definitely.

"Hi, I'm Michael Anderson."

"I'm Grace Burke." I stood to shake his hand.

"It's nice to meet you." His voice was soft, his hand warm and strong.

"It's...um, nice to meet you, too. This is my cousin, Kate," I said, trying to break whatever kind of crazy, hypnotizing, voodoo spell he'd cast over me. "We're your neighbors."

"Yeah, I know," he said, with an amused grin.

Of course he knew we were neighbors. I flushed with my stupidity. He shook hands with Kate and then studied Garrett for a moment.

"What are you eating?" he asked Garrett.

"Chocolate chip cookies. Why?" Garrett mumbled with his mouth full and tucked the almost-empty plate of cookies into his side protectively, as if afraid that Michael would take them away.

Michael scanned the kitchen. "Do I smell bread?"

"Yep. Grace here made us some homemade bread and these cookies."Garrett pushed another cookie into his mouth.

"Actually, Kate made the cookies," I corrected.

"That was very nice of you," Michael said. "Did my brother eat all the bread, or is there some left?"

Garrett snorted. "No, I didn't eat it all, but you'd better get some while you can because I make no promises. And you need to have Grace fix you up with some of that cinnamon butter. Trust me."

Michael looked at me expectantly. "Cinnamon butter?"

"I made some for the bread," I responded, and turned my focus back to the TV.

"Well, aren't you going to fix *me* up?"

Something about his voice, and the way he looked at me, made me so nervous.

"Sure." I stood from the couch and followed Michael into the kitchen. "Since I was just in here with your brother…do you mind?"

"Go ahead." He nodded with that same grin and sat on a barstool. He watched with his chin resting in his hand as I spread a piece of the bread with cinnamon butter. His expression was impassive as he took a bite of the still-warm bread. He chewed a couple of times, looked at the bread in his hand and back at me. I waited for him to say something, but he just smiled widely and continued chewing again. I took that as a good thing. After a moment his silence became unsettling, so I busied myself with wiping crumbs from the counter, being careful not to drop any on the floor.

"Thanks for the bread," he finally spoke. "You're quite a cook."

I heard a buzzing sound, and he pulled a cell phone from the pocket of his jeans, pressed a button and set it on the counter.

"So, what do you do?" he asked as he continued to enjoy his piece of bread, keeping his eyes on me.

"We—Kate and I—own the coffee shop in town," I replied. "The Open Book Café?"

He nodded with recognition. "Miles and I have been there." One side of his mouth turned up. "Which part do you own? The coffee shop or the bookstore?"

Was he trying not to laugh? I began to worry about smudges on my face or something hanging from my nose. Please, not that.

"We're equal owners, but I take care of the bookstore. I love books."

He leaned back, folding his hands behind his head. "Well then, I'll definitely have to check out the bookstore next time."

"You like to read?" I couldn't help the incredulity in my tone, but he didn't seem like the type to spend free time with his nose in a book.

"You don't think I read?" he asked with a smirk.

I shrugged. "I don't know."

He chuckled quietly, and his phone vibrated again.

"Excuse me," he said politely and pressed the phone to his ear as he disappeared down the hall.

Flustered, I returned to the living room and stood by the arm of the sofa where Garrett was intently watching the game.

"Who's winning?" I asked.

"The Raiders just scored," Garrett grumbled in disdain.

"I hate the Raiders," I muttered in equal disdain. "They're playing the Broncos in two weeks."

"Yeah, I know. Should be a good game," he said. "You gonna watch it?"

I snorted. "Does it snow here?"

Garrett laughed loudly as Michael came into the room wearing the black leather jacket I recognized from the first time I saw him standing in his driveway.

"Where ya goin', little brother?" Garrett asked.

Michael raked his hand through his hair and glanced sideways at me before answering. "I'm meeting Nina," he said. "Grace, it was nice meeting you. Thanks for the bread."

The stab of disappointment I felt surprised me. Why should I be disappointed? I didn't even know him. Besides, he was too pretty to not be with someone.

"You're welcome." I forced a smile and watched him say goodbye to Miles and Kate and then walk out the door.

No doubt *Nina* was just as gorgeous as he was.

"We should go, Gracie," Kate said. "It was great meeting you guys."

Miles and Garrett followed us to the front door.

"Thank you so much for coming over. It was wonderful meeting you both," Miles said, his voice full of sincerity. I knew he was talking to both of us, but he kept his eyes on Kate.

"Remember what I said about the bread in the morning, Garrett," I reminded him.

"I'll remember," he said.

We descended the steps of their porch and glanced at each other sideways. Kate waggled her eyebrows up and down, and I tried not to laugh. Once inside, we both flopped onto the sofa, and Kate gazed up at the ceiling while I turned on the football game.

"Are you okay?" I asked her.

She nodded and closed her eyes. "He's so sweet."

"Garrett?" I teased, knowing she was talking about Miles.

She rolled her eyes. "Miles," she said dreamily.

"He's pretty cute." I nudged her.

"He's just…pretty," she amended.

"Yeah, they're all pretty," I said. "I don't think it's normal for men to be that pretty."

"You were right about Miles and Garrett being twins," she said, ignoring my comment. "They're twenty-six, and Michael is twenty-four."

I nodded, sure she knew more.

"Miles is a Structural Engineer, Michael an Architect and Garrett a Project Manager. Their dad started the business, but he recently retired. They do most of the work from their house now and run the business themselves. Their parents live near the Springs and spend a lot of time traveling." Kate probably got more information in a thirty minute conversation than most people would get in a month.

"They lived in Denver for almost a year and decided they'd had their fill. They're originally from New York." She sighed. "I guess that's all, except, did I say how incredibly sweet Miles is?"

I had to laugh at her dreamy expression. "Yes, you mentioned that part."

There was definitely something different about the Andersons. Garrett was funny, Kate made it clear that Miles was 'sweet' and Michael…well, I couldn't be sure, but he was definitely something.

Chapter Three

The shop was a usual flurry of morning customers when Kate and I arrived. We greeted Kenny, our store manager, and Peggy, a silver-haired grandmother who works for us part time, as we headed to our office. Kate sat at her overly organized desk and started going through paperwork, while I returned to the coffee counter to steam milk for our coffees, weaving between Kenny and Peggy who were busy filling orders. I returned to the office with slices of blueberry bread and our coffees on a tray. This was our morning ritual. We sat at our desks and ate breakfast together in silence while going through mail.

I was checking an invoice for a shipment of books, and Kate giggled.

"What's funny?" I asked.

"I love it when we expect a shipment of books," she said. "You're like a kid at Christmas."

It was true. I loved books and loved that I got to work around them all day. The bookstore was my sanctuary. My happy place. Before he died, Uncle David made sure Kate and I would be financially secure, and the café was his last gift to us. Kate's degree in business made her a force to be reckoned with, and my degree in Literature? Well, I was able to keep the bookstore stocked with the best possible selections.

Our shop is right in the middle of our hometown, Fall Rivers, which is located outside the beautiful mountain community of Boulder, Colorado. Fall Rivers is so small most people pass through without realizing they've gone through an actual town.

We're next to the post-office, Sally's Diner, Fletcher's Garage and the Sheriff's Department. Uncle David saw the potential of the small brick building and the location. Originally, it was just going to be a bookstore, but he suggested adding the coffee shop, which turned out to be a fantastic idea, as well as a profitable one. Most of our customers were local college students or tourists passing through on their way to one of the many ski resorts or National Parks in the area. Even so, we had our regular customers—people we'd known most of our lives.

Kenny appeared in the doorway of our office and stretched his long, lanky arms up over his head and yawned. We've known Kenny since elementary school, and his dad was one of the teachers at our high school. Kenny received a basketball scholarship to Arizona State, but during his sophomore year his dad had a debilitating stroke, and his mom left. Kenny quit school to take care of his dad. He came to us for a job two weeks before we opened and has worked for us ever since.

"Unless you need me to stay, I'm going to head out. Peggy's staying, and I'll be back at four. I'm beat."

"That's fine," I told him. "We're supposed to get that shipment today, but I'll probably have it done before you get back."

"Yeah, I'm sure you will." He patted the top of my head patronizingly. "So, have you met the new neighbors yet?"

"Yes." Kate smiled. "We met them last night."

I tried not to laugh because Kenny wanted more information, and Kate was not accommodating him.

"So?" he said impatiently. "What are they like?"

Kate and I both glanced at each other and smiled widely.

"Oh, brother," Kenny groaned. "Let me guess, single and good-looking?"

"Actually," Kate said. "They're very nice. And yes, they happen to be single and extremely good-looking."

Kenny rolled his eyes. "Well, you two watch yourselves," he

cautioned, suddenly serious. "Make sure you keep your doors locked. They might be some kind of psychopaths. You never know these days."

This time Kate and I rolled our eyes.

"We're not worried," I assured him. "But we'll still keep our door locked. To keep the psychos out and all."

He grimaced and shook his head. "I'm outta here. See ya."

Kate and I waved as he left and then laughed.

"I hear the cackling!" He shouted from the front of the store, which just made us laugh louder.

We finished our breakfast, and I took our plates to the small kitchen area behind the coffee counter. I talked to Peggy about her newest grandbaby and then went to open the bookstore. I flipped on lights and turned on music.

I was going over receipts from the previous night's sales, organizing them for Kate, when I heard the jingling from the bells on the door of the coffee shop. I did a double take when I saw the Andersons, all three of them. They were dressed in business-type attire and just as handsome as usual, but it was Michael who caused my stomach to knot when I saw him. He looked good in jeans and a t-shirt, but in a suit? He was just sexy. Period.

I walked over to greet them. "Good morning."

"Hey there!" Garrett bellowed. "We came to see your store and get some of your great coffee."

"You don't even drink coffee." Michael rolled his eyes at Garrett and then smiled at me. "Hi, Grace."

"Hey." I smiled and made myself look away from him so I could converse coherently.

"No coffee, Garrett?" I asked. "We make other things, too. Do you like hot chocolate?"

"Do you have the little marshmallows?" he asked, with a hopeful expression that reminded me of a little kid.

I laughed and so did his brothers. "No," I told him apologetically. "But I can add extra whipped cream, and we even have sprinkles." Garrett seemed to be thinking about my proposition carefully, until Miles nudged him in the arm.

"That will be just fine," Miles shook his head at Garrett. "That's very nice of you."

Kate came out from the office then. She took Miles' and Michael's orders while I went behind the counter and started Garrett's hot chocolate. I added whipped cream and sprinkles and handed it to him, making a mental note to have mini-marshmallows here for the next time.

"This looks great." Garrett grinned. "Thanks."

I glanced over at Michael, and he was watching me with a smile.

"Can I get you guys anything else?" I asked as Kate handed him, what looked like, a regular coffee.

"Plain coffee?" I asked.

He looked at me inquisitively. "Too boring?"

I shrugged, and he chuckled.

"Okay, what do you recommend?"

I thought for a moment. "Do you like caramel?"

"Love it."

I turned and started steaming milk and preparing shots of espresso. From the corner of my eye, I could see him lean against the counter, watching me as I worked. Again, very unnerving. I drizzled caramel sauce over the heavy foam and handed the cup to him.

"Double-shot-heavy-foam-caramel-macchiato. My favorite."

He eyed me skeptically for a moment, took a sip and nodded approvingly. "Very…not boring," he said with a grin. "Thanks."

"You're welcome."

"So what are you guys up to today?" Kate asked. "Anything exciting?"

The three brothers shook their heads in unison, and Garrett let out a low groan of dread.

"I wish it were exciting," he grumbled. "We have a meeting in Denver with some new clients."

Miles glanced at his watch and then at his brothers. "Speaking of which, we should go. Kate, Grace, thanks for the coffees, it was nice to see you again."

I could feel the excitement rolling off of Kate as she looked at Miles, and it made me smile. I quickly put several muffins into a small bag and handed it to Garrett.

"For the road," I told him.

He smiled widely. "Excellent. Thanks."

Michael pulled out his wallet, but I shook my head at him.

"No charge," I said.

"Thanks."

I watched him walk away.

Even his walk was sexy.

* * *

The next two weeks were rather uneventful—except for the days when the Andersons came into the shop. Miles came by himself several times and sat with Kate at one of the tables, talking for quite a while, which made Kate absolutely giddy. When Garrett came in, the two of us talked about football, and he kept asking when I was going to make him some more bread. I'm pretty sure his thought processes consisted of food and sports, in that order.

When Michael came in, he would order a macchiato and chat casually, though he never came by himself like Miles or Garrett. I saw him almost every day during my run, but since my last embarrassing display, I was careful not to do any singing or dancing. I still blushed whenever I heard that song. When I did see him, we waved politely to each other, and I tried desperately not to maintain eye contact for too long.

On Thursday morning, Kate and I were making a list of supplies that we needed for the bookstore when the three of them walked through the door. Garrett greeted me cheerily and just seeing his giant dimples made me smile. Michael sauntered over to where I stood, one hand inside the pocket of his faded jeans and the other raking through his hair. I swallowed hard as I thought about the first time I saw him doing the exact same thing.

"Morning," I managed, as he leaned against the counter casually.

"Morning." His eyes roamed over my face, and my cheeks grew hot.

"Would you like your usual?"

He raised an eyebrow. "It's my usual already?"

"I don't know...would you like something different?" I asked.

His eyes didn't leave mine as he seemed to think about my question, and then he grinned.

"No. I suppose I will have my *usual*."

I walked behind the coffee counter to make his drink while Kate chatted with them. I handed Michael his drink just as Kenny came around the corner, his eyes widening as he assessed Garrett's size, and then cleared his throat.

"Hey, Gracie, were you expecting a shipment today? Because there's a box in the back." He slowly maneuvered his way to my side and draped his arm over my shoulder. I resisted the urge to elbow him in the ribs.

"Kenny, this is Garrett, Miles and Michael Anderson," I said. "Guys, this is Kenny Roland, our good friend and manager."

Kenny's expression turned serious as he stiffly put his hand out to shake each of their hands as they greeted him, then folded his arms across his chest with a scrutinizing expression on his face as he studied each of them.

"You guys bought the old Jenkins place?" Kenny probed, and they nodded in unison. "Well, it's nice to meet you," he said with half a smile, looked at me first, then at Kate. "Girls, if you need me..." he motioned toward the storeroom with his chin and patted my shoulder before retreating, looking over his shoulder at me.

I couldn't help my eye roll.

Garrett and Michael both chortled quietly as they watched him leave, and I made a mental note to smack Kenny upside the head the next time I saw him.

"If you guys don't have plans," Kate said. "Gracie and I would love to cook dinner for you tomorrow night, say six o'clock?"

"You two want to cook for us?" Garrett sounded surprised.

"Sure, we'd love to," she assured him. They looked at each other and then back at us.

"Hell, yeah!" Garrett said excitedly.

"That's very generous of you," Michael said. "Are you sure?"

"Absolutely." Kate smiled. "We'll see you then, huh?"

"We'll be there at six," Miles told her with a wide smile.

Kate followed Miles and Garrett to the front door, but Michael lingered back with me, fidgeting with the lid on his cup.

"So, do you run every morning?" he asked keeping his eyes down. I was sure he knew I ran every morning. We saw each other almost every morning.

"Yes," I told him. "I try to run every morning."

He cleared his throat, and his eyes met mine cautiously. "Would you like a running partner?"

My heart pounded in my ears. "Um, sure. I go pretty early, though."

"And what time would that be, exactly?"

"Seven."

"That's not so early." One side of his mouth lifted into a slight smile. "You have a nice day."

I watched as he followed his brothers to the silver Hummer. My heart was still pounding, and I felt a little giddy. He wanted to run with *me.*

* * *

The following morning, I kept my eyes on the Anderson's door as I pulled on my running shoes. Michael knew I ran every morning, and now he knew the time. I hoped he'd be running with me but after tying my laces in slow motion and walking in even slower motion to the gravel drive, I realized he wasn't coming. Disappointed, I began my run.

When I approached my turn-around point, I heard the pitiful but familiar cry of a cat. I slowed to a walk and searched the trees until I spotted the pathetic mass of gray fur several branches high in a pine tree. With a sigh, I crossed the road and stood at the base of the tree that now looked much taller than it had twenty seconds ago. Muffin looked down at me, his tail swishing back and forth.

"Seriously, Muffin?" I questioned the gray ball of fur. "How many times does this make now? Five? Six?"

"Meeeeowww..." Muffin was clearly begging for my help as he huddled closer to the trunk of the tree, the cool wind whipping around him.

"Fine. I'm coming." I grasped at the lowest branch and swung myself lithely up onto the sturdiest limb. Truth was, I'd always been really good at climbing trees. There wasn't a tree within a two-mile radius of my house I hadn't climbed at some point in my life. Obviously, tomboy was somewhere in my gene pool.

"Here's the thing, Muffin," I huffed, as I hoisted myself to the next branch. "No offense, but I've always thought of myself as a dog person. I realize we've had this conversation before, but it seems necessary to revisit the topic." I shimmied toward the cat, and he continued to 'meow' pathetically. Once beside him, I took in a deep breath as I looked at the tops of the trees swaying gently in the wind. I scratched at the soft fur behind Muffin's ears. "I guess I understand why you like it up here. What I don't understand is how you manage to get *up* the tree, but you can't manage to get down."

"Are you trying to kill yourself?"

The sound of Michael's voice made my heart jump into my throat. I searched the ground below for him, not realizing how high I'd actually climbed until I found him standing at the base of the tree. His expression was amused as he gazed up through the branches where I balanced precariously.

I grimaced at Muffin who blinked innocently at me. "See what you've done?" I whispered and tucked him under my left arm as I began the descent.

"You know she can get down if she really wants to," Michael said, and I could hear worry in his voice. "There's no need to risk your life for a cat."

When I reached the lowest branch, I handed Muffin off to Michael, and he seemed relieved when my feet were safely on the ground.

"First of all..." I brushed the loose bark from my backside and then took the cat from Michael who still looked amused, "Muffin is a *he*, not a she." Michael's eyebrow quirked up as I continued, "And second of all, the two of us go way back. I save him from a tree every couple of months." With that, Muffin squirmed from my arms, darting into the trees toward his home. "And he also never thanks me. Stupid cat."

Michael pulled pieces of bark from my hair as his crooked smile made an appearance.

"Well, I must say the way you scaled that tree was quite impressive," he said. "But you almost gave me a heart attack."

I snorted a laugh. "Do you know how many trees I've climbed in my life?"

"And how many bones have you broken?"

"What are you doing here anyway?" I hedged, hoping to change the subject.

"Running," he replied, as if the answer were obvious. "I thought you were going to run with me?"

"Yeah, I thought so too. Don't you own an alarm clock?"

He chuckled. "I couldn't make it at seven. I had a conference call with a client on the east coast at six-thirty this morning."

I nodded, and we walked in silence for a few moments, exchanging sideway glances with each other until Michael finally broke the silence.

"So, Grace Burke," he said pensively. "Maker of bread, fan of football, owner of bookstore, climber of trees and saver of cats?"

I grimaced. "I don't even like cats very much, and who names a cat *Muffin*? If I had a cat, I'd be much more creative with names. Romeo or Mr. Darcy, something like that." I realized I was rambling, but he made me nervous. Michael laughed, causing my heart to react. I tried to keep my eyes forward as we reached my driveway.

"So, dinner at six, right?" he asked.

"Six," I confirmed with a nod. "And I wouldn't be late if I were you. Kate doesn't do late."

He grinned. "Noted. Thanks for the tip."

"See you tonight."

"Have a good day." Michael waved as I walked to my front door.

It would've been impossible to remove the smile from my face; the short time spent with Michael made me unbelievably happy. In the back of my mind was the irksome reminder of Nina. The more I got to know Michael, the more I envied Nina, and the envy bothered me. I didn't like feeling that way.

Kate and I left work early to do the grocery shopping for dinner and clean the house. The menu for the evening was Caesar salad, steaks, twice-baked potatoes, homemade Italian bread and chocolate truffle cake for dessert. Not sure what the Andersons liked to eat, we concluded beef would be the reasonable choice.

We sang with Steve Perry and the rest of Journey as we marinated, grated, chopped, stirred and laughed. Kate and I loved to cook and loved cooking together even more. At four-thirty, we left the kitchen to get ourselves ready. When I got out of the shower, Kate had a pair of skinny jeans, a white cami and black v-neck cashmere sweater lying on my bed. On the floor were my black ballet flats with a silver buckle. Kate—my very own personal fashion advisor.

Kate came into my room looking fantastic in jeans, a black and white color-blocked tunic that draped slightly over one shoulder and a pair of killer black boots. Her brown hair was pulled back into a loose ponytail, and soft curls framed her heart-shaped face.

"You look fabulous, Kate."

"So do you. Let me curl your hair?" she asked eagerly. I handed her my brush, and she began working her magic. Kate always managed to make my hair look good. The usual unruly waves were smooth and soft around my shoulders, and she smiled her approval.

Back in the kitchen, I put the bread in to bake and the steaks under the broiler. Kate tossed the Parmesan into the salad and topped the potatoes with cheddar cheese, bacon crumbles and chives, sliding them into the second oven. I connected my iPod to the stereo and chose a playlist, while Kate finished setting the table. At exactly six o'clock the doorbell rang. Kate went to open the door as I pulled the steaks out of the oven.

"It smells amazing in here!"

I couldn't help but smile when I heard Garrett's voice bellow from the entry. My heart wouldn't settle down as I wiped my hands with a dishtowel and went to greet our guests. When I reached the entry, Kate and Miles already seemed to be in their own private bubble, and Garrett smiled widely when he saw me.

"Hey, Grace!" He walked over to stand in front of me. "You sure look pretty." He looked so nice in jeans and a plain white button-up shirt. I wondered where he had to shop to find clothes that actually fit him.

"Thanks." I smiled up at him. "You look great yourself. Are you hungry?"

"Does it snow here?" he asked, and we both laughed.

Just then Michael came into my view. He'd been standing behind Garrett, and I hadn't seen him. But I definitely could see him now, wearing khaki pants and a black, v-neck cashmere sweater—very similar to mine. His hand raked through his hair as he approached me slowly.

I thought my heart was going to explode right through my cashmere.

My face got hot as he leaned to my ear and his amazing smell washed over me. Wow, he smelled good.

"Trust me when I say," he said in a hushed voice. "You make the sweater look much better than I do."

I wasn't so sure about that but tried to muster some composure as he followed me into the kitchen where Garrett was already picking at a piece of the warm bread.

"Grace, did you make this homemade?"

I nodded.

"Excellent." He folded an entire slice into his mouth.

The boys took their seats, while Kate and I put the food on the table. Kate sat next to Miles, and Garrett patted the seat next to him, waggling his eyebrows at me.

"Sit here by me," he said.

Michael rolled his eyes at his brother and pulled the chair out for me before sitting on my other side.

"This looks amazing," Miles said as we passed the dishes of food around.

There wasn't a lot of talking at first, mostly just eating. Garrett hummed and moaned as he enjoyed the food, and I couldn't help but laugh. He'd look down at me with his mouth full and give me a wink. I was very aware of Michael beside me, but I made a point not to make eye contact—my nerves tumbling somersaults in the pit of my belly.

"So, who cooks at your house?" I asked Garrett. They all laughed at the same time, and Miles wiped his mouth with his napkin before he answered.

"None of us really cook, unless you count Ramen noodles," Miles said. "Garrett even manages to mess those up."

Garrett shrugged, unfazed by his brother's jab at his lack of culinary skills.

"I like Ramen noodles." I patted his giant shoulder in consolation, and he laughed.

Dinner conversation flowed smoothly, thanks to Kate, and the more I learned about them, the more I really liked the Anderson brothers. All three of them smart, kind and charming. They told us about their life in New York, a little about their business, and quite a bit about their parents, of whom they spoke very highly.

Kate suggested we have dessert in the living room, and they helped clear the table while Kate made a pot of coffee. As we ate our dessert, the conversation turned to Kate and me.

"So, where are your parents?" Garrett asked.

"My parents and Kate's mom were killed in a car accident when we were eight years old," I told them. "Kate's dad raised us. He passed away of cancer last year."

"Do you have any other family?" Miles asked with a furrowed brow, and we shook our heads in unison.

The mood suddenly shifted, and I felt uncomfortable. Kate and I weren't used to talking about our parents with others. Anyone who knew us knew about our situation, and we hadn't talked about it in a long time.

Garrett shook his head sadly. "You were only eight when you lost your parents?"

I nodded and glanced over at Michael who watched me with consternation. We gazed at each other for a long moment before I looked down at the floor nervously.

"So, what do you think of our shop?" Kate attempted to lift the dark mood.

"Best hot chocolate I've ever had," Garrett said with a weak smile.

"The bookstore is quite impressive," Michael added.

"Of course it's impressive," Kate said proudly. "That's the part Gracie takes care of."

"Of course," Michael agreed with a grin as his eyes found mine again.

"Kenny seems…nice." Garrett chuckled.

I rolled my eyes, and the boys laughed.

"Sorry about that," I said. "We've known him since Kindergarten. Since Uncle David died, he tends to be a little protective, which is sweet, in a very annoying, obnoxious sort of way."

"Nothing wrong with that," Garrett said with a reassuring smile.

When the conversation shifted to the recent remodeling of our home, I gathered the dessert plates from the coffee table and took them to the kitchen. I was rinsing the dishes when Michael came and stood beside me, pushing up the sleeves of his sweater. Can forearms be sexy?

Yes. Forearms can be sexy.

"You rinse, I'll load?" he offered.

"Sure." I handed him a plate, and he placed it in the dishwasher.

"I'm sorry about your parents." He took another plate from my hand.

"Thanks," I said. "I don't have very many memories of my parents. I'm thankful I have Kate."

He nodded. "I can see why."

"She's the most wonderful person I know," I added. "You'll see. The more you get to know her, you'll understand what I mean."

"I'm pretty sure I already understand." There was a deep sincerity in his voice that caused me to look over at him. An unidentifiable emotion shadowed his face; the green depth of his eyes searched mine for...seconds? Minutes? Then he looked away, breaking the spell, and we resumed the menial task at hand.

Too soon, we were saying goodnight. When I told Garrett they were welcome anytime, Miles cautioned me that Garrett would probably show up for breakfast in the morning, which was fine with me. They could all show up for breakfast as far as I was concerned.

Chapter Four

Saturday. I love Saturdays.

I got up at my regular time to run. As I sat on the porch to pull on my shoes, I heard the sound of gravel crunching, and my head snapped up. Michael stood in the middle of the drive wearing a black hoodie, hair in sexy disarray and a crooked smile. I strode down the porch steps quickly.

"Do you mind if I join you this morning?"

"Of course not." I tried to hide my excitement as we started a slow paced jog down the private drive.

"Don't you usually run with music?" he asked.

"Yes, don't you?"

He smiled wryly. "Yeah, but I like conversation more."

"Well, I'm not used to having conversation when I run. Kate refuses to run with me." Michael chuckled as I continued. "Besides, I tend to fall into my own little world when I run with music, which causes people to look at me funny. So it's probably better if I have conversation."

"Oh, I don't know," I could hear the amusement in his voice. "I found your concert the other morning very enjoyable."

And there it was. My jaw jutted to the side, and my face heated furiously as I looked at him. He kept his eyes forward, his lips in a tight line. I took a deep breath and decided to just let him get it out of his system.

"Okay," I relented. "I knew it was coming. Go ahead, bring it."

He laughed loudly. "Bring what?"

I ignored the question as my face continued to redden with humiliation. Surprisingly, he changed the subject.

"So, how far do you usually run?" He was attempting 'serious', but the amusement at my expense was still evident.

"Um, I've clocked the distance to some trees up here, so there and back it's somewhere around six miles. What about you?"

"Not that far," he murmured.

"Oh." I slowed to a walk. "We can turn back now if it's too far for you."

He rolled his eyes, tugging at my sleeve so I'd pick up my pace again. "No way. I may need to strap an oxygen tank to my back next time, but I'll be fine."

"Aren't you used to the altitude yet?"

"Not while running six miles."

We spent the rest of the run talking about music and decided we would switch iPods with each other to determine who had better taste in music.

"I have no doubt I will win that contest," I said confidently.

"Oh yeah? How do you figure?"

"Because, Kate and I listen to just about every genre out there. Classical, opera, rock, alternative, eighties."

His nose wrinkled. "You like eighties music?"

"Don't you? And be careful how you answer, because this could be a very short friendship if you say no."

"Oh, well then, yes, by all means, I *love* eighties music," he said with sarcasm.

"C'mon!" I was enjoying the banter. "Journey? Prince? Bon-Jovi? Def Leppard?"

"Journey? I'm not sure I've ever paid attention to any of their songs."

I stopped running and put my hands on my hips, shaking my head in disappointment.

"Okay, stop. You're killing me," I said dramatically. "Journey? Steve Perry? Possibly one of the greatest male vocalists in rock, ever! I mean he was kind of strange-looking, but still, the guy had some serious pipes!"

Michael shook with laughter, and the sound of his laugh made my heart react in strange ways.

He shrugged and tried to stop laughing. "Sorry."

"That's it," I said, shaking my head as we started to run again. "I'm going to be educating you on some of the greats. We're starting with Journey, and then we'll move on to hair-bands."

"I look forward to it. Why do you love eighties music so much?"

"Uncle David used to listen to it all the time," I told him. "He was a huge Journey fan, but we've always listened to a little bit of everything." I chuckled at the memory of my Uncle David singing along with Steve Perry whenever he drove Kate and me somewhere. Michael watched me for a moment and then turned away with a thoughtful expression on his face. When we got to the front of my house, he turned to face me and smiled.

"Grace, that was definitely the most fun I've ever had on a run," he said. "Thank you for allowing me to join you."

"Thanks for going with me. I had fun, too." I couldn't help the achingly, wide smile on my face. "I'll see you later."

He nodded and turned to go to his house.

"I'm going to be working on a playlist for you," I called to him, and he turned mid-stride to face me, walking backwards.

"Can't wait!" He called back with a wave.

I skipped up the steps to the front door. Kate was at the table reading the paper and drinking coffee in her pajamas.

"How was your run?"

"It was great." I don't think I could've been smiling any wider. I pulled my favorite mug from the cupboard and fixed myself some coffee, sitting across from Kate at the table. She studied me for a moment, and her expression turned suspicious.

"What are you smiling about?"

I shrugged. "It's Saturday."

She narrowed her eyes at me. "Gracie-Beth Burke."

"It's nothing. Michael went running with me this morning." I took a sip of coffee, looking at her over the top of my cup, and her face lit up with her sparkly smile.

"And?"

"And, he's very nice."

"Yeah. Very nice." She snorted. "And very gorgeous."

"Yes." I sighed. "Yes he is."

She giggled and looked back at the paper handing me the sports section.

We decided to have lunch and do some outlet shopping in Castle Rock. By the time we got home and unloaded our purchases, it was after four o'clock. I started a load of laundry. We stripped both beds and remade them with fresh sheets. Kate found the SC game on TV, which was in the second half, while I flipped through a magazine.

The doorbell rang, and Kate went to the door. "Hey, guys!"

"Hi, Kate."

I recognized Miles' voice and jumped from the couch to go to the door. All three of the Andersons stood on the front porch with sheepish expressions on their faces.

"Is anything wrong?" Kate asked.

Garrett snorted a laugh. "Well, we thought maybe, if you two didn't have any plans tonight, that maybe you'd want to cook for us again." Miles shoved Garrett in the arm. "What?" Garrett asked innocently. "Isn't that what I was supposed to say?"

Miles rolled his eyes, and I bit my lip trying not to laugh.

"What my brother meant to say," Miles narrowed his eyes at Garrett and then turned back to look at Kate, "is that we'd like to take the two of you to dinner, we just aren't familiar enough with the area to suggest a place."

Kate laughed. "Come on in."

The three of them filed in, and Garrett walked over to me until we stood toe-to-toe. He looked down at me, and I had to tilt my head backwards to see his face—my chin at the level of his chest.

"How's it goin?" he asked with a serious expression and an exaggerated bass voice.

I mimicked his attempt at seriousness. "I'm fine. How are you?"

He laughed and made his way to the sofa when he noticed the game. "Who's winning?"

"Trojans," I answered, my eyes meeting Michael's.

"Hey, Grace, how's your day been?"

"Good. How about yours?"

"Great," he replied with a smile.

"So anyway," Miles said. "We're sorry for just barging in like this, but we noticed you were home and thought we could repay you for the delicious dinner you made last night. We'd like to take you out. Wherever you'd like."

"We could just make something here," Kate suggested.

"No, we don't want you to have to cook," Michael said.

"I want them to cook!" Garrett called, completely at home on our sofa.

Michael shook his head. "Really, Garrett? Why don't you just make yourself comfortable?"

Garrett laughed loudly and quickly returned his focus to the game. "Where's the defense, guys?" he shouted at the television. "C'mon!"

"Do you guys like Mexican food?" Kate asked Miles.

"I love Mexican food!" Garrett hollered, not looking away from the TV. I laughed, and Michael covered his eyes with his hand and shook his head, embarrassed.

Miles grimaced. "We love Mexican food."

"How about chicken enchiladas?" Kate asked.

"Is there someplace you'd like to go?" he asked.

"There isn't any place that has chicken enchiladas as great as ours." Kate winked at him. "I would just need to run to the store for a couple of things."

"Well, then I insist on buying whatever you need." Miles raised his eyebrows. "And we'll help you with the cooking."

"Yeah," Garrett called again. "My brothers will help you with the cooking!"

I laughed loudly, and Garrett joined me.

"Don't encourage him," Michael said with a grimace. "Are you sure we aren't intruding?"

"We weren't doing anything, honestly, laundry and a movie. Exciting, right?"

"Okay, then," Kate said. "Miles, would you like to go to the store with me?" He nodded with a big smile. "Gracie, I'll get everything we need," Kate told me. "Dessert?"

"Do you guys like banana pudding?" I asked Michael.

"Love banana pudding!"Garrett bellowed before Michael could answer.

Michael closed his eyes, a small smile touching the corner of his mouth in amusement. "Yes, that sounds great."

Miles and Kate left for the store while Michael and I joined Garrett on the sofa.

"So what did you and Kate do on Saturday nights before you had intrusive, rude neighbors?" Michael asked.

"Well, we're party animals," I deadpanned, and they laughed. "It's true. I just started a load of laundry, and if you guys hadn't come, it may have gotten really crazy, like maybe a load of darks or even underwear."

"Wow, you two are wild," Michael said.

"Yeah, we're thinking of joining a support group."

They laughed, and I stood from the sofa to grab my iPod from the stereo and handed it to Michael.

"Here," I said. "Let the education begin."

Garrett raised an eyebrow at me.

"Your brother needs help with music," I explained, shaking my head. "He doesn't even know who Steve Perry is." I picked a playlist while Michael put the ear buds in his ears, and laid his head back against the sofa.

"This is Journey?" He seemed pleasantly surprised.

"Yes, and *the* Steve Perry. Good, right?"

He smiled and shuffled through songs, every now and then nodding his approval. Soon, Miles and Kate showed up with several bags of groceries, and we got busy cooking right away. We boiled chicken breasts in broth and chopped onions for the sauce. Kate took over the enchiladas while I mixed the pudding for dessert, putting Garrett in charge of layering vanilla wafers in the dish. Kate was prepared buying extra cookies, because Garrett definitely ate more than he 'layered'. Michael and Miles were in charge of shredding the chicken while Kate made the sauce.

In less than two hours we were sitting around the table enjoying enchiladas that the boys agreed were 'better than any restaurant's' and having a wonderful time. Like the night before, we had great conversation, but mostly we laughed. Garrett had me in stitches most of the night, and the way Miles and Michael got embarrassed over things he said made me laugh even more.

After dinner we talked them into watching a movie with us. Much to Garrett's chagrin, we decided it was "musical night" so they got to watch "Fiddler on the Roof", one of our favorites. They laughed as Kate and I sang along with all of the songs and pretended not to notice when we both sniffled at the end.

When the credits started, I looked up at Garrett. "You liked it, right?"

"Yeah." He rolled his eyes. "It was great."

I nudged him with my elbow. "C'mon. You liked it."

He chuckled, and they stood to leave. I went into the kitchen to get the extra pan of enchiladas we made for them to take home.

"Now, put these in the oven at three-fifty for about forty minutes," I instructed, handing the pan to Garrett. "The oven is the big silver box in the kitchen that gets very, very hot."

"Oh, you're hilarious." He patted the top of my head.

"Thanks, girls. It was great," Miles said. "We'll see you later."

"Good night," Michael said. "It was a lot of fun, and I happen to love that movie."

I nodded my approval and he waved with a smile as he turned to go. I couldn't help but be hopeful about tomorrow and another opportunity to spend time with the Andersons. Especially Michael.

Chapter Five

I hopped out of bed rushing through my morning ritual and grabbing my running shoes. Michael was already standing in the middle of the drive when I came out the front door. I waved, and he smiled as I sat down to quickly pull on my shoes and then walked over to where he stood.

"Morning." My cheeks ached from the grin on my face.

"Good morning."

We began our slow jog to the main road.

"No oxygen tank?" I asked without looking at him.

He chuckled. "Nope, no oxygen tank."We ran in silence for a long while, when he finally looked over at me. "We had a good time last night."

"So did we, it was a lot of fun," I told him. "I'm glad you guys came over."

"Where did you two learn to cook?"

"My uncle was a pretty amazing cook, but Kate and I also took a few classes together. We love it."

"You're great at it, that's for sure."

"Thanks."

"It's too bad for you, though," he said with a grimace.

"Why?"

"Because Garrett is going to drive you both crazy."

"I like Garrett, he's funny," I told him. "I can't imagine what it's like living with him, I'll bet you're laughing all the time."

"Yeah," he said, his voice dripping sarcasm. "My side hurts."

I laughed as I looked over at him, and he rolled his eyes.

"So what do you and Kate usually do on Sundays?"

"Sunday is football day."

"No laundry?"

"Nope, finished it yesterday."

"Oh, well, that's a relief. I was afraid we might need to do an intervention."

"You have no idea how boring Kate and I actually are."

"I don't think you're boring at all."

"Yeah, but you don't know us that well either. You could die of boredom if you spend too much time with us."

"I think I'm willing to risk it." He smiled the crooked smile that was, well…

Time passed much too quickly, and before I knew it we were in front of our houses. He looked at me for a moment and ran his hand through his hair, and I cleared my throat nervously.

"Well, you guys are welcome to be bored with us anytime you want," I said.

He smiled. "Thanks. I'll see you later?"

I nodded and waved as I went to my door, my heart pounding like crazy. I showered and got dressed in my favorite faded, holey jeans and Elway jersey I've had forever, drying my hair straight. I went into the kitchen for my morning coffee, and sat down at the table with the newspaper to check the times for the games that Kate and I would be watching.

Kate emerged from her room dressed in jeans and her Broncos sweatshirt—all smiles, as usual. "Mornin'."

"How are you?"

She stirred her coffee, smiling widely, and sighed. "Fabulous."

I giggled at her expression and toasted us a couple of bagels. We ate our breakfast while reading the paper.

"So what should we bake today? Brownies?" I asked.

She thought for a moment and nodded. The rest of the morning we did our usual Sunday-lounging. We played a heated game of

Scrabble while we ate leftover enchiladas for lunch, Kate arguing with me over whether 'hummock' was an actual word—which, of course, it is—she just hates losing. Later, we made brownies and while they baked, we got comfortable on the sofa.

The now familiar rumble of Garrett's Hummer echoed from the drive and made us smile.

"I would really like to invite them over to watch the game," Kate said thoughtfully. "But I don't want to scare them away."

"I was thinking the same thing, although I don't think you would scare Miles." I smiled at her. "I think he's smitten."

"I sure hope so, he's awfully sweet. He's really smart, too."

"You like him a lot," I was stating the obvious.

"Yeah, I do."

"Well, I have to say, from what I've seen so far, I can't blame you one bit. He's really a very nice guy."

"Yes, he is." She rested her chin in her hands and gazed past me. I loved that she was so excited over someone. She'd never been this excited about anyone before.

The timer went off, and Kate pulled the brownies from the oven, placing the pan on a cooling rack and returned to her spot on the sofa. The Broncos weren't on until four, so we decided to watch the rest of the Dallas game while we waited, both of us stretched out on the couch. I read my book, while Kate looked through one of her cooking magazines, but after a few minutes, she tossed it onto the coffee table and folded her arms in front of her with a huff.

"What's wrong?" I asked.

"I think it's ridiculous we're not inviting the boys over here," she said in a frustrated tone. "I mean, they seem to enjoy themselves when they're here, right?" I shrugged at her as she continued to state her case. "What's the worst they can say? No, we don't want to come over?" She stood and pushed the sleeves of her sweatshirt up with determination, walking to the door, and after a brief pause turned to me with a frantic expression on her face. "Well? Aren't you coming with me?"

I laughed and got up off the couch, and we walked over to the Anderson's house. Miles opened the door as we were climbing their porch steps, clearly happy to see Kate.

"Well, hi there," he said. "Are you two mind-readers or something? We were just talking about you."

Garrett barreled out the front door wearing the same Elway jersey he'd worn the first day I saw them. He noticed the jersey I was wearing and laughed loudly.

"We thought you guys might want to join us for the Broncos game," Kate told them. "We made brownies, and—"

Garrett didn't let her finish. Without saying a word, he grabbed my hand and pulled me down the steps toward our house. I laughed so hard I could barely walk straight as he towed me through the front door.

"What did it for you, the game or the brownies?" I asked.

"A combination of the two. Not to mention I have a thing for chicks who wear Elway jerseys." He pulled me with him to the couch and we sat down. "I thought you two would never show up, and my brothers wouldn't let me come over here. They're afraid you'll think we're stalkers or something."

I patted his shoulder soothingly. "Poor, Garrett."

"I know. What took you so long?"

"We don't want you guys to think the same thing about us."

He grimaced. "Yeah, like that would happen."

"Do you want some brownies?" I asked, and he looked down at me, rolling his eyes—I took that as a 'yes'. Miles and Kate came in as I set the plate of brownies in front of Garrett, who immediately shoved a whole one into his mouth. I resisted the urge to ask where Michael was as I returned to the kitchen and pulled some ginger ales from the fridge and distributed them.

"Thanks," Garrett said, grabbing another brownie. Kate snatched the plate of brownies and held it in front of Miles.

"You'd better be quick." She giggled, holding the plate just out of Garrett's reach. Miles grabbed two before Kate handed the plate back to Garrett. He was on his fourth brownie when the doorbell rang.

"It's Michael, he was finishing up some drawings," Miles said, as I got up from the couch to answer the door.

It wasn't Michael.

A tall blonde, with a blue sweater hugging her curves greeted me with a confused expression.

"Oh," she leaned to the side to look past me, "I must have the wrong house. I'm looking for Michael Anderson."

"Hello, Nina." Miles came up behind me.

Nina? I swallowed hard as her wide brown eyes examined me from head to toe. I was right. She was pretty, in an angular, harsh, sort of way. Her bottle-blond hair was long and smoothed into perfect waves past her shoulders. Her skin was tan and smooth, but her makeup was a little heavy for my taste. I couldn't find anything wrong with her figure—tall, mostly legs and breasts, with a tiny waist and perfect curves.

"Our house is there." Miles motioned across the street. "I don't think Michael was expecting you, though."

She arched an overly plucked eyebrow. "I'm sure he won't mind me stopping by. Nice to see you, Miles." She gave me a curt nod before turning on her heel and walking across the drive. Miles sighed and pushed the door closed for me.

"Sorry," he apologized. "Her father is one of our clients. She tends to be a little…difficult sometimes."

"Difficult, right," Garrett grumbled under his breath.

I couldn't help but feel a small amount of satisfaction. Clearly, Miles and Garrett weren't very fond of Nina. Based on first impressions, I wasn't particularly fond of her either, but I knew my reasons were selfish.

It was a long while before Michael finally joined us. My heart pounded when he smiled at me, and "Hi" was all I could manage. He grimaced at Garrett who was pushing yet another brownie into his mouth.

"What are you eating?" Michael asked him.

"Brownies, why?" Garrett answered with his mouth full and nudged me with his elbow making me laugh. It didn't take long before the brownie plate was empty. Garrett leaned back into the couch, patting his stomach and making himself more comfortable. We all watched the game, though Miles and Kate were also having a quiet conversation off and on the entire time. Michael seemed to enjoy himself—he and Garrett laughing when Kate and I would yell at the TV over a missed tackle or a bad call. After the game, we decided to go into town for pizza.

"I'll drive," Garrett said.

When we all climbed into the enormous vehicle it occurred to me *why* Garrett drove a Hummer. It was probably the only vehicle large enough for his massive size. We ordered pizza and wings, and I watched in awe as Garrett ate an entire pizza by himself, taking three pieces at a time and stacking them on top of each other. We sat for a long time after eating, just talking and laughing, and I loved every single minute.

Chapter Six

My alarm woke me much sooner than I wanted. I was tired from our late night with the Andersons, but I got up and got dressed to go for my run anyway. If I was being honest with myself, it wouldn't matter how tired I was, I looked forward to seeing Michael. I headed out the front door to put my shoes on, and disappointment quickly settled in. No Michael.

I heaved an audible sigh as I trudged to the gravel road and started my slow jog. I listened to the steady rhythm of my steps against the gravel, accompanied by the morning chirping of birds in the trees and the gentle wind rustling through the pines. Yesterday's events replayed in my mind and I smiled.

The distant hum of an approaching vehicle brought me from my reminiscent thoughts, and I moved onto the far side of the shoulder while it passed. This road was usually pretty quiet, but every once in a while, huge tractor-trailers barreled down the road at high rates of speed.

The car passed and just as I picked up my pace again, I heard it—the pathetic meowing of Muffin. After a moment of searching the treetops, I found him hunched in a ball, clinging to one of the limbs. I was really tired, and the last thing I wanted to do was scale a tree, but the cat continued to plead for my help, and I couldn't ignore the poor thing.

"Okay, I'm coming," I assured him, pulling myself up to the lowest of the branches. The cat wasn't as high in the tree as usual, so I reached him quickly. But just as I stretched my hand toward him, a bird darted from another tree close by, and Muffin lunged toward me with a hiss.

Startled, I lost my balance and was falling, grasping desperately at branches on my way down. When I hit the ground, I managed to hit feet-first, my right ankle twisting in pain, and then *THWAP!* All the air rushed from my lungs as I fell backwards and slammed into the ground. I gasped, trying to catch my breath, and there was a loud ringing in my ears. Somewhere in my mind I registered the sound of screeching tires and closed my eyes, hoping I wasn't about to become a human speed bump. When I opened my eyes, Michael's face was in front of mine, his eyes wide and frantic.

"Grace?" He searched my face in desperation. "Grace, are you okay?"

I wasn't sure if I was okay or not, but I was sure only someone as beautiful as Michael Anderson could look so amazing at seven o'clock in the morning.

Okay. I was delirious.

"Can you move?" His voice was anxious.

"I think so," I said, and tried to sit up. Michael slid his arm underneath my shoulders to help me. My face flushed with his worried gaze, and I sighed in embarrassment. "I'm fine," I said, but a throbbing pain from my ankle caused me to wince.

"Are you hurt?" Michael was still panicked, and he continued to search for visible damage. "What is it?"

"My stupid ankle," I replied, wishing I could kill Muffin—or myself, I couldn't decide which. "I twisted it."

"Which one?"

"Right," I muttered.

"I saw you fall." He shook his head, and his eyes locked with mine. "I'll be surprised if it isn't broken."

"Trust me, it's not broken," I assured him. "I know what broken feels like. This is nothing."

He didn't respond, except with a grimace, as he stood and slid his arm around my waist, lifting me gently.

"Let's get you home, or should I take you to the E.R.?"

"Home is fine." I tried to keep my weight off of the sore ankle as Michael helped me into his car. The Yukon was warm and smelled of leather and another heavenly scent I couldn't pinpoint. I surmised it was just him. Classical music played—Bach—which made me smile in spite of the pain emanating from my ankle. Michael climbed into his seat and turned the car around, driving toward the house. I was more embarrassed than guilty that he had to disrupt his day because I felt the need to rescue a stupid cat.

"What about Muffin? Did you see him?" I turned in my seat as if I would actually be able to see the cat now. Michael reached across and grasped my hand. This did not escape my attention as my eyes flitted between his face, and his hand wrapped around mine.

"Muffin is fine," he assured me. "She," he stopped to correct himself, "*he*…ran home. I told you he could get down from that tree if he really wanted to. You scared me to death, you know that?"

I swallowed hard and noticed what he was wearing. The top of a gray dress shirt and tie peeked beneath a black wool coat. I imagined how gorgeous he probably looked in a dress shirt and tie.

"I'm sorry," I said. "You were obviously on your way somewhere."

He squeezed my hand, which caused a thrill of excitement to radiate through me. "Don't worry about it, really. It's nothing that can't wait."

"Thank you," I said, and he finally released my hand. "I'd probably still be lying there if you hadn't stopped."

"Where's your cell phone?"

"I don't bring it with me when I run. I never think I need it."

"And what do you think now?"

"That I should probably start bringing my phone," I muttered, making him chuckle.

We pulled in front of my house, and I started to open the door.

"Just wait a minute," he instructed as he got out, walking around to open the door and help me out of the car. Once again, his arm slid around my waist, and I leaned into him as we made our way to the front door.

"What happened?" Garrett yelled from across the road. "Is she okay, Michael?" Before I knew it, Garrett was on the porch opening the front door for us, looking at me worriedly. "Gracie, you okay? What happened?"

"I'm fine." I felt uncomfortable with all the fussing, though my ankle was screaming at me. Michael helped me to the couch and Garrett sat beside me, folding his hands together nervously.

"She fell. Out of a tree," Michael said the last part with disdain, and Garrett chuckled.

"Um, Gracie?" Garrett scratched his head. "What were you doing in a tree?"

"Saving a cat," I mumbled. Garrett's lips pursed together in an effort to keep his laughter at bay, and I felt the need to defend myself. "He gets stuck! I can't just leave him up there!"

"Actually," Garrett said matter-of-factly, "if he wants to get down, he'll get down."

"I told her the same thing," Michael interjected.

"Okay well, thanks for your help," I said, wanting the entertainment at my expense to cease. "I'll be fine now." I bent to untie my shoe and bit my lip to keep from yelping in pain. My ankle really hurt.

"Here, let me," Michael said, kneeling in front of me. I watched as he untied my shoe, pulling it off slowly, and I tensed from the pain. "Sorry," he said with a grimace. He took my sock off, and I was thankful I'd recently given myself a pedicure. My ankle was already red and swollen.

"Do you girls have an ice pack?" Garrett asked, and I heard him rummage through the freezer.

"It's in the door," I called to him.

He came back to the couch handing the pack to Michael, who lifted my foot gently, propping it on a pillow and laying the ice pack over it.

"I think it might be a sprain," he said. "We'd better go to the E.R."

Another thrill coursed through me with his use of the word *we,* but I shook my head.

"No, really. I just twisted it, it'll be fine."

"Grace," Michael said patiently. "The swelling is already bad. You need an X-Ray to make sure it isn't broken."

"I can take her," Garrett said. "Michael, you'd better get to your meeting. You'll be late."

I felt terrible.

"I can reschedule the meeting," Michael stood and loosened his tie. "Sandler won't be there anyway."

Garrett and Michael exchanged a look, Garrett raised an eyebrow and Michael scowled at him before walking to the front door.

"I'm going to change clothes, I'll be right back."

"Okay," I said. "Thanks."

He nodded and left, pulling the door closed behind him. Garrett chortled.

"What?" I asked.

He shook his head. "Nothing."

Just then Kate came down the hallway dressed for work.

"Hey, Garrett!" she said cheerily. Her smile disappeared when she saw my ankle with an ice pack on it, and she walked over to the couch quickly, kneeling next to me. "What'd you do?"

"She's okay," Garrett said soothingly. "We think she sprained her ankle."

Kate pulled something from my hair. "Why do you have bark in your hair?"

Garrett coughed, trying to hide his laugh, and Kate scowled. "That stupid cat," she grumbled.

"I'm fine. Garrett and Michael are going to take me to the E.R."

She nodded. "I'll go, too."

"You can't. You have to meet with the accountant today," I

reminded her. "I'll be fine."

"I'll take good care of her, Kate. I promise," Garrett assured her.

"Okay, if you're sure," she said hesitantly, watching me worriedly.

"I'm sure. Just ask Kenny to work the bookstore for me." Then I remembered something. "Oh, crap! Kenny's not working today, he's rafting."I started to get off the couch, but Garrett pushed down gently against my shoulders. "But I need to go to work," I argued. "My ankle isn't hurting that bad."

Obviously, I was a terrible liar. Garrett snorted and lifted the ice pack. Even with the ice on it, the swelling had gotten worse. Kate winced when she saw it.

"Yeah, I don't think so," Garrett said. "I'll call Miles. He'll be happy to help out."

Kate's eyes lit up with his suggestion, though she still tried to show concern over my ailment.

"That's a great idea," I told Garrett as he went for the phone. I smiled and gave Kate a wink.

She smiled weakly. "I'm sorry you're hurt."

"I know." I squeezed her hand. She *was* sorry, but she was also happy for the opportunity to spend the day with Miles, and if Kate was happy, I was happy.

"It's all taken care of," Garrett said. "Miles is on his way over."

"Thank you," Kate called from the kitchen. "Gracie, you need to eat something."

"I'm not hungry." I couldn't even think about food, my ankle was hurting too bad.

The front door opened, and Miles poked his head in while he knocked.

"Come on in," Garrett said.

Miles walked over to the couch and looked at my ankle, shaking his head sadly. "I'm sorry you're hurt. Is there anything I can do for you?"

"Actually you're already doing it," I told him. "Thank you so much for helping Kate today, I felt terrible leaving her short-handed."

Kate came into the living room, and Miles smiled widely at her.

"It's my pleasure," he said to me, but his eyes didn't leave Kate's as she practically bounced over to where he stood.

"You're a life saver. Thank you," she said.

"I don't know how much I'll be able to help, but I'm all yours," he replied.

I swear they grinned at each other like the Cheshire Cat, and I'm pretty sure they'd forgotten Garrett and I were even in the room. Garrett nudged me with a wink and we both stifled a laugh. Kate helped me to the bathroom so I could freshen up, and when we came out Michael was there.

"Ready then?" he asked, and I nodded.

"Make sure you keep me posted on what's going on, okay?" Kate said.

I nodded, and she kissed my cheek before walking out the door with Miles, Garrett following close behind.

"Garrett's driving," Michael said.

"That's good," I said. "I'm not sure he'd fit in my Jeep."

The Hummer rumbled in front of the house, and Michael helped me into the backseat. The drive to the E.R. was fairly quiet, aside from Michael talking on the phone with Nina. I couldn't hear what she was saying, but she seemed to be annoying Michael. Garrett got my attention in the rearview mirror and rolled his eyes, making me giggle.

"I'm sorry, Nina," Michael said patiently. "I didn't mean to mess up your day. We should reschedule the meeting for when your father can attend anyway. No. I understand that." He sighed and raked his hand through his hair. "I've apologized. What more can I do? Fine. We'll talk about it later." He disconnected the call and slid the phone in the pocket of his jacket.

"Everything okay, little brother?" Garrett asked.

"She's exasperating," Michael muttered, rubbing both hands

over his face.

"I don't understand why you—"

Michael cut Garrett off with an icy glare then glanced sideways at me. I quickly focused my attention out the side window, pretending not to notice the exchange.

After more than an hour in the waiting area of the E.R., we were taken to an examination room. The throbbing from my ankle was getting more intense, but I didn't want to complain in front of Michael and Garrett. The nurse took my vitals and promised a doctor would be with us shortly.

"Can you give her something for the pain?" Garrett asked.

The nurse huffed. "And you are?"

Garrett squared his large shoulders. "I'm her brother."

I pursed my lips together as the nurse looked to Garrett, then to me, then to Michael.

"Uh-huh," she said dubiously. "The doctor will be here in a minute." She left, pulling the door shut behind her.

"Do you think she believed me?" Garrett asked, and Michael chuckled.

The door opened, and a familiar, fresh-faced doctor with honey-blonde hair and soft blue eyes came in the room. He assessed Garrett and Michael and then looked at the file in his hand.

"So, Miss Burke," he said, stepping to the side of the bed. "I don't recall you having brothers."

That's when I recognized him.

"Evan Taylor? Is that you?"

He laughed, and gave me a tight hug. "You've grown up, Grace."

"So have you." I couldn't help but laugh, too. "What are you doing here? Last I heard you were somewhere on the east coast."

"I moved here a little over a month ago," he said. "Dad had a heart attack."

"I'm sorry. I hadn't heard. Is he okay?"

"Oh, you know him," Evan waved his hand dismissively, "if

he'd end his love affair with bacon, he might live a little longer. Stubborn old man."

Garrett chortled, and I remembered we weren't alone in the room.

"Evan, this is Garrett and Michael Anderson. They're our new neighbors…friends," I corrected myself, making Garrett and Michael smile.

Evan cleared his throat and leaned closer. "You mean brothers," he whispered conspiratorially.

"Exactly," Garrett said with a laugh, shaking Evan's hand. "Nice to meet you."

"Evan," Michael said, with a nod as they shook hands.

"So, how do you know Gracie?" Garrett asked.

Evan smiled widely. "She and her cousin were at my house almost constantly during high school."

"Evan's sister, Erin, was our closest friend," I clarified. "Evan was in college and much too mature to socialize with lowly high school students."

"That's not true," he said with a laugh. "I remember being the taxi service to the mall plenty of times, not to mention sneaking you into R-rated movies."

I was a little embarrassed. "How is Erin? We haven't seen her since Uncle David's funeral."

"She's doing great," he said and his expression turned somber. "I'm sorry I wasn't here for the funeral. Kate's dad was a great man and one of the reasons I became a doctor."

My heart ached with the thought of Uncle David, and Evan patted my hand consolingly.

"Now," he said, clearing his throat. "Looks like you've done some damage here. What happened?"

"She was climbing trees," Garrett said, and I frowned at him.

"I guess some things never change," Evan shook his head, making Garrett laugh.

Michael stood quietly in the corner of the room, arms folded across his chest, watching quietly as Evan examined my ankle. I tried not to make a noise, but I couldn't help the wince as he pressed the swollen area with his fingertips. "Let's get an X-Ray and something for your pain."

Sure enough, my stupid ankle was sprained. Evan gave me a big, ugly, black plastic boot with Velcro straps to wear, along with prescriptions for pain and inflammation.

"You're going to need to take it easy for a couple of days," Evan said as he scribbled out my prescriptions. "No running or climbing trees."

Garrett and Michael both laughed, and I rolled my eyes.

"Very funny," I grumbled.

Evan handed me two prescriptions. "One is for inflammation, the other for pain." He pointed to my boot. "Keep the boot on."

"Why would I take it off?" I asked sarcastically. "It's so pretty."

"It's great to see you again." Evan gave me a one-arm hug. "Tell Kate I said hello."

"You should come check out our coffee shop. You might be impressed."

"I'm sure I would be." He winked at me and turned to Garrett and Michael. "It was nice meeting you both. Take good care of her."

"We will." Garrett shook his hand. "Thanks a lot."

"Thanks, Evan," Michael said. "Nice meeting you, too."

We dropped off my prescriptions and stopped by the shop to see Kate and Miles. Miles was working the register while Kate and Peggy filled orders, and I was impressed with how smoothly things seemed to be going. Kate made me a vanilla latte, as well as a hot chocolate for Garrett and a macchiato for Michael. She sent me home with a kiss on the cheek and assurance that everything was under control. When we got home, Michael helped me hobble to the couch, and Garrett sat next to me.

"Do you mind if we keep you company, Gracie?"

"I would love for you to keep me company," I said, unable to hide my excitement at the offer.

"Actually," Michael said, raking his hand through his hair. "I need to go."

"Oh." My disappointment was obvious, and I tried to cover it with a smile. "Thank you so much for taking me to the E.R.—I'm sorry for messing up your schedule."

"You didn't mess up anything," he corrected. "I'll see you both later. Garrett, behave yourself."

Garrett snorted a laugh, rolling his eyes as Michael walked out the door.

"You hungry?" Garrett stood from the couch and looked down at me.

"Yeah," I said. "There's some yogurt in the fridge."

He disappeared into the kitchen, and I heard cupboards and drawers opening and closing, as he tried to find everything he was looking for. He managed to find one of our serving trays, where he had a container of yogurt, a huge bowl of leftover banana pudding from Saturday night and a ginger ale. I raised an eyebrow at him.

"The pudding is for me." He shook his head. "I don't do yogurt."

I pursed my lips together and patted his arm when he sat down next to me. "Thanks, Garrett. I really appreciate you doing this."

"You're welcome." He took a bite of pudding. "Banana pudding for breakfast. Excellent." His phone rang, and I laughed at the ring tone: "Sexy and I Know It.

"Hello?" he mumbled, his mouth full of pudding. "Hey, Michael."

I took a sip of my coffee, trying to ignore the heart fluttering that took place at the mention of Michael's name.

"Pudding, why?" Garrett answered, and I almost spit out my coffee. Michael was obviously asking his routine 'What are you eating?' question. Garrett heard me and showed me the pudding in his mouth.

"Ewww," I groaned, and his shoulders shook as he laughed quietly, trying to listen to whatever Michael was saying.

"Yeah, she's fine. Uh-huh. Okay." He rolled his eyes. "Don't worry, I will." Garrett hung up the phone, and I resisted the urge to ask what Michael had said. Garrett picked up his pudding again taking a big bite.

"You and your brothers seem very close," I said.

"We are close," he said simply. "You and Kate, too."

I nodded and smiled, thinking of Kate. "We've been together all our lives. I'd do anything for her."

"It's the same for me and my brothers." He set his bowl down and leaned back into the couch. "That's the way it should be."

I nodded my agreement, feeling a sense of appreciation for his parents, though I'd never even met them.

"Old fashioned values," I said. "They're definitely a rarity these days."

Garrett shook his head in disagreement. "There's no such thing as old-fashioned values. There are just values. Right has always been right and wrong has always been wrong. Old-fashioned really has nothing to do with it. People have just lost sight of what's truly important."

I'd never thought of it that way. He was absolutely right.

"I don't know you that well," he said. "But I can tell the relationship you have with Kate is like the relationship I have with my brothers. Maybe that's why we feel so comfortable together, eh?" He winked at me as he got up from the couch and walked over to the shelves that held our movie collection. "So what sounds good?" he asked, and then with a shocked expression, he pulled out one of the DVDs and held it towards me. The Replacements. One of my many favorites.

"I can't believe you have this movie in your house," he said with a huge grin.

"What can I say?" I replied dryly. "Pain heals. Chicks dig scars. Glory lasts forever."

He guffawed loudly, shaking his head at my Keanu Reeves impression.

We laughed and cut up with each other while we watched, and when it was over he told me to pick the next movie. I convinced him to watch a classic. He grumbled as he put "The Sound of Music" into the DVD player and then sat down next to me. I laughed at the perplexed expression on his face as he watched the opening scene.

"Why is she in a maid's uniform singing on a mountain? Maids aren't that happy."

I giggled. "It's not a maid's uniform. She's a nun, and she's singing on a mountain because she's Julie Andrews, and she can sing anywhere and work it."

We listened to how the hills were alive.

"She does have a nice voice," he mused.

"Nice?" I snorted. "She's fabulous. I have so much to teach you." I wagged my head, and he reached around my shoulders putting me in a headlock, rubbing the top of my head roughly before releasing me. I blew the loose strands of hair from my forehead, and we settled into the couch. Garrett watched quietly until the ending when the Von Trapp family hid from the German soldiers.

"I hate Nazis," Garrett grumbled.

"Yeah, they suck," I mimicked his grumble, and he chuckled. My cell phone buzzed, and Garrett handed it to me. It was Kate.

"Ooh, let me answer it," Garrett snatched the phone back. "Hey, Kate! How's it going? You teaching my brother to make all those fancy coffees? Yeah, she's fine, but she's making me watch Sound of Music, so we're both in pain."

I could hear Kate's laughter, and Garrett's eyes widened with her non-stop chatter.

"Okay, I'll tell her. See you soon." He set the phone on the coffee table, shaking his head as if trying to clear it. "Um, Kate says hi."

I sniggered and leaned back into the couch getting comfortable again, and we watched the rest of the movie. As the end credits rolled, I waited for his reaction.

"So, what'd you think?" I asked.

"Honestly, it wasn't that bad. You were right about Judy Andrews. The hills really were alive."

"*Julie* Andrews," I corrected. "You liked it?"

"Yeah, I liked it, but let's try to spread the true classics out to about one a month," he said. "I mean, I'm still trying to recover from the weird little violin player that kept following the Jewish guy around."

I busted up laughing. "'Fiddler on the Roof'! And that was symbolism, goof-ball!"

"Whatever." He rolled his eyes. "That little dude was creepy."

I had to wipe my eyes because I was laughing so hard, which made Garrett laugh. He stood up and stretched, glancing at his watch. I couldn't help but feel guilty. Surely he had other things to do besides babysit me.

"Garrett, if you need to leave, I totally understand."

"No way, I said I'd stay. Besides, I'm having way too much fun." He scanned the family photos displayed by the TV and pulled one from the shelf. "Is this your mom?" He held a black and white picture of my mom, and I nodded.

"I see where you get your looks," he said. "She's a beauty. You have the same eyes."

"She and my aunt were twins," I informed him proudly.

"No kidding?" he asked with a raised eyebrow. I pointed to one of the pictures of my mom and my Aunt Beth.

"Wow. You and Kate," his voice was quiet. "It's no wonder you look more like sisters."

"I'm named after my aunt, you know," I told him. "Grace Elizabeth. Sometimes Kate calls me Gracie-Beth." He chuckled as he continued looking at the different pictures, every now and then selecting one from the shelf to get a closer look.

"Hmmm, Gracie-Beth. I like that," he said thoughtfully. "What's Kate's middle name?"

"Elise. She's named after my mom, Katherine."

"Why did your parents name you Grace instead of Elizabeth?"

"I was really sick when I was born, they didn't think I was going to survive. I had some kind of issue with my heart."

Garrett's eyebrows came together as he listened.

"My parents were going to name me Elizabeth, but when I was so sick and survived, they decided to name me Grace instead." I shrugged. "I guess they thought it was fitting."

He quickly retrieved another picture from the shelf, turning it around so I could see. It was me in a pink ruffled dress and black patent-leather shoes, standing next to a piano.

"My first piano recital. I was eight."

"You play the piano?" He seemed happily surprised.

"Kate and I both play. Our mothers were amazing pianists. We have a piano in a storage facility in town," I told him. "We remodeled shortly after Uncle David passed away, and there just wasn't room for it, so we never brought it back." He looked at the picture for a minute, and then set it back down, picking up a photo of me with my mom and dad.

His expression was sad, and he seemed hesitant. "What happened with your parents and Kate's mom?"

"You mean the accident?"

"Yeah," he studied the picture in his hand. "What happened?"

"We were on a ski trip in Vail for the weekend. Uncle David couldn't join us until Saturday afternoon. He was a Neurosurgeon and busy at the hospital, so he drove up by himself." I looked down at the floor as I remembered. Sometimes it seemed like yesterday. "He promised to take Kate and I to our favorite ice cream place on the way home, so we rode with him. Mom, Dad, and Aunt Beth were eager to get home," I swallowed hard. "Anyway, I guess Dad hit a patch of ice on the road."It had been so long since I'd even thought about the accident, but, it still caused the familiar ache to return, even after all the years that passed.

"I'm sorry, Gracie," Garrett said sweetly. "I'm sorry you lost your parents."

"Uncle David was wonderful to me, he was like my dad," I said with a smile. "And, I have Kate."

Garrett sighed as he set the picture carefully back on the shelf. "Did you know we had a little sister?" He shoved his hands into his pockets and kept his eyes on the photos, not looking at me. I swallowed the knot that formed in my throat.

"No," my voice was quiet. "I didn't know that."

"Rachel." A smile touched the corner of his mouth. "She died eight years ago of cancer. She was only fourteen."

My breath hitched with his words, and I shook my head. "I'm so sorry."

He looked at me then. "You know, you remind me of her. She had blue eyes, too." Grief came over his face, and I wanted to go to him and just hug him. I looked down at my hands, the ugliness of cancer familiar to me. He turned suddenly and walked to the kitchen. "You hungry?"

"Um, not really." I was still trying to recover from our conversation, and pretty sure he was doing the same thing. "You need to help yourself to whatever we have. There are leftover enchiladas, unless you're tired of them."

"Excellent. You should probably eat something too."

"Okay, I'll have an enchilada."

"On it."

Plates clanked and the microwave beeped. He brought me a plate with an enchilada on it, then returned to the kitchen.

"Hey, I think I found some leftover steak, do you mind?" he called.

"Not at all, but it's leftover from Friday. It may not be that great."

He snorted a laugh, obviously disregarding my warning. After a few minutes, he came into the living room again, holding a plate piled high with leftover steak, several enchiladas and two bottles of ginger ale. He took a big bite of steak, his eyes rolling back into his head as he chewed. His cell phone rang, and he answered it with his mouth full, again.

"Hey, Michael," Garrett mumbled and I smiled waiting for the inevitable. "Steak, why?" He shrugged as he looked at me innocently, and I was about to fall off the couch laughing.

"We're good," he said. "Yes, I'm behaving myself. Just a sec." He pulled the phone away. "Do you need anything?"

"No, I'm good. Thanks."

"Did you hear that?" Garrett asked Michael. "Okay. See ya." He pressed a button and tossed his phone on the coffee table.

"Was he calling to check on me?"

Garrett grinned while he chewed. "You could say that."

"That was nice of him."

"Yep. He's a pretty nice guy."

I thought about how Michael rearranged meetings to take me to the E.R., Garrett had given up his day just to sit with me, and Miles was busy helping at the store. I'd never known anyone quite like the Andersons, and even though we'd only known each other for a few weeks, I already cared for them. It seemed so strange to feel this way about people I hardly knew. I was comfortable with Garrett. I liked him so much, and it was the same with Miles and Michael.

"What's wrong?" Garrett interrupted my reverie.

I smiled at him. "Nothing's wrong, I was just thinking…I've never met anyone like you and your brothers."

"Is that good or bad?"

"It's good," I told him. "It's just surprising, that's all."

He nodded thoughtfully, and then smiled widely as if something had suddenly come to his mind.

"Providential," he said matter-of-factly.

"Providential?"

"That's the word Miles used the night you and Kate came over to introduce yourselves. Providential. And I would have to agree."

I couldn't help my smile. "Me too."

There was a knock on the front door, and then it opened slightly.

"Can I come in?" Michael peered around the door.

"Of course," I said.

I noticed every detail about him every time I saw him, and I'm pretty sure that made me pathetic. He smiled when he saw his brother in the kitchen doing dishes.

"Hey, little brother." Garrett waved. "How was the meeting?"

"Stimulating," Michael said dryly, and then he looked down at me. "How are you doing?"

"I'm good. Thanks."

"Does it still hurt?"

"Not too bad," I said with a shrug.

"When did you take your last pain pill?"

I smirked at his line of questioning. "Um, this morning."

He checked his watch and went to the kitchen. He returned with a glass of water and the bottle of pain medication, shaking out a tablet and handing it to me.

"Thanks," I said.

"You're welcome." His eyes didn't leave mine, and I felt the trembling begin, confused by the strange effect he had on me. I swallowed the pill and leaned into the couch, trying to escape his gaze.

Deciding I couldn't put off a shower any longer, I excused myself to my bathroom. After my shower, I hobbled into the kitchen where Kate and the Andersons were all sitting around the table.

Garrett saw me and patted the chair next to him. "Sit here, Gracie. You feel better now?"

"I know I smell better," I quipped.

Kate dished Chinese take-out onto a plate for me. I looked over at Michael as I started to eat, noticing he was watching me.

"How's the ankle?" He asked.

"Fine. Thanks again for everything today. I really appreciate it."

"It's no problem." He smiled warmly. "I'm glad we could help."

For a long moment he watched me and then abruptly pushed away from the table.

"Thanks for dinner, Kate," he said. "But I have some things I need to finish up. Grace, feel better."

"Thanks." I was disappointed he left so quickly and tried not to dwell on it, but did anyway.

"So, Miles," Garrett said. "Do you know how to make all those fancy coffees now?"

Kate giggled while she gazed dreamily at Miles, and Garrett nudged me gently under the table, obviously noticing the same thing.

"I think I actually got the hang of it," Miles said proudly. "Have you ever heard of a 'half-caf-non-fat-double-shot-full-foam-latte?"

Garrett looked at him dumbfounded.

"Exactly." Miles replied.

"Was the bookstore busy?" I asked.

"Yeah," Kate said. "It was pretty busy all day."

Miles nodded in agreement. "Grace, I have to hand it to you. You have an impressive selection there. Kate tells me you run the bookstore."

"Well, I don't do it by myself. The bookstore just happens to be the part I like best," I told him. "I love books."

"So I've heard." Miles smiled, watching Kate as she got up and started doing dishes. "She talked about you most of the day," he said in a low aside. He winked at me and then went to help Kate.

Garrett stood up, pulling my chair out for me, and I hobbled to the couch in the stupid, ugly boot. I wasn't sure I'd be able to keep the annoying contraption on for two weeks like Evan instructed. I hadn't even had it on for eight hours, and I hated its guts. Garrett chuckled at my irritated expression as I sat down on the couch next to him. I wasn't surprised anymore at how comfortable I was with Garrett, because he made me comfortable. He flipped through the channels, looking for something to watch as I laid my head back and closed my eyes. My ankle throbbed dully, and I was tired. He put the TV on ESPN, and we watched baseball highlights.

"Yankees?" he asked, cocking an eyebrow.

I snorted. "Of course."

He grinned, giving me a fist bump.

When Miles and Kate came into the living room, Garrett stood from the couch and helped me to my feet. As I looked up at my new friend, I felt a surge of love for him. It was bizarre feeling so close to him, so quickly.

"Thank you, Garrett. Thank you so much for everything today."

Without warning, he picked me up, tightening his arms around me in a bear hug.

"Aw," his voice was gentle. "I had so much fun with you today, really. You don't need to thank me." He swung me back and forth so my feet swayed above the floor—even with the stupid boot—making me giggle. He set me down and kissed the top of my head before walking out the door.

"Miles, thanks for your help today," I said. "I really appreciate it."

"It was my pleasure. You get better, okay?"

I nodded and turned to go to my room as Kate walked with him outside. I took the boot off of my foot and slid under the covers of my bed, feeling a little drowsy. I heard the front door close, and soon Kate was sitting on the edge of my bed.

"You need anything, Gracie?"

I shook my head and remembered my conversation with Garrett.

"Kate, did Miles tell you they had a sister?"

Her expression was instantly troubled as she shook her head slowly.

"Her name was Rachel. She died of cancer eight years ago." My throat tightened. "She was only fourteen."

Kate's eyes welled with tears, and I brushed mine away. Kate grabbed my hand and lay down next to me as we both stared up at the ceiling. Memories of Uncle David flashed through my mind, and though I'd never met her, I thought of Rachel and the heartache the Anderson family must have suffered with their loss.

Kate stayed with me that night, neither of us willing to leave the other alone. Both of us so thankful we had each other.

Chapter Seven

I woke to the smell of coffee and bacon, wondering why Kate would be making breakfast on a workday. I rolled over to look at my alarm clock, which I'd forgotten to set last night. It was after nine o'clock. I quickly got out of bed and was instantly reminded of what I'd done to my ankle.

"Ow!" I clinched my teeth and hopped toward the bathroom for my shower. Kate came into my room, dressed and ready for the day.

"You okay?" she asked.

"Why didn't you wake me up?"

She strolled past me into the bathroom and turned on the shower for me. "I thought you could use the sleep. Don't worry about it, I called Kenny, and we're covered."

"Okay, I'll be ready in just a few."

"Take your time. I invited Miles to join us for breakfast." She hummed as she started making my bed for me.

"Kate, it's only a sprained ankle. I can make my bed."

She shrugged, and I knew better than to argue. I showered quickly, got dressed and strapped the big, ugly boot onto my foot and limped out to the kitchen. Miles sat at the table with Kate dishing up scrambled eggs, bacon and her cinnamon-streusel muffins.

He smiled sweetly at me. "Good morning. How's the ankle?"

"It's fine, thanks." I replied. "Where are your brothers?"

"They had to go to Denver. We're starting a remodel project at St. Joseph's Hospital."

Kate handed me a cup of coffee and sat next to him. We ate quietly for a moment, when Miles broke the silence.

"Grace," his voice was soft. "Kate told me Garrett talked about Rachel yesterday."

I nodded warily.

He seemed hesitant. "I feel the need to explain something."

"Okay."

Miles took a deep breath and rested his arms on the table, his expression wistful.

"We all loved Rachel very much, but Garrett was closest to her, and her death was a devastating blow to him." He looked down at his hands as he continued. "Her last two weeks, Mom and Dad brought her home with a nurse, wanting her to be as comfortable as possible. Garrett only left her side long enough to shower because Mom and Dad insisted." He smiled, but it didn't touch his eyes. "He ate and slept right next to her bed, and when she died it was Garrett's hand she held. He wasn't himself for a long time after that."He shook his head sadly, and I felt tears coming. Kate reached over and placed her hand over his, and they watched each other for a moment before he turned to me again.

"I'm telling you this because, I know that Garrett can be…a lot to take, and I say this with all the love in my heart for him. I just don't want him to scare you or make you uncomfortable."

I wondered for a moment if maybe I should feel uncomfortable with Garrett, but when I thought about him, the only thing I felt was happy.

"He's a gigantic, massive guy, with the biggest heart of anyone you'll ever meet," Miles continued. "He's never spoken of Rachel's death with anyone. Not even Michael or me. The fact he said anything to you…he already thinks a lot of you."

Sadness and happiness surged inside me at the same time. Sadness for the loss Garrett and his family suffered, and happiness that Garrett felt some sort of comfort in our new-found friendship.

"I already think a lot of him, too, and he doesn't scare me one bit," I assured him. "He hasn't made me feel uncomfortable either. In fact, I've only been surprised at how quickly I felt comfortable with him."

Miles seemed relieved as he leaned back in his chair."Well that's good. I know he would never want to give you the wrong idea or make you feel uneasy in any way. I've never seen Garrett take to anyone so quickly. And that's a compliment."

"That's exactly how I take it, as a compliment," I responded. "And you know, I've never had a big brother."

He laughed and nodded. "I think it's safe to say, you do now."

* * *

Over the next several weeks, the Anderson's became an intricate part of Kate's and my life, and we loved each one of them. They were three of the most generous, compassionate and warm-hearted people I'd ever known in my entire life, and it didn't take long for the five of us to feel more like family than neighbors.

I was closest to Garrett. It was so easy to be comfortable with him. Miles was right—Garrett was the goofy, over-protective, big brother I never knew I wanted. We'd razz each other constantly and argue about which one of us knew more about football. I knew he did, but I would never admit it, even if I had to spend time on the Internet looking up facts just to impress him. I tried to educate him on music and books, and he'd pretend to be bored, but I knew he listened. He'd break into his loud, gut-busting laugh when I quoted verbatim most of the lines from the first three "Rocky" movies and pat my shoulders in comfort when I sniffled during a sad movie.

Miles was gentle and soft-spoken, and I loved the way he loved Kate. They adored each other and were blissfully in love. Their happiness was infectious. It made the rest of us happy just being around them. He and Garrett treated me like a little sister, and I loved it.

And then, there was Michael.

After my ankle healed and I got rid of the stupid boot, we ran together almost every morning. I really loved having that time together, even though he made me quite nervous in the beginning. We'd laugh a lot and ask probing questions about each other, from favorite color to favorite ice cream, and talk about everything from politics to childhood memories. I loved being with him, and the more I was around him, the more at ease I felt. We enjoyed each other's company, and I was determined not to make things awkward because of my feelings for him, even though I wasn't really sure what those feelings were. He was in my every thought, his presence always felt. I lay in bed at night, seeing his face when I closed my eyes. Even with everything I knew about him, I wanted to know more.

The boys were eager for Kate and me to meet their parents, so, they arranged for a weekend visit. Will and Ava Anderson were a visible explanation of why their three boys were so gorgeous. Their dad, tall and lean, had the same dark curly hair as Garrett, not to mention the same enormous dimples flanking the movie-star smile each of the boys inherited. Mrs. Anderson was also tall, and graceful, reminding me of a ballerina. Her features were delicate and her hair the same chestnut color as Michael's.

We stood in the Anderson's living room and I watched as Miles introduced Kate, the exultant pride in his voice and on his face. Garrett grabbed my hand and pulled me toward him, draping his giant arm over my shoulders.

"Mom, Dad, this is Gracie."

Mrs. Anderson smiled warmly and reached for my hand taking it into hers. "It's wonderful to finally meet you. We've heard so much about you from all of the boys."

"It's great to meet you too, Mrs. Anderson."

"Please, call me Ava."

I nodded and put my hand out to Mr. Anderson, and he shook it gently.

"It's nice to meet you, Grace. You can call me Mr. Anderson."

Ava nudged him in the ribs with her elbow, and he didn't release my hand as he continued to laugh, and I saw a reflection of Garrett's personality.

"Call me Will," he said with a wink.

We spent the weekend getting to know Will and Ava. The love the Anderson family had for each other was overwhelming to see and it caused my heart to ache. Not with pain, but with joy.

* * *

It was Saturday morning, and I returned home from a run alone, because Michael didn't show up. The house was empty, and I walked straight to shower and get dressed in my comfy jeans and crimson USC sweatshirt. The Trojans were playing Stanford, and Garrett and I were going to watch it together. While I made a pot of coffee, I noticed a note from Kate on the fridge saying she was with Miles and Garrett getting groceries.

I listened to the *drip, drip* of the coffee maker and retrieved a cup from the cupboard. After stirring cream and sugar into my coffee, I decided to grab the paper and catch up on football scores. When I picked up the paper from the front walk, I noticed a cherry-red Porsche parked in front of the Anderson's house. Before I made it inside, I heard voices from across the drive.

Michael and Nina walked together arm in arm to her Porsche. She was dressed impeccably, her hair perfectly styled and laughing at something Michael had said, tossing her hair and rubbing his arm.

A twinge of anger flashed through me when she touched him, even though I knew I had no right to be angry. They looked like they belonged together—both of them beautiful. My anger turned into plain old jealousy.

Michael opened the car door for her and just as she was getting ready to climb inside, they looked over at me. Caught staring like an idiot, I panicked for a moment, wishing I could blend in with my surroundings somehow, and gave an awkward wave with the newspaper in my hand. Michael grinned widely in amusement, and I quickly walked into the house closing the door behind me, embarrassed.

Every time I saw Michael with Nina it made me miserable.

I grabbed my coffee and heard the *click* of the front door opening, thinking it was Michael. Too embarrassed by my earlier scene of stupidity, there was no way I was going to face him. No way. I sprinted to my bedroom and closed the door silently. I turned the lock on the doorknob, hearing his footsteps as he came down the hallway toward my room. I put my ear to the door and tried not to breathe. There was a soft knock, and I clamped my hand over my mouth.

"Grace?" He knocked again. "Are you in there?" Another knock. "Grace?"

I stood frozen, sure he could hear my heart pounding through the door. There was a soft chuckle and quiet steps as he walked down the hallway, and then the front door closed. I exhaled and waited for a moment. Not hearing anything, I returned to the kitchen setting my coffee on the table and pulled out a chair.

"Ahem."

I jumped about a foot in the air and spun around to see Michael leaning against the wall in the kitchen, arms crossed over his chest, a huge smirk on his face.

"Holy crap," I muttered.

He laughed quietly as he watched me try to pull myself together.

"Playing hide and seek?" he asked with a smug grin. I sat at the table with my back to him so he wouldn't see how red my face was.

"No." I opened the newspaper in an attempt to ignore him, which, of course, was a complete waste of time. Michael Anderson was impossible to ignore.

I knew he was still there, though he wasn't speaking. It felt like he was boring a hole through the back of my head with his eyes, and I wanted to go back to my room and hide. I also wanted to ask him about Nina, but there was no way I was going to do that.

Finally, after a long silence, he came around the table and sat in front of me, resting his chin on his hands, watching me with a grin. I raised the paper to block his view, but he sniggered so I lowered the paper slightly, giving him an angry look.

"What?" I spat.

"Is something bothering you this morning?"

"No," I lied.

"Well, don't you think you'd be able to read better if the paper was right side up?" He was biting the corner of his mouth, enjoying my discomfort.

Crap. I was trying so hard to ignore him—the stupid newspaper was upside-down. With a sigh, I turned it around while my face reddened. He laughed quietly as he got up to pour himself a cup of coffee and returned to his chair. My body tensed as he walked past, but I kept my face hidden behind the paper, feeling his eyes on me again.

"You look cute today," he said, casually opening a section of the newspaper. I snorted a laugh and continued trying to focus on the sports section, since it was right side up now.

"Are you sure there's nothing bothering you?" he asked.

I lowered the paper to meet the full force of his gaze."You decided not to run this morning?"

His expression turned apologetic. "I had a last minute appointment this morning. Did you miss the stimulating conversation?" His eyes sparkled with humor, and I couldn't be mad at him anymore.

"Actually, I was able to run much faster today for some reason." I smiled smugly.

"Oh, you're so witty." He groaned.

The front door opened and Kate, Miles and Garrett all filed into the kitchen carrying bags of groceries.

"Hey, guys!" Garrett said cheerfully as he came over and kissed the top of my head, which he now did on a regular basis.

I glanced at Michael, and he watched me as we pushed away from the table to help put groceries away.

Garrett grinned down at me. "Stanford. USC. Fight on, right?"

"Fight on. Two o'clock," I said. "You want brownies?"

He rolled his eyes. "Uh, yeah."

"Are you coming?" I asked Michael, and he nodded. "Good. You can help me make the brownies since your brother never does," I said, raising my eyebrows at Garrett.

"No kidding," Garrett said, shaking his head as he patted Miles' shoulder. "Miles, you really should help out once in a while."

Miles shook his head at his brother while the rest of us busted-up laughing.

Chapter Eight

It was Monday before Thanksgiving, and Michael and I went for our run, having our usual casual conversation. Kate and I were invited to spend the holiday with the Andersons at their parents' home just outside of Castle Rock. He talked about his family's Thanksgiving traditions and asked about Kate's and mine. This was difficult to answer because we didn't really have many.

"Uncle David was usually at the hospital on holidays," I explained. "I'm not sure why it always worked out that way, but it did."

"So what did you and Kate do?"

"We always made a traditional dinner, and then, of course, football. I guess that's it."

"That makes me a little sad."

"Why?" I asked. He stopped running and I stopped in front of him. His expression was troubled, and I didn't like to see him that way.

"I guess I feel a little selfish," he said.

I snorted a laugh. "You're the least selfish person I know, Michael Anderson. Why would you feel selfish?"

His gaze shifted between the ground and me.

"Because you never really had the chance to make holiday traditions with your own parents." He smiled weakly. "But I'm also glad you and Kate are part of our family now, so it makes me feel selfish."

Without thinking about it I stepped toward him, wrapping my

arms around his waist, and he embraced me.

"You don't have to feel sad about that, it's just how things were for Kate and me. We never realized we were missing out on anything." I looked up at him. "You and your brothers…you can't even imagine how thankful we are that you're a part of our lives. Everything we missed with our own families, each day we spend with you guys, we're making new memories. We aren't missing anything."

I watched him, hoping he understood what I was trying to say. He pulled me close to him again, and I could feel my heart pounding, the sensation of his arms around me making me feel like I could fly. He released me with a fervent smile, and we continued our run.

"Make sure you bring your running shoes with you to my parents'," he told me as I walked toward the house. "You didn't want to take a vacation from running, did you?"

"Not if you don't." I wanted to spend every minute possible with him.

* * *

Wednesday finally arrived and we were in Garrett's Hummer, making our way to Will and Ava's house in Black Forest. The drive went quickly, and soon we turned onto a paved driveway that wound between massive pine trees and ended in front of a magnificent house.

The red brick house was two-stories high with tall arched windows and white columns that stretched from the roof line, to the front porch. A warm glow of light shone through the windows, making the house look like something you'd see on a greeting card.

"It's beautiful," I said.

"Michael designed it," Garrett said as he walked to the back of the car to get our bags. "They just finished construction a couple of months ago."

Michael stood next to me, a suitcase in each hand and a duffel bag over his shoulder, while I stared at the house in astonishment. I reached for the duffel bag, but he shook his head with a smile.

"You designed this?" I asked, pointing to the house.

He shrugged, and I shook my head.

"What?" He asked.

"I guess I shouldn't be surprised, you're very talented."

He smiled. "I'm glad you're here."

Will and Ava greeted us warmly, and I took in the beauty of their home, overwhelmed by the fact Michael had designed such a spectacular place.

A grand staircase was the focal point of the entryway, with a stunning chandelier hanging from the high ceiling. The colors of the fabrics and décor were richly colored reds, golds and coppers and the wood floors a dark mahogany.

"Girls, make yourselves at home," Ava instructed. "Anything you need, just ask."

We followed the boys up the staircase into a wide hallway, several doors on both sides. Rows of family portraits hung along the walls, and the boys pointed out who was who, as Kate and I looked over each one; Will and Ava at their wedding, baby pictures of the boys and more of them at various ages.

At the end of the hallway was a picture that seemed to be separated from the others. It was a portrait of a young girl, in her early teens, with long, wavy hair and blue eyes. The dark-haired beauty was all smiles and dimples, and I swallowed the lump in my throat as I studied the portrait closely, realizing it was their baby sister, Rachel.

"She's beautiful," I whispered, examining each detail of her lovely face. Garrett put his arm over my shoulders, but didn't say anything.

"Yes, she is," Michael said, the sadness in his voice causing my heart to ache. "It happened so fast. She was diagnosed and died six weeks later."

Since we'd met, I believed the Andersons stepped out of some kind of fairy tale story land. Smart, wealthy, handsome, talented. But just like the rest of us, they weren't exempt from heartache. I glanced up at Michael, and his eyes met mine. The pained expression on his face was heartbreaking. I wanted to comfort him in some way, but I knew when you've lost someone you love, comfort was difficult to find. It doesn't matter if it's one year or eight, the heartache is always there. I reached for Michael's hand, squeezing it gently, and he smiled as we followed Garrett into the room where Kate and I would be staying.

"Mom said dinner will be ready in about fifteen minutes," Miles said. "We'll see you downstairs."

"Hey, Gracie," Garrett said as he walked toward the door. "Mom and Dad have a piano downstairs, and I told them you and Kate play." He waggled his eyebrows at me and I felt the blood drain from my face.

"Yeah, I don't think so."

"Aw, c'mon," he whined. "I wanna hear you play."

"No." I shook my head adamantly. "Absolutely not."

Garrett's shoulders dropped, and he followed Miles out the door. Michael leaned toward me.

"I would love to hear you play," he said in a quiet voice before pulling the door closed behind him.

"Do you think Ava and Will really expect us to play the piano for them?" I asked Kate anxiously.

"Oh please," she said, exasperated. "You could play in your sleep. Stop worrying."

Of course Kate wasn't worried, because she was the one that could play in her sleep. I dug the toiletries bag out of my suitcase and followed her into the bathroom to freshen up for dinner. We made our way down the stairs to the kitchen where everyone was already gathered around the table, and Garrett patted the seat between him and Michael, waiting for me.

Ava made a delicious dinner of green salad, beef stew and yeast rolls. There were several conversations going on at once while we ate. Miles, Kate and Will were talking about our store, while Garrett and Ava were talking about something that had to do with Thanksgiving dinner.

"Grace," Ava said my name sweetly. "I've been informed you and Kate play the piano."

"It's been a while," I answered nervously. "But yes, we do play."

"You don't play anymore?"

"They took the piano out of the house when they remodeled," Garrett explained for me. "And they never brought it back."

"There wasn't really room for it anymore," Kate amended.

"That's a shame," Ava said. "Did you ever play duets?"

Kate and I actually did play duets. Uncle David always loved it when Kate and I played the piano together.

"They did more than just play, Mom," Garrett answered again. "They've won state competitions and everything." I looked at him in shock, wondering how he knew this because I never told him, and I'm sure Kate hadn't either.

"Really?" Ava smiled. "That's wonderful! I can't wait to hear you."

"Well, it's been a while," I said again.

Garrett chuckled, and I narrowed my eyes at him, nudging him under the table.

He shrugged. "Kenny told me. I think it's pretty cool myself."

After dinner, Kate and I insisted on doing the dishes and Ava relented. Michael and Miles helped while Garrett, Will and Ava went into the family room. When we finished the dishes, Miles took Kate's hand, pulling her from the kitchen.

"We want to show you something," he said with a big smile. "You too, Grace."

Michael motioned with his head for me to follow them. Miles led us into a large room decorated completely in white, and right in the middle of the room was a beautiful, grand piano. Not just any piano, mind you, but a Steinway, and it was beautiful. I touched the smooth ebony finish reverently, while Kate sat on the tufted, leather bench and lightly ran her fingers over the ivory keys.

"This is wonderful," I said. "Who plays?"

"Mom," Michael replied. "She always tried to teach us, but none of us were really interested. I think it makes her a little sad."

Kate played a C-scale quietly, and we both smiled at the perfect pitch and tone, each note clear and beautiful. I knew she wouldn't be able to stand it, because I barely could. She began playing, her fingers gliding over the keys smoothly and flawlessly as the music filled the room. Miles was awestruck as he walked slowly to the piano, sitting beside Kate. He watched her face as she played, his expression so full of love.

"This is one of Gracie's favorites," Kate said.

"'The Swan'," I murmured and closed my eyes, listening to each note of music. I remembered my mom playing the same piece when I was little, and a pang of sadness caused a lump to form in my throat.

When I opened my eyes, Michael stood next to me, his eyes intense and sincere as he gazed into mine. It was at that moment, I realized I loved him.

I loved Michael Anderson.

It became clear why I'd never understood the feelings I had for him. I'd never been in love before. There was no doubt in my mind now.

I knew if I was asked to explain it, I wouldn't be able to. The feelings and emotions reached deeper than I knew possible but also offered a strange sense of comfort. My heart clenched with happiness and pain at the same time.

What if he didn't feel the same? And what about Nina?

Fear eclipsed the happiness as the thought made my heart ache even more. Michael's expression changed as he watched me, and I looked away quickly, afraid he'd see right through me.

The beautiful song came to an end, and it was quiet.

“That was amazing,” Miles said, taking Kate’s hands in his.

“Thanks, Kate,” I told her, and she winked at me.

Ava, Will and Garrett had come into the room unnoticed.

“That was absolutely beautiful,” Ava said.

Kate stood and did a quick curtsy, and everyone laughed as they turned to leave the room.

“So, when are you going to play for us?” Garrett asked me with a grin.

“Kate’s much better than I am, she pulled that off without touching a piano in almost a year. I don’t think I should even try.”

“I’m thinking you should,” Michael urged, but I avoided looking at him.

Garrett grabbed both of my hands excitedly. “Let’s go kill some zombies!”

“I’m sorry, what was that?” I asked, having no idea what he was talking about.

Michael laughed. “It’s a video game.”

“C’mon,” Garrett pleaded. “It’ll be fun!”I was tired, but I didn’t want to hurt his feelings. He studied my expression and grimaced, pulling me into a tight hug.

“Okay, fine. But you’re playing tomorrow.”

“Okay,” I agreed, and he bent down so I could kiss his cheek. I started to follow him into the living room, when Michael tugged at my sleeve.

“Are we going to run tomorrow?”

I tried to smile. “Sure, I’ll be ready. Regular time?”

He nodded, his expression somewhat perplexed. “What’s going on in that head of yours?”

My thoughts became muddled as he gazed at me.

“Is something wrong?”

I shook my head and smiled nervously. “No,” I tried to sound convincing. “I’m fine.”

I could tell he was dissatisfied with my response, but he followed me into the living room without further questioning. Kate and I said goodnight to everyone and headed to our room where I sat on the edge of the bed.

So many things were running through my mind. The biggest thing, of course, being I could finally admit to myself I loved Michael. Not the same way I loved Garrett or Miles, but in a way I'd never expected. Kate sat next to me, eyeing me speculatively.

"So," she said with a slight smile. "When are you going to tell him?"

I should've known. Sometimes Kate knew me better than I knew myself. I laid my head on her shoulder, and she sighed impatiently.

"Are you going to tell him or not?"

I shrugged. "I don't know. I'm not sure he feels the same way, and I don't want to ruin our friendship."

"I understand, but it's going to make things awkward anyway if you keep it to yourself."

I sat up straight and looked at her. "What do you mean?"

"I mean, you love Michael, and you know it," her tone was matter-of-fact as she continued. "You may decide not to tell him, but the love is still there. Are you going to be able to pretend nothing's changed?"

She was right. I flopped backwards onto the bed, covering my eyes with my arm.

"I'm not that good of an actress," I said with disdain.

She flopped down next to me and giggled. "True. Neither of us was ever very good at acting."

"So what should I do?" I turned my head so we were facing each other.

She shrugged. "Tell him."

As usual, she made it sound so simple. I lay in bed that night and worried about being alone with Michael in the morning, hoping I wouldn't turn into a babbling idiot during our run. I had a hard enough time trying to form coherent sentences before I knew I was in love with him. If I didn't want things to change between us, I was going to have to become an actress overnight, literally. As much trouble as I had looking into his eyes on a regular basis, I was going to have to be friggin' Meryl Streep.

Chapter Nine

I got out of bed carefully, so I wouldn't wake Kate, pulled my clothes from my bag and went into the bathroom to get dressed. I grabbed my shoes as I closed the bedroom door behind me quietly.

"Good morning."

I flinched and turned around to see Michael leaning against the wall next to his bedroom door, grinning as he tied his shoe.

"Sorry, I didn't mean to scare you," he whispered.

"Uh-huh." I narrowed my eyes at him. "I think you like scaring me."

He chuckled, and we walked quietly down the stairs to the front door. Once outside, I sat on the front porch to pull my shoes on, and he waited at the bottom of the steps with his arms folded across his chest, watching me. I felt the relentless thudding of my heart as I started toward the driveway.

This was going to be even more difficult than I'd thought. Just having him near me caused strange sensations and feelings. He came up beside me, and I could feel him watching me, but I kept looking straight ahead as we walked down the driveway.

"Everything okay?" he asked.

"Sure," I replied, my voice shaky. "Why?"

"I don't know. You just seem a little…distracted."

Yep. Meryl Streep indeed.

We were both quiet during our run, and I was thankful. I'm not sure how far we ran, but it seemed further than usual. When we reached the driveway, we slowed to a walk, and I put my hands on my hips, taking some deep breaths.

"Did I run you too much?" He asked, sounding a little smug.

"Ha-ha," I said dryly. "I think it's the altitude."

"Um, except we're lower. So, I don't think so."

"Maybe that's the problem. The air is too thick down here."

He laughed as I followed him up the porch steps and through the front door. I could hear voices and dishes clattering from the kitchen, and the aroma of bacon and coffee filled the house. When we entered the kitchen, Michael kissed Ava on the cheek as she flipped slices of French toast on a large griddle, while Garrett, Miles and Will watched the Thanksgiving Day Parade in the family room.

"Good morning, Ava," I said. "Is there anything I can do to help?"

She smiled sweetly. "If you'd like to help Kate set the table, I think we're about ready." I went to the sink and washed my hands.

"So, how's it going, Meryl?" Kate whispered over my shoulder with a giggle.

"Very funny," I whispered back, nudging her in the ribs.

Ava called everyone in, and we sat down and started to eat the huge breakfast that she'd prepared.

"So did you girls sleep well?" Will asked as he took a bite of French toast.

"We did, thank you," Kate replied.

"Ava, our room is absolutely beautiful," I said. "Thank you so much."

"Your whole house is really beautiful," Kate added.

She smiled. "Thank you. But most of the credit has to go to Michael. He's brilliant."

Brilliant, kind, generous, beautiful...

His eyes met mine for a moment, and I quickly turned back to Ava.

"So, what can we do to help with dinner today?" My voice was shaky because of Michael's gaze, and I tried desperately to get a grip on myself.

"Actually, I've got the turkey ready to go into the oven and other than that, there's not much more to do," she assured me. "I did most of the cooking yesterday."

"Well, I wish you would have allowed Kate and I to contribute something. We would've been happy to help."

"I just want you to enjoy your time here. Besides, from what I hear, you've been taking good care of my boys."

"We've heard reports that you and Kate are quite the gourmet cooks," Will said.

"I don't know how *gourmet* we are, but we do enjoy cooking," I said.

"Well, the boys sure love your cooking," Will laughed. "Especially that one there." He pointed to Garrett with his fork, and Garrett winked at me.

Kate and I helped with the dishes, and Ava hummed sweetly as she worked, reminding me of my mom and Aunt Beth. They were always humming or singing. As little girls, Kate and I would sit at the table watching our moms cook and hum happily.

My eyes blurred with tears as I looked at Kate, a single tear falling down her cheek. I was never surprised how often we knew what the other was thinking. It had been so long since we'd been around a family, we watched the Andersons and some of the memories we thought were forgotten, returned.

I noticed Michael leaning against the counter, watching me with sadness etched on his face. He approached me, draping his arm over my shoulder, and we went into the living room to watch the parade with the others.

After the parade and a barrage of ESPN hype for football, Ava told us dinner would be at four o'clock. Miles tipped us off that everyone dressed up, so after Ava convinced us she didn't need any help with dinner, Kate and I went to our room to get ready.

I showered after Kate, and she had my outfit laid out on the bed: a flared black silk skirt, and white silk fitted blouse with three-quarter sleeves. She cinched a wide sequined black belt around my waist and gave me her peep-toed black suede heels. I kept my hair down, smoothing the curls into soft waves. Kate wore a copper-colored satin dress that draped low in the back and hugged her figure. She looked beautiful.

Miles met Kate at the bottom of the stairs, and they disappeared down the hallway toward the kitchen. I stopped to adjust my shoe and Garrett wolf-whistled.

"If I didn't love you so much like a little sister, Gracie, I'd ask you to go out with me," he said with a huge grin. "You're gorgeous."He bent down and pointed to his cheek for a kiss.

"You're way too good for me, Garrett Anderson," I told him. "But thank you."

Garrett glanced behind me where Michael stood at the top of the stairs. He was wearing all black and was so beautiful it was difficult to look at him. Our eyes held each other's for a long, intense moment, and I cleared my throat nervously as he descended the stairs.

"You look very nice," I said.

An unidentifiable expression crossed his features as he stepped closer, leaning down to kiss my forehead tenderly. I closed my eyes as he held his lips against my skin, and my breathing became unsteady.

"You're stunning," he whispered, his breath was warm against my skin. A shiver ran through me, and I was reeling emotionally, not to mention physically, at his unexpected display of affection. Garrett continued grinning as he offered his arm, leading me down the hallway.

The dining room was grand with rich mahogany furniture and a graceful chandelier hanging over the center of the long table. The china place settings were ivory with a silver band around the edges, crystal glasses and sterling silverware sparkled and shimmered from the flicker of candlelight, and classical music played softly in the background. Michael pulled my chair out for me as I sat down between him and Garrett. The table was overflowing with traditional

Thanksgiving dishes—turkey, gravy, chestnut stuffing, cranberry sauce, sweet potatoes, fresh green beans and homemade rolls. We all ate until we couldn't eat another bite.

"Ava, everything was simply fabulous," Kate said. "Thank you so much."

"Yes, thank you," I echoed Kate. "It was all delicious."

"I'm so glad you enjoyed it. Are we ready for dessert?" Everyone groaned and Ava laughed. "Okay, well maybe later."

"The men are doing the dishes today," Will announced.

"Girls, why don't we go into the music room?" Ava suggested.

Kate and I followed her out of the dining room as the guys all cleared the table and started the cleaning process. Ava sat down at the piano and began playing, while Kate and I sat on the sofa, listening intently.

This Thanksgiving was so different from any Kate and I ever had. It almost didn't seem real. The beautiful home filled with a beautiful family I never expected. I'd always known I was blessed to have Kate. Now I was blessed with the Andersons.

While Ava continued to play a piece by Bach, the men joined us. Will sat beside Ava on the piano bench, and when she finished he kissed her shoulder while the rest of us applauded.

"Thanks, Mom," Miles said to her. "I miss hearing you play."

Will stood and looked at me with a grin, and I felt my face turn red because I knew what was coming.

"Grace, will you play for us?"

Garrett squeezed my shoulders, and I looked up at him, my stomach knotting nervously.

"C'mon," he said quietly. "I've wanted to hear you play ever since I saw that picture."

"What picture?" Michael asked.

Kate smiled proudly. "He's talking about the picture of Gracie at her first piano recital. She was eight."

"You were eight, too." I shook my head, embarrassed, and Garrett nudged me again, his expression pleading. I sighed as I stood up and walked over to the piano.

"It's been almost a year since I've played," I muttered. "So be kind."

Everyone chuckled as I adjusted the bench and smoothed my skirt. I looked at Kate, who was smiling eagerly, as I picked through my memory for a song.

"Okay, this is Kate's favorite," I said, and Kate clapped her hands happily.

I took a deep breath as I placed my hands on the keys and began to play. It had been over a year, but I remembered every note of this song. It had always been Kate's favorite and when we had our piano, she asked me to play it constantly. I listened to the music I was making and realized how much I really missed playing. I continued to play, my hands shaking slightly but thankfully, not missing a note, the melody of the familiar song making me smile. Michael left his chair to stand by the piano, watching me carefully. The music flowed from my fingers to the keys, as memories flooded my mind—hazy memories of my parents, the haze clearing with the memories of Uncle David, and Kate, always Kate, her love and kindness. Now, the new and fresh memories of the Andersons. As my hands hit the final notes, it was Michael's face I saw, and my heart was full.

"Thank you, Gracie," Kate's voice was quiet.

Michael was gazing at me intently as I returned to the couch.

Garrett took my hand. "Thanks. I think we need to get that piano out of the storage facility, don't you?"

I nodded in agreement.

"Well, who's ready for some football?" Will asked clapping his hands together. Garrett hopped up from the couch and everyone made their way to the living room, talking about who was playing. I noticed Michael still standing beside the piano with a distant look on his face.

"Aren't you coming?" I asked.

"That was really something, Grace." He tilted his head toward the piano and smiled wryly. "I guess I shouldn't be surprised. You're very talented."

I rolled my eyes, because I'd said the exact thing to him when I saw this house he'd designed so brilliantly.

"Thanks," I said. "I didn't realize how much I missed playing."

He looked at me thoughtfully and nodded, taking me by the hand as we walked into the living room where everyone gathered around the big screen. After a while, Ava went into the kitchen to get dessert for everyone, and Michael followed to help. I watched him in the kitchen, laughing with his mom, and a lump formed in my throat.

I needed some air.

Excusing myself, I walked quietly down the hall and went outside, pulling the door closed silently. I sat on the porch steps and breathed in the cool air. I shivered and rubbed my arms, trying to create friction. The front door opened, and a quilt came around my shoulders. Garrett stood over me as he zipped his jacket. He sat next to me, and I pulled the quilt tightly around my shoulders. "Thanks, Garrett."

"You're welcome." He shoved his hands into his coat pockets. I leaned my head against his shoulder, looking out at the trees, and he rested his head on top of mine.

"Gracie, why don't you just tell him?" I leaned away so I could look at him, but he just put his arm around me, pulling me to him, and settled his chin on the top of my head again.

"How did you know?" I asked him.

He snorted and squeezed me tightly. "I'm a friggin' genius," he said sarcastically. "Honestly, we all know. The only one clueless is my little brother."

I sighed. "I can't tell him, I don't want to ruin our friendship, and if he doesn't feel the same way about me…"

He chuckled softly, and I looked up at him.

"What's funny?" I asked, irritated.

He patted my shoulder. "You worry too much. What makes you think he doesn't feel the same?"

"I don't know, but it's scary."

Garrett didn't say anything.

"What if he doesn't feel the same? Or what if he's just not interested in anything more than friendship? And he's dating Nina!"

"I wouldn't worry too much about her," he said dismissively. "I think you should tell him."

I rested my head on his shoulder again, and he squeezed me tightly as we sat quiet for a moment.

"Garrett, why don't you date?"

"I love you, Gracie, but you're not my type." He chortled, and I elbowed him in the ribs.

"I'm serious. You're an amazing person," I said, lifting my eyes so I could see him grinning. "I know there has to be girls throwing themselves at you."

"Oh yeah," he snorted. "I'm fighting them off left and right. Look at you, you're all over me."

I rolled my eyes, and he took a deep breath.

"I had a girlfriend in New York," he said. "We were pretty serious, but it didn't work out."

"What happened?"

He shrugged. "We wanted different things. I wanted to treat her like a princess and to love me. She wanted to be treated like a princess and see other guys on the side."

"What?" I felt a burning anger at the thought of anyone hurting Garrett. "She cheated on you?" The thought was so preposterous I couldn't even comprehend it. "What is wrong with her?"

Garrett laughed. "Settle down, Gracie," he said, patting my shoulders. "It was for the best, and I'm not even sorry. Why would I want someone who treated me that way? Life's too short. I haven't found the right one yet."

"I don't think there's anyone out there good enough for you."

"Thanks," he said. "Everything's going to work out fine, you'll see. You and Kate are family now. We all love you, even if one of us is having a difficult time realizing that fact." He winked at me as he stood. "Now come on, let's get inside. It's cold out here, and I want pie."

That night, as I lay in bed, my mind wondered about a hundred different things—all of them involving Michael. I thought about how his touch made me feel. When he kissed my forehead, it was different. His lips touched me, and my body reacted in a way completely unfamiliar to me, causing sensations that made me feel like I was dissolving into a puddle of goo. Accompanied with the heart-flutters and stomach-knots, I was a mess.

I wondered about Nina. I couldn't tell Michael how I felt while he was with her, it wouldn't be right. If he had feelings for me, he wouldn't be with her. Even if he wasn't with Nina, I wondered if I'd ever have enough courage to tell him how I felt.

Chapter Ten

Friday night we returned home to a blanket of fresh snow on the ground. It continued to snow most of the weekend, so Michael and I didn't run because it was just plain cold. Garrett and Miles spent Saturday and most of Sunday with us, but Michael worked on a project he had to finish.

Honestly, I was thankful for the diversion. It had given me time to think and contemplate what I needed to say to Michael, if anything. I hadn't come to any conclusions. Actually, I was more at odds with myself. I was a coward. Too afraid to let my true feelings be known, and too afraid to lose Michael as my friend.

The Broncos were playing at seven o'clock, and Garrett promised to watch the game with me. Around five, Kate went grocery shopping while I did some cleaning and finished up the last of the laundry. When I was done, I decided to take a shower before the game started. I pulled on my comfy sweats and tee shirt, and towel-dried my hair. When I came out of my room, Kate already had the groceries put away and was talking with Miles by the front door.

"We're going to go get a bite in town, Gracie. You wanna come?" she asked.

"No, that's okay. Garrett's coming to watch the game in a few minutes, you two have fun."

They left, and I got comfortable on the couch while I waited for Garrett. Seven o'clock arrived, and he still hadn't come. I went to the front window and looked across the road. His Hummer was there and so was Michael's Yukon. I went back to the couch and found the game, pulling a quilt over my legs. The first quarter was underway and still, no Garrett. It wasn't like him to just not show up.

I went to the front window again. All the lights were on at the Anderson's house. Why hadn't he come yet? If he wasn't going to come, he would have called.

Something wasn't right.

I was wearing my holey sweats and a tee shirt, and my hair was still pretty wet, but I didn't care, I opened the front door and started toward their house. It was cold, really cold, which caused me to quicken my pace. I had my slippers on, but even with snow covering the ground, I could feel the sharp edges of gravel poking the bottoms of my feet. I hurried across to the Anderson's front steps and then to their door. It was partially opened, so I just walked in. I'd been in their house a hundred times, but for some reason I felt like I was being intrusive. I heard murmurs coming from their offices in the upstairs loft.

"Guys?" I called, not very loudly.

No answer, so I stomped the snow off of my now-damp slippers and walked through the entry to the stairs. I shivered from the cold as I climbed the stairs, the voices becoming clearer. I heard a woman's voice, and then the same woman laughed. I stiffened, unable to move because I recognized the laugh. Nina Sandler.

The low murmuring of Michael's voice was followed with more of Nina's incessant giggling, and I couldn't help my eye-roll. Michael was funny, but he wasn't *that* funny. I turned to make my way to the front door, really not wanting to be seen. The footsteps and voices grew louder as they approached the top of the stairs.

"Grace?" Michael called just as I reached the front door.

Damn!

I turned slowly to face him, completely humiliated.

"Is something wrong?" he asked worriedly.

"Um…no…sorry for disturbing you," I stammered, trying to remember the reason that would explain why I was standing at his front door in my pajamas and slippers. With wet hair.

"I-I was just looking for Garrett," I could feel my face turning red. "We were supposed to watch the game."

"He probably fell asleep." Michael surveyed my appearance with his eyebrows pulled together. "What are you doing with wet hair and...are those your slippers? You're going to catch pneumonia."

"Okay then," I said quickly. "Bye."

Michael bit the corner of his mouth as if trying not to laugh, and I turned to go, again.

"Oh, Grace?" he called, and I turned around slowly, wondering why he was determined to prolong my humiliation. When I faced him, his eyebrows were raised in amusement. "This is Nina Sandler." He motioned with his hand to the perfect blonde standing very close to him. "Nina, this is Grace Burke."

"Hello," Nina smiled a perfect smile. "It's nice to meet you." Something in her tone gave me the impression she didn't think it was 'nice' to meet me at all. As I looked at her in all of her blonde perfection, I suddenly felt very self-conscious.

"It's nice meeting you, too." I tried to smile. "Sorry for disturbing you."

They watched me, and Michael looked like he was enjoying my embarrassment. A grin touched the corner of his mouth, and I narrowed my eyes in an attempt to give him an angry look. I don't think I succeeded because I heard him chuckling as I went out the door.

I ran back to my house, kicked off my wet slippers by the door, plopped onto the couch and tried to focus on the game. My teeth chattered from the cold, and I shivered. I grabbed the quilt from the back of the sofa, wrapping it around my shoulders and went into the kitchen to make myself a cup of hot tea. I put the kettle on the stove, turned the burner on high and pulled a cup from the cupboard.

The front door opened, and I figured it was Kate and Miles, but when I looked up, Michael was walking toward me with his hands in his jacket pockets.

"Hey." He smiled and slipped his jacket off, still looking a little amused.

Irritated that he was enjoying my humiliation, I tried not to look at him as I answered.

"Hey." I was still shivering as I opened the cupboard to get the box of tea, and Michael came around the corner to stand beside me.

"Are you cold?" he asked.

I nodded as I pulled a tea bag out of the box and dropped it into my cup.

"Well, it's no wonder," he said. "What are you doing outside with wet hair?"

"Your brother," I said disdainfully. "He was supposed to be here at seven, and I was worried."

"Ah," Michael said in understanding.

The kettle began to whistle, and I pulled it off the burner and poured the boiling water in my cup. I could feel his eyes on me, which made me uncomfortable because I knew I looked completely ridiculous.

"Would you like some tea?" I asked, not making eye contact.

"Sure." He opened the cupboard and retrieved a cup, setting it beside mine. I dropped in a tea bag and poured the hot water. "Thanks."

I could hear the smile in his voice as I took my tea and walked over to the couch, curled up on the end and wrapped my hands around the cup, trying to get warm. The linen closet door closed in the hallway, and Michael came over and spread another quilt over my legs.

"Thanks," I said. Why did he have to be so thoughtful all the time?

He went back into the kitchen for a moment and then sat down across from me on the couch holding his cup of tea, grinning smugly while he watched TV.

"What's so funny?" I asked him, more irritated than before. He shrugged casually, and I turned to face the TV in time to hear him laugh quietly.

"What are you laughing at?"

"You," he said unapologetically.

"Thanks so much."

He didn't say anything, though he was still grinning, and I wanted to smack him. Then I realized how ridiculous I probably looked at his house earlier, and I couldn't really blame him for laughing.

I sighed. "Sorry. I probably embarrassed you. I didn't know you had company."

Now he looked irritated as he turned to face me. "Why on earth would you think you embarrassed me?"

I swallowed hard and looked down at my cup nervously. "Well, I just barged in on you and your guest, and I know I look ridiculous in these stupid, grungy sweats."

He shook his head slowly with an exasperated look on his face.

"First of all, she wasn't a guest," he said plainly. "She's just a client, and she was just picking up some drawings."

What? Just a client? I tried to pay attention to what he was saying.

"Second, you are always welcome in our home. There's nothing you would ever disturb, okay? And besides, you always look beautiful." He turned back to the TV as he took a drink of his tea. "Even in your stupid, grungy sweats."

My face heated from his compliment, and I heard him laugh again. We sat quietly, watching the game when Miles and Kate walked in.

"Hey, guys!" Kate chirped. "Where's Garrett?"

"I think he fell asleep," Michael replied. "I swear, whenever we go to Mom and Dad's, he stays up all hours playing those video games."He watched me for a moment before standing up and walking to the kitchen, setting his cup in the sink. "I'm heading home. Good night." He patted the top of Kate's head. "Night, Grace. Thanks for the tea."

"Night," I murmured, still trying to process that Nina was *just a client.*

He chuckled and shook his head as he walked out the door. I got up from the sofa and started to my room, saying good night to Miles and Kate, who watched me with curious expressions. I closed the door to my room and fell onto my bed, still embarrassed over my display of stupidity in front of Michael.

"Stupid wet hair and grungy stupid sweats," I grumbled to myself.

After tossing and turning for an hour, I decided I was done thinking. I put on a Mozart CD and tried to concentrate on the intricate melodies until I fell asleep.

* * *

It was a typical Monday at the store, slow. Kate and I spent most of the day decorating the store for Christmas, and it looked really great. Miles showed up early in the afternoon to help Kate with some kind of paperwork, so I spent the remainder of the afternoon dusting shelves and returning misplaced books to their correct spots while I waited for five o'clock to come around.

As I arranged cookbooks, a deep voice interrupted my boredom.

"I'd like to speak to your boss, please."

Evan Taylor stood beside the register with his hands deep in the pockets of his faded jeans and a wide grin covering his face.

I laughed as I strode towards him. "What are you doing here?"

He surprised me with a strong hug. "I'm looking for a gift for my mom and she loves to read, so I figured I'd come to an expert." He pointed to my foot. "How's the ankle?"

"Completely healed, I had a great doctor."

He grinned. "True."

"So a gift for your mom, huh?" I asked.

"It's her birthday, and I don't even know where to start when it comes to books."He looked around, pulling a random book from the shelf next to him without paying attention, as he continued scanning the store.

"Um, Evan?" I bit my lip and tried not to laugh. "I've met your mom, and I'm not sure she'd be interested in that one." I pointed to the book in his hand. He looked at me with a raised eyebrow and then at the title of the book he was holding. His face turned a deep shade of red. He placed the book of *Kama Sutra* back on the shelf and shook his head in embarrassment.

"What kind of bookstore is this, anyway?" he asked, feigning shock.

The door to the coffee shop opened, and Michael walked in looking beautiful in a cream v-neck sweater and brown leather jacket. He smiled and my stomach did a complete back flip. I smiled in return and attempted to return my focus to Evan.

"Well, does she enjoy the classics? Or does she prefer more recent authors?" I asked.

"I have no idea."

I grimaced and motioned for him to follow me. I showed him a beautiful collection of Jane Austen books I had on display. Michael leaned against the coffee counter, watching me.

"You can't really go wrong with Jane," I told Evan. "Especially for classics."

"Okay, Jane it is," he agreed.

"Would you like me to wrap them for you?"

He nodded with an appreciative smile, and we walked to the counter. My eyes involuntarily found Michael again, who still watched as I rang up the sale. I chatted casually with Evan as I wrapped the books.

"Where's Kate?" Evan asked.

"She's in the office," I told him. "I'll get her so you can say hi."

I walked around the counter to hand him the gift bag and pulled him by the elbow to the coffee counter where Michael stood.

"Michael, right?" Evan asked.

"Yeah," Michael said, and they shook hands. "Nice to see you again, Evan."

"Evan Taylor!" Kate shrieked and threw her arms around his neck.

"Hey, Katie-Bug!" Evan gave her a hug. "It's great to see you."

Kate introduced Evan to Miles excitedly. "What brings you here?"

"I needed a birthday gift for Mom, and if she doesn't like it, I'm blaming Grace."

I rolled my eyes at him. "Oh yeah, because I'm sure she'd love the first book you chose." We laughed, and I glanced over at Michael still leaning against the coffee counter, his eyes on me. I felt my face get red as I looked back at Evan. "Really, if she doesn't like it, just bring it back. I'm sure we can find something else."

"I'm sure she'll love it," he said, glancing at his watch. "I'd better get going. It was great seeing you both."He lifted the bag, examining it closely. "Nice job on the wrapping. Do you mind if I take the credit?"

"Whatever you feel is necessary," I said.

"Thanks. I'll see you soon?"

I nodded, and he waved goodbye. I watched as he got into a white Land Rover that looked brand new. Michael came towards me, looking out the window at Evan.

"Hey." I smiled at him.

He looked at me, running his hand through his hair, and smiled weakly. "Hey. How's your day?"

"Um, very boring. And yours?"

"I was hoping you'd join me for one of our favorites." He motioned toward the coffee counter, and I nodded.

He followed me behind the counter, helping me make our macchiatos. We sat at one of the tables, and he shrugged out of his jacket. I forced myself to look away, but I could smell his cologne and it caused my head to whirl.

"So, you've known Evan since high school?" he asked, eyeing his coffee cup.

"Since ninth grade."

He started to say something, but Garrett came through the door and strode to our table. I glowered at him.

"I think you're in trouble, big brother," Michael cautioned him, and Garrett surveyed my expression.

"Now, stop giving me the stink-eye, Gracie." He held his hands up defensively. "I didn't mean to, but I fell asleep."

"Fell asleep?" I asked raising an eyebrow skeptically. "A Sunday night Broncos game and you fell asleep?"

He pulled a chair next to me and sat down, watching me with amusement.

"I'm really mad at you," I told him. "I went over to your house looking for you."

"That's true," Michael said. "I'm surprised she doesn't have pneumonia. She came over in slippers, with wet hair."

"Yeah, it was a sight." I continued glaring at Garrett. "I embarrassed your poor brother."

Garrett laughed then, reaching over and putting me in one of his head locks, rubbing the top of my head with his knuckles.

"You're in big trouble, mister!" I said between squeals.

"Yeah, I'm scared." He let go of me, and I blew my hair out of my face, scowling at him.

"I'll make it up to you," he said. "I'll make you some brownies for tonight's game."

I snorted a laugh. "You can't make brownies."

"Oh, yeah. Well, I guess you'll be making them."

Garrett kissed the top of my head and strutted to the office.

"So, are you going to watch the game with us tonight?" I asked Michael.

He shook his head, keeping his eyes on me. "I have some drawings I need to get done."

"For Nina?"

He nodded.

"Well, I promise I won't disturb you tonight." I smiled, making an attempt at humor. He folded his arms across his chest, leaning back in his chair.

"You weren't disturbing me last night."

"Oh. Well, that's good." I laughed nervously.

Garrett came from the back, holding my coat and purse.

"Michael and I are going to take you home, Miles and Kate aren't ready to leave yet."

On the drive home, Garrett and I made bets and talked trash to each other about the football game. The red Porsche was parked in front of the Anderson's and my stomach sank.

"We'll see you later, little brother," Garrett told Michael as he climbed out of the car.

Michael turned to me. "See you in the morning for our run?"

"Absolutely." I tried to paste a smile on my face. "See you at seven."

He waved and started toward their house. Nina stepped out of her Porsche, all legs and blonde perfection, greeting Michael with a kiss on his cheek. I was unable to repress the sigh that escaped, and Garrett chuckled.

"She's just a client." He patted the top of my head. "Stop worrying. Let's go make some brownies."

I looked up at him with my eyebrows raised in surprise. "You're going to help?"

"No." He shook his head. "I'm going to supervise."

Chapter Eleven

I was humming along with the music playing in the store, organizing a shelf of children's classics when someone cleared their throat, getting my attention. Evan stood with a wide smile, the blue sweater he wore making the blue of his eyes more vivid.

"Returning some books?" I teased.

He laughed and shook his head. "No, she loved them. I wanted to thank you."

"You're welcome. I'm glad she liked them."

"If you're not too busy, I thought maybe I could buy you a cup of coffee?" He motioned to the coffee shop with his thumb. "Unless this is a bad time."

"Sure, what would you like?"

"Just regular coffee. Do you have that here?" he asked with a smirk.

"Hmm, regular coffee? I'll have to check."

He chuckled and followed me to the counter.

"Where's Kate?" he asked.

"In the office." I motioned with my head to the back of the store. "You should go say hi, or I'll never hear the end of it."

"Be right back."

When he returned, I was carrying a tray with our coffees and some blueberry bread to a table and sat across from him.

"Have you moved to Fall Rivers permanently?" I asked.

"Yep." He took a sip of coffee. "Over Thanksgiving weekend. I'm still at St. Joseph's every now and then, but mostly I'm in

Boulder. Did you know the Andersons are building the new Oncology wing?"

I nodded.

"I saw Garrett there just last week. He seems like a great guy."

"He is a great guy," I clarified. "All three of the Andersons are great guys."

"Garrett is, uh…" he paused for a moment.

"A goofball?"

We both laughed.

"Yes," Evan said. "He's also huge! You could show a movie on the guy's back!"

"True."

"He sure thinks the world of you and Kate," he added. "Not that I blame him."

I smiled and took another sip of my coffee. There was a somewhat uncomfortable moment of silence as he turned his cup around on the table, keeping his eyes down.

Something was different about Evan. I remembered him as a teenager with his All-American good looks, curly blonde hair smoothed into a low ponytail, collecting girls' phone numbers as he waited tables at Mario's. I used to watch him, thinking he was so wonderful, but because I was so much younger, it was more of a schoolgirl crush than anything else.

But now, he was different. All grown up. A doctor, with a great sense of humor and the same all-American good looks.

"So, I'm thinking we should have dinner sometime," he said abruptly.

My mouth went dry, and I swallowed hard. This caught me completely off-guard, and my expression must have been proof because he laughed.

"Well—" I was interrupted by all three Anderson brothers coming through the door.

"Hey, Gracie!" Garrett said as he came over and kissed the top of my head. "Evan, it's great to see you, man!"

Evan chuckled as they shook hands. “How’s it going, Garrett?”

Miles greeted Evan before retreating to the office to see Kate, while Michael stood next to Garrett, watching me with his eyebrows pulled together.

“Hi, Michael,” Evan said. “Good to see you again.”

Michael nodded curtly.

“What are you doin’ here, Evan?” Garrett asked. “Don’t you work for a living?”

“I’ve got a night shift in Boulder,” Evan laughed. “What’s your excuse?”

Garrett guffawed. “Early meeting in Littleton. What’s goin’ on?”

I couldn’t concentrate on their conversation, I was anxious about Evan’s dinner invitation and Michael’s glare.

“Well, sorry for interrupting,” Garrett said. “Evan, see ya later.” Garrett nudged Michael, and they walked to the back.

Evan looked at his watch, then at me. “I should probably go,” he said, standing and pulling his coat on. “Thanks for the coffee.”

“Sure.” I collected the cups and plates, setting them on the tray. Evan reached into his pocket, retrieving a business card and handing it to me.

“I’d really like to take you to dinner sometime, or we can just have coffee again,” he said with a wide smile. “Give me a call.”

He didn’t wait for me to respond, just waved and walked out the door. I studied the card for a moment and set it on the tray with the dirty dishes. When I turned, Michael was there and took the tray from my hands.

“Let me help you.” His voice was soft, but his jaw clenched.

My heart thudded relentlessly as I followed him to the back. I took the cups and plates from the tray and put them next to the dishwasher, noticing Michael reading Evan’s business card. I took a cloth, wiping the tray, and he held the card in front of me.

“You left this on the tray.” His mouth was tight as I took the card. He continued to watch me with tension emanating from him.

"He seems like a nice guy."

"Um, yeah," I replied, keeping my focus on the tray I continued to wipe needlessly."He's really nice."

It was quiet for a moment, and I glanced up at him.

"So, are you going to go out with him?" His expression was tense, and his eyes didn't leave mine.

"I haven't really had time to think about it."

He nodded stiffly and walked away without another word. Puzzled, I stood there for a moment before returning to the bookstore.

What was that? Was he jealous? Why? He hadn't shown any interest in me, other than friendship, so why would he be jealous? The more I thought about it, the more upset I became. I felt a headache coming on as I tried to sort through the confusing emotions. I closed my eyes, rubbing my temples with my fingers.

"It's four o'clock, Gracie, you ready?" Kate chirped. "I'm going to ride with Miles."

I nodded and walked to the back to get my things, passing Michael without making eye contact. When we got to the parking lot, Kate handed me the keys to the Jeep and walked with Miles and Garrett to the Audi. I was opening the door of the Jeep when Michael came up beside me.

"I can drive you home," he said quietly.

"Why?" I couldn't hide the acidity in my tone.

He shrugged. "Because I like driving your Jeep."

I only agreed because my head hurt, and I really didn't want to drive. While climbing into the passenger seat, Michael attempted to fold himself into the driver's seat—his knees wedged between the steering wheel and his chest. I pursed my lips together as he fumbled for the button to slide the seat back, so he could actually fit. He glanced at me, and I quickly looked out the window.

"What are you giggling at?"

I shrugged but didn't look at him. It was a quiet drive home, except for the radio. I wanted to ask what his problem was earlier, but he seemed fine now, so I didn't bring it up.

Standing by the front door, he handed me my keys and ran his hand through his hair.

"You want something to drink?" I asked as I shrugged out of my jacket.

He nodded and followed me into the kitchen where I retrieved two ginger ales from the fridge. We sat across from each other at the table.

"How's the head?" he asked, looking at me carefully.

"How'd you know I have a headache?"

He shrugged casually and took a sip of his soda, while I spun my bottle cap on the table.

"What are you thinking about?" he asked. It was so easy for me to get caught in his stare, mesmerized by his eyes, not to mention the rest of him. I wondered if I should ask him about his behavior earlier.

"Grace," he said. "Did you hear me?"

"Yes, I heard you."

"So are you going to answer me?"

"I was just wondering," my voice was quiet, "why you seemed so angry earlier?"

He leaned back in his chair and pursed his lips together tightly.

"It's not a big deal if you don't want to tell me," I told him. "It just seemed like you were upset with me."

"I could never be upset with you, Grace."

I lifted my eyebrows, as I looked at him in disbelief.

"I wasn't upset with you," he amended. I waited for him to finish, but I guess he had. The front door opened and Miles, Kate and Garrett came in holding bags of Chinese food.

"I got you some Lo Mein," Garrett informed me proudly.

As we ate, Kate decided to discuss my brief conversation with Evan.

"What did you and Evan talk about today?"

"Nothing much," I replied with a shrug.

She eyed me skeptically. "Oh? Well, he was there for a while."

I gave her a look, hoping she would change the subject but no such luck.

"Did he tell you he's moved back to Fall Rivers?"

I could see Michael from the corner of my eye, his jaw clenched tight.

"Yes. He told me." I twirled noodle remnants with my fork. "But he's still working at St. Jo's occasionally."

"I saw him there last week," Garrett said. "Great guy."

Kate giggled. "Gracie had a crush on him in high school."

My face heated, and I wanted to crawl under the table.

"Gracie!" Garrett nudged me with a huge grin. "Is that true?"

I rolled my eyes. "I was fourteen, for crying out loud."

I narrowed my eyes at Kate, daring her to say a word, and she stifled a laugh as I got up from the table quickly, trying to escape the questioning. I gathered the plates from the table, taking them to the sink and rinsing them. Michael came and stood next to me and helped me load them in the dishwasher without saying a word.

When the dishes were done, the boys headed for the front door to leave. Garrett kissed the top of my head, and Miles and Kate were talking quietly with each other. Michael walked out, not saying anything, and I felt nauseous.

* * *

It was earlier than usual when I rolled out of bed to get ready for my run, wondering anxiously if Michael would even be joining me. I sat on the porch tying my shoes when I heard the familiar crunching of gravel coming from the road. Michael stood there, hands pushed deep into the pockets of his hoodie and a look of trepidation on his face. I smiled uneasily as I walked toward him, my heart pounding so hard I was sure he could hear it.

"Morning," I said.

He nodded and eyed me cautiously as we started a slow jog

down the drive. After a long silence, he finally spoke.

"Grace, I was wondering something."

"What's that?"

"I was just wondering why you don't go out with Evan?"

I kept my eyes forward, as he continued, trying to explain his question.

"Actually, I'm wondering why you don't date at all," he clarified. "I mean, I know you get asked out a lot, so I'm just curious."

I snorted a laugh. "I get asked out a lot?"

His eyes narrowed with impatience, and I cleared my throat.

"It's kind of a long story." I shrugged. "And it'll probably sound stupid to you."

He stopped running, grabbed the sleeve of my jacket, pulling me to a stop, and folded his arms across his chest with an obstinate expression.

"Try me."

I took a deep breath and kicked at the gravel by my feet.

"It's just something Uncle David drilled into Kate's and my head when we were in high school. He told us to never sell out."

A confused look came over Michael's face. "Sell out?"

"Well, according to my uncle, most people—girls especially—tend to settle. Settling for the first guy that says she's beautiful or the first guy that gives her attention.

"She gives pieces of herself away to each guy, searching for that *one* guy. The one guy who thinks she's truly beautiful, seeing her inner beauty more than anything else."

I watched him carefully, wondering if he thought I was insane.

"Piece after piece goes to guy after guy, until all that's left are broken pieces that have been used. Used and given back. Then one day, the right guy does come along, but there are so many pieces, she has to be put back together. And even though she can be put back together, the scars from stitching those broken pieces together are there forever."

Michael continued to study my face as he listened.

"Anyway, Kate and I decided together that we would never sell out. We wouldn't give pieces of ourselves away. We want to give ourselves away in one piece to the right person."

I swallowed hard as his gaze became intense.

"That's how I know Miles is so amazing for Kate because that's what she's done. He doesn't just have her heart, he has all of her, and it's a beautiful thing. I think it could be that way for everyone if they wouldn't sell out."

"Was he talking about giving yourself away physically?"

"Mostly," I said. "But, you can give yourself away emotionally, too."

He was contemplative for a moment.

"How do you know it's the right person if you don't spend time with them?" he asked. "I mean, dating someone is how you get to know them, right?"

"You don't sell out by dating. I've dated before," I tried to explain. "But sometimes, the more you're with someone, the more you try to convince yourself that person may be the right one, even though you know in your heart they're not. You're afraid the person you've built up in your mind will never come, so you settle."

"I understand," his voice was quiet. "But you didn't really answer my question about Evan. He seems like a good guy."

It seemed like he wanted me to go out with Evan, and that hurt.

"He is a good guy, but like I said before, I haven't really thought about it too much." I looked past him to avoid eye contact. "I don't think he's what I'm looking for."

"What are you looking for, Grace?" Michael's voice was sincere and full of curiosity.

I wanted to summon the courage to tell him how I felt, but no courage could be found.

"I'm looking for the same thing everyone else is looking for."

"Which is?"

"To be taken care of, watched after, loved. To be the most

important thing in someone's world."

I finally met his eyes, and something changed. There was no more curiosity, only sadness. We continued our run in an uncomfortable silence.

Chapter Twelve

Things seemed a little off after my conversation with Michael about Evan. He didn't show up for our run the following morning, and because of snow, we'd been unable to run for the three days following. I barely saw him because of the work he was doing for Nina Sandler. Technically, he was working for Nina's father, but Nina was in charge of the design aspect of whatever project was underway.

Nina was an entirely different issue. I knew she was a client, but whether it was work-related or not, she and Michael were spending a lot of time together. The few times I'd spoken with her were less than comfortable. Each time, she appraised me while looking down her surgeon-sculpted nose, and after making a snide comment about my hair, or my choice of clothing, she'd force a smile as fake as her boobs.

Kate and Garrett both tried to convince me to tell Michael how I felt, but every time I saw him with Nina ate away my courage a little more. Besides, I was convinced Michael only saw me as his friend and nothing else.

After spending an entire afternoon organizing the storage room, I got a text from Garrett saying we were all going to meet for dinner. Kate and Miles had the Jeep, so Michael picked me up. The ride to the restaurant was quiet and a little tense. Michael's jaw clenched and unclenched, but he wouldn't say anything.

"So do you think we'll ever get to run again?" I asked, trying to break the tension. "It's been a while."

"I've just been busy." He sounded aggravated, and he'd misunderstood what I was saying.

"I just meant because of the snow," I explained. "It's been so cold."

"Oh." He glanced at me and then faced the front again. "Yeah. It's been cold."

When we pulled into the parking lot, he turned off the engine and sat quietly for a moment.

"Is something wrong?" I asked. He was acting so strangely, and I wanted him to talk to me about whatever was bothering him.

He smiled weakly and shook his head. "Nothing's wrong. Let's go eat."

A lump formed in my throat as we got out of the car and walked in silence into the restaurant. Kate, Miles and Garrett were already seated, and Garrett patted the chair next to him when he saw me. I scanned over my menu and decided on a bowl of soup, my appetite diminishing with every sideways glance at Michael. The waitress brought our food, and we all ate while conversation ensued about our plans to spend Christmas with Will and Ava. Halfway through dinner, I noticed Nina approaching our table, as if my night hadn't been uncomfortable enough.

"Hello, everyone."

As usual, she was a beauty wearing a low-cut hot pink dress, her hair in gorgeous curls that fell over her shoulders. Everyone said 'hello' as her eyes found Michael.

"Hello, Michael," she said sweetly. "I just wanted to make sure we were still on for Friday?"

Michael shifted in his chair. "Yes."

She stared at him for a moment, and then her eyes slid to me. I was holding my soda, playing with the straw.

"Tracy, right?" She pointed her manicured finger at me.

"Grace," I corrected her, even though I knew she didn't care what my name was. We'd met more than once, and each time she never managed to remember my name.

"Oh, that's right." She twittered a giggle and flipped her hair over her shoulders. "It's nice to see you again. Are you feeling okay?"

I nodded, confused by her question.

"Your complexion looks a little sallow," she said with a sniff. "I know a great place that gives fabulous facials. If you're interested let me know, and I'll give you the number."

Ouch.

My face got hot, and I couldn't even think of a snarky response. Garrett draped his arm over my shoulder as he leaned back in his chair—he didn't like Nina much either. She lingered, maybe waiting for someone to speak to her, but no one did.

"Okay then," she said. "Enjoy your dinner. Michael, I'll see you on Friday."

I continued to focus on my soda as she sashayed toward the front of the restaurant. Garrett squeezed my shoulders.

"You okay?" he asked.

I nodded and took a bite of my soup, but now I really wasn't hungry. Everyone was quiet for a moment, and Kate cleared her throat delicately, trying to ease the tension.

"How about brunch tomorrow? Miles, I'll make banana pancakes."

He grinned at her, and she giggled. Banana pancakes were Miles' favorite. "Sounds great to me," he said. "I'll be there."

"Me, too," Garrett said, and I snorted a laugh—as if there were any doubt he wouldn't show up for pancakes.

"What are you laughing at?" He nudged me.

"Nothing," I replied with a shrug.

He headlocked me, casually taking a sip of his drink, while I squirmed and everyone laughed. Finally, he kissed the top of my head swiftly and let me go. I scowled at him, but he just grinned.

After dinner, we walked to the parking lot, and I followed Miles and Kate to the Jeep.

"Grace," Michael called from beside his Yukon. "Will you ride with me?"

"Okay," I said hesitantly.

He opened the door for me and I climbed inside, fastening my seatbelt as he got in his seat and started the engine. It was quiet as we pulled out of the parking lot and onto the main road, but then he sighed.

"Nina was rude to you," he said sympathetically. "I'm sorry."

"It's okay." I shrugged. "You don't need to be sorry for what she does."

"I don't understand why she has such a problem with you," he said.

"Maybe she thinks we're more than friends," I replied. "She obviously thinks of you as more than a business associate."

He seemed surprised by my response. "I told her that you and I are good friends, but we're not together or anything."

The truth of his words hurt. I nodded minutely and turned to look out my window. I tried hard to swallow the lump in my throat as he pulled in front of the house.

"Do you ever think of me as more than just your friend?" My voice was quiet, and I looked down at my hands, too afraid to meet his eyes, and instantly regretted my question.

"Do you?" he asked.

"Yes." I exhaled—relieved to finally say it. "Yes, I do."

I looked at him then—his expression pained, and my stomach sank.

He shook his head sadly. "You don't know what you're saying."

"Yes, I do. I've wanted to tell you since Thanksgiving."

He took a deep breath. "Grace, I care about you a great deal—"

I felt nauseous because I knew what he was going to say next.

"It's okay," I told him quickly. "You don't have to say anything."

"I just," he stammered. "I really care about you and our friendship but—"

"Michael," I interrupted him, I didn't want him to finish. I couldn't bear it. I had to get out of the car before I got sick. "It's okay. Really."

It wasn't okay. Nothing was okay.

I grabbed my purse and started to open the door, but he grasped my wrist.

"I'm so sorry," he said shaking his head. "I just—you don't know—"

"Please," I said, the sob building in my throat. "Let's just forget about this, please?" I pulled my hand away and opened the door, trying to get out of the car as quickly as possible.

"Do you want to run in the morning?" His voice was desperate.

I avoided eye contact, my voice shaking now. "No. I should probably help Kate with breakfast. I'll see you then." I closed the door and ran up the steps to the front door, unlocking it quickly and closing it behind me.

When I got to my room, I tried not to think, as I got ready for bed. I crawled slowly onto the middle of my bed, pulling my knees to my chest and replaying what happened over and over in my head, until it felt like my heart was breaking into a hundred pieces.

There was a soft knock on my door.

"Gracie?" Garrett called. "Can I come in?"

I didn't answer. I just sat there.

"I hope you're decent because I'm coming in." The door opened, and Garrett stood there for a moment. He closed the door behind him and stepped toward my bed. "What happened?"

I shrugged, not looking at him. "He doesn't want me."

Did I say that out loud? I felt so strange, like I'd been punched in the stomach. My chest ached, and I was trying not to cry.

"He told you that?"

"No. He didn't say those words, but I told him how I felt, and he said he was sorry. He didn't have to say it." Tears spilled now. "He just doesn't want me."

I hated that I was crying because Garrett couldn't stand to see me cry. He pried my hands from around my knees and brought me with him as he sat down on the chair, pulling me onto his lap. I hugged his neck and sobbed, wishing the ache would stop.

Garrett didn't say anything—just rubbed my back softly and let me cry. After a while, I got up and went into my bathroom to blow my nose. Garrett patted the ottoman, and I sat down in front of him. He rubbed his face with both hands and leaned back into the chair.

"What happened?"

I recounted the conversation with Michael. How it started about Nina. How he told me he was sorry, but he just couldn't…I wasn't sure exactly how he was going to end that sentence, but I told Garrett I didn't want to know.

"I've ruined everything. He won't even be my friend now."

Garrett folded his hands behind his head with a calm expression, though his eyes were sad.

"You haven't ruined anything, Gracie."

"Yes, I have," I argued. "It's going to be uncomfortable, especially for me. I told myself I'd tell him how I felt, and it didn't matter what he said because I just wanted him to know. But it does matter because he doesn't feel the same. Now I'm humiliated, and he probably doesn't even want to be around me anymore."

Another tear came down my face, and I swiped at it angrily. Garrett leaned forward and held both of my hands in his.

"I'm sorry," he said softly. "I really am, but listen to me. You just keep doing what you've always done."

I sniffled. "What do you mean?"

"You just keep being our Gracie." He smiled weakly. "Keep doing your thing, Michael will see soon enough."

I wanted desperately to believe what he said, but I was hurting too much. Garrett stood and kissed the top of my head softly.

"Love you, Gracie-Beth."

I watched him leave my room, closing the door behind him. I climbed under my covers, turned off my lamp, and as I laid my head on my pillow, the tears came again. It wasn't long before Kate's arms came around me, causing me to cry even more.

"It's going to be okay," she whispered.

She held me for a long time, and eventually I fell asleep, Kate's arms still around me.

* * *

I woke up and rolled over to check the time, it was almost eight o'clock. Even though I'd told Michael I wasn't going to run, the idea of running sounded really good to me. My head pounded relentlessly as I made my way to the bathroom slowly. I flipped on the light and studied my reflection in the mirror.

Scary.

My eyes were bloodshot and puffy, my face blotchy. I brushed my teeth, washed my face, got dressed in black running pants and pink fleece, and pulled my hair into a ponytail. Kate was busy in the kitchen and when she saw me, she came over and kissed my cheek.

"Morning." She tried to smile. "Enjoy your run."

As I walked down the porch steps toward the gravel drive, I resisted the urge to look over at the Anderson's door, fighting between wanting to see Michael and dreading that I would. I put the earbuds in and searched for a playlist on my iPod as I walked. From the corner of my eye I saw him, standing in the front window of their house. My heart sank, but I started my run without looking at him.

I kept the volume of my music loud to keep from thinking about anything, and it worked. My feet pounded a strong, steady rhythm against the pavement and as my muscles worked, my mind cleared. When I approached the house, I saw the red Porsche, Michael and Nina standing there, and nausea returned. They both turned when they saw me, and I quickly focused on the ground, pretending not to see them.

When I opened the door, the aroma of coffee and bananas wafted over me.

"Hey, Gracie," Garrett greeted me from the table with his dimply smile, but his smile left quickly as I approached him—probably noticing my puffy, red eyes.

"You have time for a shower if you want," Kate told me. "We're not quite ready."

I went to my room, showered and dressed, braided my hair loosely, and put makeup on, attempting to cover the ugliness my emotional breakdown caused.

When I walked into the kitchen, Michael was standing beside the fridge and my body tensed. Quickly, I turned to the cupboard to get a cup. I felt him step behind me and nausea returned full force.

"I thought you weren't going to run this morning," he said quietly.

Without looking at him, I shrugged and poured myself some coffee. "Changed my mind."

When I started for the fridge to get cream, Michael held the carton out to me.

"Thanks." I added the cream and sweetener to my cup, stirring quickly. I could feel him watching me, and as much as I wanted to look at him, I didn't.

"I think we should talk, don't you?" he asked.

"Not really," I said. "There's nothing to say, and I'd much rather forget about the whole thing."

"Really?" he asked incredulously. "Is that true?"

"Yes." It was the truth. I was humiliated, and now I was angry he was pushing the issue further.

"What if I want to talk about it?" he said, stepping closer to me.

"We're ready to eat," Kate announced.

Relieved, I turned away from him and went to the table. I cringed at my usual seat between Michael and Garrett. I walked around the table and started to pull my chair out, but Michael was there, doing it for me. Why couldn't he just leave me alone? Did he not understand how embarrassing this was for me?

I ate rather quickly, not really paying attention to the conversation and got up to take my plate to the sink.

"So, little brother," I heard Garrett say. "What was Nina doing at the house so early this morning?"

I resisted the urge to look at Michael, not to mention the sudden urge to vomit, as I waited for his response.

"She was picking up drawings for the L.A. building," Michael replied.

It was quiet, and I returned to the table to pick up everyone's plates. Michael stood with his plate and walked to the sink where I was rinsing. He always helped me do the dishes, and I always enjoyed that, but now I felt tense. We were both quiet as we worked, and he continued to help me until everything was done. The others were still sitting at the table, drinking coffee and talking. I wandered into the living room and sat on the sofa, turning on the television. Michael sat down next to me. I kept turning the channels, trying to find something to watch, wishing I was better at acting casual.

"Are you ever going to look at me again?" His voice was quiet.

I looked at him then, mostly to prove I could, but when our eyes met I looked away, embarrassed.

"Grace," he said. "I feel terrible about last night. I think we should talk."

I shrugged. "You don't need to feel terrible. I'm fine."

"If you were fine, you would look at me."

I sighed, keeping my eyes down, knowing he was right.

"Okay, I'm not fine," I admitted. "But I will be, I just don't want to talk about it."

"Well, maybe I do want to talk about it."

When I looked at him, he was scowling. I scowled right back at him, folding my arms across my chest. Why was he angry? He wasn't allowed to be angry.

"Grace, I don't want to lose your friendship."

"You haven't, but I just can't pretend like everything's okay when it's not."

"Fair enough," he agreed. "But how can I fix this if we don't talk about it?"

"There's nothing to *fix*," I corrected him. "I told you, everything will be fine."

He ran his hand through his hair with exasperation.

"At least let me explain why—"

"You can't help feeling the way you feel," I interrupted him. "There's no explanation needed."

"But—"

I stood up and glared down at him, wishing he would just drop it.

"Please just leave it alone." My voice shook. "I never should've said anything, it was stupid. This is my problem, not yours."

He stood and glared down at me. The others were quiet as they watched.

"How can you say that?" he fumed. "How can you say that to me?"

"Because it was me that ruined everything by being honest with you in the first place."

His jaw clenched. "You are the most stubborn…frustrating…" His hand raked through his hair, demonstrating his irritation. "So, you just want to leave it alone, huh?"

The last thing I wanted was to fight with him. This wasn't his fault.

"Michael, I don't want to fight with you." My throat tightened as his expression softened. "Please believe me, I'm not angry with you or anything you said. You were being honest with me. I can't be upset with you for being honest."

His eyes were full of remorse, and I felt the ache in my chest return.

"I'm so sorry I made you feel bad or guilty about anything. This is not your fault, and everything will be fine." I tried to smile. "I just want things to be like they were before…before I said anything."

"I'm not sure things will ever be like they were before," Michael said quietly.

I'd thought my heart had broken so much it couldn't possibly break any more, but I was wrong. The pain returned. It was just as

I'd feared. My honesty had ruined our friendship. My eyes blurred with tears.

"I understand." My voice was barely a whisper.

"No, you don't understand," he said. "Because you won't let me explain anything."

I waited for him to continue, but he didn't.

"Um," I stammered. "I need to go."I walked past him to my room, grabbing my coat and purse and then back to the kitchen to get the car keys.

"Gracie?" Kate said. "Where are you going?"

"I just remembered something I forgot to do at the shop yesterday. I'll be right back."

She started to say something, but I shook my head minutely and she responded with a nod. I needed to leave, and she knew it. Michael followed me to the door and put his hand on top of mine, causing me to tremble.

"I'll be right back," I said quietly.

I kept my eyes down as I opened the door and hurried to the jeep, climbing in and starting the engine. Michael watched from the porch as I backed out of the driveway and pulled away.

Emotions took over once I was on the main road, and I was bawling. Of course there was nothing for me to do at the shop, but there was really nowhere else for me to go. I unlocked the front door and went inside, locking it behind me, and walked back to the office. I flipped the light on and sat at my desk, taking deep breaths to stop the tears.

Why was this so hard? Miles and Kate knew they loved each other right away. Maybe I just needed to come to the realization that Michael and I were only supposed to be friends, and he really wasn't the one for me. With that thought, I laid my head on the desk and sobbed, my heart breaking again.

I felt guilty for getting so angry with Michael. After all, he couldn't help the way he felt, and I knew I was feeling sorry for myself. I sat in the office for a while, not really paying attention to the time. The longer I sat, the more ashamed I felt for being such a baby.

"Grace?"

I jumped out of my seat, and Miles stood at the office door, smiling apologetically.

"You scared the crap out of me," I muttered.

"I didn't mean to scare you," he said softly. "I thought you'd hear me come in." He twirled his car keys around his finger as he watched me."Could I talk to you for a minute?"

"Of course you can."

He pulled a chair over and sat down across from me. I wiped my eyes and took a deep breath. I don't know why I was nervous, Miles never made me nervous, but I had a feeling whatever he wanted to tell me wasn't going to be good.

"Kate's worried about you," he said.

"I'm okay. I just needed to leave for a minute, that's all."

"I understand. I'm sorry about all of this."

"It's not your fault."

"It's not yours, either," he said. "My brother…wouldn't want me to say anything, and I would never want to betray his trust—"

"I would never want you to," I interrupted him.

He smiled knowingly. "I want you to know, you're wrong about him."

My thoughts began to spiral in ten different directions with Miles' words.

"Grace, it's not my place to tell you what's happened, but he cares for you a great deal."

I sighed."I know, Miles. The problem is I care for him more than he cares for me."

"I wouldn't be so sure about that if I were you," he said assuredly. "Like I said, it's not my place to say anything, but you're wrong about how he feels about you. Trust me."

I trusted Miles completely, but I was confused and the ache in my chest remained. Miles reached for my hands, holding them tightly.

"I wish there was something I could do for you."

As I looked into his eyes, I was overcome with the warmth and understanding they held, and I could smile then.

"You do something for me every day. You love Kate. You make her happier than I've ever seen her, and that's saying a lot."

He smiled widely and stood, pulling me into a tight hug, which caused more tears to come.

"I love you, Grace. You know that, right?"

I nodded against his chest.

"Please give my little brother a chance," he said. "I know it's not easy for you, but when he's ready, he'll explain."

I sniffled. "Okay."

"Let's get back," he said and handed me the keys, following me to the front of the office. He started to open the door, and I cleared my throat.

"Miles?"

"Yeah?"

"I love you, too."

* * *

The following week was quiet. I didn't see Michael at all, and I wasn't sure if it was a good thing or a bad thing. I missed him. I missed our talks, his face, his laugh, everything. I was miserable.

Garrett and I spent time together when he wasn't working. Kate always invited me to tag along with her and Miles, but that only made me feel pathetic. Basically, I was working. A lot.

On Tuesday afternoon I had my nose in a book, waiting for four o'clock to come around so I could leave. The low growling of a motorcycle caused me to look up. I watched as Evan parked his motorcycle in the front of the store and removed his helmet before coming inside.

"Nice ride, man." Kenny gawked from behind the counter.

"Thanks, Kenny." Evan unzipped his leather jacket and draped it over the back of a chair.

"I wouldn't have pegged you as a motorcycle type," I said with a smirk.

"Why? Because I'm a doctor?" His cheeks were rosy from the wind, and he smiled widely. "Doctors have to let loose every now and then. Our job is very stressful, you know."

"I'll bet. Especially working in an E.R. where people come in with broken legs, arms, and faces because of motorcycles."

He laughed and sat down across from me. "I've never dealt with a broken face. Besides, until you ride one, don't knock it."

"Is it new?"

"Yep." He smiled proudly. "Does it make me look cool?"

"Nah." I shook my head. "You're still a doctor."

He pursed his lips together, and I giggled.

"Can I get you something, Evan?" Kenny asked.

"Just a coffee. Regular."

We sat for a while, sipping coffee and talking, and even though my heart still ached for Michael, I found myself comfortable with Evan.

"So, how about a ride?" He motioned with his thumb to his motorcycle. "It's like sixty degrees out there, and the roads are clear. I'll take you for a bite to eat."

I swallowed hard, my emotions warring with each other. Evan was a friend, but Michael was still in my heart, unmoving.

"Look, Grace," he said, folding his hands on the table. "I know there's something going on between you and Michael. I'm not blind."

He couldn't have been more wrong. There was nothing between Michael and me. I wasn't even sure there was a friendship anymore.

"I just want to take you for a ride and get a slice of pizza. That's all."

"I don't have a helmet."

"You can have mine."

I grimaced at him. "Then you won't have one. I thought you were a doctor?"

"Oh, come on," he said with a laugh. "You ski some of the most difficult slopes in Colorado, but you're afraid of a little motorcycle? I know you better than that. Let's go."

He tugged on my arm and followed me to the back where Kate was tapping away at her computer. She smiled when she saw us.

"Hey, Evan!" she said cheerily. "What are you doing here?" "I'm taking your cousin for a ride on my bike," he said, helping me with my jacket.

"Oh?" Kate eyed me quizzically. "That sounds like fun."

I knew there'd be a line of questioning later.

"You want a ride, too?" Evan asked.

Kate shook her head. "Uh, no, but you two have a good time."

I pulled the strap of my purse over my head and followed Evan outside. He put the helmet on my head and took a step back to survey my appearance.

"It suits you." He patted the top of the helmet with a grin.

I rolled my eyes, and he laughed as he climbed onto the motorcycle and motioned for me to follow. I straddled the black leather seat and looked for a place to put my hands.

"You're going to have to hold onto me," he said, grabbing my hands and pulling them around his waist. "Don't let go."

I'm sure I was blushing as the engine snarled to life. When he pushed away from the curb, Garrett's Hummer pulled into the space next to us. Garrett's forehead creased in concern, and Michael came around the front of the Hummer, jaw clenching and eyes flashing. My stomach sank, but I managed a small wave to Garrett as Evan took off down the main road.

It was exhilarating. The cool wind whipped around us, trees blurred past, and I released a nervous squeal. Evan must have heard me because with a flick of his wrist we were going even faster.

When we got to Mario's, I made a beeline to the ladies room to brush through my helmet-hair. My phone buzzed, and I fished it from my purse. Garrett's name flashed on the screen, and I smiled.

"Hi."

"Hey." He paused. "You okay?"

"Sure. I'm scraping bugs off my teeth."

He chuckled half-heartedly. "I just wanted to check on you."

"Thanks. We're getting a piece of pizza, and then I'll be home."

"Okay. Gracie?"

"Yeah?"

"Michael's really upset. I thought he was going to put a hole through my windshield."

"Why?"

"Why do you think?"

I closed my eyes. "I don't know what you want me to say."

He sighed. "I just thought you should know. Be careful, and I'll see you later."

I stayed in the bathroom for what seemed like a long time. When I got to the table, Evan eyed me suspiciously.

"You look a little pale," he said. "Did I drive too fast?"

"Yep. That's it." I tried to smile as I sat down.

The waiter came to the table, and Evan ordered two root beers and a large sausage and mushroom pizza.

"You still like root beer with pizza, right?" he asked.

I nodded, impressed with his memory. Kate and I came into Mario's almost every Sunday night during high school, and Evan was our waiter almost every time. We ordered the same thing: sausage pizza with mushrooms and root beers.

"So, why don't you tell me what's going on," he said, breaking a bread stick in half and taking a bite. I wasn't sure what he was referring to, but when he saw my expression, he frowned. "With you and Michael."

I shifted uncomfortably in my seat and tried to look past him, but he leaned into my line of sight.

"Hey," he said. "We're friends, aren't we?"

"Sure."

"Well, friends talk about these things." He took another bite of breadstick. "You never know, I might be able to help. I am a doctor, you know."

I had to smile at his expression. "Yes. I know."

"Okay then, talk."

"There's not really much to talk about," I said with a shrug, pulling my napkin between my fingers. "I told Michael how I felt about him, and he told me he didn't feel the same. That's it."

Evan raised an eyebrow. "And how do you feel about him?"

The waiter delivered our drinks, and I took a long drink of my soda, feeling embarrassed.

"I'm sorry, Grace."

I shook my head. "There's nothing for you to be sorry about."

"Well," he said, leaning back in his chair. "I guess I was wrong. I can't help you with that at all."

"Yeah. Some doctor you are," I said with a smirk.

He shook his head in disappointment, fighting a grin. "I know. I suck."

We both laughed, and it felt good. The two of us sat for a long time, talking about med school, Erin's job in California, his parents, Kate, the bookstore, everything. When I looked at my watch, I was surprised we'd been talking for over three hours. Evan glanced at his watch and raised his eyebrows.

"Wow," he said. "I have to be at work in two hours."

He tossed a few bills on the table while I pulled on my jacket, and then we were back on the motorcycle heading home. The wind was much colder now, and I kept my head ducked behind Evan's shoulder the entire way. He stopped in front of the house and helped me climb off the seat. I handed him the helmet and pulled my fingers through my tangled hair.

"Thanks for the ride and the pizza," I told him. "I had a good time."

"So did I." He smiled warmly. "We'll have to do it again sometime."

I hesitated, not wanting to commit to anything. He chuckled and reached for my hand, giving it a quick squeeze.

"Night, Grace. I'll talk to you soon." He started up the motorcycle; giving a quick wave before speeding away, gravel spitting behind the back tire. I looked across the drive at the Anderson's house and noticed all three cars were in the garage. For a long while I stood in front of the house, gazing at the stars and listening to the wind move the pines.

"You're going to freeze to death out here."

Michael was suddenly beside me, zipping up his jacket. I silently wished my heart wouldn't react the way it did whenever I saw him, but there was no halting the fluttering against my chest with his proximity.

"How's Evan?" he asked, looking up at the dark sky.

"Good."

"Garrett says he's a really nice guy."

"He is," I agreed. "He's a good person."

He nodded and raked his hand through his hair. "Grace, I miss you," he said. "I miss seeing you every day. Talking to you…I just…miss you."

"I miss you, too," I admitted, and at that moment I'd have given anything for things to go back to normal. "Will you run with me tomorrow?"

He smiled his crooked smile, and it made my heart ache. I'd missed that smile so much.

"I would love to run with you tomorrow."

"Okay," I said with a nod of affirmation. "I'll see you here at seven."

* * *

Over the next two weeks, Michael and I ran together every day, and each day things felt a little more comfortable. After the misery of *that* night, I tried very hard to pretend things were okay between the two of us, and I guess for the most part they were. Though I was heartbroken Michael didn't feel the same way for me that I did for him, I still wanted to be with him every chance I had.

Kate and I frantically prepared for Christmas, excited to spend the holiday with the Anderson's. Before I knew it, we were piling into Garrett's Hummer, making our way to Black Forest. The huge vehicle overflowed with luggage and presents, and Garrett blared Christmas music from the stereo.

As we approached the tree line of Black Forest, it began to snow. We pulled in front of Will and Ava's house and I was awestruck. White lights covered the trees closest to the house, while lit wreaths and garland graced each window and the railing of the front porch—lights reflecting off the sparkling snow that was already covering the ground.

Will and Ava greeted us on the front porch with hugs, and we all filed into the house that was even more festive on the inside. Christmas music was playing, and the smell of cinnamon and cloves filled the air. Ava told us to get settled into our rooms quickly because she had hot cider and a movie ready to go.

It took several trips to get the suitcases and presents from the car, and then we were all in front of the television, sipping hot cider and watching "It's a Wonderful Life". After the movie, we had a dinner of cold cut sandwiches and pasta salad. Garrett dragged me to the basement/game room, where he taught me how to kill zombies since I'd never learned during Thanksgiving. Michael joined us later, and the three of us played until late.

"Okay, you guys, I have to go to bed," I said, rubbing my temples. "I think I may need a Dramamine before I play next time. I'm dizzy."

"Come on, Gracie, don't wimp out on me now," Garrett whined.

"Hah! Wimp out! You know I was kicking your butt," I told him. "I have to go to bed."

Garrett led the way through the dark house to my room.

"Night, Gracie." He kissed my head and went to his room.

Michael stood next to me. "I think you may be right about the Dramamine," he whispered as he rubbed his head. "I don't know how he plays that thing for so long."

"I'm surprised he isn't cross-eyed," I whispered, and he chuckled.

"So shall we run in the morning?" he asked. "Or take the day off." We looked at each other and nodded in unison.

"Take the day off," we said together and then laughed quietly.

"Night, Michael."

"Night." He watched me for a moment before walking across the hall to his room.

I tiptoed into my room and then to the bathroom, closing the door quietly. Kate had my pajamas and toiletries lying on the vanity, and I got ready for bed quickly, slipping under the covers. The room was dimly lit by moonlight, casting a soft glow. It was beautiful, and I fell asleep quickly.

* * *

I woke to Kate's humming in the bathroom and rolled out of the bed, trudging in to see her fixing her hair.

"Hey," I said groggily.

"Morning, sleepy," she sang. "Did you kill all the bad guys?"

I laughed and rubbed my eyes."Garrett's insane."

By the time I got out of the shower, she was already downstairs. I dressed in jeans, black turtleneck sweater and pulled my hair into a clip. When I came out of the room, I was met by Michael smiling widely as he looked me over.

"You look pretty today."

Of course he always looked pretty, but I couldn't say that.

"Good morning. How's the head?"

He laughed. "I was just about to ask you the same thing. Don't worry, Mom has plenty of aspirin downstairs." He took me by the hand, and we went to the kitchen where everyone was sitting at the table, already eating. Just like at home, there was an empty chair for me beside Garrett. Ava handed me a plate of scrambled eggs, and we ate with several conversations going on at once. After a while, Michael nudged me with his elbow.

"Do you and Kate like snow-tubing?"

"We love it," I replied quickly, unable to hide my excitement.

"Good. After breakfast we're going. There's a hill not far from the house that's crazy."

"Excellent," I said excitedly.

He laughed and looked over at Garrett. "You in, big brother?"

Garrett snorted a laugh—which in 'Garrett language' meant 'yes'.

* * *

We met everyone in front of the gigantic garage that was big enough for five cars but only had two. It also had four snowmobiles, and an ATV. Everyone grabbed an inner tube, and we followed Will and Garrett around the back of the house. We hiked for about ten minutes through drifts of fresh snow and came to a long, steep hill. Just like Michael said, it was crazy. My eyes widened as Kate and I surveyed the hill they wanted us to fly down, Kate's expression mirroring mine. We'd been tubing many times, but never down a hill this steep. I could hear Garrett laughing at my expression.

"You're not afraid are you, Gracie?" he scoffed. I rolled my eyes at him, but yeah, I was a little afraid.

"You want to go with me the first time?" Michael whispered in my ear.

I nodded, trying to hide my fear.

"Okay." He laughed as he took my hand. "Come on, coward."

I looked at Kate with what I'm sure was panic. She just giggled and winked at me. Michael and I got situated in our tubes, and he locked his arm with mine.

"Don't worry," he assured me with a smile. "I won't let go."

My heart pounded in reaction to his promise, and his eyes held mine as I nodded. Garrett was behind us and had a hand on each of our backs, waiting for our consent.

"Ready?" Garrett asked, and Michael and I both nodded.

Garrett gave a push, and we were flying down the hill. The butterflies in my stomach fluttered and jumped with the cool air whipping in my face, and I screamed in exhilaration. Michael kept his promise and didn't let go of me until we reached the bottom. We were both laughing so hard I could barely get to my feet. Michael put his arms around my shoulders and hugged me as we both continued to laugh. His hair was windswept, his cheeks red from the cold, and his eyes sparkled with excitement.

"How was that?"

"Excellent!" I exclaimed, unable to stop smiling, not just from the thrilling ride, but also from his arms, which still held me tight. "Let's go again!"

We grabbed our tubes and started the hike back to the top, watching as Kate and Miles went down next, Kate's high-pitched squeal making everyone laugh. Garrett went down on his stomach, spinning and bouncing all the way to the bottom, followed by Will. Ava managed to slide down the hill looking completely graceful and lovely. I don't know how long we were out there, but my toes had started to lose their feeling when Ava announced it was time for some lunch. After we changed clothes, everyone sat in front of the fire and ate leftover pasta salad and homemade pizza. Our cheeks were rosy from the cold, and I was just starting to get feeling back in my toes, when Garrett decided we needed to go again.

* * *

It was Christmas Eve, and Kate and I were getting dressed for dinner. We'd been having a fabulous time, and neither of us could stop smiling. Though we had some wonderful memories of Christmas with our parents, after they died the holidays were never the same. Uncle David did his best, but the older we got, the more he worked at the hospital during the holidays. Kate believed it made him happier helping patients at Christmas and Thanksgiving, so we celebrated Christmas with each other, and that's all we really knew. Being with the Andersons showed us what we never realized we were missing. I couldn't imagine having a more fabulous holiday.

Kate was wearing a black organdy and silk dress, with delicate ruffles around the bust-line and sleeves, and it silhouetted her figure so beautifully. Once again, she had chosen my attire for the occasion—a red silk, sheath dress that draped slightly off one shoulder. She put my hair up, with loose curls around my face and had a pair of suede high-heeled pumps that were the exact shade of red as the dress. As we came down the stairs, Miles was waiting with his dimpled smile as he took in the vision that was Kate.

"You're stunning, as usual," he said quietly and then looked over at me and gave me a wink. "Grace, you're beautiful in red." He smiled and offered me his other hand as he led us into the living room where everyone was already gathered.

My eyes found Michael right away, wearing a charcoal gray suit coat with a crisp black shirt and pants. He was so gorgeous it made my heart ache just looking at him. Our eyes met, and he started towards me, running his hand through his hair.

"You look…amazing," he said.

I tried to form a coherent sentence in my head before I spoke. "You look amazing, too."

"Gracie!" Garrett strode toward us smiling widely and bent down, pointing to his cheek for me to give him a kiss. "You're beautiful," he said, taking my hand and pulling me with him into the living room, where we sat by the fire and talked with Miles. Kate was talking and laughing with Michael, while Ava and Will excused themselves to get dinner on the table.

"So, Kate told me the two of you have a surprise for us tonight," Miles said. "I can hardly wait."

Actually, I'd forgotten all about it. Kate and I had a piano duet we were going to play for everyone tonight. We hadn't played it in over a year, but it was one we'd performed so often, Kate was confident we could pull it off. I wasn't nearly as confident.

"What surprise?" Garrett asked.

"They're going to play a Christmas duet on the piano," Miles said.

"Really?" Garrett was excited, and I smiled at him. "Excellent."

We were gathered around the beautifully decorated dining table eating a delicious dinner of prime rib, roasted red potatoes with parsley, glazed baby carrots, homemade yeast rolls and green salad. After dinner, Kate, Miles, Michael and I helped Ava with the dishes, and we had them done rather quickly. Ava had made several varieties of pies for dessert, and I started a pot of coffee, while Kate assembled the dessert plates and forks.

"Okay, Mom and Dad," Miles announced loudly. "Before we have our dessert, Kate and Grace have a surprise for you."

Kate was standing next to me, and I grabbed her hand nervously as everyone watched us expectantly, and I regretted our decision.

"Well," Kate said with a smile. "At Thanksgiving, you asked if Gracie and I played duets, so we've decided to play one for you."

"Wonderful!" Ava exclaimed. "Let's go." She led the way to the music room and everyone followed. Will and Ava sat in the chairs closest to the piano, and I glanced at Michael, who was smiling widely at me. I shrugged, and he chuckled as he lined up next to Garrett and Miles, who stood beside the piano with eager expressions on their faces.

Kate and I took our places on the piano bench, she on the left and me on the right. She looked over at me with her eyebrows raised.

"Ready?" she whispered.

I nodded, and we placed our hands on the keys. She counted off and we began our rendition of "Sleigh Ride". We played it every year for Uncle David, and he always loved it. I couldn't be sure, but I think Kate and I had more fun than anyone else. It was like it had always been—she and I played together perfectly—neither of us missing a note. At one point, I glanced over at her and our eyes met, both of us grinning from ear to ear, and I heard the boys laugh. When we hit the last chords, everyone clapped, and Garrett whooped and hollered as we stood and just like in the music competitions, gave a curtsy.

"That was wonderful, girls," Ava said. "Thank you so much."

"You two are incredibly talented," Will said. "Thank you."

Garrett laughed as he picked me up in one of his bear hugs.

"That was amazing. You might have to do that again."Garrett set me down, and Michael was standing beside him, smiling at me.

"It sounds like you two have been practicing for weeks," he said. "How'd you do that?"

"We've played that so many times, we could probably do it in our sleep," Kate said. "We were hoping we could pull it off since it's been a while."

Michael shook his head in disbelief as Kate left the room with Miles. My heart raced as he stepped toward me, smiling his crooked smile.

"And I didn't think you could surprise me anymore." He held my gaze, and I tried to smile as my heart thrummed in my ears. Garrett cleared his throat loudly and winked at me.

"So are we going to kill zombies or what?" I asked him.

Garrett grinned. "That's my girl."

I turned to Michael. "What about you? You wanna help save the world from the undead?"

He took my hand. "Let's go."

We went downstairs, and I kicked my shoes off, sitting on the sofa between the two of them as we started the game. We played until late again and when we finally made our way to our rooms, Garrett reminded me they got up early to open presents.

"I'll be ready," I promised and for the first time in years, I was excited for Christmas morning.

Chapter Thirteen

"Gracie. Wake up."

Someone gently shook my shoulder. I opened my eyes to see Garrett hovering over me, smiling widely, still in his tee shirt and flannel pants.

"Merry Christmas. Come on. Hurry." He left the room, and I rolled over to see Kate still trying to wake up.

She yawned and stretched. "I swear. He's like a giant kid."

"For sure," I said groggily. "Merry Christmas, Kate."

"Merry Christmas."

The Andersons were all sitting around the enormous tree in their pajamas and robes, with smiling faces. I sat down on the couch beside Michael, and he handed me a cup of coffee.

"Merry Christmas."

"Merry Christmas." I smiled and took a sip of the coffee he'd prepared for me, nodding my approval. "Perfect. Thanks."

Garrett was rooting through the presents and just like a kid, looked at Ava, asking permission to start. She nodded for him to proceed, and Garrett pulled presents out for Ava and Will first, then one for the rest of us.

"Okay, I'm opening Gracie's present," Garrett announced.

The first present was two CDs, one of Mozart's Requiem and the other a collection of Chopin nocturnes. He made a funny face—like a kid who had just opened a present with socks inside—and then he opened the next box. It was an official Denver Broncos practice jersey worn and signed by Champ Bailey—one of Garrett's favorite players. It was evident I'd made a good choice because he jumped from the floor and crushed me into the couch trying to hug me.

"Gracie, you're the best," he said. "Thanks."

"You're welcome. Merry Christmas."

He kissed my forehead and folded the jersey carefully, putting it back inside the box, and handed me a present.

"This is from me," he said waggling his eyebrows. I laughed at him as I opened his present—a Yankees cap and matching Derek Jeter jersey.

"Just what I wanted." I put the cap on my head. "Thank you, Garrett."

He grinned his dimpled grin and turned to pull another present from beneath the tree.

"This says it's for all of us from Gracie." Garrett read the attached card and handed the gift to Michael.

"There's actually one for your mom and dad, too," I told Garrett, pointing to the identical package under the tree. "I wanted you to open them together."

Garrett handed the present to Ava, and she smiled at me.

"It's for all three of us?" Michael asked, and I nodded.

Garrett sat on the sofa next to Michael, while Miles leaned forward trying to get a closer look. Michael and Ava tore away the wrapping at the same time. When Michael opened the box, his brows came together, and Garrett and Miles were quiet. I got nervous right away, afraid I'd made a bad decision.

I cleared my throat nervously.

"Um, your mom gave me most of the pictures, and I made copies," I stammered. "I also found some at your house."

Michael opened the scrapbook I'd made, and the three boys looked over each page carefully. Black and white photos of their sister Rachel, beautiful pictures with her three big brothers who loved her so much. There were also photos of Rachel with Ava and Will. Each picture was evidence of the love and adoration they had for each other. I loved every picture in the album. As I made the album for them, I fell in love with the Andersons even more, not thinking that was even possible.

The minutes seemed to tick by slowly as I waited nervously for them to say something, but they kept looking through the pages. I glanced at Michael and noticed his bottom lip quivered slightly, which made my heart sink. He looked up at Ava, who was smiling sweetly at him; she wiped a tear from her cheek. Garrett and Miles watched me intently, and I started fidgeting with my fingers.

"I'm sorry," I said nervously. "I just thought they were so beautiful, and I didn't think you'd mind." Everyone was quiet, and I looked at Michael worriedly. "Don't you like it?"

Michael set the album on the coffee table in front of him and stood. He pulled me up from the sofa, removing the baseball cap from my head and wrapped his arms around me tightly.

"This is the most thoughtful gift anyone has ever given us," he whispered. "I couldn't love it more." My heart pounded as he squeezed me again and then released me, gazing into my eyes. "Thank you."

Garrett stood, his eyes glossed with tears. "Thanks, Gracie." He hugged me tightly. "It's beautiful."

Miles embraced me without saying a word, and returned to his seat beside Kate. Ava and Will both thanked me, Ava wiping at tears and Will rubbing her shoulders in comfort. I sat back down next to Michael, and he took my hand in his, squeezing it tightly as I breathed a sigh of relief.

When the presents were opened, Kate and I made a breakfast of bacon and mushroom quiche, fresh fruit and biscuits with sausage gravy. We all sat around the kitchen table, enjoying Christmas breakfast together.

The time went too quickly, and soon we were saying goodbye to Will and Ava. The same twinge of sadness I felt at Thanksgiving returned. I was going to miss them. On the way home, I fell asleep on Miles' shoulder, those late night video game battles obviously catching up with me. When we pulled onto the private drive, Miles nudged me gently, and I jerked awake. Michael turned around and gave Miles a pointed look. Garrett pulled up in front of the house and got out quickly, running to our house, unlocking the front door and closing it behind him.

"What in the world?" Kate said. "Is he okay?"

Miles didn't respond as we got out of the car. When I started toward the back of the car to unload our bags, Michael took me by the hand and led me to the front door with a wide smile.

"We have a surprise for you and Kate," he said. "But you have to close your eyes."

I glanced at Kate who just shrugged and closed her eyes. Kate loved surprises and never took much convincing when it came to the 'close your eyes' part. Miles chuckled and put his hands on her shoulders, guiding her through the front door.

"Come on, Grace," Michael encouraged. "Trust me."I closed my eyes, and he took me by the hand, leading me inside the house slowly, and then turned me so I was positioned where he wanted.

"Now you two, keep your eyes closed," Miles said. "Promise?"

We promised, and I could feel Kate fidgeting next to me. I reached for her hand, and she giggled. There were loud, rustling noises and the boys were murmuring quietly to each other. I noticed a familiar smell, like sawdust and lacquer. After what seemed like forever, Miles told us to open our eyes. I took in a quick breath as my brain attempted to catch up with my eyes.

A music room.

And in the center of the beautiful room, on a raised floor, was our piano with a small but elegant chandelier hanging over the center. A lump formed in my throat, and I tried hard to swallow it down.

The Anderson brothers built us a music room.

"It's Michael's design," Miles said proudly. "Garrett and I took care of the rest."

The room extended from our living area with an A-frame roof. The wall to the left had built-in shelves painted white to match the shelves in the living room, while the back wall and the wall to the right was floor to ceiling windows. The floor was the same knotted pine that ran through the rest of our house. There were two off-white, tufted chaise lounges in either corner, as well as a bench seat that extended across the length of the back wall, covered in the same fabric as the chaises. Pillows and a quilt with the same palette of soft blues and yellows that matched the rest of our décor covered the bench.

The shelves had old music books that Kate and I had put in storage with the piano, along with newly framed photos I'd never seen before. Photos of my mom and Aunt Beth sitting at the piano, Kate and I in our Christmas costumes playing for the school pageant, some of me and my dad, and Kate and I with Uncle David. The top shelf was lined with trophies and music awards that Kate and I had won over the years.

I stepped onto the raised floor and ran my fingers across the familiar piano. It wasn't a Steinway, though it was a grand piano. It was so beautiful to me because it was the same piano my mom and aunt Beth used to play.

"Kenny gave us the key to the storage facility," Garrett said. "He also arranged to have the piano tuned."

I felt tears coming down my face, and Kate too, had tears.

"How did you guys do this?" I asked, still trying to take in every detail.

"Gracie, it's what we do," Garrett replied. "We've been planning since we left Mom and Dad's at Thanksgiving. We pulled permits and ordered materials so we could start as soon as we left for Christmas."

I wiped my cheek and looked over at Michael.

"When we saw you and Kate play at Mom and Dad's…" his voice was quiet, "we knew we needed to do this for you. We've had our crew working day and night to finish."

"Kenny told us about the trophies and photos in the attic," Garrett added. "Miles took the photos to get framed." He handed me a portrait I had never seen. "This one is my favorite."

The photo was black and white, with yellowing around the edges from aging. My mom and Aunt Beth were sitting at this very piano, with Kate and I on their laps. We weren't much older than five, and we were laughing, while our mothers smiled at the camera. I cried as I looked at how beautiful they both were.

The boys were standing together by the back wall, watching Kate and I carefully, and I felt so much love for them I could hardly stand it. Kate jumped into Miles' arms and cried. I set the picture on top of the piano and strode toward Garrett, and he bent down so I could put my arms around his neck.

"Thank you, thank you," I sobbed. "I can't believe you did this."

He hugged me and chuckled softly. "*We* did this because we love you."

"I love you too, Garrett," I said, still crying. "Thank you."

Michael's expression was uncertain as I stepped over to him. He pulled me close to him and rested his head on top of mine. Whether it was the gratitude I felt because of the music room or the overwhelming love I felt for Michael at that moment, I cried even more.

"Michael, thank you so much, it's just beautiful." I choked between sobs. "No one has ever done something so wonderful for us before. Thank you."

"You're welcome," he continued to hold me, stroking my hair softly.

"I love you," I whispered.

The words came out before I had the chance to think, but I'd said it. I didn't care if he thought I was talking about loving him as my friend or not. He pulled me tighter, and I closed my eyes, wishing I could stay in his arms forever. When I pulled away from him, his eyes studied my face intently and then the corner of his mouth turned up into the crooked grin I loved. At that moment I wondered if there was a possibility he might love me the way I loved him.

Chapter Fourteen

During the following week, the TV was rarely on, except for football games because Kate and I played the piano almost constantly. Sometimes just one of us, other times we'd play duets. We'd found the music for a "William Tell Overture" duet and had been practicing.

New Year's morning I was on the porch tying my shoes, freezing my butt off, waiting for Michael to show up for our morning run. Even though our New Year's Eve was rather uneventful, we'd still stayed up way past midnight, and I'd wanted to stay in bed. But who was I kidding? I'd never pass up any opportunity to be with Michael.

It was after eight when I trudged to the middle of the drive. I glared at the Anderson's door, waiting for it to open because Michael was late. I stood there for a moment, kicking the gravel at my feet and then turned to walk back inside. I heard a door close and turned to see Michael jogging toward me. I narrowed my eyes at him and pointed to my watch.

He winced as he looked down at me. "Sorry."

"Mm-Hmm," I said, shaking my head. "You were almost in some serious trouble, mister. I wanted to stay in bed today."

He chuckled, and we started our jog. We ran in silence for quite a while, until he cleared his throat. "So did you make any resolutions this year?"

"Yeah," I said, scowling at him. "I resolved never to make my running partner wait when it's friggin' freezing outside."

He laughed and shook his head. "I said I was sorry, I forgot to set my alarm."

I rolled my eyes.

"So did you make any resolutions or not?" he asked with a grin.

"Just the usual: quit smoking, lose ten pounds, try to stay away from alcohol—"

"Okay." He laughed. "So I'm guessing there were no resolutions this year."

"I kind of forgot about the whole resolution thing this year," I told him. "But I'm sure there's more than one thing I could change."

He snorted a laugh.

"What?" I raised an eyebrow. "You think I need to work on some things?"

"No, that's why I laughed. I can't think of a single thing you need to change. Well, except for the smoking thing."

I laughed. "What about you? Did you make any resolutions?" He shrugged.

"Care to share?" I asked him. "Or is it personal?"

He smiled. "I resolved to be more honest with myself."

I nodded, even though I had no idea what he was talking about. I couldn't help but stare at him. He was so gorgeous, and I loved that smile. He glanced over at me, catching me in my stare. I turned quickly feeling my face heat and heard him chuckle.

"What's so funny?" I asked, not looking at him.

"Nothing," he said, reaching over and tugging the end of my ponytail gently. "I just love it when you blush."

Once in front of our houses, we each walked toward our own doors.

"What's for breakfast?" he asked

"Um, waffles I think. You coming?"

"I'll be there."

"Are you going to be late?"

"Very funny, Burke."

I waved with a smile, and he laughed as he turned to go inside. I went into the kitchen where Kate was making breakfast, looking adorable in her USC sweatshirt, and Miles was stirring something on the stove.

"Morning," I said.

"Morning, Gracie," Kate said as she poured batter on the waffle iron. "You have time to shower if you want."

"Are you sure?" I asked. "Do you need any help?"

"We've got it," Miles assured me.

I went to take a quick shower and got dressed in jeans and my favorite USC sweatshirt. I dried my hair straight, pulling half of it up into a barrette and put on a little makeup. When I returned to the kitchen, Garrett greeted me cheerily, and Michael was leaning against the counter. He was wearing the USC sweatshirt I gave him when I found out he had no SC garb.

"I like your shirt." I nodded my approval. "Fight On."

"Fight On." He draped his arm over my shoulders. "Are you still mad at me for being late this morning?"

"No, but don't let it happen again," I warned with a smirk.

He folded his arms across his chest and grinned, watching me as I made my coffee. When my face turned red, he stifled a laugh, still watching me. I pulled the cream from the fridge and when I turned around, he was still staring with the same grin on his face. I pursed my lips together as I stirred my coffee and then turned to look at him.

"What?" I asked. "What are you staring at?"

He smiled and shrugged casually. "I'm staring at you."

His eyes didn't leave mine, and my heart thrummed against my chest. After an uncomfortable moment he chuckled, releasing me from his gaze as he walked over to sit at the table with his brothers.

Kate high-fived me when she saw my USC shirt, and we did our traditional, hip bumping while we hummed the 'Fight Song', making the boys laugh. We all ate waffles with strawberries, talking about the Bowl games and the Rose Parade. Kate and I planned on making homemade pizza, hot wings, and of course, brownies. I refilled everyone's coffee cups, and we sat for a long while at the table, just visiting and laughing.

Eventually, I got up and started clearing dishes, and as usual, Michael helped me. When we finished, we all went to the living room and watched the parade and drank our coffee. We spent the rest of New Year's Day, watching football, eating pizza and having a great time. USC won the Rose Bowl—again—and Florida won their game, so we were all pretty happy. We all talked about getting back to work and into our regular schedules. Garrett had to go to Denver to check on the St. Joseph's job, Miles and Michael both had blueprints and proposals to present to a client in Denver for a new hotel. And Kate and I would be busy getting back into our schedule at the shop.

Michael asked if I was going to run in the morning, and I said yes, but if he was late, I was leaving his butt in the driveway. He just rolled his eyes and tousled my hair as he walked out the door.

* * *

The remainder of the week was fairly uneventful, the boys stayed busy with their work, and Kate and I stayed busy with ours. By the time Friday arrived, I was tired and looking forward to a quiet evening at home. Kate and Miles had dinner plans, Garrett was going to Kenny's apartment with Evan to play video games—I was invited, but declined the offer—Michael had a late meeting in Denver, so I had a date with Haagen-Dazs and some laundry.

When I arrived home, I changed into my comfy jeans and a sweatshirt, moved the clean towels from the washer to the dryer, starting a new load of Kate's and my clothes. I went into the kitchen and grabbed a carton of chocolate-peanut butter from the freezer and channel-surfed looking for something worth watching.

Nothing good.

I decided to watch a movie, but went to pull the towels from the dryer first, carrying them to the sofa. I put on a CD of Grace Potter and the Nocturnal sand turned up the volume, singing and dancing as I folded the warm towels. "And if I was from Paris, if I was from Paris, I would say Ooh-la-la-la-la-la-la-la…"

I picked up the folded towels to take them to the bathrooms and when I turned, Michael was leaning against the wall, arms folded across his chest with a giant smirk on his face. I jumped, dropped the towels on the floor and clamped my hand over my mouth to keep from screaming.

"Holy. Crap." I glared at him. "Why do you do that?"

"Sorry." He sniggered. "I rang the doorbell."

My heart pounded as he watched me, and I was completely embarrassed. He walked toward me slowly, faded jeans, gray sweater, and black leather jacket, hair in its usual gorgeous disarray. I tried to be casual, but didn't pull it off too well. I was still breathing heavy as I bent down to pick up the towels.

"How long have you been standing there?" I asked, trying not to look at him.

"Long enough to know that if you were from Paris, you would say ooh-la-la-la-la-la-la-la."

I closed my eyes and wondered if I'd ever be able to make it through a twenty-four hour period without humiliating myself in front of Michael Anderson.

He pursed his lips together in an attempt to hide the humor he found in the situation and then reached over and turned the stereo volume down.

"I thought you might be hungry, I brought Chinese." He looked at the coffee table and saw the empty carton of ice cream and smiled. "Or have you already eaten?"

"Very funny," I grabbed the carton and spoon to take to the trash. "Chinese sounds great."

Michael picked up the bag of Chinese food from the floor and went into the kitchen, while I took the towels to my bathroom. He got us drinks, while I grabbed plates and forks, and I sat across from him as we started eating quietly.

"Thanks for bringing dinner." I twirled some Lo Mein on my fork. "That was nice of you."

"My pleasure," he said. "How has your week been?"

"Pretty busy," I told him. "What about you?"

"Same."

We ate in silence, except for the music playing, and after the dishes were done, we went into the living room.

"So how about a movie?" I asked.

"Sure."

I went to the shelf with our DVD collection and decided to take a gamble, sliding one of my favorites from the shelf and holding it up to Michael, ready for his usual reaction.

He rolled his eyes with a groan.

"Oh come on!" I pleaded. "I've been begging you to watch this for months!"

He tossed his head back against the couch like he was in pain.

"Your brother didn't want to watch it at first either," I informed him. "And now it's one of his favorites."

"Well, which one is this? I mean weren't there like ten?"

"Okay," I said. "I'll admit that after the third they went downhill fast."He grinned as I started my much rehearsed and always ready 'Defense of the Rocky Films' speech. "But I will have you know, this was nominated for ten—that's right, ten—Academy Awards and it won three."

He was looking at me like I was nuts.

"One of them for Best Screenplay which was written by Sylvester Stallone himself, not to mention, it is listed as one of the 100 Best Movies of All Time."

Michael laughed now, but Rocky was one of Kate's and my absolute favorite movies, and we would defend it to the end. Plus, I had a thing for Sly.

"Okay, okay." He continued to laugh. "I'll watch it, settle down."

"That's right you'll watch it." I narrowed my eyes at him.

"Don't be trashing Rocky."

He watched me with a grin as the movie started, and I pointed to the TV. We watched the movie without saying anything, though I glanced at him often to watch his reactions. When it was over, I sighed my Rocky sigh, wiping my eyes and he turned to face me, his lips pursed together tightly.

"Okay," he said. "You were right and I was wrong. It was really good, I had no idea."

I smiled and clapped my hands, which made him laugh.

"You see?" I raised an eyebrow. "And you thought I was crazy."

He chuckled. "Well, you are a little. I've never seen anyone get so defensive over a movie."

His expression changed as he watched me, as if warring internally over some kind of dilemma.

"What?" I asked him.

"May I ask you something?"

My throat got tight as I nodded reluctantly.

"I was just wondering," he said quietly. "That night, in the car…"

Oh, no.

I felt my face turn red right away, and I wanted to crawl under the couch. I was confused why he wanted to bring this up when things were just getting back to normal.

"Michael," I shook my head. "I really don't want to go back to that again—"

"I understand," he interrupted. "But I just wanted to know if you think I don't care about you."

"No, I don't think that." I picked at the hem of my shirt. "I know you care about me as a friend."

He tilted his head slightly, and his eyes were sad.

"But you were hoping for more."

I looked down, unable to meet his eyes, and took a deep breath.

"I knew by saying anything I could be risking losing you as my friend," I confessed. "But—"

"But," his voice was quiet. "You were willing to risk that."

"I suppose I was, but now that I know how you feel, I would never do anything to risk our friendship again."

"What do you mean?"

"I mean that no matter how I feel," I tried to explain. "I would rather have your friendship than nothing. If I ever lost you as my friend…" I shook my head, the thought too heartbreaking to even consider.

"You'll never lose me as your friend, okay?" he assured me. "I don't want you to ever doubt that, but I need you to understand why I said what I did."

I nodded reluctantly and braced myself for something bad.

"Two years ago, I was engaged to be married," he said quickly.

A broken engagement didn't seem like a big deal to me, so I was a little more than confused, but I waited for him to continue.

"Her name is Allison Landers, our families have known each other since we were in elementary school. Our parents were close, and Allison and I were always very good friends. Our families would always tell us how great we'd be together and how wonderful it would be if we ended up getting married."

His eyes dropped to his hands.

"She's a very kind and caring person, and she loved me." He took a deep breath. "After two years of dating, I proposed."

He glanced sideways at me, as if ashamed, but I just nodded.

"She accepted, and our families were thrilled. We planned for our wedding. Neither one of us felt it necessary to have a long engagement, so the wedding was planned for six months after I proposed. It was going to be Allison's dream wedding, and she was ecstatic. But, two weeks before the wedding…I called it off. She was so devastated," he said quietly. "I broke her heart, and I'll never forgive myself for that."

"Why didn't you marry her?"

He shrugged his shoulders.

"Because as much as I loved Allison as a person and as my

friend, I wasn't *in* love with her. I'd known it all along, but believed as much as I cared about her, the love I had for her would grow into something more. The only thing I accomplished was hurting Allison. My family supported my decision, saying I'd done the right thing by calling it off."He heaved a sigh. "I hurt someone I really cared for because I was too much of a coward to be honest with her or myself."

"So, you wish you wouldn't have called it off?" I asked, not sure I was ready for the answer. "Because you *do* love her?"

"There's more," his voice was quiet. "A week after I called off the wedding, she called to tell me she was pregnant." He kept his eyes down. "When I asked why she hadn't told me, she said she'd wanted to surprise me after the honeymoon—she was less than eight weeks along. She'd made it more than clear she didn't want to see me. I tried. I called her, I went to her house, but she wouldn't have anything to do with me, until--" his voice broke for the first time. "When I finally got her on the phone, she told me the baby was gone. She'd had an abortion that very morning."

I tried to swallow the lump that formed in my throat. Sadness for Michael. Sadness for the baby. Even sadness for Allison.

"I'll never forgive myself." His fists clenched, and he finally looked at me, eyes glistening from unshed tears. "Remember that day on our run when you were talking about giving pieces of yourself away?"

I nodded.

"Grace, my problem isn't that I gave myself away. My problem is I'm the one who broke someone."

I shook my head, feeling guilty. "I had no idea."

"There's no way you could have," he said. "But you have to understand, I think about Allison every day and the pain I caused her." His eyes bore right through mine. "It scares me to think about hurting anyone like that again. Do you understand? You deserve someone who will make you happy."

"And you don't think I deserve you?"

"No." He squeezed my hands tightly. "It's me that doesn't deserve you."

"That's ridiculous, Michael. You're one of the most wonderful people I know."

"You deserve better."

I pulled my hands away, feeling nauseous, because I knew what he was trying to tell me. My heart battled with my head over the pain and guilt Michael carried because of Allison. Whatever fault was his, he clearly recognized and took responsibility. What she took from Michael angered me, yet, at the same time, it gripped me with sadness over his loss.

"It wasn't your fault, Michael. It wasn't. It was her doing. Not yours." I realized he hadn't answered a question I'd asked earlier. "Do you still love her?"

"No," he said with certainty. "I never did and that's the problem, Grace. If I'd been honest with Allison from the beginning, none of this would've happened. It's *my* fault."

"So, who do *you* deserve then? Someone like Nina?"

His forehead creased. "What do you mean?"

"I'm trying to understand what you're saying. You feel guilty about what happened with Allison and you don't deserve me." I shrugged. "So, you must think you deserve Nina. I mean, obviously she's what you want and what you feel you *deserve*."

"Grace, I—"

"You deserve so much more than Nina Sandler. How someone like you could be with someone like her, I'll never understand."

He stood from the couch and glared at the floor. "You don't understand what I'm saying."

"You're right. I don't understand," I agreed. "You don't believe you deserve happiness. I don't understand that at all."

When he didn't respond, I began to feel guilty for my rant.

"I don't believe for a moment you would ever intentionally hurt anyone. I'm so very sorry for what happened with Allison, and I won't pretend to understand how painful it must be for you." The grief in his eyes made me want to hold him. “You’re an amazingly good and kind person, Michael. You deserve to be happy.”

As much as I wanted happiness for him, I knew he didn’t want happiness with me, and that fact was suffocating. I stood to leave.

“Grace,” he whispered and reached for my hand, but I stepped away.

My heart broke all over again. His touch would be too painful.

Chapter Fifteen

The following week seemed like the longest of my life.

I hadn't seen Michael since our conversation that night. Garrett said he was working a lot, which meant he was most likely with Nina. My head told me it was time to move on, but my heart missed him. Missed him so much it hurt.

It was snowing, which normally would have given me an excuse to go back to bed, but I went out to the drive and started my run alone. There was nothing but the silence falling snow brought. The ground was barely covered, and there was no wind, so it wasn't too bad.

I ran, not really thinking about anything, the only sound being my feet against the pavement that was lightly dusted with the fresh snow. I heard a car coming from the road ahead of me, and I moved over to the shoulder waiting for it to pass. As the engine got louder, I saw the familiar red Porsche winding its way up the two-lane road.

It was, Nina's car, of course, and when she saw me, she slowed to a crawl. I thought about pretending not to notice her and keep running, but it was too late. I stopped, staying where I was, and her window came down slowly. She smiled the usual sweet smile that I knew was a façade.

"Hello, Grace."

"Good morning," I stood with my hands on my hips, waiting for her to say whatever she was going to say, wishing she would just get on with it so I could finish my run.

"You're very dedicated to run in this." She looked up at the falling snow.

"I suppose." I'd dealt with Nina enough to know she was about to pull something from her arsenal of 'Grace Insults'.

"I guess some people have to be dedicated when it comes to exercising." She chuckled, as she looked me up and down. "It's good you make the time."

And there it was. Bull's-eye.

I looked down at the ground, attempting to recover from her hit on my self-esteem, and trying not to say anything I might regret.

"Well, it was nice to see you," she lied. "I'm just on my way to see Michael. We have an early appointment."

"Okay then," I said.

I turned away to continue my run.

"You know, Grace," she said sweetly, and I turned to face her again. "I hope you won't take this the wrong way or anything…"

Something was coming and it wasn't going to matter how she said it, it was going to be ugly.

"I know how you feel about Michael," she was attempting to sound concerned. "But I think you should know he'll never really be interested in you."

I felt anger stirring in me, and I narrowed my eyes at her.

She shook her head. "I mean really, what could the two of you possibly have in common?"

"Unlike the two of you." They had nothing in common except money. The two of them were polar opposites, and I knew it.

"We have more in common than you might think."She laughed. "Michael and I have become very…close, and I think the sooner you accept that, the easier it will be for you."

My stomach rolled over. "Is that all?"

She watched me for a moment, and her expression gave nothing away. I turned and started my run again. I felt uncomfortable having my back to her, but kept going, hearing the engine of her car rev and continue up the road.

The sickening knot formed in my stomach as I ran, thinking

about what she said. I knew that once again, she'd tried to hit where I was the most vulnerable, and once again she succeeded.

I didn't turn around at my usual spot. I just kept running. It was a good five miles into town, and that's where I decided to go. I'd just call Kate or Garrett to pick me up later.

I needed some time to recover—alone.

When I got to the coffee shop, Kenny and Peggy were both busy with customers. Kenny gave me a confused look when he saw me, but I just nodded and walked back to the office, taking off my coat and gloves. I went into Kate's and my private bathroom—which was always stocked with our personal hygiene items—to wash my hands and brush through my hair, returning it to the ponytail again. I put on some hand lotion as I flopped down in Kate's chair in front of the desk and stared at the ceiling.

"Gracie?" Kenny had his head poked through the doorway. "You okay?"

"Yeah, I'm fine."

He looked at me skeptically. "Then why are you here?"

"I don't know, but if I'm making you uncomfortable, just pretend I'm not here."

He chuckled."No, I was just checking. Can I get you something?"

"Thanks, Kenny, but I'm good."

He nodded with a half-smile and returned to the front.

I picked up a pen and doodled random geometric patterns on a legal pad and thought about what happened with Nina. I realized what she said didn't aggravate me nearly as much as the fact that I let her words get to me. I knew she was wrong about Michael and I having nothing in common, but I also knew it didn't matter how much we had in common. Michael didn't love me the way I loved him which made her twisted words cut even more.

"Hi there."

I looked up, and Evan was standing in the doorway with a grin. His hair was windblown, and his blue eyes sparkled against the silver-gray of his sweater.

"This is a nice surprise, what are you doing here?"

I stood from the chair and smiled. "I work here. What are *you* doing here?"

"I happen to come here every Saturday," he said matter-of-factly. "Which is why I know you don't work on Saturdays." He surveyed my appearance. "So what are you doing here? You okay?"

"I'm fine. I was running and just kind of kept going."

He looked puzzled, and I shook my head.

"It's a long story," I said. "How are you doing?"

"I was getting some really great coffee from my favorite place."

I pulled a face at him."You'd think gas station coffee is good. You're comparing it to hospital coffee."

"True." He laughed. "Why don't you join me?"

I didn't hesitate to follow him to the front. Kenny handed Evan his coffee, and they talked football while I made myself a latte. Evan went to a table in the corner, and I joined him.

"So how's the new year progressing?" He asked, folding his hands on the table with a smirk.

"Swimmingly," I answered dryly. "And yours?"

He laughed. "What are you up to today?"

"Nothing really," I shrugged. "What about you?"

A slow grin spread across his face. "Well, I just decided to go to the movies with this gorgeous brunette I know."

My face flushed, and I sipped at the foam from my cup.

"So how about it?" he asked. "Why don't you let me take you to the movies. Looks like you could use some entertainment of the Hollywood kind. We could see the new Meryl Streep movie, you love her."

My mind bolted in a hundred different directions, and I didn't know what to say. I loved Michael, that hadn't changed. I liked Evan, felt comfortable with him, but only as a friend.

"Grace? Did you hear me?"

"Yes, I heard you." I looked down at my hands. "I just don't want to give you the wrong idea."

"Wrong idea about what?" he argued. "We're just two friends going to a movie. You can even buy the popcorn if that'll make you feel better."

I had to smile. Evan was a good friend, and maybe a night at the movies was what I needed.

"Okay," I agreed. "I don't know what the gorgeous brunette has planned, but I would love to go to the movies with you."

"Gorgeous brunette," he said thoughtfully. "Oh, did you think I meant you?"

I groaned, and he laughed again, checking his watch.

"I'll pick you up around four o'clock?" He stood, and pulled his coat on.

"Sounds great. I'll see you then."

He nodded with a smile as he headed for the door, and I walked back to the office. It had stopped snowing, so I decided to walk home instead of calling Kate. I pulled my coat and gloves back on, and started to the front of the store.

"Bye, Gracie," Kenny said.

"You're still coming to the Super Bowl party, right?"

"Wouldn't miss it." He tossed a bar towel over his shoulder. "Do I still get to bring a date?"

I rolled my eyes. "Yeah. Do I know her?"

Kenny never had trouble getting dates, but he was a 'one date' kind of guy.

"Don't know who I'm bringing yet." He shrugged. "But I'm sure I can find someone."

"Well, if you need the phone book there's one on my desk," I said smugly. "Or have you exhausted the female resources in the Boulder vicinity? Perhaps Denver?"

"Go home." He snapped the towel at me playfully. "Tell everyone hi for me."

He chortled as I wagged my head and pushed through the door to start my trek home. The snow was now wet slush because the sun had made an appearance, but it was still chilly and I could tell the sun wouldn't be out much longer.

When I was about halfway home, Michael's Yukon came speeding down the road, skidding to a stop less than five feet away from me. He flew out of the driver's seat, furiously slamming the door behind him and strode toward me. Reflexively, I took a step backward as he got closer. I'd never seen him this angry.

"Where the hell have you been?" His nostrils flared and his jaw clenched as he leaned over me.

"I-I was at the shop," I stammered. "What's wrong?"

"You've been gone for over three hours!"

I flinched back and looked at my watch, swallowing hard. He was right. I didn't say anything as he continued to glower at me, his anger not dissipating.

"Kate called the shop," he said slowly. "Kenny said you just left? What were you doing? Why didn't you call?"

"I went for a run," I replied quietly. "I just kept going, and I had some coffee."

I decided not to mention Evan.

"Well, did it ever occur to you that we've all been at home worried sick about you? Why would you run all the way to town?"

I argued with myself on whether or not I should tell him why.

"I don't know," I lied. "I just did."

"Where's your cell phone? We've been calling it all morning."

He folded his arms over his chest and looked down at me, still angry. But now *I* was angry. Who did he think he was? He hadn't spoken to me in over a week and now he was lecturing me?

"I can run anywhere I please," I snapped. "I'm not a ten year old."

He raised an eyebrow at me, either surprised by my response, or he really did think of me as a ten year old. Both of those possibilities made me even angrier. I folded my arms in front of me, mirroring his stance and scowled back at him.

"It wasn't my intention to worry everyone," I told him. "I'll apologize when I get home."

I stepped around him to leave, but he grabbed my arm, causing me to stumble backward.

"Where do you think you're going?"

I jerked my arm away. "I'm going home!"

"I'll take you." He reached for my arm again.

"No, thank you." I stepped away from him. "I'll walk."

He heaved a sigh and walked to his car, opening the passenger door.

"Why are you so stubborn? Just get in the car, Grace."

"Don't tell me what to do."

He stood by the open door, the muscles in his jaw working hard. I wasn't sure whether he'd come after me if I walked away, but I was willing to risk it. I started walking, passing his car and heard the passenger door slam. I didn't look back as his door slammed shut. The tires squealed as he made a u-turn and followed me at a snail's pace. Apparently, he would be escorting me home whether I was in the car or not. I kept walking, the engine humming close behind me. I glanced over my shoulder at him, and he watched me with a smirk, his eyebrows lifted in amusement. I stopped, put my hands on my hips and shook my head in irritation.

I turned and slowly made my way to the vehicle. He reached across and pushed the passenger door open. I climbed in, and slammed the door angrily, folding my arms across my chest. I refused to look at him, as I kept my body turned toward the passenger window, seething in silence.

He cleared his throat, and I could tell he was probably grinning, which made me want to smack the crap out of him.

"Grace." His voice was calm. "I'm sorry I yelled at you. I was worried. We all were."

I didn't say anything. I just kept my back to him and heard him sigh as we pulled in front of the house. I quickly opened my door and got out, angrily making my way to the front porch.

"Hey, hold on a minute," he said, grabbing my arm again.

I stopped walking, glared at his hand on my arm and then at his face. He released his grasp, biting the corner of his mouth. Was he trying not to laugh?

"What?" I spat.

He grimaced and shook his head. I turned and opened the front door. Kate practically tackled me, throwing her arms around my neck.

"You had me scared to death!"

"I'm sorry, Kate, I didn't mean to worry you."

She nodded, still squeezing me. I looked at Miles standing behind her, his mouth in a tight line.

"Sorry," I mouthed silently to him, and he nodded.

Garrett stepped up next to Miles and glared down at me. I sighed and walked over to him, but before I could open my mouth to apologize, he grabbed me up in a tight hug. My feet hovered over the floor as I hugged him back.

"Don't you ever do that again, Gracie-Beth," Garrett ordered. "Do you understand?"

I nodded, and he gave me another squeeze before setting me down. I smiled up at him, and he put me in a headlock as we walked to the kitchen. They hadn't eaten breakfast because of me, which made me feel worse than I already did.

"Why don't you shower," Kate said. "I'll get breakfast ready."

I nodded and started to my room. Michael was in the hallway, leaning against the wall by my door, watching me. When he didn't say anything, I brushed past him into my room and closed the door.

The hot water of the shower calmed my nerves, which was a good thing because I was still mad at Michael Anderson.

I joined everyone at the table, sitting in my usual seat between Michael and Garrett. Michael was pushing scrambled eggs across his plate but not eating. When I glanced at him, his eyes met mine for a moment, before he looked away. Part of me wanted to apologize for worrying him. He was the only one I hadn't apologized to, and I felt bad. I also wanted to tell him about Nina. She was psycho-scary, but

I couldn't say anything about her without sounding like a jealous teenager. Maybe part of me was jealous, except I couldn't imagine Michael liking someone like Nina because she was…foul.

"Gracie," Kate interrupted my thoughts. "Did you hear me?"

I looked at her and shook my head.

"Miles and Garrett are taking me to town to get the things for the Super Bowl party," she said. "Is there anything you need?"

"Just what I wrote on the list."

She nodded and started to get the plates from the table.

"I'll do the dishes," I told her. "You guys go ahead."I stood up and started clearing plates, while they got ready to leave. Michael got up from the table, but instead of helping me with the dishes like he usually did, he headed for the front door.

"Thanks for breakfast, Kate," he said.

"Where are you going, little brother?" Garrett asked.

Michael glanced at me and raked his hand through his hair. "I've got work to do."

Garrett pursed his lips and nodded.

Michael walked out the door with Miles and Kate, without saying anything. Garrett kissed the top of my head and waved with a sympathetic expression on his face as he followed them. I finished the dishes and went to collect the dirty laundry, starting a load in the washer. I went into my room, and picked up the current book I was reading from my bedside table, returning to the living room. I turned on music and curled up on the couch, pulling the quilt over me. A light snow was falling, and I watched it for a few minutes before opening my book.

The front door opened, and I knew it was Michael. I didn't move as he walked over and sat at the opposite end of the sofa. Even though I hadn't read past the first word, I kept my eyes on my book.

It was quiet for a moment, and he leaned back to make himself comfortable.

"How's the book?"

I shrugged without making eye contact with him. Maybe I was

being immature, but at the moment I didn't care. His chuckle got my attention, and he watched me with a slight grin as he shook his head.

"You have a temper," he said smugly.

I snorted, looking at him incredulously.

I have a temper?

When I didn't acknowledge his statement, he leaned forward, resting his elbows on his knees.

"You have got to be one of the most frustrating, hard-headed, stubborn…"

Apparently, he'd run out of adjectives.

He rubbed his forehead with his fingertips, staring at the floor. I closed my book and waited for him to finish whatever he was going to say.

"I don't suppose you'd like to tell me what happened this morning? Because it's just not like you to do something like that."

I didn't respond, and he still watched me.

"Was it Nina?"

Maybe my silence answered his question because he leaned back against the couch, staring up at the ceiling with a sigh.

"What did she say this time?"

The way he phrased the question told me he either assumed there had been more than one incident regarding Nina, or Kate had told him. He turned to face me, waiting for my answer.

"She didn't say anything that matters," I responded quietly.

That was the truth. Nina made it sound like Michael and I had some kind of relationship other than friendship, and obviously, we didn't. So, no matter how much the things she said bothered or hurt me, it didn't matter.

"Why don't you tell me anyway?"

"Because, it doesn't really have anything to do with you, Michael. She just dislikes me, so she tries to get to me, that's all."

"Well, it must have worked this morning. You ran over five miles just to avoid coming here."

"I wasn't avoiding coming here," I argued. Then I realized, I did run to town to avoid coming here, but it wasn't *here* I wanted to avoid, it was Nina. "Okay," I admitted. "I just wanted to keep away from her. I told everyone I was sorry for making them worry."

"What. Did. She. Say?" He enunciated each word impatiently, ignoring my statement and making me angrier by the second. "Why does it matter to you what she says to me?" I finally said. "She seems to think we have some kind of relationship other than friendship. She's delusional. And I don't know what I've ever done to her, but she takes every opportunity to rip into me." I rambled out of frustration now. "She takes shots at everything from my hair to whatever I happen to be wearing at the time. Not to mention the fact that she enjoys telling me how *close* the two of you are and how I'm not good enough for you. She's vile!"

I stopped and stared at my hands, twisting my thumbs nervously, trying not to cry. I was angry. He'd pushed me into telling him things I didn't want him to know.

"Look," my voice was quiet. "It doesn't matter what she says, and it has nothing to do with you."

I stood from the couch, doing my best not to look at him.

"It's my fault I let her get to me today," I glanced at him, and he was watching me worriedly. I could feel tears coming, and I wasn't going to cry in front of him. "I'm not feeling very well, I think I need to lie down. I'll see you later."

He didn't stop me as I turned and walked to my room, closing the door behind me. I crawled to the middle of my bed, lying down and squeezing my eyes closed. Tears escaped as I tried to take a deep breath and relax. I wasn't angry with Michael anymore. He obviously cared about me, but he didn't love me—at least not the way I loved him. Every time I thought about that fact, it felt like my heart was being broken apart again, and it was awful.

Chapter Sixteen

I didn't realize I'd fallen asleep until my eyes opened, and I saw it was after three o'clock. I could hear talking and music playing in the kitchen. I rolled off my bed and my head pounded. I went into my bathroom, washed my hands and brushed through my hair as I cursed at my red, puffy eyes in the mirror before going into the kitchen.

Garrett looked at me with his brows pulled together. "We've got some pizza, you hungry?"

I smiled and nodded at him. Michael was sitting in his regular chair, watching me with a sympathetic expression, which made me uncomfortable.

I didn't want his sympathy.

I opened the fridge and pulled out a bottle of water before going to the table. Garrett draped his arm over my shoulder and hugged me to him.

"Michael said you aren't feeling too well," he said. "Are you okay?"

"I'm fine."I felt everyone's eyes on me as I pulled a piece of pizza from the box and took a bite. I looked up at Kate, and she smiled tentatively at me.

"I hope you're better for the party tomorrow," she said.

"It's just a headache."

She nodded, though I could tell we'd be discussing the matter later. I ate my pizza quietly, while everyone chatted about the Super Bowl party. There was a bet on whether Kenny would be bringing the same girl he was with on New Year's Eve. I doubted that, and so did everyone but Miles, he was giving Kenny the benefit of the doubt.

There was a loud pounding on the door that made me jump, and everyone looked at each other, puzzled. Kate started to get up, but Miles shook his head at her and went to the door, followed by Garrett and Michael. Kate and I looked at each other anxiously, as we heard the front door open.

"You have some nerve, Michael Anderson!"

I could hear Nina screeching from the front porch, and my stomach knotted nervously.

"How dare you leave my father a message like that! You can't just back out of your contract with our company!"

"Actually," Miles said sternly. "If you had read the contract, Nina, you would know we reserve the right to pull out at any time we feel it is detrimental to our company."

"Detrimental? Detrimental! You have no idea who you're dealing with!" She continued to screech.

"We know *exactly* who we're dealing with," Garrett said, an edge to his voice. "That's why we're not working with you anymore."

"Nina, your company hasn't given us a penny," Michael said. "You've lost nothing, except time."

Kate watched me worriedly as I pushed away from the table, and she followed me to the entryway. Nina stood in front of Michael, with Garrett and Miles behind him. Nina continued to rant until she saw me. Her eyes widened, and she started towards me, but Michael stepped in front of her. Garrett was behind me quickly, placing his hands on my shoulders.

Nina sidestepped Michael and narrowed her eyes at me angrily.

"You…" her voice was a snarl. "This is all because of you!"

I had no idea what was going on, and my expression must have been proof.

"Don't pretend you didn't have anything to do with this!" She shouted. "You've been feeding him lies about me from the beginning!"

"This has nothing to do with Grace," Michael said angrily. "This has to do with you and the way you do business."

She continued to glare as if Michael hadn't spoken.

"The hell it doesn't!" She screeched. "This has everything to do with her!" As if a switch had been flipped, her expression changed to a smile, and she tossed her hair over her shoulders, looking at Kate and then back at me again. "Doesn't it, Grace?"

Her tone was acid and sugar at the same time, and it rolled my stomach.

"Get out of my house," I told her. "Get out. Now."

She laughed humorlessly and turned to leave. Michael opened the door, and she glanced over her shoulder at me.

"You're a bitch," she snarled. "And this isn't over, Grace."

"Hey!" Garrett shouted, making me flinch. "Watch yourself!"

Nina didn't even acknowledge him as she stepped closer to Michael and stroked the side of his face with the back of her hand. He jerked away from her, but she just smiled at him.

"Goodbye, Michael. When you're done slumming," she threw a smug glance over her shoulder at me, "give me a call."

Michael's jaw clenched as she walked out the door, and he closed it behind her. I felt nauseous as I closed my eyes, taking a deep breath, and Garrett squeezed me to him.

"Well, you've never seen that side of her, have you, little brother?" Garrett spoke tensely but was trying to lighten the mood. "I'm pretty sure she's all colors of crazy."

Michael ignored Garrett's question and looked at me apologetically.

"I'm sorry, Grace," he said. "She had no right to be here. I never thought she'd do something like this."

"What was that about anyway?" I asked.

"Anderson Industries dropped her father's company," Miles explained. "As of today."

I swallowed hard. "Because of what happened today?" I asked, looking at Michael.

"No," he assured me. "Like I said, it's because of how she does business."

I believed that partially, but I also felt like it was far too coincidental.

"This is going to cost you a lot of money." I shook my head, focusing on the floor. "You should have left it alone."

"Grace," Miles said softly. "We won't do business with Nina or her father."

I kept my eyes down, and Miles stepped in front of me, taking my hands in his.

"Yes, they were a big client, but our dad taught us not to compromise our integrity for any reason. Especially money." He smiled encouragingly as he continued. "There's no way we could do work for Nina's family without compromising our integrity."

Michael nodded in agreement. "If I'd known how Nina was treating you, I would've quit a long time ago."

"Yeah, that's why I didn't tell you," I said. "What she does to me has nothing to do with you or your business."

Michael's expression became angry, and Miles squeezed my hands.

"It has everything to do with our business, Grace," Miles said calmly. "We saw what she really is, and we won't ignore that for money. It's construction," he said matter-of-factly. "We don't have that job now, but another will come, and we didn't compromise. That's how we were taught."

He kissed the top of my head before going into the kitchen with Kate, Garrett following. Michael stepped toward me, anger etched in his features.

"And for you to say that the way she's treated you has nothing to do with me—" he took a deep breath and shook his head. "You should've told me."

He walked past me into the kitchen with the others, and my

heart sank.

This was too hard.

When it came to Michael, I seemed to do everything wrong. I'd believed I could settle for friendship, but I wasn't good at being his friend. It was too hard being Michael's friend, because I loved him too much. I was making things difficult on myself by loving Michael.

But how was I supposed to stop loving him? I didn't know the answer.

For the first time in my life, I doubted the whole selling out theory. How long was I supposed to wait for someone who'd made it completely clear he didn't want anything more than friendship?

I had nowhere to go with Michael because he didn't want me.

He doesn't want me.

Saying the words again, even in my head, caused the dreaded ache to return. With all the different feelings of love I'd experienced with Michael, what I felt now was different.

Now, it was just hurt.

I stood by the front door, wanting to leave. To go somewhere… anywhere.

Just then the doorbell rang. The boys were back at the door in a heartbeat, and Kate held me close to her as Garrett opened the door. Apparently, we all thought the same thing: Nina was back.

"Hey, everyone." Evan was on the front porch with a big smile, until he noticed the obvious tension, and his smile disappeared quickly. "Is everything okay?"

There was an awkward moment of silence, but I was relieved to see him.

"We're still going to the movies right?" Evan asked me skeptic-cally.

I tried to smile. "Absolutely. Come on in."

Evan came in closing the door behind him, looking at all of us nervously.

"Are you sure everything's okay?" he asked again. "Is this a bad time?"

"Hey, Evan," Garrett said quietly. "How's it goin', man?"

They shook hands, and Evan greeted the others.

"Evan," I said. "Can I have just a minute?"

"Sure."

Kate followed me to my bedroom, and I closed the door behind me. I told her what happened with Nina that morning, and how I saw Evan at the shop.

"I completely forgot," I said. "I feel terrible."

Rushing to the bathroom, I ran a brush through my hair. Kate watched as I put on my shoes and jacket.

"I'm not sure you should go," she said. "Nina just threatened you."

"It'll be fine," I said, not sure it was going to be fine at all. "Nina's crazy, but she doesn't scare me."

"What about Michael?"

"Evan's just a friend, but it wouldn't matter anyway," I told her. "I mean, I keep loving Michael and hoping, and he—"

"Oh, Gracie," Kate whispered as she wrapped her arms around my neck.

She held onto me tightly, and I swallowed hard to keep from crying. There was a knock at the door, and Garrett stepped inside, closing the door behind him. His face was crumpled with worry, and I stood on my toes so I could kiss his cheek.

"You have your cell phone?" he asked.

I pulled my phone from my purse and showed it to him.

"I'm going to be calling you," he cautioned me. "And you'd better answer, okay?"

I nodded.

"I mean it, Gracie-Beth." His expression was serious. "Evan told me where you two are going. I'll come and drag your butt out of that theater if you don't answer, got it?"

"Garrett, Evan wouldn't—"

"This isn't because of Evan," he interrupted. "This is because of

Nina. Were you not in the room just a few minutes ago when she threatened you?"

He was watching out for me, and I loved him for it.

"I'm not afraid of Nina," I told him.

He scowled."I know," he said. "Why am I not surprised?"

"Be careful, Gracie," Kate said.

I kissed her cheek as I started to drop my phone back into my purse, but Garrett stopped me.

"Keep it on you—in your pocket."

I tucked the phone into the front pocket of my jeans, and walked out to the living room. I noticed Michael watching me indignantly, leaning against the wall as Miles and Evan talked with each other.

"I'm ready," I said.

"Great." Evan smiled. "We'll see you guys later."

Evan opened the front door, and I followed him to his car. I looked over my shoulder as Garrett waved half-heartedly. I climbed into the passenger seat of Evan's Land Rover, he closed the door and walked around to his side. The engine revved, and I buckled my seatbelt as Evan drove down the private drive toward the main road.

"So," Evan said hesitantly. "You could actually cut the tension in there with a knife. Are you all right?"

"It's just been a weird day, that's all."

"We have a bit of a drive if you want to talk." He raised his eyebrows with a smirk. "I am a doctor, you know."

I laughed. "You say that a lot."

"Well, tell me what's going on. Maybe I can help."

I knew he couldn't help, but I didn't see any harm in telling him what was going on. I started by telling him about Nina. How she stopped me on my run that morning, and about her appearance at the house this afternoon. I didn't go into details about Michael. Evan already knew how I felt.

We pulled into the parking lot at the theater, and he turned off the engine with a troubled expression on his face.

"Well," he said. "No wonder the Andersons were so uncomfortable with you going out. I can't say I blame them."

"They told you that?"

"Not really." He shrugged. "But I kinda picked up on the tension."

"I suppose it was easy to pick up on."

He smiled in response.

"That's why Garrett will probably be calling every half hour."

Just then, "I'm Sexy and I Know It" hummed in my pocket, and Evan laughed.

"Garrett picked that ringtone," I explained with a laugh as I pulled the phone from my pocket."Hey, Garrett."

"You okay, Gracie?"

"Yes, we just got to the theater."

"Okay, just put the phone on vibrate when the movie starts. I just want you to say hello and then you can hang up."

I chuckled. "Okay."

"Well, I don't want you to miss the movie or anything, but I want to make sure you're all right."

Evan was sniggering, and I rolled my eyes.

"Is the doc laughing at me?" Garrett asked, and Evan waved his hands in front of him, shaking his head back and forth.

"Um," I giggled. "No."

"Yeah, right." Garrett snorted. "Have fun."

I snapped the phone shut, and Evan smiled at me.

"He looks after you," he said.

I nodded with a smile, my heart full of love for the Andersons, but then I thought of Michael and the ache returned.

"I couldn't help but notice tonight," Evan said. "Michael didn't seem too happy about you going out with me."

I wasn't sure what to say.

"I don't think he has a problem with me," he said. "But I'm not sure you're right about how he feels about you."

I shrugged, still not sure what to say. He smiled and pulled the keys from the ignition.

"You ready to see a movie?"

I nodded, and we both got out of the car and walked into the theater.

"So what's it going to be?" He asked as we studied our film choices. "Blood and guts, romantic comedy, scary?"

"What do you like?" I asked.

"Well, I kind of get my fill of blood and guts working at the hospital."

"Because you're a doctor," I said dryly.

"That's exactly what I was going to say." He grinned. "How about scary?"

"Sure," I said. "I can always watch a masochistic killer chase a college co-ed in her underwear through the woods."

He busted up laughing and shook his head.

"I thought we were going to see the Meryl Streep movie?" I said.

"Oh, that's right. Meryl, it is."

He bought the tickets and when we got inside, I stepped up to the concession counter.

I smiled at the young guy working. "Hi. How are you?"

"I'm good. What can I get for you?"

Evan leaned against the counter, rested his chin on his hand and watched me with half a smile.

"Well," I glanced at the guy's nametag, "Josh, I'll take a large popcorn with extra butter. Two large drinks, one diet, and…" I looked over at Evan questioningly and he held up two fingers. "Make that two diets, a pack of plain M&Ms," I paused again, and Evan pointed out his candy selection. "A pack of chocolate covered raisins." I wrinkled my nose at the raisins, making Josh laugh as he started getting our snacks.

"I like a woman who takes charge." Evan grinned. "Not to mention a woman who knows how to eat junk food at a movie."

I snorted a laugh, and he pulled out his wallet, but I stopped him with a raised eyebrow.

"The deal was I buy the popcorn, remember?"

"Right," he said. "What was I thinking?"

Josh lined up our snacks on the counter, as I opened my wallet.

"So how much are we looking at here, Josh? Fifty bucks?" I smirked. "First born child? What's the damage?"

He grinned and rang up the total.

"That'll be sixteen seventy-five."

"Are you allowed to accept tips?"

He turned to the girl working next to him, and she nodded.

"Keep the change then, Josh." I smiled, and handed him a twenty. "Thanks."

"Thanks a lot," Josh said appreciatively.

I handed the drinks to Evan and dropped the candy in my purse, grabbing the popcorn. We managed to find good seats even though the theater was crowded and got settled.

"You haven't changed a bit," Evan said as I handed him his box of candy. "You still talk to strangers like you've known them for years. I think poor Josh is smitten."

I rolled my eyes.

"He's probably working up the courage to ask for your phone number."

"I doubt that," I said. "But if he asks for my number, I'll just give him Garrett's."

We both laughed as my phone rang.

"Okay." Evan shook his head. "That's just eerie."

I chuckled as I pulled the phone from my pocket.

"Hey, Garrett."

"It's Michael."

I swallowed hard.

"Grace?"

"Um, yeah."

"You okay?"

"Yes."

"Good."

The phone went silent, and I turned it to vibrate before putting it back into my pocket. Evan munched on popcorn and watched advertisements flash on the screen. I wondered if Michael was hurting, too. That wasn't what I wanted.

"That was Michael, huh?" Evan asked without looking at me.

"How'd you know?"

He shrugged with a grin as he chewed. "You're welcome."

"What does that mean?" I glowered at him, and he chuckled as the lights dimmed and the previews started. I found myself enjoying the movie and Evan's company, both a welcome distraction from the drama of Nina and Michael.

When the movie was over, Evan and I both applauded, and he grinned at me.

"What'd you think?" he asked.

"I loved it."

"Me too," he said. "But I'm wondering, was this considered a chick-flick?"

I pursed my lips together. "Um, probably."

"Okay." He nodded. "Then you have to tell everyone we saw the blood and guts. You know, because—"

"You're a doctor?"

He laughed. "I was going to say because I'm a guy."

We left the theater, and Evan walked extra slow as we passed the concession counter, trying to see if Josh was going to ask me for my number. I finally pulled him out the doors by his arm.

"Come on, Grace," he teased. "I had to give the poor kid his chance. He's going to be heartbroken."

I rolled my eyes at him as he opened the car door for me, and I climbed inside. The phone vibrated, and I answered it quickly.

"I'm out of the movie now."

"Okay."It was Michael. "Are you on your way home?"

"Um, I think so."

"Well, if you go somewhere else, make sure you call."

The phone went silent before I could say anything else, and I shook my head. Evan started the car and pulled out of the parking lot.

"Are you hungry?" he asked. "It's still early. We could get a bite to eat."

I wrinkled my nose. "I'm too full from the popcorn and M&Ms."

"I can't believe you still mix your M&Ms and popcorn," he said. "Reminded me of when you were just a kid with braces, sitting with Kate and my sister on the ugly plaid couch in the basement."

We both laughed.

"Yeah," I said. "And you enjoyed putting on your hockey mask and scaring the crap out of us, if I remember correctly."

"Yes. Yes, I did." He nodded. "I enjoyed that a great deal."

When we pulled in front of my house, Evan smiled warmly.

"I had a great time," he said. "Good luck with…everything."

"Thanks, Evan."

I climbed out of the car and watched as he pulled away. When I turned to go inside, Michael was coming through the front door of my house, zipping up his coat. My heart flailed as he walked towards me.

"Hey," I managed, though his expression made me wish I could retract my greeting.

"So," he shoved his hands into his pockets, "how was your *date*?"

"It wasn't a *date*," I corrected him.

"Oh really?" He cocked an eyebrow. "He picked you up, and you went to a movie. That's not a date?"

"He's a friend, and we went to the movies," I replied, irritated with his tone and his line of questioning.

He shook his head, and sighed. "I think we should talk, don't you?"

I stared down at the ground, warring internally with everything I really wanted to say.

"Not really. Whenever I talk, it just seems to make things

worse."

He snorted a laugh, and I looked up at him, wondering why he would think that was funny.

"You're being a baby," he said. "Why do you have to be so stubborn?" he asked, though I don't think he was expecting an answer. "Why would you think it was okay to not tell me what Nina was doing? Why wouldn't you tell me?"

"Because it didn't have anything to do with you."

"Why do you keep saying that?"

"Didn't we cover this already?" I asked acerbically. "I didn't tell you about it because I knew there was no truth in the things she was saying, and honestly, I just wrote it off as her being a little nuts."

He nodded. "Okay, you're right about that. Is that it?"

"Is what it?"

"Is that all you want to talk about?"

I heaved a sigh. "No, but, I really don't think you want to hear the rest."

He tilted his head, and my heart raced with his gaze."Try me."

The internal warring continued—loving him and hurting at the same time.

"Grace," he said impatiently.

"Okay," I said, exasperated. "Sometimes, I think it's too hard being your friend."

The hurt on his face caused me to instantly regret my words.

"I always say the wrong things because I'm feeling the wrong things."

He was quiet as he waited for me to continue.

"I told myself I wanted to be your friend no matter what, but it's just so hard, and it's because of the way I feel about you, Michael."He looked away. "Every time I'm with you or see you, I feel like an idiot teenager waiting for something to happen that I know isn't going to happen because—"

I didn't want to say it. He looked up at me then, his eyes sad.

"Because—" he prompted me to continue.

I swallowed hard. "Because you don't want me."

An unreadable expression crossed his face, and his eyebrows knitted together. In one long stride he was in front of me, his eyes burning into mine. He lifted his hand and traced my bottom lip with his finger, his touch an electric current right to my core.

"Did he kiss you?" His voice was barely a whisper, and I wasn't sure I'd heard him correctly. "Evan," he clarified, his eyes following his fingertip as it continued around my mouth. "Did he kiss you?"

My mouth went dry. I swallowed hard and shook my head minutely.

"Good," he murmured. Then his lips were on mine.

My breath left my lungs in a rush, and my brain was in a tail-spin. I'd waited for this, dreamt about it, and it was so much sweeter than anything I could've imagined. His mouth was soft, and his breath was warm as his lips grazed my jaw back and forth.

"Grace?" he whispered against my mouth. "Will you take a ride with me?"

He pulled away then, his eyes on mine, a hint of a smile on his beautiful mouth. I only nodded, still reeling from his kiss, and he took me by the hand. We walked to his Yukon, and he opened the passenger door for me.

"Where are we going?" I asked as I climbed in.

He leaned in close to me, his face inches from mine, and I had a hard time breathing as he took my seatbelt and reached across to buckle me in, the 'click' of the seatbelt making me flinch.

"You're awfully jumpy," he smiled wryly. "Don't you trust me?"

His face was so close to mine, it took every ounce of self-control I had not to attack him right then and there.

"Um, yes," I told him. "I trust you."

He kissed me tenderly before closing my door. I watched him walk around, climb into his seat and start the engine.

"Are you nervous?" he asked with a smirk.

"With you?" I raised an eyebrow. "Nah."

He laughed at my sarcasm and turned on the heater, then plugged his iPod into the radio. Def Leppard came through the speakers, and I giggled. He glanced over at me with a shrug.

"Kinda grows on you, doesn't it?" I asked with a smirk.

"Yeah," he said dryly. "A lot like mold."

He turned up the volume as we got on the main road. During the drive, he reached for my hand, twining our fingers together, which made me smile more than I already was. Every part of me was on sensory overload. The sudden shift of his emotions confused me, but I was too nervous to ask questions. We drove for almost forty-five minutes, making small talk and listening to music, when Michael pulled into a construction site. We circled around to a chain link gate with a giant ANDERSON INDUSTRIES, INC. sign. A security guard was sitting in a small booth watching television and when he saw our car, he came outside while Michael lowered his window.

"Good evening, Jason," Michael said.

"Oh, good evening, Mr. Anderson." The man smiled in recognition. "How can I help you this evening?"

"I just want to check on the progress," Michael said. "We won't be long."

"No problem. Let me get the gate."

The guard walked over and unlocked a massive padlock, pulling the gate open for us to drive through. Michael parked the car and walked around to open my door for me.

"Thank you, Mr. Anderson." I smirked.

He rolled his eyes and pulled on his coat, then took my hand and led me toward the building that looked like mostly steel beams. Jason handed Michael some kind of radio and flashlight, and led us into the building to an elevator. Michael stepped inside, and I followed.

"Just radio me when you're ready to come back down," Jason said.

Michael thanked him as he pushed a button and the silver doors slid closed. He smiled at me as the elevator climbed for several floors and came to an abrupt stop. Michael switched on the flashlight.

"Watch your step," he cautioned and stepped off the elevator while I followed closely, wondering why on earth he would bring me to a construction site. I kept my eyes on the floor as we stepped around construction debris, gripping his hand tightly. We stopped walking, and Michael pointed out the side of the building, smiling excitedly.

"Look."

I turned in the direction he was pointing and gasped. We were at the top of a building—nothing but steel beams and concrete floors, no walls and no ceiling. I wasn't sure how high we were, but we were definitely high. City lights sparkled below. Above, stars seemed close enough to touch. There was no noise from traffic, only the sound of a gentle wind that blew through steel beams causing eerie, creaking noises.

Michael stepped over to a corner and pulled some kind of cushioned tarp along the concrete floor to where I stood. He motioned for me to sit down and then sat beside me.

"Where are we?" I asked.

"Outside of Denver. This is one of the high rises we're building," he replied. "We're eighteen stories in the air."

My eyes widened. "Your design?"

He nodded.

"Michael, this is so amazing!" I was in awe. "We're sitting at the top of something you designed, and your brothers are building!"

I felt so much love for him I could hardly stand it. He smiled and grasped my hands in his.

"Every time I see you," he said quietly. "I'm overwhelmed with how beautiful you are, even when you're not trying."

His words didn't register. He thought I was beautiful? He turned so we were face-to-face. It was quiet for a brief moment, as he seemed to be deep in thought.

"I brought you here, because I want to tell you," he paused. "I love you, Grace. I love you more than I could ever tell you. More than I could ever put into words."

I was dizzy, and his words swirled in my head as I tried to comprehend what he'd said. What I knew was happiness felt like an ache in my heart.

He watched me for a moment, and a slow smile spread across his face.

"I love everything about you. I love your crazy taste in music and movies, the way you get excited over a book, or a song on the radio. I love the way your eyes sparkle when you laugh, I love when you get angry at the referees during a football game. I love your cooking, I love your sense of humor. I love how your face turns red when you're embarrassed or angry, I love how your jaw juts to the side when you're frustrated. I love watching you play the piano—I love watching you do anything." He stroked my hair gently. "I love your eyes and your smile. I love how you look beautiful in a pair of sweats and tee shirt. I love how you look beautiful in jeans and a turtleneck sweater. I love how you look beautiful in a red silk dress."His eyes never left mine."I love your kindness, your generosity, your selflessness. I love how you love Kate, and Garrett, and Miles, and Mom and Dad."

He leaned closer to me as he brought his hands to the sides of my face.

"I love how you love me, Grace, and I hope I'm not too late in telling you this, because I don't want to waste another second not loving you."

A single tear slid down my cheek. He wiped it away with his thumb and pressed his lips against my forehead. His thumbs stroked my jaw as his lips brushed down along my cheek. A shiver went through me as his lips met mine tenderly. This wasn't like our kiss before. It was much more.

It was everything.

Our lips moved together in feathery-light kisses as he brought his thumb to the corner of my mouth, and my mouth opened slightly so he kissed only my bottom lip. He continued to brush his lips with mine, until I thought I would pass out from happiness. His mouth moved from mine, to my forehead again, and he kissed the tip of my nose and chuckled quietly.

"Your nose is cold."

I opened my eyes, feeling dizzy, sick, and giddy all at the same time. I thought of all the things I'd wanted to tell him for weeks. Now, the words came to me in a rush of emotion as I looked at him, but I had questions.

"Why now?" I sniffled. "You told me you didn't want me because of what happened with Allison."

He squeezed my hand tightly.

"Grace, I always wanted you," he amended. "The first time I met you, I wanted you. The guilt I felt about Allison was an excuse. I was afraid of the feelings I had for you. The first time I saw you it scared me to death."

"I scared you?" I snorted a laugh. "I could hardly remember my name when we first met, and I scared you?"

"I'd never felt that way before." He shrugged. "And everything that happened with Allison made it worse, because the thought of hurting you was unthinkable."

He squeezed my hand.

"I'd loved Allison as my friend and still had guilt over hurting her," he swallowed. "Guilt over the baby. I knew I'd done the right thing by calling off the wedding, and I knew I had to let go of the guilt if I was ever going to be happy." He smiled. "I knew I loved you, but I used Allison as an excuse because I was a coward."

I couldn't get over the beauty of his face, and I traced my fingertips over his eyebrows and under his eyes.

"I was scared, too," I said, my finger tracing his mouth. "I never thought you'd love me."

"Grace," he sighed. Suddenly, his lips were on mine again, still sweetly, but with more intensity. I wound my arms around his neck, brushing my hands through the soft strands of his hair. He hummed softly and I opened my eyes, continuing to comb through his hair with my fingertips.

"I love you," I whispered against his mouth, tasting the sweetness of his breath. It felt so good to say it out loud, and if I said it a thousand times it still wouldn't be enough.

"You have no idea," he murmured, and I shivered involuntarily. "We should go before you freeze to death."

"No," I told him. "I'm fine."

I was cold, but I didn't want to leave. He chuckled and kissed the top of my head as he stood.

"Of course, you are," he said, pulling me up with him. "But being in love with you and all, I'd prefer it if you didn't have to be hospitalized for pneumonia because of me."

"Okay," I sighed. "I guess we wouldn't want that on your conscience."

The drive home was quiet. Michael held my hand, kissing my fingers every now and then, while my mind still tried to grasp that all of this was really happening. I leaned my head against the back of the seat, feeling sleepy as I watched him drive.

"What about Nina?" I asked.

His eyebrows came together. "What about her?"

"Well, you were…dating her, right?"

He heaved a sigh. "Do you really think I could ever be interested in someone like Nina Sandler?"

I kept my eyes forward, knowing he was right. It never did make sense to me.

"She was never anything more than a client," he said.

"Did she know that?"

His lips pinched together. "I explained it more than once. She was persistent."

I couldn't help my snort of laughter, and he glanced sideways at me.

"Can I ask you one more question?" I asked.

"Of course." He kissed my fingers.

"If you'd known about the baby, would you have married Allison? Even though you weren't in love with her?"

I could see his brow furrow in concentration as he contemplated my question.

"I used to think so," he said. "I mean, at the time I thought marrying her would be the right thing. I definitely would've taken responsibility." He was quiet for a moment. "After Allison told me what she'd done, Garrett asked the same question. When I told him yes, he said, 'so you'd marry someone you don't love because of a baby? What kind of life would that be for a kid, being raised by parents who don't love each other?'" He shrugged. "I suppose he's right. A baby isn't a mistake. Making another mistake wouldn't solve anything, it would only cause more pain."

Though he seemed sure of his words, I realized there was still heartache. Michael may have been able to let go of the guilt over what happened with Allison, but I knew the grief would always be there—missing the unborn child he never had the chance to meet. He was too caring of a person to completely let go and forget.

"Grace."

I felt Michael's lips against my forehead.

"Wake up," he whispered. "We're home."

I opened my eyes, not realizing I'd gone to sleep. He got out of the car and walked around to open my door, holding me to him as we slowly made our way to the front porch.

"You sleep well," he said. "And I'll see you tomorrow."

"Are we going to run?"

He shook his head and brushed the hair from my face.

"It's late, you should sleep."

I didn't try to hide my disappointment, and he smiled.

"I'll see you in the morning." He brought his hand to my cheek and stroked it gently with his thumb. "I love this face." He pressed his lips to mine. "Good night."

I watched as he walked down the porch steps, and my heart pounded.

"Michael?"

He turned around with a smile, and I jumped into him, throwing my arms around his neck, causing him to almost fall backwards.

"You're crazy." He laughed as he held me tightly.

"Well, I forgot to tell you something very important." I buried my face in his neck, smelling his wonderful smell. "I love you."

I felt his breath as he sighed."I love you so much," he murmured. "Good night, my Grace."

He set me down, kissing my forehead, and waited until I was inside.

Kate was waiting for me, curled up on the end of the sofa, watching television. When she heard the front door close, she shot up straight. Obviously my expression said it all, because in a flash she was across the room with her arms around my neck. It was late when Kate and I finally said good night. I'd given her every detail of my time with Michael, and she listened with teary eyes and a smile.

As I lay in bed, I closed my eyes and thought of Michael just like I did every night, but tonight was different. I was so happy. The tears came, just like they had so many other times, but these were tears of happiness and love. These tears didn't bother me at all.

* * *

I woke before my alarm went off. Michael told me I should sleep in, but I was too wide awake to stay in bed for another hour. I got dressed for my run and after finishing my morning bathroom ritual, grabbed my shoes and iPod. I zipped up my fleece as I walked down the porch steps, and made my way to the gravel drive. I didn't even bother to wait for Michael, even though I really wanted to see him, I was sure he'd be sleeping. I glanced over at his house and smiled as I put in my earbuds and started my slow jog down the drive, turning up the volume as I picked up my pace.

Before I got to the end of the drive, two arms snaked around my waist from behind. My heart pounded as my feet left the ground, and

I was spun around. When my feet found the ground again, I pulled the earbuds from my ears. Michael laughed as he kept his hold on my waist and kissed the side of my neck from behind, causing me to shiver.

"What do you think you're doing?" he asked as I turned to face him, his arms still around my waist. "I thought we agreed to sleep in?"

I took a moment to study his face, the sparkle in his eyes, the stunning smile.

And he loves me.

"I just woke up and didn't want to lie in bed for another hour. You scared me to death!" I narrowed my eyes at him. "What are you doing up?"

"I knew you'd run anyway." He shrugged as he ran a hand through his hair. "You tend to be a little stubborn, you know."

I made a face and he tugged at the end of my ponytail with a grin, and we began our run. Together. Being around Michael was so different than it had been. I wasn't tense or nervous, just incredibly happy.

That afternoon, we were making food for the Super Bowl party, and the guys were helping. Michael and I were cutting brownies into the shape of footballs and decorating them with icing. After two failures, he decided I should take care of the decorating part.

"Don't you draw for a living?" I asked with a grin.

He kissed my neck. "You smell good," he whispered and nuzzled into my hair.

My face heated because everyone was watching with ridiculous grins on their faces. I cleared my throat, and Michael stepped behind me, wrapped his arms around my waist, and rested his chin on the top of my head.

"All I wanna say is," Garrett crossed his arms over his chest, "it's about damn time."

Everyone laughed as Garrett winked at me.

It was about an hour before game time, and I went into my bathroom to freshen up. When I came out, I was pleasantly surprised to see Will and Ava standing in our living room.

"I didn't know you were coming!"

She laughed as she embraced me. "It's wonderful to see you."

"You, too," I said. "I've missed you both so much."

Will cleared his throat loudly and stretched his arms in front of him. I practically jumped at him, making him laugh as he hugged me tightly.

Soon, Kenny showed up, with a different girl—Emily. Garrett held out his hand to Miles, and Miles slapped a ten-dollar bill in it, shaking his head. Everyone made themselves plates of food as the game started, and soon we were all watching, eating, laughing and having a great time. The Andersons were rooting for the Jets, while Kate, Kenny, Emily and I cheered on the Cowboys. The truth was, none of us cared about either of the teams playing, but we had to cheer for someone, and it definitely made things more fun.

When the game was over, no one made a move to leave, and I was glad. We just continued to eat and talk.

"Girls," Will said, looking at Kate and then me. "The boys told us about a duet you've played for them, and I would love to hear it."

"Come on, Gracie," Garrett said.

Michael squeezed my hand and pulled me from the couch, leading me to the piano. Kate skipped into the room with a big grin on her face, and everyone gathered around the piano as she sat on the bench next to me.

Kate nudged me. "Ready?"

I nodded, and as was our practice she counted us off, and we began the rendition of "William Tell Overture", the driving, quick-tempo melody making us smile while we played. When we finished, everyone applauded. Will shouted 'bravo' a couple of times, and Garrett whistled loudly.

Michael took Kate's place on the bench next to me, while the others made their way back to the living room.

He kissed my fingers. "Play the song you played at Thanksgiving."

There was no hesitation. With him so close, the music seemed more beautiful and I wondered if it would always feel this way. The song ended, and he squeezed my hand gently.

"Thank you," he said. "That was beautiful."

Everyone continued visiting until late into the night. Will and Ava were staying overnight at the boys' house and promised to come by the shop in the morning before returning home. Kate, Miles and Garrett were still talking by the front door as Michael and I walked out to the porch.

"Shall we run tomorrow?" he asked as we walked down the steps.

"Of course." I pointed to the middle of the drive. "I'll meet you right there at seven. No lateness."

"No lateness," he repeated with a grin and stroked the side of my face with his thumb softly before gently pressing a kiss to my mouth. The sensation of his kiss lingered on my lips as I told him good night and watched him walk into the darkness.

Chapter Seventeen

The following morning, I hopped down the porch steps and walked toward the drive, stretching my arms and breathing in the cool air.

"Good morning."

I turned to see Michael standing behind me with a big smile. I'm sure my smile was just as big. We'd started our slow jog down the drive, when I noticed him watching me with a smirk.

"What's so funny?" I asked.

"Did I see you *hopping* down the porch steps?"

I shrugged. I was feeling good, so yeah, I hopped down the porch steps. He continued to grin as he shook his head.

"Your parents are still coming to the shop before they go home today, right?" I asked.

"I'm going to bring them by later this morning."

"Good. They can have breakfast there."

"I'm sure they'd love that."

I was excited. Will and Ava had never seen our bookstore, and I couldn't wait to show them what Kate and I had managed to accomplish. The thought made me smile. Will and Ava Anderson felt like parents to me. I loved them as much as I loved the rest of their family.

Except Michael. My love for Michael exceeded anything I'd ever expected.

When we got home, Michael assured me he and his parents would be at the shop before ten. He waved as I made my way toward the house. When I reached the porch steps, I turned to make sure he watched as I hopped up each step, one at a time, exaggerating the movements. He laughed loudly and shook his head as he turned to go into his house.

On the way to work, Kate chattered about the party and how much everyone enjoyed themselves.

"We need to get some more duet music," she said. "Maybe some more Gottschalk?"

She waggled her eyebrows, copying Garrett's signature move.

"Wow, the hard stuff," I said.

We laughed as we pulled into the parking lot, both of our smiles disappearing when we saw Nina's Porsche parked in our usual spot. Kate looked over at me, and I took a deep breath as she parked as far away from Nina as possible. Kate reached into her purse and pulled out her cell phone, quickly sending a text. We paused for a moment before getting out of the car, and Kate gripped my hand as we made our way toward the shop. Nina got out of her car smoothly.

"Don't stop, Gracie," Kate whispered. "Let's just go inside."

We didn't look at Nina, but right before we got near the entrance she stepped in front of us.

"Good morning," she smiled.

Kate gripped my hand tighter.

"Hello, Kate," Nina said sweetly. "Grace, may I speak with you?"

I wasn't afraid of Nina—she made me uncomfortable, but I wasn't afraid of her. Besides, I was sure the text Kate sent was to Miles and I knew that at least one of the Andersons was on his way. Kate glanced at me worriedly.

"Go ahead, Kate," I said, trying my best to look at ease. Kate hesitated for a moment then hurried inside. A moment later she and Kenny stood in the opened door of the shop. Nina, with her back to them, was staring at me icily. The look on her face was enough to irritate me.

"What do you want, Nina?"

She shifted her monstrous bag over her shoulder. "Well, I wanted to apologize."

I didn't believe that for a second.

"I shouldn't have gotten angry with you because of what happened with Michael." Her voice was calm but laced with sarcasm.

I waited for the venom she was going to spew—no doubt in my mind there would be spewing.

"Obviously, you're manipulative and conniving," she shook her head, "but Michael is the one stupid enough to believe everything you say. So, it's really not your fault."

I snorted a laugh. "Wow," I said dryly. "You really suck at apologies."

She laughed humorlessly. "Well, you have to admit that Michael never would have backed out of his contract with my father's company if you hadn't manipulated him."

Her condescending tone caused a flicker of anger inside me. I folded my hands in front of me and looked down at the ground, feeling the heat rise in my face."Are you finished?"

"No." She shook her head, blonde waves bouncing over her shoulders. "I also want you to know that you and Michael will never last anyway."

"If you believed that, you wouldn't be standing here trying to…what exactly are you trying to do? Scare me? Intimidate me?"

"I *do* scare you." The smile never left her face, and if I were being completely honest, it was a little scary. Her voice lowered to almost a whisper. "Do you really think I'm going to let you just have him?"

"*Have him*?" I asked. "He's not yours, Nina. Never was. Never will be. You're delusional."

Just as she took an angry step toward me, the rumble of Garrett's Hummer squealing into the parking lot distracted her, but my eyes stayed fixed on her face. A moment later Miles strode calmly past us to where Kate and Kenny watched from the doorway. Garrett stood behind me, his hands heavy on my shoulders, Michael beside me.

"What's going on?" he asked. "Nina, why are you here?"

Nina appeared to be relaxed, despite their somewhat sudden appearance.

"Actually," I began, "She was here to apologize."

"Oh, really?" Garrett asked derisively.

I nodded pointedly at Nina. "Yes, but she was just leaving."

She flipped her hair over her shoulders, and I glanced at Michael, his jaw clenched in anger. I was angry, too, and I was done with her.

"Except, now it's my turn to talk." I took a step toward Nina. Michael moved with me and Garrett tightened his grip on my shoulders. "If I ever see you near my house or near this shop again, I'll be calling my good friend, Sheriff Henderson."

She snorted a laugh and rolled her eyes, but I ignored it.

"I know you want me to be scared of you, Nina," I spoke slowly. "But, truthfully? The only thing I feel when I look at you is pity. You're just angry, miserable and bitter."

She glared at me, but I was still angry.

"You're not moving, Nina. Maybe you didn't hear me. Leave. Now."

Nina shifted her glare to Michael. "Your company is through," she said calmly. "I'll make sure of it, and so will my father." Her eyes found mine again, her voice still uncomfortably calm. "See you later, Grace."

I didn't miss the not-so-hidden threat in her words. Garrett pulled me to him as Nina shoved her way past us and stormed to her car. The Porsche squealed out of the parking lot, and I started to shake from the confrontation as she drove out of sight. Michael pulled me inside the shop, and Kate hugged me tightly.

"I need to sit down," I said.

Kate led me to one of the chairs, and I laid my head down on my arms, trying to catch my breath. I despised confrontations, and any anger I'd felt was now just trembling, shaking and nausea working its way through my body. I heard Michael and Miles talking quietly as Garrett crouched down next to my chair, rubbing my back. I turned my head to look at him.

"Are you all right?" he asked.

"Yeah," I said. "Thanks for showing up. I never used to be afraid of her, but she's starting to scare me a little."

He snorted a laugh. "You'd never know that."

"I'm glad you were here," I told him.

He pointed to his cheek, and I gave him a kiss.

"I've gotta go. Mom and Dad will be here soon."

"You can't stay?" I asked, disappointed he was leaving.

He stood and stretched. "I have to go check on St. Jo's. I'll see you this afternoon."

"Thanks again, Garrett,"

He winked as he turned to leave, waving goodbye to everyone. Kenny sat a caramel macchiato on the table in front of me.

"You okay?" he asked.

I nodded with a smile, and he started wiping tables. Michael sat next to me, worry etched in his expression.

"I'm fine," I assured him.

He shook his head, his expression changing to frustration. "I should have dropped the contract a long time ago." His jaw clenched. "My brothers were right."

"It's okay, Michael," I tried to assure him. "She's just trying to scare me. She's all talk."

He brought my hand to the side of his face and kissed my palm before smiling weakly. I knew he was concerned, but I didn't want Nina to have such an effect on either of us. He joined me in opening the bookstore, and I was able to put the incident to the back of my mind for the time being.

It was almost ten o'clock when Ava and Will came into the store. Michael helped me make their coffees, and we assembled several different muffins and breads on a platter and delivered them to the table. We visited and drank our coffees, gave them a tour of the bookstore, and before I was ready they had to leave.

Will thanked me for the girly breakfast as he hugged me. When I said goodbye to Ava, a lump formed in my throat as she wrapped her arms around me.

"I'm going to miss you," I whispered.

She tightened her embrace. "We'll see you soon. Take care of my boys, okay?"

"We'll walk you out," Michael said, and he and Miles followed their parents out the door. Kate and I watched as they walked to the parking lot and said their goodbyes. Ava cradled Michael's face in her hands, saying something with a smile. He nodded in response and hugged her. We continued to watch as they drove away, and the boys came back inside.

"We'd better go," Miles told Kate. "Michael and I have a lot to do."

Michael took my hand and pulled me a few steps away.

"Will you have dinner with me?" His eyes searched my face. "Tonight?"

"I'd love to," I said. "What time?"

His smile made my heart thrum. "Meet me at my place. Six o'clock?"

I nodded excitedly. "I can't wait."

He laughed and tucked my hair behind my ears. "I can't wait either." He kissed me tenderly and followed his brother out the door.

Kate stepped beside me. "Going on a date?"

"Sure am," I said, unable to hide my grin.

She giggled. "I have to run some paperwork to the accountant and then to Boulder to pick up some office supplies. I'll be back in a couple of hours."

I resumed my position behind the bookstore counter and tried to focus on something besides my watch. Six o'clock seemed like a long way away.

When we pulled into the driveway, I barely waited for Kate to turn off the ignition before dashing into the house. Kate followed, and I asked her to pick something out for me to wear while I showered. When I wrapped the towel around me, Kate came in and pushed me down on the toilet, starting to work on my hair. I tried not to laugh because she was in her hummingbird-mode. She was almost as excited for my date as I was. Almost.

My hair was soft and shiny with curls everywhere. I never knew how she did it, but Kate always made my hair look great. She applied my makeup and then pulled me into my bedroom and pointed to the clothes laid out on my bed. Jeans, a soft pink turtleneck and a black cashmere cardigan sweater with a ruffled hem and a satin bow that tied at the waist.

"Don't mess up your hair when you put the turtleneck on," she ordered and exited my room.

I was incredibly nervous as I fidgeted with the satin bow, trying to get it just right.

"You look fabulous." Kate appeared in the bathroom door, and I turned so she could fix the darned bow because my hands were shaking.

We walked out to the living room. Garrett was on the couch with Miles, and when he saw me he gave a wolf-whistle.

"Wow, Gracie." He smiled widely. "You look gorgeous."

"You sure do," Miles agreed.

I fidgeted with the hem of my sweater. "Thanks."

"Michael's waiting for you," Garrett said.

I checked my watch. "It's not even five-thirty. He said six."

"Trust me," Garrett said with a laugh. "He's ready."

Miles nodded in encouragement. "Have a great time."

Kate kissed my cheek. "Go," she whispered excitedly. "You've both been waiting long enough."

Chapter Eighteen

Kate pushed me gently out the front door with a smile, closing it behind me. I felt a million butterflies in my stomach. It had just started to get dark, and the air was cool as I took a deep breath and made my way across the drive.

I climbed the front steps to the Andersons' door and opened it slowly. I could hear the beautiful "Flower Duet" from Lakme echoing through the house as I entered. There were no lights on, but the house was dimly lit by dozens of small votive candles that lined the floor of the entryway.

My heart pounded furiously as I walked slowly into the living room and gasped.

Most of the furniture had been removed. Several strands of white twinkle lights were extended across the ceiling, making it resemble a starry sky, and on the floor a red blanket was spread out with candles and crystal champagne flutes. It was the most romantic gesture I'd ever seen, and I swallowed hard as I took it all in.

Then I saw Michael and everything else seemed to disappear. He was gorgeous in black pants and dress jacket, a crisp white shirt and black tie. He held a single pink rose, and my breath hitched as he gazed at me with his crooked smile.

"Um, hi," was all I could manage.

I couldn't take my eyes off of him as he walked smoothly toward me, bending down to kiss my cheek tenderly.

"You're beautiful," his voice was almost a whisper as his eyes burned into mine. He handed me the rose, and I brought it to my nose to take in the fragrance.

"Thank you."

He only nodded, his gaze unrelenting.

"You look really…great," my voice was shaky.

Actually, he looked more than great. He looked amazing. He took my coat from my arms, setting it on one of the bookshelves behind him and then glanced around the room.

"So," he said. "What do you think?"

"It's absolutely beautiful," I told him. "Did you do all this?"

He shrugged casually and took both of my hands in his, smiling fervently at me.

"My brothers helped." He stepped closer to me and wrapped his arms around my waist. "I wanted our first date to be special."

"Nicely done," I said, and he chuckled.

"Are you hungry?" he asked.

I nodded, and he motioned to the blanket on the floor. Once I was seated, Michael disappeared into the kitchen. There was 'clanking' of dishes, and I heard the oven door close. He appeared moments later with two plates and sat across from me, handing me one of the plates.

"This is Kate's homemade ravioli," I said, inhaling the aroma of mushrooms and Parmesan cheese. "I've been asking her to make this for weeks."

"I know," he said. "She told me."

"So, today when she was running errands—"

"She was here," he interrupted. "Making dinner for us."

He filled each champagne flute, handed one to me and raised his in front of him.

"Okay," he said. "Let's drink to…beginnings."

Our glasses made a delicate 'clink', and we both took a drink. He picked up his fork, and we started eating, though I was nibbling more than eating because I was such a giddy, nervous wreck.

I looked around the room as I took another sip from my glass, smiling at the twinkle lights.

"I always thought a picnic under the stars would be a pretty romantic first date," he said. "But it's too cold for a real picnic, so I thought this would be the next best thing."

I nodded in agreement as the CD player, which had been playing some beautiful operatic pieces changed, and Michael Bublé was singing "Crazy Love". Whenever I heard this song I had to smile, it always made me happy.

Michael set his plate aside and stood, holding his hand out to me.

"Dance with me?"

He didn't have to ask twice. I'd dreamt about dancing with him more than once. I reached my hand to his as he led me to the middle of the room, pulling me toward him gently. And then we were dancing.

We were dancing to "Crazy Love".

I laughed as he twirled me around, and as close as he held me, I wanted to be closer. I rested my head against his chest and closed my eyes as we swayed to the music. The song stopped, but he didn't let go of me as the next song came on, and I felt his head rest on the top of mine as we danced slowly, one hand holding mine gently, the other holding me to him. I'm not sure how many songs played as we danced, but when we sat down on the blanket again, Adele was singing "To Make You Feel My Love".

Our ravioli wasn't hot anymore, but we both ate anyway. When we finished, Michael took our plates. I started to get up to help, but he just gave me a look that said 'stay put', so I did. He returned with a plate of chocolate dipped strawberries for dessert and set them between us.

He ran his hand through his hair. "You look beautiful tonight, Grace. Pink is my favorite color on you."

"Really?"

He nodded.

"Pink is my favorite color," I told him.

"Yeah, I know," he said, winking at me.

Did he have any idea how sexy he was?

When we finished eating, we stretched out on the blanket and gazed up at the electric stars above while our favorite music serenaded us. We talked and laughed, my head against his chest, his arms holding me tight. I loved being in his arms, and we talked for a long time about a little bit of everything.

The night air was chilly, our breaths leaving in smoky puffs, as we said goodnight on my front porch.

"We have an early appointment in the morning in Boulder," he said. "But the rest of our day is free. How about we bring you and Kate some lunch?"

"Sounds great." I stood on my toes to kiss him. "Thank you for a wonderful evening. This was the best date I've ever had."

"You make me so happy." His arms came around me and his mouth was on mine. "I love you."

"I love you," my voice was barely a whisper. "So much more."

Chapter Nineteen

I was having a difficult time not smiling while getting dressed for work. Every thought was about Michael and every thought made me happy. As I left my room, I could hear Kate humming in the kitchen.

"How was your date last night?"

I guess my expression said it all because she hugged me excitedly.

"I'm so glad. He wanted last night to be perfect."

"It was perfect."

I told her every detail on the way to work, and by the time we got to the shop she was smiling almost as much as me.

"Hey, girls," Kenny greeted us cheerily. "How's it goin'?"

We chatted as I prepared Kate's and my breakfast, and after eating, I went to open the bookstore, noticing several boxes in the store room.

"Those came yesterday afternoon," Kenny informed me. "You need any help?"

"Nope, I've got it."

He laughed and nodded. "Yeah, I figured that's what you'd say, but I have to offer."

I rolled my eyes and got busy going through the new shipment of books I'd ordered after Christmas, humming as I worked.

"Hey, Grace." Miles was coming toward me with a smile. "New books?"

I nodded as he peered into the boxes.

"Anything good?"

"It's all good," I said matter-of-factly.

He laughed as he turned to go see Kate in the office, and I walked over to stand next to Garrett. Without a word, he put me in one of his headlocks, making Kenny laugh. Kate and Miles emerged from the office, and Miles shook his head at Garrett.

"Garrett, release Grace and come with me to get lunch for everyone," Miles said.

Garrett released me, and I punched him in the arm.

"Ow." He rubbed his arm, even though I knew I didn't hurt him in the slightest. "You wanna come with us, Gracie?"

"Michael's supposed to be here soon." I looked at my watch. "I thought he'd be with you."

"He's on his way," Miles said. "I told him I'd pick up lunch."

"I should get these boxes unloaded."

"You need some help?" Garrett asked.

"Maybe after you've eaten," I patted his stomach. "You think better when you're not hungry."

"True," he said, and they went to the door. Before walking out, Garrett paused and looked at me. "Cobb salad?"

I nodded, and he smiled widely at me.

"What?" I asked.

He shrugged. "You're in love, and it makes me happy."

I sighed, overwhelmed with love for my best friend. He gave me a wink as he followed Miles out the door. Kate gave my shoulders a squeeze.

"I'm going to get those books coded," I told her, and she returned to the office.

I was on the floor rearranging one of the display shelves, making room for some of the new books, when I noticed someone coming toward me. I got angry right away when I saw Nina, smirking as she watched me get to my feet.

"No, no," she said sweetly. "Don't get up. You're so comfortable on the floor."

I ignored her comment and slid a book onto the shelf.

"Why are you here?" I asked. "Did you not believe me when I said I'd call the sheriff?"

"I believed you." She pulled a random book from the shelf, seeming to look at it carefully. "I just thought I might look around for a minute. Maybe I'll buy a book."

She slid the book back in its place, pulling out another one. There was something about her that didn't seem…right, and it made me uncomfortable. I glanced around the store. No customers. I couldn't see Kenny, which meant he was either in the kitchen or the storeroom. From the office, Kate wouldn't have seen Nina come in.

"What's wrong, Grace? You look nervous."

"Yeah, you make me nervous," I admitted. "Why don't you say what you came to say and get out of here?"

She smiled. "Okay. I think you're a lying, manipulative bitch."

I folded my arms across my chest. "Haven't we covered this already?"

Her smile disappeared, and she looked past me.

"I knew it the first time I saw you." She shook her head. "I knew you were going to be trouble, and I tried to tell him, but he wouldn't listen."

"Okay, you're done here." I pointed to the door. "Get out."

She seemed amused as she took a deliberate step toward me. I ignored the instinct to step away from her.

"He thinks he loves you, but he doesn't." Her expression went blank as she spoke. "I saw him with you last night. I saw you dancing with him." Her eyes glistened, and she blinked rapidly. "But the thing is, you don't deserve him."

A chill went through me, like my blood had run cold.

"I'm leaving, Grace." The smile returned as she turned on her heel to leave.

I watched her walk slowly toward the door and released a deep breath. I bent down to pick up books from the floor and when I stood, Nina was in front of me again.

A sudden jolt of pain throttled my torso. A burning, searing pain radiated from my stomach and traveled through the rest of my body. The books in my arms fell to the floor with muted thuds. Nina kept one hand on my shoulder, her eyes void of all emotion as she watched me.

"Are you afraid of me now?" she whispered, then turned calmly and unrushed, exiting the store.

Everything blurred as I dropped to my knees. A painful electric current pulsated through me, and I crumpled to the floor. I tried to wrap my arms around the heat, but it wouldn't turn off. It only got hotter. Something warm and wet seeped through my fingers. The pain was excruciating. An eerie darkness crept over me, while nausea and dizziness made it difficult to focus.

Michael's face flashed through my mind. Nina had watched us last night, and she wanted to hurt him. I needed to get up. No one could see me here, hidden between the shelves. The room was getting darker by the second. I grabbed at the shelf next to me and managed to get on my feet. The burning took over my whole body as I tried to make my feet move. Books tumbled from the shelf as I struggled toward the front of the store and collapsed again.

"GRACIE!" I heard Kate scream, but it sounded far away. "Kenny! Help!" She stroked my face frantically, but I could barely see her.

I recognized Kenny's voice. "Oh, no."

Kate sobbed, still stroking my face and holding my hand tightly. The bells from the shop door jingled, and Garrett's laughter caused my pain to subside for the briefest of moments.

"Miles!" Kate shouted.

"Kate? What—" Garrett sounded far away too, but a second later I felt his arm go under my neck, cradling me to him. "What happened? Gracie, can you hear me?"

I tried to blink away the tears so everything wouldn't be so blurry, but it didn't help. I struggled to make my eyes focus.

"No. NO!"

Michael. He was with me, and he was safe.

He pleaded as his hands searched for some place to offer comfort. "No…no…"

"I know, little brother," Garrett muttered anxiously, holding me to him. "There's so much blood. Gracie, can you hear me?"

I could hear him, but now I couldn't see anything. It was too dark.

"Please," Michael whispered in my ear, so much sadness in his voice. I wanted to see him. I wanted the darkness to lift so I could see his face. "Please open your eyes, Grace. Please."

I didn't realize my eyes were closed.

"The ambulance is coming." It was Kenny."I'm so sorry. I didn't even hear anyone come in. You know I never would've let this happen."

This wasn't Kenny's fault. I swallowed hard, trying to find my voice.

"Nina," my voice was barely a whisper. "It was Nina."

Garrett shouted a string of profanities and tightened his hold on me. "I'll kill her. I'll kill her myself!"

He let out another string of profanities as Kate sobbed louder.

"You stay with us, do you hear me, Gracie?" Garrett's hand came to the side of my face.

I tried to open my eyes. Michael's face was there for a moment, and then it was dark again. Why did it have to be dark?

"Miles," Michael pleaded. "Why aren't they here? What's taking so long?"

"They're coming, little brother," Miles' voice was shaky. "They're coming."

A siren from far away came closer, and voices shouted at the same time.

"Back here! Hurry!"

I felt several hands on me, and my body moved. The movement caused the pain to intensify, and I cried out.

"Be careful with her!" Garrett shouted.

"I know it hurts," Michael was by my ear. "They have to move you. I'm so sorry."

"What happened?" An unfamiliar voice was close to me, and something tightened around my arm.

"We aren't sure, but it looks like she's been stabbed," Garrett answered, and then another string of profanity.

"We have to move her now," the unfamiliar voice said. "She's lost too much blood."

I couldn't feel anything except the pain.

"We're going with you," Garrett said.

"I'm sorry, but only one."

"Go, little brother. We're right behind you."

A siren squealed, and my body shivered. I was so cold, but I couldn't find my voice to tell someone.

"She's cold," Michael's voice was anguished.

"It's because of the loss of blood."

Michael's lips were against my ear murmuring something I couldn't understand, and after what seemed like forever, I was moved again. There was a lot of shouting and many voices, as something soft came underneath me. There was the sound of fabric being torn and cool air hit my torso.

A familiar voice called my name. "What happened to her?"

"Evan!" Garrett sounded almost relieved. "She's been stabbed!"

Evan began shouting orders frantically, and there was a sense of relief because he was with me. There was motion all around me, but I could only focus on the pain that jolted my stomach. There was a loud cry, and I realized it was mine.

"Get the morphine in her! Now!" Evan shouted. "I know it hurts, Grace. I'm sorry, I'm going to make it stop."

"You can't be in here!" someone yelled.

"Please!" Kate pleaded. "Please let me stay with her! I can't leave her alone!"

"Katie-Bug," Evan's voice was loud, as if he were next to my ear. "I'm going to help her, but you have to leave and let me do my job. I promise I won't leave her alone for even a minute, okay?"

Someone grasped my hand, then let go, and for the first time I was afraid.

I listened for the voices of the people I loved, Michael, Kate, Garrett, Miles, but only heard the beeping of machines and Evan speaking in a clipped, even tone. The pain became more excruciating, every minute feeling like an hour.

"Grace," Evan said loudly. "Honey, can you hear me?"

My voice wouldn't let me respond.

"If you can hear me, please squeeze my hand." A warm hand came around mine, and I tried to squeeze, but I couldn't. "Squeeze my hand, honey. Come on!"

I used all my strength to try and squeeze his hand.

"Good girl." He kissed my forehead. "I know you hear me. You're going to be fine, okay? I know you must be scared, but you're going to be fine. I'm going to make sure you're fine. You hold on."

I thought about the people I loved. I wanted to be on the couch watching the Avalanche game with Garrett or in the kitchen baking with Kate. I wanted to be running with Michael.

I wanted to be anywhere with Michael.

It was so dark, and I couldn't hear anything except my own breathing. The pain was gone, but the darkness became a heavy weight.

"Hold on, Grace. Please, hold on…"

Evan's plea became an echo in the darkness, and I wanted to hold on, but the dark was too heavy. It pushed and pushed until I was under it, helpless.

* * *

"Grace, can you hear me?"

I knew that voice, and I wanted to hear it again. I tried to open my eyes.

"Grace Elizabeth, I want you to hear me," Michael said.

"Gracie," Garrett spoke. "Please wake up."

Their voices came to me like a dream.

"We have to get her into surgery now," Evan's voice was clinical and calm. "There's no more time, the damage is too severe."

"I love you," Michael whispered in my ear. "I love you so much."

I love you, too.

Garrett's voice shook with emotion. "We all love you, and we're here waiting for you."

"Don't leave me, Gracie," Kate cried as she kissed my cheek. "Please."

My heart was breaking with all of their words, and I wanted to tell them how much I loved them, how much they meant to me.

"Come back to us," Miles said softly. "We love you."

"We have to go," Evan said.

"Evan, please…I—" Michael's voice trembled.

Evan's voice was still calm. "Dr. Murphy is a brilliant surgeon, she's going to be in the best of hands. I promise."

"But, you'll stay with her?" Michael asked. "Please, Evan, don't leave her alone."

"I won't leave her," Evan promised, his voice shook for the first time.

"Come on, little brother," Miles spoke quietly.

"I love you, my Grace," Michael whispered. "Please come back to me."

Michael's plea was the last thing I heard as the silent darkness submerged me.

Chapter Twenty

The light was bright. Reflexively, I closed my eyes again, and my head pounded from the slight movement. Something covered my nose and mouth, blowing a low, cool stream of air with a medicinal odor that made me nauseous, and my throat was sore. Electronic beeps and hums echoed around me and something on my arm tightened for a moment, then loosened. A sharp pain emanated from my stomach making my nausea even worse, but I couldn't seem to move.

When I opened my eyes again, Michael's face was there. Overwhelmed, I tried to lift my hand to touch him but was unable to move. Tears escaped my eyes as I looked at him, wishing he would hold me and make the terrible pain stop.

A high-pitched tone reverberated in my ears. Two women, dressed in brightly colored scrubs appeared, and Michael watched them with concern. I kept my eyes on his face, afraid the darkness would come again, and I wouldn't be able to see him.

"What is it?" Michael asked them worriedly. "What's wrong?"

"Her heart rate accelerates with the pain," one of the women responded. "We need to keep her sedated, or she could go into cardiac arrest again."

His expression was anguished as he held my hand to his lips, kissing my palm. Then he leaned into me, burying his face in my neck. His breath was warm against my skin as he shuddered with quiet sobs. I wanted to wrap my arms around him, but it felt like they were strapped down, and I couldn't move them. With a deep breath, he sat back and wiped his eyes roughly with the back of his hand.

Our eyes held each other's as he kissed my fingertips, until my eyes became too heavy to keep open.

* * *

"Oh, she's waking up."

I recognized Kate's voice right away and could hear the electronic tones of machines and the rustling of movement as I felt someone grasp each of my hands in theirs.

"Are you sure?"

It was Garrett.

"Yes, I just saw her eyes open," Kate said softly. "Gracie? Can you hear me?"

My eyes fluttered opened. Her face was close to mine and tears fell down her cheeks.

"Oh, Gracie." She took a deep breath, choking back a sob.

Miles stood behind her, smiling sweetly at me. "Hey there," he said with relief. "Boy, are we glad to see you."

Garrett's hulking figure was on the other side of the bed. His eyes glistened as he kissed the back of my hand and held it to his cheek.

I tried to clear my throat, and the pain made me moan. I lifted my hand to try and move the irritating piece of plastic away from my face, but every movement caused even more pain.

Kate pulled my hand away. "You have to leave that alone. It's helping you breathe."

My throat burned as I swallowed, and I winced.

"It's going to be sore," she said. "You had a tube down your throat."

Michael. I searched the room for him, wondering why he wasn't with me.

"Gracie?" Garrett watched me worriedly.

The pain intensified, and the monitors by my bed reacted with high-pitched tones, alerting everyone to my pain and panic.

"Get the nurse," Michael's voice was next to my ear. I turned my head toward his voice, but the movement caused my eyes to blur with tears because everything hurt.

"I'm here," he said quietly. "I've been right here."

My body relaxed as I strained to look at him, and he moved closer.

"Do you need something for the pain?" he asked.

A tear escaped the corner of my eye, and Michael brushed it away with his thumb. His eyes were sad as he looked over at Garrett. Garrett pressed a button on the side of my bed, and I closed my eyes, wishing the pain would stop. A nurse strode into the room, and Miles said something to her in a hushed voice. Minutes later, she returned and injected something into the tube taped to my arm.

Michael stroked my forehead, and my eyes became heavy as a numbing sensation crept over my body. I continued watching him, afraid to close my eyes because I wouldn't be able to see his face.

"Sleep." He spoke as if he knew my fear. "I'm not going anywhere. I promise."

* * *

I woke to an unfamiliar face.

Jet-black hair was smoothed into a ponytail, eyes almost as dark as her hair. She studied me carefully, with a stethoscope around her neck. She smiled when she noticed I was awake, and it registered that I was in a hospital. I struggled to remember what happened, but everything was muddled and foggy.

"Hello, Grace," she said, checking the fluids in the I.V. bags. "My name is Abby. I'll be taking care of you tonight." She put the stethoscope in her ears and listened to my heart. "Do you know where you are?"

I nodded minutely.

"Do you know why you're here?"

Again, I tried to remember, but was unable to think of anything except the ache in my stomach.

"We just gave you meds an hour ago, but if you need more just let me know," she instructed. "Don't wait until its unbearable, okay? It's better to keep it under control."

I nodded again, and she typed something into the computer next to my bed.

"Is there anything I can get for you?"

I shook my head and winced from the pain.

"Just push the button if you need me." She pointed to the red button on the railing of the bed and walked out of the room.

My eyes closed, and someone stroked the side of my face. I tried to focus on Michael's face as he rested his head next to mine on the pillow.

"Hi." He smiled softly at me and held my hand my hand to the side of his face.

"Where is everyone?" It hurt to talk, and I didn't move my eyes from his.

"They went to get something to eat," he answered. "The hospital doesn't like all of us in here at the same time, but Evan has managed to convince them it won't be a problem."

I nodded and tried to smile, every movement causing a current of pain to go through me.

"How long have I been here?"

He sighed and stroked my hair. "Five days. You've been in and out of consciousness."

"Five days?" I was confused. "What happened?"

"You don't remember?"

I shook my head slightly, trying to remember what had happened. Then a vision of Nina flashed through my mind. I squeezed my eyes shut as the floodgate opened. Memories played in my mind like a dream. Nina's blank emotionless stare, the excruciating pain, Kate's screams, Garrett's anger, Michael's pleading.

"Nina," I could barely say her name. "Nina did this."

The grief in Michael's eyes added to my pain. "Yes," he whispered. "Nina did this."

"Are *you* okay?"

He shook his head in confusion at my question. "Why on earth would you be worried about me?"

"She hates me," I reminded him. "And she knows how I feel about you. I was afraid she'd try to hurt you."

He leaned toward me, brushing his lips over my eyes and down the sides of my face. I felt the familiar heart fluttering when his breath was at my ear. A high-pitched tone echoed through the room.

"I love you." He chuckled softly.

Abby came in and looked at us, Michael's face close to mine as he grinned.

She narrowed her eyes at Michael with a half-smile. "You're going to have to behave yourself, or you won't be allowed within five feet of her."

"Yes, Ma'am," Michael told her, as she checked the machines.

"How's the pain?" she asked me.

I felt the throbbing, and it was getting worse, but I didn't want to sleep.

"Grace, if you're in pain you need to tell her," Michael instructed.

I looked at Abby and nodded. She smiled and then left the room.

"And it would take the National Guard to keep me away from you," Michael added with a grin, as he brushed the hair from my face.

The throbbing intensified, and I winced.

"What is it?" he asked worriedly.

"It just hurts."

He shook his head sadly. "I'm so sorry, sweetheart."

Abby returned, and Michael kept his eyes on mine as she injected the medicine into my I.V.

"There ya go, Grace, that should help." She patted my shoulder gently.

"Thanks, Abby."

Michael leaned close to me, brushing his fingertips over my cheeks. My eyelids became heavy, and the numbing sensation slowly blanketed my entire body. The memory of lying in the floor at the shop and searching for Michael's face in the dark came to me.

"I couldn't see you," I told him.

"What?"

"When you found me," my words slurred together. "It kept getting dark. I could hear you, but I couldn't see you, because it was too dark."

He frowned sadly. "You're just going to sleep."

"It scared me when I couldn't see you," I argued.

My eyes were closing, and I fought to keep them opened.

"I'm not leaving, Grace," he promised. "I'll be right here when you open your eyes. I promise."

I nodded, remembering his promise, and drifted.

* * *

Just like he promised, Michael's face was the first thing I saw when I opened my eyes.

"You kept your promise," my voice was gravelly.

"Of course, I did," he replied.

"Grace?"

I turned and saw Ava's lovely face and swallowed the sob that wanted to come out.

"I'm so glad to see you," I said.

She smiled, bending down to kiss my cheek, and wiped at her tears. Will stood behind her, rubbing her shoulders.

"Hello, Mr. Anderson." I smiled weakly and heard quiet chuckling all around.

His eyes narrowed playfully. "Hey, now. None of that nonsense."

I heard Kate's giggle and found her at the foot of my bed,

painting my toenails a hideous shade of blue.

"The blue matches your fabulous hospital gown," she chirped with a shrug. "Garrett wouldn't let me paint his nails. I was bored."

Garrett snorted a laugh and then smiled widely at me.

"Hey," I said to him.

"Hey, yourself. How are you?"

"I'd really like a shower." I knew it had been much too long.

"Oh, I wouldn't be worried about that," Miles laughed. "Kate sends us out of the room every day, so she can…do whatever she does."

Kate winked at me before returning to my pedicure.

"So, when do I get to go home?"

Michael's expression became grave, and he shook his head.

"It's going to be a while. You were bleeding internally and they had to do some serious repairing—" his voice trailed off.

"You went into cardiac arrest twice," Garrett continued for Michael. "You've been in critical condition."

I closed my eyes and nodded, still feeling quite a bit of pain with each movement.

"What day is it?"

"Saturday," Michael answered.

"Don't worry, Gracie," Garrett smiled proudly. "I've got our games on the DVR, I haven't even watched them because I'm waiting for you. However, the Avs are looking suh-weet."

Everyone chuckled, but Michael rolled his eyes.

"Of all the things to worry about, only you two would worry about the NHL."

"I wasn't worried," I said confidently. "I knew Garrett would take care of me."

Garrett smiled smugly and nodded. "Damn straight."

Something occurred to me suddenly, and panic returned.

"What's wrong?" Garrett asked.

"Did they catch her?"

Garrett's jaw clenched while he shook his head. "No. When you were in surgery, Sheriff Henderson was here. We told him about Nina, and Kenny gave him the security recordings from the shop. They're looking for her. She obviously didn't know about the cameras."

"Didn't know or didn't care," Miles amended.

Nausea rolled in my stomach as I remembered something Nina had said. I squeezed Michael's hand.

"She was watching us," I told him in a hushed voice, though I knew the others could hear. "The night we had our date, and you danced with me…she was watching."

Garrett muttered something unintelligible, and Michael's eyes narrowed as he studied my face, his anger palpable. "They'll find her, Grace, don't worry. She won't hurt you again," Michael assured me.

"I'm not worried about me," I argued. "She could hurt you or Kate or Garrett or Miles…what about your mom and dad?"

The thought of Nina coming near any of the people I loved caused the pain in my stomach to flare, and my breath quickened with my panic.

Michael took my face in his hands and locked eyes with me. "Grace, you need to calm down."He waited while I tried to slow my breathing. "Do you really believe my brothers and I will ever allow anything like this to happen again?"

Garrett grunted in agreement, and I shook my head. He was missing my point.

"But what about you?" I said. "She wants you. She could hurt you."

"The only way she can hurt me is to hurt you. And that will never happen again."

Ava stroked my forehead soothingly. "You shouldn't worry about this right now," she said. "You need to rest and get better."

As much as I wanted to do as she asked, my mind wouldn't allow me not to worry. No one really knew what Nina was capable of doing. Even though I believed Michael when he said he wouldn't let her hurt me again, I couldn't shake the feeling that she'd be back. I remembered the emptiness of her eyes as she stared at me with no fear. No remorse. I didn't even see hatred in her eyes. I just saw—nothing. *"Are you scared of me now?"*

"Grace, it's okay," Michael whispered. "Please don't worry about this right now."

He watched me, his expression soft, his eyes tired and red. Bronze stubble covered his jaw, and I wondered how long it had been since he'd slept.

"You're so tired," I told him. "You should go home and get some sleep."

"I sleep just fine here," he said obstinately. "I'm not leaving."

"It's actually a good idea, son," Ava said. "At least for one night, you would sleep so much better in your own bed."

Michael kept his eyes on me."You don't be worrying about me, you just get better. That's the only thing you need to worry about right now."

I didn't want him to leave, but I was worried about him.

"Kate and I will stay, little brother," Miles told him. "She's right, you need to get some rest. You haven't had a full night's sleep in almost a week."

"Michael," I shook my head sadly, "you need to sleep."

He rested his head on my pillow and stroked my chin with the tip of his finger.

"I like being the first person you see when you wake up," he whispered.

"Well, be here before I wake up." I smiled. "Because I like that, too."

He traced his finger along the edge of my bottom lip and nodded reluctantly. "Only because I don't want you to worry."

Michael stood from the chair and leaned down to kiss my forehead and then each cheek, causing the machines to betray my usual reaction. Everyone laughed quietly, including Michael.

Stupid machines.

"I'll be back first thing," he promised with a smirk.

"I'll just wait here," I said.

He rolled his with my attempt at humor.

"Very funny." He left with Will and Ava, while Garrett took Michael's place next to me, holding my hand.

"Garrett," Miles said. "Kate and I are going to go home to pick up a few things, and then we'll be back for the night."

As they left my eyes became heavy, but I couldn't shake the feeling of anxiety I had about Nina. Garrett noticed my drooping eyes and patted the back of my hand.

"Gracie, you rest now, I'm going to stay with you until Kate and Miles get back."

As I looked at him, the panic increased.

"And...what about you? You'll be with Michael and your parents, right?"

He squeezed my hand tightly. "Most of Colorado is looking for Nina Sandler. Not to mention…" he shook his head, attempting to censor himself. "Not to mention the fact that my brothers and I would kill her ourselves before we let her get anywhere near you. So stop it. You should know better."

I felt tears welling in my eyes. No one understood I wasn't worried about myself.

"It's not me," I tried to explain. "I couldn't stand it if anything happened to any of you, Garrett."

He held my hand to the side of his face. "We're all looking after each other and you. Don't worry, okay?"

I nodded, and my eyes closed involuntarily. Garrett kissed my forehead.

"Hey, Gracie?"

I opened my eyes and tried to focus.

"How come the machines don't beep like crazy when *I* kiss you?"

Chapter Twenty-One

The room was dark, but I could see Miles sleeping on the sofa in the far corner of the room, and Kate was curled up in a chair close to my bedside. The door opened slowly, allowing light to filter in from the brightly lit hallway, and my heart raced as Nina entered my room slowly. Her face reflected the glow of the multicolored lights from the machines and monitors that surrounded my bed, and she smiled that same sweet smile she always did.

The blade of a large butcher knife shimmered in her hand, reflecting the lights as she walked toward Kate. I tried to move but was paralyzed. She raised the knife up over Kate, the smile still on her face.

"NO!" I screamed. "NO!"

I still couldn't move. My arms felt strapped to my sides, and my heart pounded painfully against my chest. Nina's blank, expressionless stare was a shot of ice in my veins.

"Please!" I begged between sobs. "Please, don't hurt her! Please!"

I closed my eyes, tears running down my face.

"Gracie!" Kate was calling for me, and I opened my eyes. She stood over me, her hands on the sides of my face. "Gracie! Wake up! It's okay."

Miles was on the other side of my bed, squeezing my hand, watching with the same expression of panic as Kate.

"Nina," I hiccoughed. "She was here." I pointed to where I'd seen Nina standing—my hand trembling. "She—she had a knife—" I closed my eyes and tried to slow my heart rate. The nurse came in and pushed buttons on the machine next to me.

"She had a nightmare," Kate told her and brushed at the hair that clung to my forehead from the sweat. Miles disappeared for a moment and returned with a cold cloth, placing it on my forehead.

"It didn't seem like a dream," I sobbed. "I was awake. She was right there."

Kate stroked my hair, and I shook uncontrollably.

"Grace, honey," Miles said soothingly. "We've been here the whole time, nobody's come in."

"It's the medication," the nurse said matter-of-factly. "It can cause hallucinations."

"Okay," Kate shook her head, "I don't think she'll want that medication anymore. Maybe the doctor should prescribe something different."

The nurse nodded and left after checking the I.V. bag. I was still shaking as Miles continued to wipe my forehead softly with the cloth. Kate sat down holding my hand, and then I was embarrassed.

"It seemed so real—"

"It's okay." Miles said soothingly. It's okay now."

I tried to take a deep breath. "What time is it?"

"Almost six a.m."

"You two must be tired," I said. "You should go home and get some sleep."

Kate snorted a laugh. "And you must be delirious. Go back to sleep, Gracie."

They both remained next to the bed, and eventually I drifted to sleep once again.

* * *

"What happened?"

"She thought Nina was in the room."

I could hear the conversation between Michael and Miles, but my eyes were so heavy I couldn't manage to open them.

"It's okay, Michael," Miles said. "The nurse said it was probably because of the medication, it can cause hallucinations. Kate already spoke to the doctor about changing it."

"I shouldn't have left," Michael murmured. "Is she okay?"

"She's fine, little brother, but I've never seen anything like that. She thought it was real."

The fresh scent of Michael's body wash invaded my senses, and his hand grasped mine.

"The doctor said they're going to move her to a regular room today," Kate sounded excited. "She'll be able to take a shower."

"That'll make her happy," Michael said. "That's all she's asked about since she woke up."

"Like you aren't going to be glad I'm going to smell better?" My eyes opened, and I focused on Michael's clean-shaven, gorgeous face.

"You smell fine to me." He kissed my cheek and smiled warmly. "Hey."

He smelled so good. I was suddenly aware of the horrible taste in my mouth, sure my breath matched. I covered my mouth with my hand and glanced at Kate. She giggled and went to get my toothbrush and toothpaste. Michael rolled his eyes and stood so Kate could pull the curtain around my bed. She handed me my toothbrush with toothpaste on it and a basin. While I brushed my teeth, she brushed my hair out and braided it loosely over my shoulder.

"I brought your pink plaid pajamas, but they're going to let you shower today so you can just put them on after that," she chattered. "Miles and I are going home for a little while, and I'll bring your shampoo and conditioner. You don't want the hospital crap."

Kate and Miles went home, Kate promising to return with all the necessities from home for my shower. It wasn't long before the nurse took me to Radiology for tests, which showed the bleeding had stopped. Since the test showed no more bleeding, I was moved to a room in the main wing of the hospital. I was excited there was an actual window in the room. At least I'd be able to tell my days and nights apart.

Kate and Miles showed up, Miles carrying one of my large duffels full of…I had no idea actually, but I knew Kate would have it stocked with the essentials as she promised. Michael helped me to the bathroom while Kate graciously kept my hospital gown cinched behind me. I was extremely sore and dizzy, and Michael stayed with me until I was sure I wouldn't fall.

I stared into the mirror, the reflection of myself hardly recognizable.

My complexion was sallow. There were dark circles under my eyes, and I could tell that I'd lost weight. Kate sighed as she stepped behind me.

"You're still gorgeous." She smiled encouragingly.

I saw nothing in my reflection that was familiar, much less gorgeous.

She helped me out of the hospital gown and peeled a large bandage from my torso. For the first time, I saw the injury Nina had inflicted. It was directly above my belly button and about three inches wide with multiple stitches and terrible bruising. I ran my hand over it gingerly, feeling a twinge of anger. Kate pressed a waterproof bandage over the wound and helped me into the shower.

The familiar fragrances of my shampoo and shower gel made me homesick, but it felt so good to be clean. Kate helped me into my favorite pink plaid pajamas, which felt soft and comfortable, especially compared to the scratchy hospital gown. I felt like a new person, but I was completely exhausted.

When we came out of the bathroom, Michael was there waiting. He wrapped his arm around my waist and helped me to the bed, which had fresh linens. Pain flared in my stomach as I climbed onto the bed, and I winced. Michael murmured a quiet "I'm so sorry" as he tried to make me comfortable. I closed my eyes and took a deep breath, feeling the exhaustion even more.

"That took a lot out of you," he said. "You need to rest now."

"I'm fine."

He shook his head, probably a little irritated, as Garrett approached the side of the bed and bent down so I could kiss his cheek.

"I brought you something," he said, handing me a cup. "Kenny made your favorite."

I brought it to my nose and inhaled the familiar aroma. My hands shook, and Michael watched me worriedly.

"Thank you, Garrett." I smiled up at him.

"I also brought you these." He showed me a stack of movies and pointed to a TV and DVD player across the room. "Evan got it for us. We can watch some movies, huh?"

I nodded excitedly, though dizziness was causing my head to swim.

"Mom made some homemade muffins this morning." Miles opened a plastic container, and I took one out right away taking a small bite. My arms felt like gelatin, and Michael grabbed my coffee because I almost dropped the cup. Everyone watched as he took the muffin from my hand, and my eyes closed.

He reclined my bed, so I was lying down. I wanted to argue, but was too exhausted. I reached my hand to him, and he kissed my palm.

"Rest," he said. "I'll be waiting for you to wake up."

I tried to nod but could barely move my head.

"Gracie," Garrett said. "Go to sleep. We're not going anywhere."

Michael leaned toward me and kissed beside my ear.

* * *

The next few days in the hospital seemed like some of the longest days of my life, and even though the others never complained, I was sure they felt the same. We passed the time, playing cards, watching movies, and then more movies. I was allowed to take short walks through the hospital halls, and every day I felt much better.

Michael stayed every night, leaving in the mornings for a shower and then coming right back. Kate, Miles and Garrett would come in the morning and stay all day. Will and Ava came every day. They were staying in the guest room at Kate's and my house, taking care of Kate and the boys.

Garrett and Miles kept assuring me their work could wait, though Garrett took a couple of trips to Denver to check on St. Jo's and the high-rise under construction.

Kenny came to see me frequently, excited because he'd hired another part-time employee, which gave him a little more freedom. Apparently, she was a student at the University and was doing a 'fine job', which in Kenny-language meant she was nice to look at. Evan came every day and became quick friends with Garrett. After several visits, I was convinced he came to see Garrett more than he came to see me, which was fine with me.

I wanted to go home.

I wanted to get back to work.

I wanted to feel normal again.

Chapter Twenty-Two

Finally, I was going home.

Garrett and Miles loaded my things into the Hummer, while Kate helped me get dressed. The doctor gave Michael and Kate my instructions—no lifting or strenuous exercise for at least two weeks, lots of rest and pain medicine as needed.

Michael held me close to him in the backseat, and I watched out the window as snow fell, covering the ground in a fluffy blanket of white. Will and Ava came out the front door, waving excitedly as we pulled in front of the house. Garrett helped me out of the backseat and carried me into the house.

"Gracie, you've lost too much weight." He shook his head. "We need to fatten you up."

A WELCOME HOME banner stretched across the entryway, my favorite classical music played, a fire crackled in the fireplace, and the house smelled of something wonderful. Garrett brought me to the couch, and I breathed a deep sigh of relief as I took in the comfort of my surroundings. Michael leaned against the wall by the door watching me, and I smiled at him. He ran his hand through his hair as he walked over and sat beside me. I pressed into his side, and he rested his chin on the top of my head.

"Welcome home," he said quietly.

I sighed. "It feels wonderful."

"Grace, I hope you're hungry," Ava said. "I made a big dinner."

"I'm starved," I told her. "I can't thank you enough for everything you've done to help me, Ava. Thank you, so much."

She smiled and took my chin in her hand. “It’s my pleasure. I’m glad you’re home.”

Garrett plopped in the chair beside the couch, crossed his feet on the ottoman and folded his hands behind his head. “Gracie, I put your things in your room, but you don’t have to worry about putting any of it away. Kate has it done already.”

I laughed. “Of course she does.”

I closed my eyes and rested my head against Michael’s chest, listening to the chatter and laughter coming from the people in my life. Ava hummed as she prepared dinner, Will and Miles talked quietly, Kate giggled and Garrett guffawed as they bantered about something.

I listened to all of them—the people I loved.

Michael gave me a squeeze. “Do you want to go to your room so you can sleep? It’s kind of noisy out here.”

“It’s not noisy at all,” I said. “It’s wonderful.”

After a delicious dinner, Michael helped me to my room, with Kate following. When we walked through the door, I gasped as I looked around. Vases of pink roses were everywhere, filling the room with their heavenly fragrance. Strands of twinkle lights draped across the ceiling, reminding me of my first date with Michael.

Kate smiled. “Michael did this for you.”

Michael shrugged casually. I swallowed hard, admiring his face and overtaken with love for him. He kissed the top of my head and led me the bathroom where Kate had the shower running.

“Kate, do you need anything?” Michael asked.

She shook her head. “I think we’ll be fine. Just don’t go too far.”

“I’ll be right out here.” He gestured to the hallway.

Kate closed the bedroom door. As I undressed I noticed a chair, similar to the one at the hospital, sitting in the middle of the shower floor. I turned to Kate quizzically.

“Michael.” She snickered. “I had to talk him out of hiring a full-time nurse to take care of you.”

I was surprisingly grateful for the chair as I completed my shower, my body tiring quickly. I put on a soft pair of flannel pajamas and brushed my teeth. Kate dried my hair and then helped me climb into bed. I felt myself relax instantly as I slid between the sheets, inhaling the familiar scent. Kate had the medication bottles on my nightstand, along with a bottle of water. The twinkle lights cast a soft glow around the room, and I smiled, closing my eyes.

"Amazing."

My eyes flipped open. Michael leaned against the frame of the door; shaking his head with the crooked grin I loved so much.

"What's amazing?" I asked.

"That someone can look so beautiful in flannel pajamas."

I held my hand out to him, and he pushed away from the doorframe, coming to the side of my bed.

He smiled. "You look happy."

"Mm-Hmm," I hummed. "But there is one thing I'm going to miss about the hospital."

"What would that be?"

"I'm going to miss not seeing you when I open my eyes." I lifted my hand and stroked the side of his face, wondering if I would ever get tired of looking at him. I doubted it.

"Hmm," he said thoughtfully.

I chuckled at his expression, and he shook his head.

"I don't think Mom would approve of me staying here all night." He grinned and looked around the room. "I suppose I could sneak in the window."

"I'll leave it unlocked." I waggled my eyebrows, and he laughed.

"You need to sleep," he said. "How's the pain?"

"No pain, just sore."

"Is there anything I can get for you?"

"Will you do something for me?" I traced over his eyebrows and along the side of his face with my fingertips.

He closed his eyes. "Anything."

"Will you stay with me until I fall asleep?"

He stepped over to the chair by my window and pulled it to the side of the bed. He sat down and rested his head on my pillow—just like he did at the hospital.

"How's this?"

I studied every detail of his face that I had already memorized, falling asleep quickly— Michael's face the last thing I saw before my eyes closed.

* * *

"How bad was it?"

"Pretty bad. She was so scared."

Michael and Ava spoke quietly outside my door.

"Kate told me the same thing happened at the hospital," Ava said.

"The nurse said it was from the morphine, but she's not taking that anymore. This isn't from the medicine." I could hear the stress in his voice, and I imagined him running his hand through his hair.

"Michael," Ava said soothingly, "what happened to Grace was extremely traumatic. It's going to take a while. We just have to be patient. She's strong."

I didn't feel strong at all. In fact, I was sure I wasn't strong. The pain in my stomach flared as I sat up slowly, feeling groggy. I leaned against my bed for support and tried to make my way to the bathroom.

"Hey." Michael was at my side in a moment. "What are you doing?" He wrapped his arms around my waist, and I leaned into him as he called for Kate.

"Morning," she chirped, and I had to shake my head. I'd kept her up all night, and she still was in a good mood. "I've got her, Michael. You go eat. I'm sure Gracie wants a shower."

Michael nodded, brushing my cheek with his fingers. Kate didn't mention what had happened while she helped me get dressed.

She just chattered about different things, in her usual Kate-style.

When we came into the kitchen, everyone was seated at the table, except for Ava who stood at the stove stirring a large pan of sausage gravy. Michael came to my side when he saw me, wrapping his arms around my waist and kissing the top of my head.

"Are you hungry?" he asked.

"Starving."

Garrett left the table long enough to give me a gentle hug, and I received dimpled, Anderson-smiles from Will and Miles before Michael helped me to the sofa. He knelt down in front of me and studied my face.

"You had another nightmare," he said quietly. "I'm sorry I wasn't here. Do you want to talk about it?"

I stared down at my hands, folded in my lap. "Your mom says I'm strong, but I'm scared to death because of stupid nightmares."

Michael put his finger under my chin, lifting my face so I could meet his gaze.

"First of all," he stroked my face with his thumb, "you are strong, Grace. These nightmares have nothing to do with your strength. These nightmares have to do with the reality of something terrible that happened to you. They don't mean you're weak; they're proof of your strength because you survived. Nina didn't win. Even if they never find her, she didn't win because here you are...here *we* are...together."

I rolled my eyes as tears came down my face and wiped my cheeks roughly with the sleeve of my sweatshirt. "Yeah. I'm strong."

"Crying doesn't mean you're weak. I know better."

I leaned toward him and kissed him softly. "I love you."

He studied our hands, our fingers laced together. "I've asked myself if I'll ever get tired of hearing you say that." He met my eyes. "I've decided I'll never get tired of hearing those words."

"Good," I said. "Because I don't feel like I can say it enough."

* * *

Every day that passed my strength returned, and I didn't have to take any more pain medication. I went for my follow-up appointments with Dr. Murphy, who said I was healing extremely well and though I wasn't allowed to run yet, I could go for extended walks.

After two weeks, Will and Ava returned home. Kate went back to the shop but only on the days when Garrett or Michael could be with me.

Michael worked on the plans for two hotels in Florida. There were times I went with him to his house, sat in Garrett's over-sized leather swivel chair while Michael focused intently on his drawings at the drafting table. He'd catch me staring and then we'd end up kissing…a lot. After that, he said I couldn't be at his house when he was trying to get work done because he had a difficult time concentrating.

Though I hadn't had any more nightmares, I wasn't sleeping very well at all since the last one. Kate and Miles did some research on the computer and found I'd experienced night terrors. Similar to nightmares, but much more frightening because the person believes he or she is awake. Just thinking about them made me nauseous, and I wouldn't sleep.

Afraid of what I might see.

Chapter Twenty-Three

Michael and I were sitting on the sofa watching the evening news, everyone gone for the evening.

"We should talk to the doctor about something to help you sleep." Michael stroked the dark circles under my eyes with his thumb. "You're so tired."

"Sleeping isn't the problem," I told him. "It's what happens while I'm sleeping."

"Maybe there's something to help you sleep deep enough that you won't dream," he argued. "You need to sleep."

I knew he was right, but the thought of taking more medication when I'd just gotten off my pain meds didn't appeal to me. I didn't like feeling groggy all the time.

"Grace." He looked down at our hands. "I'm going out of town for a few days."

I felt a knot form in my stomach, and he lifted his hand to brush the side of my face.

"I know the timing is terrible, but Miles and I have to go to Florida."

"The hotels?"

He nodded. "We have to meet with our clients and go over my drawings," he said. "Make sure that we're on the same page, so to speak."

"You're brilliant. They're going to love them."

His forehead creased with worry. "I can't stand the thought of leaving you, but we've put it off as long as we can."

I knew this wasn't something he wanted to do, and I didn't want to make it more difficult.

I forced a smile. "It will only be for a few days, right?"

"Five. We're leaving tomorrow morning, and we'll be home Friday night."

So soon. I quickly tried to swallow the panic attempting to make its way into my voice.

"Okay," I said. "So, you probably need to pack and everything, right?"

"Already done. I wanted to make sure I had the whole evening with you."

"I'm going to miss you," I said.

He shook his head. "I can't even tell you how much I'm going to miss you. You have no idea."

"Um, I have some idea."

The corner of his mouth turned up in a small grin, and he leaned down to kiss me sweetly, gently brushing his lips with mine. A shiver went through me, and he smiled against my lips. I pulled away.

"What's so funny?" I narrowed my eyes at him.

"Nothing. Nothing's funny." He was more than a little smug. "You just have this...*power* over me. I like it."

I eyed him skeptically and started to get up from the sofa, but he pulled me firmly onto his lap, the look in his eyes causing my breath to quicken. He traced his finger around my lips, down to my throat and I swallowed hard. His eyes followed the steady movement of his hand as it slid to my shoulder and then down the length of my arm. The backs of his fingers seared an invisible trail against my bare skin, and when his eyes met mine again they radiated an energy that caused my heart to thrum in my ears. I combed my fingers through his hair and he closed his eyes with a sigh.

"Grace," his eyes opened and held my gaze. "I love you so much."

Then his lips pressed to mine, and we kissed tenderly at first, but it quickly escalated with an intensity that made every part of my body come alive.

It was exhilarating. It was frightening. And at that precise moment, it was everything.

Everything I'd waited for and more.

A quiet moan reverberated in his chest, which only increased every sensation to an impossible pitch, and I pulled him closer. I couldn't get close enough. His mouth nipped along my jaw to my ear, where the heat of his breath caused me to shiver like before, and then his lips were on mine once again. He ended the kiss and leaned his forehead against mine, both of us breathing heavily. I could feel the rise and fall of his chest against mine, and I reluctantly loosened my hold around his neck.

When I opened my eyes, he was watching me closely, his gaze still searing.

"I think we'd better stop, don't you?" His voice was quiet.

No.

"Okay," I said, still trying to catch my breath. "If you want."

He held my face in his hands, kissing me once more and smiling softly.

"No," he said. "It's not what I *want*, but—"

I slid from his lap, hoping I wouldn't fall over from dizziness.

"You are so wrong," I muttered under my breath.

"What?"

I shook my head, embarrassed, as I smoothed the front of my shirt.

"What did you say?" he asked again.

I glanced sideways at him, unwilling to meet his eyes.

"I said," I spoke slowly. "You are so wrong."

"What am I wrong about?"

"You just said I have some kind of power over you. And I think you're wrong. You're the one with all the power."

He laughed quietly, and I looked over at him.

"Trust me just this once." His smile was mesmerizing. "I am

completely powerless when it comes to you, Grace Elizabeth Burke."

I just shrugged and looked back at the television. He leaned to my ear, and I closed my eyes.

"You have no idea the effect you have on me," he whispered. "I'm fighting the urge to throw you over my shoulder and carry you into that bedroom right now. That's not power. That's weakness."

My heart felt like it was in my throat, and I swallowed hard as I looked over at him, surprised by his statement.

"Trust me," he said. "I have no power at all."

I couldn't help the snort of laughter that escaped. "And you need to trust me," I argued. "After you kiss me like that, it feels like I'm going to explode, and my vision is impaired for a short period of time."

His crooked grin made my heart pound.

"See?" I pointed at him accusingly. "That right there."

"What?" His expression was confused.

"That gorgeous, sexy smile of yours," I said. "Power."

"Hmm," he seemed to be contemplating what I'd said.

"Not to mention the rest of you." I felt my face turn red.

He was enjoying my embarrassment, and I just shook my head at him.

"I would continue," I told him. "But I don't want your ego to get out of hand."

He laughed and pulled me to his side, pressing his lips to the top of my head.

"I have something for you." He turned to pull something from the pocket of his jacket draped over the back of the sofa. I recognized the Tiffany-blue color of the box immediately.

"We kind of missed our first Valentine's Day," he said, placing the small box in my hand. "So I wanted to give this to you before I leave tomorrow."

"Valentine's Day?" My mind tried to catch up with the date, and sure enough, Valentine's Day had come and gone.

"Michael—"

"Don't," he interrupted angrily, "or I'm taking your present back."

I sighed, feeling miserably disappointed. "But I missed our first Valentine's Day, I missed it." I felt tears coming, but I swallowed them away. He put his hands on both sides of my face.

"We were together on Valentine's Day." He smiled. "That's all that matters."

I was probably unconscious that day. He heaved an exasperated sigh.

"Grace, if I'd known it was going to upset you, I would've waited for your birthday. Please just open it."

I pulled the small white ribbon loose, lifted the lid from the small box and opened the smaller velveteen jewel box. Inside was a delicate silver chain with a silver heart charm. I held it in my hand, admiring its simple beauty, the familiar Tiffany & Co. stamp on one side.

"It's engraved." He turned the charm over in my hand.

There, in elegant script were three words that were so familiar to me, but now meant so much more than I ever dreamed possible.

Forever Yours, Faithfully.

"I thought it was fitting." He shrugged. "It's because of you I can truly understand what these words even mean." He took the necklace and clasped it around my neck. "Not to mention," A slight grin touched the corner of his mouth, "it's because of you I heard this song in the first place."

My lip quivered, and my voice shook. "It's the most beautiful necklace I've ever seen. Thank you. Thank you." I threw my arms around his neck and planted kisses on his cheek, making him chuckle. "Thank you for my present."

I continued to study the charm, rubbing it between my thumb and index finger, feeling the words engraved there, as we watched television together.

Too soon, we stood by the front door, our arms around each

other.

"What time are you leaving?"

"Early. We have to be in Denver by seven thirty." He pressed his lips against the top of my head. "Grace," he said quietly, "I don't want you going or doing anything outside of this house while I'm gone okay? Garrett is going to be here. I'm going to be calling you. And you can call me, too."

"What if you're in a meeting or something?" I said. "I don't want to interrupt anything important."

He pulled away and leaned down so he was eye-level with me.

"Nothing in my world is more important than you. Call whenever you want." I nodded, and his eyebrows furrowed together. "I'd better go. The longer I stay, the more difficult it's going to be to leave."

"You be safe," I said, leaning into him again. "I'll see you on Friday."

"You'll see me on Friday," he repeated, "but you'll be talking to me a lot in between now and then. I love you, Grace Elizabeth."

He kissed me softly and then walked out the door. My arms felt empty, and tears welled in my eyes. I went to my room and sat in the chair by the window, staring at my heart charm, when I had an idea. I quickly went to my closet and pulled out my monogrammed stationery. I jotted down some quick letters to Michael, telling him how much I loved him, how much I missed him, and on a few, I wrote lyrics to some of our favorite songs. He'd have one note for every day he was gone. I put the five letters in five separate envelopes and labeled them for each day he'd be gone.

When I heard Miles and Kate come through the front door, I went to meet them in the kitchen.

"Hey there." Miles smiled. "What are you doing up so late?"

I only shrugged, not wanting to tell him I was busy feeling sorry for myself.

"Hi, Gracie!" Kate said. "Sorry we took so long. We stopped at the shop to unload everything."

She noticed my necklace and smiled her sparkly smile as she turned it over in her hand.

"It's gorgeous," she said. "Perfect."

Miles chuckled as Kate turned to face him.

"They're leaving." She jutted her bottom lip into a pout.

Miles wound his arms around her waist. "Hey, I thought we agreed no pouty face."

She giggled, and he kissed her forehead.

"Miles?" I stepped close to his side. "I was wondering if you would do me a favor?"

He let go of Kate and turned to face me. "Sure."

"Do you think you could put these in Michael's suitcase?" I held my letters out to him, and he took them from me.

"Of course I will."

"Thanks," I told him. "You have a good trip."

He hugged me tightly, and I gave him a swift kiss on the cheek.

"I'm going to bed," I told them. "Good night."

I went to my room and got ready for bed slowly, brushing my teeth and putting on my flannel PJs. I dreaded going to bed at all. It was fairly tolerable when I knew I'd see Michael the next day, but he was going to be gone for five days. I climbed into bed and turned on the television, looking for something to watch. I glanced at the cell phone resting on my nightstand.

I picked it up and sent Michael a text: *Is it Friday yet?*

Seconds later, there was a response:

I wish.

I smiled and sent another: *Just checking.*

I held the phone in my lap, waiting for a response. When the phone stayed quiet, I plugged it into the charger. Not finding anything worth watching on television, I decided to watch a movie. The opening credits to "When Harry Met Sally" began, and my phone vibrated.

I snatched it up quickly to read the message.

What are you doing?

I smiled as I typed: *Watching a movie, what are you doing?*

I waited for his response.

It's late. You're supposed to be sleeping.

What about you? You have a plane to catch tomorrow.

Not tired. What are you watching?

Harry and Sally. Good stuff.

I waited, but the phone was quiet. I sighed and tried to focus on the movie, when the phone vibrated with another message.

I was just wondering, are you wearing your flannel pajamas?

I giggled as I typed: *Yes. Why?*

Just remembering how cute you are in those.

I snorted a laugh, unsure of how to reply, when I received his next message.

Grace?

Yes?

Go to your window.

My heart lurched into my throat as I jumped out of bed and pushed the curtains away from the window. There he was, the dim light from his cell phone illuminating his crooked smile. I opened the window and leaned out, the chill of the wintry air hitting my face.

"Hi," he said. "Can I come in?"

I smiled, stepping aside and holding the curtain back. We both laughed quietly as he climbed clumsily through my window. When he was inside, I closed the window and pulled the curtains closed. He stood there in black plaid flannel pants, gray tee shirt and leather jacket. His hair was going in a hundred different directions, and I tried to tame the wildness by running my fingers through the strands.

"What exactly are you doing?" I asked.

He shrugged and glanced over his shoulder at the television.

"I want to watch a movie with you." His tone was matter-of-fact.

"You know it's after midnight, and you have to leave in less than six hours?"

"I don't care. I'm not going to be able to sleep anyway."

No way was I going to argue with him. I climbed under the covers while he took off his jacket, draped it over the chair and kicked off his shoes. He watched as I propped up several pillows against the headboard, patting the bed next to me. He climbed onto the bed and got comfortable. I leaned against him, his arms around me, and we watched Harry and Sally saying, "Waiter, there is too much pepper on my Paprikash."

"Have you seen this before?" I asked.

"Mom loves this movie, and I used to have a thing for Meg Ryan."

I sat up, eyeing him quizzically. "Really?"

His expression was amused. "Does that surprise you?"

"No." I shrugged. "Not at all. She's very cute."

"Well, you have a thing for Sly," he pointed out.

"True." I sighed dramatically, and he poked my side playfully, making me giggle.

"You know he's like seventy now," he said dryly. "He's way too old for you."

"Yeah," I snorted. "And Meg is just your age."

"I said I *used* to have a thing for her," he clarified. "I don't any more. I have a thing for this brunette I know."

He raised his eyebrows at me, and I leaned against him again. He traced invisible patterns on my back lightly, and my eyes began to get heavy.

"Michael?"

"Hm?"

"I'm glad you're here."

He sighed and kissed the top of my head, holding his lips there.

"Will you stay?" I asked. "Until you have to leave in the morning?"

He nodded against my head, and I could feel the warmth of his breath in my hair.

"I want you to sleep," he whispered.

My eyes closed, and I drifted happily in his arms.

* * *

I draped my arm over my eyes to block the light that was still on and smiled remembering Michael climbing through my window last night. I rolled over and looked at the clock. It was just after six. I turned onto my back again, draping my arms over my head. There was a rustle of paper against my elbow, and I sat up, seeing a note lying on my pillow. I opened it and read Michael's words:

Grace,

I'm going to miss you every day, loving you even more.

When you sleep, dream of me because I'll be dreaming of you.

Yours Always,

Michael

I returned the note to the pillow, feeling the ache in my chest as I thought about him leaving. I glanced at the clock again. Maybe he hadn't left yet. I jumped out of bed and ran to my bathroom, brushing my teeth quickly to rid my mouth of morning breath and then pulled on my slippers and robe. I hurried to the front door, opening it as quietly as I could. It was cold, and there was a thin layer of snow on the ground.

Michael was loading his suitcase into the back of his Yukon, and I sighed in relief and trudged across the gravel drive.

"Grace?"

I ran to him and buried my face in his chest, as he held me.

"You're going to get sick." His voice was worried, and honestly I felt a little silly, but I didn't care.

"I just wanted to see you before you left." I squeezed him tightly.

Their front door closed, and Garrett came to the driveway in his pajamas, his hair a mass of untamed waves.

"Gracie-Beth." He shook his head disdainfully. "You're gonna catch your death."

Michael nodded in agreement. "He's right. Go inside, I'll see you soon."

He kissed me softly, and smiled. Garrett pulled me toward him just as Miles came out the door, grimacing when he saw me standing there.

"Grace—" He shook his head.

"I know, I know," I told him. "I'm going."

Michael chuckled quietly, and Garrett squeezed my shoulders.

"I'm going to go into town, and then I'll be over," he said. "You want me to bring you something from the shop?" I nodded, and he gave me a wink, knowing my answer, and then pointed to my house. "Go home."

I glanced at Michael again, the ache in my chest returning as I turned to go, walking slowly back home. The car doors closed, and the engine started as I went inside and shut the front door. I stood at the window, waiting for his car to go by. The Yukon crawled to a halt in front of the house and the driver's window came down slowly. Michael leaned out of the window, smiling widely as he watched me for a moment before driving away. I returned to my room and looked at the note still on my pillow, deciding to leave it there.

* * *

The five days Michael was gone were brutal.

I'd barely slept, except for the occasional nap when Kate and

Garrett were with me. I'd lost track of how many hours it had been since I closed my eyes for longer than thirty minutes. In addition to resembling a zombie, I was also overly emotional. Thursday night, Kate and I were sitting at the kitchen table, and I wept over a song on the radio. It was a good song, but still, I was a disaster.

Kate tried to make me feel better by going Dr. Phil on me. She was convinced my emotional-rollercoaster-ride was a combination of trauma from the attack, medications and separation anxiety. I couldn't argue because she was so sure of herself, as usual.

When I went into my room to check my phone, there were several texts from Michael.

Where are you?

His 'tone' grew more impatient with each text.

If you don't respond to this in five minutes I'm calling and I won't be happy.

Two minutes...

I had to giggle as I typed quickly to make the deadline:

Go ahead and call. I'd rather hear your voice anyway.

It wasn't even two minutes when my phone rang.

"Hey."

"Hey. Where were you?" He sounded irritated. "I was getting worried."

"Sorry. I was in the kitchen being psychoanalyzed by Kate."

"What?"

"Never mind. Hi."

He chuckled. "How are you?"

"Pretty miserable. You?"

"The same. Only a few more hours."

"Sixteen, approximately," I amended.

"I miss you."

"I miss you more."

"Have you been sleeping?"

I didn't want to answer that particular question.

"Grace?"

"I'm here."

He sighed. "Honey, have you been sleeping?"

"Not really, but I'll be so much happier when you're home," I hedged.

"I know. Me too."

I changed the subject by asking if the clients liked his design. Of course they did. He laughed when I asked if he and Miles were going to visit Disney World, and then he yawned.

"You're tired," I said. "I'll let you go."

"Sorry about that. It's just been a little busy, and I hate hotel rooms."

"Well, I'll see you tomorrow night."

"Yes, you will, and I can't wait."

"What time does your flight leave?"

"I think it leaves at two-something. I'll let you know."

"Okay."

"I love you, Grace Elizabeth."

"I love you, too. Sleep well."

He sighed, and I heard the sadness in his voice. "I would tell you to sleep well, but I know better."

"I can't help it."

"I know. I just wish there was something I could do."

I swallowed hard at the lump in my throat. "Come home. That's what you can do."

"I'll see you tomorrow."

When I returned to the living room Kate was sitting on the sofa, talking with Miles on the phone. She motioned for me to sit beside her. I laid my head in her lap, and she played with my hair.

"Okay, I love you too," she said with a giggle. "I know. See you tomorrow."

She set the phone down and sighed. "I miss him."

"Me too," I said. "Where's Garrett?"

"He called a little while ago," she said. "He and Evan were meeting for pizza."

I felt my eyelids get heavy.

"You need to sleep," she said. "Do you want me to sleep in your room tonight?"

"Thanks." I yawned. "But I can't expect everyone to change their lives around more than they already have just because I have nightmares like a two-year-old."

I didn't have to see her face to know she rolled her eyes at me.

Chapter Twenty-Four

I woke up on the sofa, a quilt spread over me. It was after two in the morning and the room was dark except for the light in the hallway. I folded the quilt and draped it over the back of the sofa before going to the front door to make sure it was locked. I flipped on the porch light and looked over at the Anderson house. The porch light was on, and their front door was open.

I swallowed hard.

Garrett's Hummer was in the driveway, but he wouldn't be awake, and he definitely wouldn't have left the front door open. My hands shook as I opened the door. Cold air hit me like a brick wall, stinging my skin through my sweats and tee shirt. The wind whistled loudly through the trees, and sharp rocks dug into my bare feet as I made my way across the gravel drive. My legs felt heavy as I climbed the steps of the Andersons front porch.

When I reached the door, it became blurred. I rubbed my eyes roughly with the palms of my hands and pushed the door all the way open.

"Garrett?" I slowly made my way through the entry and cleared my throat before calling his name again. "Garrett? Are you okay?"

The house was eerily quiet. A single lamp lit the living room, the rest of the house dark. I looked around, feeling a little dizzy, a thin sheen of sweat forming on my forehead.

My voice shook with fear. "It's-it's Gracie." A sob pushed against my throat because something was wrong. I could feel it.

A light came on in Garrett's bedroom, shining dimly in the

darkened hallway, and my breath hitched.

"Garrett?"

Nausea and panic took over as I walked slowly toward the bedroom, dreading painfully what I was going to find. I wrung my hands together anxiously as I looked around the door into his room.

Garrett was asleep. Sprawled across the bed on his stomach, the blankets in a tangle around his legs. The wide, dimpled grin on his face made me sigh in relief. I walked to his nightstand to turn off the lamp, when I felt something cold and wet under my feet.

Confused, I looked closely. Garrett's arm was draped off the side of the bed and something dripped from his hand. I reached out to touch him. His fingers were cold. Trembling, I turned his hand over. His palm was covered with blood. Then I noticed his face. Even with the grin, his lips were a sickly shade of blue, and his face an icy gray. I reached up to touch him with my fingertips, and he was so cold.

Tears came. "Please, Garrett. Please don't do this. Open your eyes. Please."

My heart raced as I quickly pulled the covers away from his hulking figure. The sheets were nothing more than a pool of Garrett's blood. It felt like something heavy pressed on my chest as I backed out of his room slowly, my breaths short and shallow.

I knew he was dead.

And I knew Nina killed him.

I shook my head as if I could erase what was in front of me, but all I could see was my best friend dead. My feet wouldn't carry me out of the house fast enough. I cried out for Kate when I was finally outside, but the sound of my voice didn't carry over the wind.

The cold air stung my skin as I tried to make my way back home, desperately wanting to reach Kate. I could see my house, but it seemed so far away.

"Kate!" I sobbed. "Kate!"

Dizziness took over, and my stomach surged with the need to vomit. My legs didn't hold my weight, and I fell. The gravel was like a dozen sharp knives as my face scraped across the ground.

"Gracie!"

The taste of blood was on my tongue, and I tried to push myself up. I could hear my name being called. Arms came underneath me, and I was being carried.

"Garrett's dead! He's dead!" I wanted someone to hear me.

The warmth of the house came over me and then I was on the sofa, but I continued to sob, wishing someone would listen about Garrett.

"He's dead. Garrett's gone," I hiccoughed.

"Gracie, it's okay. Kate, she's bleeding."

I opened my eyes and saw Garrett's face. I sat up quickly, trying to make my brain catch up with what I was seeing.

"It's okay." Garrett leaned over me, his eyes full of distress as he tried to soothe me. "Gracie, it's okay. I'm here."

I moved my hands frantically over his chest and then his arms, searching for blood.

"You were hurt." When I saw the blood streaked across his shirt, my body shuddered. "You're bleeding! She hurt you! I hate her! I hate her!"

"I'm fine!" Garrett was shaking me. "This is your blood! You fell!"

He wiped at his own tears roughly, and I shook my head trying to dispel the memory of him lying dead in his own blood. I covered my face and sobbed as reality confronted me.

The whole thing was a dream.

I was embarrassed. Embarrassed and relieved Garrett was alive. He pulled me onto his lap and cradled me against him tightly. I turned my head against his chest and tried to slow my breathing, feeling relief wash over me because he was safe.

"Gracie," Garrett said quietly. "You're bleeding. Kate needs to check the cuts on your face."

He set me on the couch, and Kate kneeled in front of me, sniffling as she took a wet cloth and blotted the left side of my face.

She shook her head sadly as she saturated a cotton ball with hydrogen peroxide and dabbed gently at the cuts I was now starting to feel.

"They aren't deep," she said. "Let me see your hands."

I held my hands out in front of me and saw the shallow scrapes on my palms. Kate took the cloth again and started the same routine she'd just finished on my face. I turned to Garrett, and he watched me with his eyebrows knitted together. Sadness and worry etched in his face.

"I thought I was awake," I tried to explain to him. "I fell asleep on the sofa, but then I woke up."

He nodded, waiting for me to continue.

"Your front door was open." I swallowed hard. "I was worried, so I went over to check on you. When I called your name, you didn't answer." I looked down at my hands now folded in my lap. Kate kneeled in front of me, listening as I recounted the nightmare.

"I saw a light on in your room so I went to check." I took in a ragged breath. "You were asleep…and you were…smiling. But then…" I squeezed my eyes shut, "I saw how pale you were. I touched you, and you were so cold and then I pulled the covers back."

Everything was so vividly clear and terrifying.

"There was so much blood." I felt a surge of anger go through me. "I knew you were dead, and I knew she killed you."

The cuts on my hands stung as I tightened them into fists.

"I hate her," I said. "I hate her."

Kate cried as Garrett wrapped his giant arms around me and pulled me to him.

"Gracie, I'm so sorry," he murmured against my hair.

"They have to catch her." I clung to his shirt and continued to tremble. "If she hurts one of you—"

"They'll find her," he assured me. "She can't hide forever."

I tried to take comfort in his words, but they offered none. When I closed my eyes, I still saw him in a pool of his own blood, and I hated her. I'd never used the word 'hate' when I talked about someone, and I despised her even more for making me feel so much hatred. It was like some kind of sick circle with no end and no beginning. Everything I felt at that moment—the sadness, the nausea, the exhaustion and the hatred—was all because of Nina Sandler. And I hated her for it.

"You're so exhausted," Kate said.

I heard the worry in her voice and she was right, but there was no way I would sleep now.

No way.

Garrett gave me a squeeze. "Come on, Gracie."

He stood from the couch, bringing me with him, and kept his arm around my shoulders as we walked to my room. Kate turned on my stereo, took the throw pillows from my bed and pulled the blankets back.

"I don't want to go to sleep," I said quietly. "I'll be fine."

Garrett climbed onto my bed and patted the spot next to him, pulling his eyebrow moves and making me smile. He held his arms open with a dimpled grin on his face. I climbed next to him, resting my head on his chest, and he wrapped his arms around me.

Kate pulled the covers over me and kissed my cheek before leaving the room. I could hear Garrett's heart beating and it comforted me.

"Are you going to stay until I fall asleep?" I asked.

"I'm staying until you wake up."

I tried to look up at him so I could argue, but he tightened his hold on me, making it impossible to move.

"Garrett, you can't do that. You won't get any sleep."

It was quiet for a moment, then his chest rumbled with a loud snore. I nudged him in the ribs, and he shook with quiet laughter. "Don't worry about me." He patted my head. "You sleep."

It was quiet for a moment except for the lull of the nocturne coming from my stereo.

"I like this music," he said. "What is this?"

"It's Chopin's Nocturne five in F-Sharp."

He sighed loudly, and I giggled, sure that what I'd said made no sense to him.

"I gave you this same CD for Christmas," I reminded him. "Haven't you listened to it yet?"

When he didn't answer, I nudged him again, making him laugh.

"Sorry, Gracie."

"Mom and Aunt Beth used to play his music for Kate and me when we couldn't sleep, it always helps me relax."

He sighed. "It's nice. I guess I need to listen to that CD."

I nodded, and again it was quiet for a moment.

"Garrett?"

"Hm?"

"I love you."

He kissed the top of my head. "I love you, too. Now go to sleep, Gracie-Beth."

* * *

When I opened my eyes, I still had my head on Garrett's chest, and I sat up slowly, feeling stiff and sore. Garrett rubbed his face with his hands and then stretched. The side of my face stung and I winced.

Garrett put his hand under my chin and studied the left side of my face.

"Ooh," he shook his head in disdain. "Michael's not going to be happy with me when he sees this."

"It's not your fault. I'm the one who did it, not you."

"It happened on my watch," he said matter-of-factly.

I frowned. "He'd better not blame you."

"I'm more afraid of you than I am of my little brother."

I rolled my eyes at him, and he grinned.

"Thanks, Garrett," I said. "Thanks for staying with me."

"No problem, Gracie." He yawned loudly.

Kate came in the room, passing Garrett on his way out.

"Morning." She smiled at him, and he patted her head. "Breakfast?"

"Excellent." He scratched his head as he disappeared down the hall. "I'll be back in about twenty minutes."

I noticed she wasn't dressed in her usual work attire. "Aren't you going to work?"

She shrugged. "No. I'm staying with you and Garrett today."

I started to argue, but she held up her hand to stop me from saying anything.

"I'm not leaving," she said stubbornly. "So just get over it. Besides, the boys are coming home today, and I wouldn't be able to focus on work anyway."

I nodded in agreement as she on the edge of my bed and gently touched the scratches on my face.

"Michael's going to think I'm crazy," I told her.

"You're not crazy." She pushed herself off my bed. "I'm going to make us some breakfast. I can't wait to see Miles."

Her sparkly-Kate-smile appeared on her face as she disappeared into the hallway. I went into the bathroom and stared at my reflection in the mirror. It looked like I'd been dragged across asphalt by my face, which I suppose wasn't too far from what truly happened.

Shallow scrapes ran from the hairline of my temple to the middle of my left cheek, and my left eye was badly bruised underneath. A ragged cut on the corner of my mouth explained why I'd tasted blood last night. I washed my face gingerly and brushed my teeth and hair before going into the kitchen.

Kate and I made pancakes, and we sat with Garrett eating our breakfast, making small talk. I was glad no one brought up last night because I knew when Michael saw the self-inflicted damage on my face, I'd be talking about it plenty.

"So," Kate smiled, "I think we need to have a special dinner tonight. What do you think?"

She was asking me, but Garrett answered.

"Sounds great to me. What are we…I mean what are you going to make?"

"I was thinking about—"

"Steak." Garrett interrupted her. "You were thinking about steak and homemade bread. Right?"

Kate slapped her hand down on the table with a big grin. "How did you know, Garrett?" She said sardonically. "That's exactly what I was thinking!"

"Really?" he asked, surprised.

"No," Kate said flatly. "But that's what we'll be having anyway."

* * *

After breakfast, I showered and got dressed in jeans and a pink cable-knit sweater. Michael liked me in pink, and I hoped the pink sweater might distract from the ugliness of my face. I didn't even attempt make-up. It was hopeless.

I went into the living room and sat next to Garrett as he watched TV. He draped his arm over my shoulder, and I leaned into his side.

"How you feelin', Gracie?"

"Fine. How about you?" I asked. "Are you tired?"

"No, not really," he said. "But I think you should know, you snore."

I frowned at him. "I do not."

"Okay. You don't." He cocked an eyebrow at me, and I elbowed him in the ribs, making him laugh.

Kate returned from the store with steaks and everything needed for dinner. I'd asked her to buy the ingredients for my coconut cake. I'd never made that for Michael before.

There were only a couple of hours until Michael and Miles would be home. The steaks were marinating in the fridge, I had the cake done and the bread dough was rising. I decided to go lay down because, including last night, I'd had less than six hours of sleep all week. My face was evidence. The dark circles had taken permanent residence beneath my eyes, and said eyes were a regular shade of bloodshot as well. Not to mention the cuts and partial black eye. All in all, I'd have to say I was looking pretty rough. I realized a nap would not help this, but it definitely couldn't hurt.

"Go rest," Kate told me. "Miles is supposed to call when they land, and I'll wake you up."

I nodded and went to my room, turning on my music as I climbed onto my bed. My phone buzzed with a message from Michael.

I'm counting the minutes now.

I smiled as I sent my reply: *You're just now counting minutes? I've been doing that since last night.*

I closed my eyes while I waited for his response.

* * *

"It's one of the scariest things I've ever seen, aside from seeing her that day at the shop."

Garrett talked quietly outside my door.

"She was outside, lying in the middle of the driveway in the cold, asleep. She really thought I was dead. I've never seen her like that."I could hear the sadness in Garrett's voice. "It scared me to death, and I couldn't do anything."

His voice shook with emotion, and I felt terrible for putting him through that.

"It was awful." Kate was talking now. "The side of her face is all scraped up, and she's completely exhausted from lack of sleep."

"What did she see?" Miles asked, and Garrett recounted what I'd told him and Kate.

I didn't want to hear anymore. I pushed myself to the edge of the bed, rubbing my eyes.

When I turned around, Michael was standing at my bedroom

door holding a bouquet of pink roses. He was trying to smile, but the smile didn't reach his eyes as he watched me. My stomach knotted, and without thinking I ran and jumped into him. I heard the flowers fall to the floor as I buried my face in his neck.

"Oh, I missed you," he murmured and tightened his arms around me.

I kept my face nuzzled in the crook of his neck, smelling his wonderful smell. His arms made me feel safe again, but he couldn't hold me tight enough or close enough.

Without breaking our embrace, he sat on the edge of my bed and pulled me onto his lap. He tried to loosen my arms from his neck, but I didn't want him to see my face. I was embarrassed about what had happened.

"Sweetheart, look at me," he said.

I let go, but didn't make eye contact.

"Grace," he whispered and gently touched the scrapes along my face. "What did you do to yourself?"

I swallowed hard as the nightmare flashed through my mind. "I didn't mean to."

He sighed and brushed his lips tenderly over the scrapes and scratches along the side of my face. I closed my eyes and he kissed the bruises on my eyelid.

"I'm so glad you're home," I told him.

He pressed his mouth to mine, holding my face with his hands. Our mouths moved together sweetly.

"I'm so sorry." He shook his head and kissed the scratches on my face again. "What are we going to do with you? You're so tired."

"These dreams…aren't like dreams," I tried to explain. "I think I'm awake. Everything I see…it's not like a dream at all." I closed my eyes as I thought about what I'd seen with Garrett. When I shuddered, Michael tightened his hold on me.

"What I see," I whispered. "It's real. And it's more frightening than what happened with Nina, because she's hurting the people I love."

He pulled me to him, and I rested my head on his shoulder. After a long while, I stood from his lap, and he reached for both of my hands, holding them tightly in his.

"Are you okay?"

"I am now," I told him. "Next time you have to leave it may be necessary for me to stow away in one of your suitcases."

"I'm not going anywhere for a while," he assured me. "So don't even worry about that."

I picked up the roses from the floor and held them to my nose, inhaling their heavenly scent.

"They're so beautiful." I smiled. "Thank you."

"You're welcome. Thank you for my letters."

"You liked them?"

"How could I not? They were from you, and they helped me through the five days."

"Well, I just wanted you to think of me while you were gone."

His eyes burned into mine. "Trust me," he traced along my bottom lip with his finger, "I didn't need letters for that. I thought about you every minute."

A shiver ran through me and he kissed me sweetly. I could smell the steaks broiling in the oven. "Are you hungry?"

"For your cooking?" He grinned. "Always."

He took my hand as I led him to the kitchen. Kate and I got dinner ready while Michael and Miles filled Garrett in on the business details of their trip to Florida. The clients loved Michael's designs, and it was likely he wouldn't have to return. Garrett and Miles would be making quick turn-around trips while the hotels were being built, but construction wouldn't be underway for several months.

After dinner, we sat on the sofa and watched basketball highlights on ESPN. The phone rang and Kate answered, talking quietly in the kitchen. When she hung up, she came into the living room, her expression grave.

"What's wrong?" Garrett's voice was full of concern, and I

knew what she was going to say.

"She's here."

Chapter Twenty-Five

"That was the Denver P.D." Kate looked at Miles while she spoke. "They received an anonymous tip that Nina is here in Fall Rivers. They wanted us to know."

She sat beside me and took my hand in hers, but nobody spoke. After a moment, Garrett stood up angrily from his chair, muttering profanities as he switched off the TV. Michael's arm tightened around me, and I closed my eyes trying to fight the nausea threatening to take over.

The silence screamed as I waited for somebody to say something. Anything. Finally, I stood and walked over to the window, staring into the darkness. I imagined Nina peering from behind a tree, watching from the shadows, and a shudder went through me.

"I think we should go somewhere," Michael's voice broke the silence. "Anywhere. Maybe we could go to New York."

The anger toward Nina stirred inside me. She wanted me to be afraid, and I wasn't going to give her anything that she wanted.

I turned from the window to face Michael. "Run? No way am I giving her the satisfaction of running."

Michael pushed himself from the couch and glared down at me. "Grace, I'm not going to argue with you about this."

I glared right back. "You said she'd lost because I wasn't dead. Do you really think she's going to just give up?" He ran his hand through his hair, frustrated, but I didn't back down. "If we run away, she'll wait. She's probably sitting out there right now waiting for a chance for me to be alone, or worse—" I tried not to choke on my words. "Waiting for one of you to be alone. Are you going to take everyone I love to New York?"

As I said it, there was a part of me that actually liked the idea.

"Gracie," Kate said quietly. "I think Michael's right. We should go somewhere just for awhile. Give them a chance to find her."

Michael hadn't moved from in front of me.

"They know she's here," Kate continued. "They're going to catch her."

"Little brother," Garrett said. "I agree with Gracie."

Michael's glare shot to Garrett, and then Miles stood up beside Garrett.

"I think she's right," Miles agreed. "We shouldn't run."

"It's not running," Michael argued. "It's keeping Grace safe. Like Kate said, giving the police a chance to catch Nina—"
"And how long do we stay away, Michael?" I interrupted him. "A week, a month?"

He turned and paced angrily for a moment, stopping in front of me again.

"Dammit, Grace," Michael muttered. "This subject is not up for debate. We're leaving."

"No." I argued. "You heard your brothers, they don't think we should leave."

"They don't have as much to lose as I do either!"

I flinched away from him. Garrett wrapped his arm around my shoulders, the muscles in his arms tense.

"Michael," Miles said quietly, his voice sad. "How can you say that?"

Michael sighed and sat back down on the couch, holding his head in his hands. He kept his eyes down, and Kate rubbed his shoulders soothingly. After a moment, he pushed himself from the sofa, and walked over to where I stood with his brothers. His expression was full of remorse as he placed his hand on Garrett's shoulder.

"I'm sorry," he said to both of them. "I didn't mean that. Please forgive me."

Garrett heaved a sigh. "I know you're worried, little brother. We all are."

Michael nodded in agreement.

"Let's at least wait to make any decisions until Mom and Dad come," Miles said. "They'll be here tomorrow, and we can talk to them about this, okay?"

I stepped to Michael, winding my arms around his waist and resting my head against his chest. His chin came down on my head as he sighed in defeat.

"Okay. But I do think we should take some precautions," he said.

I didn't let go of him as he spoke.

"Kate, no going anywhere by yourself for a while. One of us will be with you when you're at work."

"He's right," Garrett agreed. "I also think one of us should sleep here at night. The girls shouldn't be alone."

As I listened to the conversation, my hatred flared. The lives of everyone I loved being disrupted because of Nina Sandler. Angry tears filled my eyes, but I kept my hold on Michael.

"Grace did you hear me?" Michael asked.

I looked up at him and shook my head. He put his hands on the sides of my face and smiled softly. "I want to take you to see Dr. Murphy about getting something to help you sleep."

I didn't want to argue with him. It wouldn't have done any good, and besides that, I really wanted to get some sleep.

He cocked an eyebrow. "No argument?"

I shook my head. "No argument."

Michael turned to his brothers again and I started to sit down, but he kept a tight hold on my hand. He embraced Garrett tightly, then Miles, all the while gripping my hand tightly. Garrett kissed the top of my head, before returning to his original position in the overstuffed chair.

"Don't worry, Gracie," he said with a grin. "Everything's going to be fine."

Michael led me to my room, closing the door behind us. He sat in the chair by the window and pulled me onto his lap. I wound my arms around his neck, burying my face in his neck.

"I owe you an apology," he said. "I never should've spoken to you that way. I'm sorry."

I just nodded, not saying anything. I held onto him, feeling an ache in my stomach as I thought about Nina skulking around in the darkness, waiting for someone I loved to be alone so she could harm them in some way. I fought the tears trying to come and squeezed my eyes closed.

"Grace, please look at me."

I loosened my hold on his neck. He tucked my hair behind my ears and ran his fingertips gently across the scratches on my face.

"I know how scared you are—"

"No," I interrupted him. "You don't know how scared I am."

I was scared. But, not for the reason he was thinking.

"You think I'm scared for myself, and that's not why I'm scared at all."

His jaw tensed, and a fiery glint flashed behind the green in his eyes.

"And you're forgetting a couple of things." I could tell he was trying to keep his voice calm, but he was also clearly irritated. "First, you're forgetting that I know you. I am well aware you're not scared for yourself. I think we all know that. Second, you're forgetting it was me, and Kate, and my brothers, who watched you almost die."

He closed his eyes as if trying to push away the memory. When he opened them again they were no longer fiery, they were anguished.

"*I* thought I was going to lose you. *I* saw you lying on that floor bleeding. *I* saw what Nina had done."

There was an ache in my stomach as I remembered struggling to see Michael in the darkness, wondering if I would ever see him again. I stroked the side of his face with my fingers, and he leaned against my hand.

He sighed. "So, though I may not know exactly how you feel, I think I have a pretty good idea."

I rubbed his cheek with my thumb, feeling bad for underestimating his love for me. He held my hand to the side of his face and kissed my palm.

"I know you're scared, but we're going to get through this. They'll find Nina, and everything's going to be fine."

I wanted to believe what he was saying, because I knew he truly believed it. But as I looked at him, the anger stirred once again. I thought about how I would've felt had it been Michael on the floor of the bookstore. Or Kate. Or Garrett. Or Miles. Or anyone dear to me. Even though I wished it hadn't happened at all, I would do it a hundred-times over if it meant keeping Michael and the others safe.

"What are you thinking about?" he asked.

"I hate her," I said flatly. "And I hate that I hate her."

I waited for him to ask what I was talking about, but he didn't, he just kept watching me.

"Because of her, everyone's having to change their lives around, and because of her, everyone's scared and worried. I hate her for that." I shook my head, fighting the sob in my throat. "We've found each other, but we can't just be happy because we have to be worried and scared for each other all the time. Because of her, and I…hate her."

Tears came, and I swiped them away angrily.

"Grace," Michael said softly. "Every single day since you and Kate first came to our house, and I saw you sitting on the sofa with my big brother, I've been happy I met you."

He smiled as he brushed my hair from my shoulders.

"Every day we're together, I'm happy. Even when I was sick with worry over losing you when you were hurt, when I look at you I'm happy. I'm happy because I love you, and I know you love me." He smiled sweetly. "There's nothing Nina Sandler or anyone else could ever do to take this happiness from me."

Another tear escaped my eye, and he wiped it away with his thumb.

"I've had hatred for Nina, too," he said. "But hatred turns to bitterness. And bitterness is ugly, Grace, it is."

"I know." I shook my head. "That's why I'm so angry, because I feel that hatred at all. I don't know how to not hate her, and I hate feeling this way."

He held my face in his hands.

"With all the heartache you've had in your life, if anyone could be bitter, it's you. But you've been able to rise above that petty emotion to be the loving and caring person you are now. You were those things before Nina, and you're those things now. She hasn't changed you."

"Then why do I feel so much hatred for her?"

"She did a terrible and vicious thing to you," he said matter-of-factly. "But don't you see? With all of her money, fancy cars, and expensive clothes, it's just like you said. She's nothing more than a miserable, lonely, bitter girl who was jealous of you the first time she saw you." He smiled warmly. "You have everything she wants and more. You have people in your life that love you more than their own lives. Nina wants what you have. Hating her for what she did is not going to affect her, it will only affect you, and I love you too much to let that happen. I'm too happy loving you to let that happen.

"But until she's found, I'm going to do everything in my power to keep you safe. That's the only thing that matters to me. Keeping you safe."

As I listened, there was a sense of awe with his beauty. Not his physical beauty, but the beauty of his character and his heart.

"What?" Michael smirked. "What are you thinking about now?"

I shook my head and pressed my lips against his neck again, resting my head there.

"I just love you," I whispered. "I love you so much."

He sighed and kissed the top of my head. "It's late. You need to sleep."

I nodded reluctantly, feeling a twinge of panic at the thought of him leaving.

"Grace," his voice was quiet, "I want to stay here. I know you sleep better when someone's with you, and I'd rather it be me than anyone else."

I felt relief wash over me, and I took a deep breath. "Thank you."

I stood from his lap, and he smiled as he watched me pull my pink plaid PJs from the dresser drawer and go into my bathroom, closing the door behind me. As I got ready for bed, I heard several voices outside the door and then Garrett's laughter. When I came out, Kate was sitting on my bed with her arms folded across her chest and a playful scowl on her face.

"What's wrong?" I asked. "Where did Michael go?"

"Grace Elizabeth Burke," she said, shaking her head disdainfully.

I waited for whatever was coming, and something was definitely coming.

"You think we're going to allow your boyfriend to sleep over?" Kate shook her finger at me. "Really, Grace. Shame."

I heard Garrett's chortling from the hallway. I peered around the partially open door to see Garrett, his lips pursed in a tight line, trying not to laugh.

"What are you laughing at?"

He stepped inside my room. "We've had a family meeting and decided that Michael will be sleeping here tonight." He waggled his eyebrows. "Is that okay with you?"

"Ha, ha," I said dryly. "Maybe you'd prefer to stay again."

He shook his head. "No way. You snore."

I picked up a small pillow from my bed and whacked him on the arm, but before I could get in another swipe, he had me in a headlock. Kate left giggling down the hallway. Garrett kept me that way, rubbing the top of my head roughly. I heard Michael chuckle, and Garrett let go of me, kissing the top of my head.

"Night, Gracie," he said, and turned to Michael. "Night, little brother. Good luck trying to sleep with Gracie snoring like a freight train."

I lunged at him, and he retreated quickly out my door.

"I don't snore," I pouted.

Michael laughed. "Of course you don't. Garrett snores so loud we had to soundproof his room. We could light firecrackers in his bed, and he wouldn't hear them over his own snoring."

Michael walked over to sit in the chair, and I noticed he'd changed into a pair of gray sweats and USC tee shirt. I took pillows off the bed, as he turned on the television and channel-surfed. After I climbed under the covers, I watched him, waiting. He glanced sideways and smiled his crooked grin, standing to kick off his shoes. I propped pillows against the headboard, and he leaned against them, making himself comfortable. I snuggled to him, laying my head on his chest.

I yawned. "Michael, you don't have to stay all night. You'll be miserable."

He squeezed me to him.

"How could I possibly be miserable when I'm with you," he whispered. "Besides, I've wanted to sleep with you since the first time I saw you."

My head snapped up in surprise, and he just laughed quietly. "Shhh. Go to sleep."

My eyes closed, happiness surging through me, as I lay there in Michael's arms, safe and happy.

* * *

After a dreamless night, I awoke to the sound of Michael's steady breathing, his arm draped over my shoulders. I tried to sit up, but his arm felt like a dead weight too heavy to move. I chuckled quietly and attempted to wriggle my way free from his hold. His breath hitched and then continued steadily as I sat upright, pulling my knees to my chest as I gazed at him. His face was peaceful as he slept soundly. I resisted the urge to touch him, not wanting to wake him.

I got up carefully and silently pulled the drawers to my dresser open to retrieve my clothes for the day, before going into my bathroom and closing the door quietly. As I showered, I realized that for the first time since my injury, I actually felt somewhat rested. This realization brought a smile to my face as I finished my personal hygiene rituals. I dressed in jeans and an Avalanche sweatshirt, dried my hair and pulled it into a loose braid and smoothed some Aloe-Vera gel over the cuts on the side of my face.

When I came out of the bathroom Michael was gone, but Kate was there all smiles, looking adorable as always, making my bed for me.

"Morning," she said happily. "You look like you got some sleep."

"I did," I said. "Where's Michael?"

"He went home to shower. He'll be back in a few minutes."

After helping her make my bed, we went to the kitchen where Miles was reading the paper at the table.

"Morning." He smiled sweetly.

I kissed his cheek and went to the stereo, turning on a Lenny Kravitz CD to accompany us while we made stuffed French toast, scrambled eggs and bacon. Kate and I sang along with Lenny as he asked, '*Are you gonna go my way?*' It was difficult for Miles to focus on the newspaper because he was laughing.

Garrett arrived first, poured himself some orange juice and sat at the table with Miles. Then Michael came in, and I strode over to him quickly.

"Well, good morning to you, too." He laughed, hugging me tightly, and I sighed, enjoying feeling his arms around me.

"Good morning," I said.

He kissed my forehead tenderly, and then kissed along the scratches on my face before meeting my eyes with a warm smile.

"You look better," he said. "How'd you sleep?"

"No bad dreams," I told him. "I slept great. What about you?"

He took both of my hands in his and shrugged. "Are you kidding? I was with you. I've never slept better."

I eyed him skeptically, and he smirked. "Let's go eat some breakfast. I'm hungry."

He took my hand, pulling me to the kitchen. I poured him some coffee and he sat down in his usual spot while Kate and I put breakfast on the table. We all had a very enjoyable breakfast together, all things considered. Everyone helped do the dishes, and we were done quickly, all of us sitting at the table, drinking our coffee when Will and Ava arrived. I scooted away from the table quickly and ran to meet them, hugging Ava's neck.

"I'm so glad you're here," I told her.

Will held his arms open with a big smile, waiting for me to hug him. I laughed and embraced him tightly. When the greetings were finished, Will and Ava sat down at the kitchen table, and I poured them both a cup of coffee while casual conversation was made about the boys' business trip to Florida.

The conversation switched to Nina, and I sipped my coffee uncomfortably while Michael began to fill in Will and Ava about the phone call from the police and the discussion last night. Michael's arm wound tighter and tighter around my waist as he talked about wanting to leave in order to keep me safe. Ava's eyes were sad and Will's were concerned, as they listened to their son.

Will assured the boys that they were doing everything they could, and that unfortunately, until Nina was found we would just have to be patient. Patient and cautious.

Chapter Twenty-Six

Will and Ava stayed at the boy's house, and Garrett stayed on our couch. It was after midnight, and since I really didn't want to sleep, I turned on "Pride and Prejudice" and watched as poor Mr. Darcy tried to tell Elizabeth that he loved her 'most ardently'.

My cell phone vibrated, and I retrieved it from the nightstand quickly and read the text from Michael: *Hey.*

I smiled as I responded: *Hey, yourself.*

His response was quick: *Are you asleep?*

I giggled. *Yes. I'm sleep-texting.*

Very funny. Why are you awake?

Why are you awake?

I miss you.

I smiled as I responded: *I miss you, too. Aren't you sleepy?*

Nope. What are you doing?

Watching Pride and Prejudice.

Ah, poor Mr. Darcy.

Would you like to come watch it with me?

It took a while for his response. *I'd better decline that offer.*

I frowned, because I really wanted to be with him. After a moment, he sent another text: *Are you pouting?*

How did he know? *Are you laughing because I'm pouting?*

Yes.

"Hmph," I grumbled as I typed a response. *Well if you're not going to come and watch the movie with me, what will you do?*

I'll just think of you watching the movie in your pink flannel pajamas.

I rolled my eyes. *I'm not wearing the pink flannel PJs, I'm wearing sweats and Elway tee-shirt.*

Hmm, that's even better.

Hah. Okay.

Good night, my Grace.

Good night.

I released a sigh and focused on Mr. Darcy. *"...But one word from you will silence me forever. If, however, your feelings have changed, I will have to tell you...you have bewitched me body and soul, and I love-I love-I love you. And I never wish to be parted from you from this day on."*

My eyes were heavy, and I looked at the clock—it was after one, but I didn't want to sleep. I put another movie in the player and fought sleep as long as I could.

* * *

Muffled voices came from the kitchen, and I fought to open my eyes. I wasn't sure what time it was when I'd finally fallen asleep, but I knew it was after five. I rolled over slowly and groaned, draping my arm over my eyes. I heard a quiet chuckle and sprang up quickly—my heart thudding.

"I'm sorry." Michael was sitting in the chair next to my bed, looking half-worried, half amused and completely gorgeous.

"Holy crap," I muttered and flopped back onto my pillow, pulling the covers over my head.

He laughed. "I didn't mean to scare you."

"Yeah," I mumbled. "You always say that."

He tugged on the covers, but I held them tight.

"Would you please let me look at you?"

I could hear the amusement in his voice. "No."

"Why not?"

"Because I'm a mess."

"You're beautiful."

"Very funny," I argued. "How long have you been sitting there?"

"Um, since about six-thirty."

I moved the covers slightly so I could see the clock. He'd been there for almost two hours.

"Grace," he pleaded. "C'mon, I want to see your face."

He tugged gently on the covers, and I relented, letting go and covering my face with my hands. He pulled me by my arms until I was upright. I lowered my hands just below my eyes so I could see him. As usual, he was so stunning it made my heart ache.

"It's not fair," I complained, my words muffled through my hands.

"What?"

"That you can look so…good…this early in the morning."

He rolled his eyes and pulled me onto his lap. I buried my face in his neck as he rubbed my back softly.

"Good morning," he said with a chuckle. "Why don't you get your shower? Mom's making breakfast." I started to get up, but he held onto me, studying my face carefully. "What time did you go to sleep last night?"

I shrugged, but he narrowed his eyes at me.

"The last time I looked at the clock it was after five." I kept my hand over my mouth as I spoke. "I'm not sure exactly."

He grimaced and pulled my hand away from my mouth, rubbing underneath my eyes with his thumbs, shaking his head sadly. I stood up, going to my dresser to pull out my clothes for the day, as he walked toward my door.

He smiled weakly. "I'll see you out there."

I nodded, and he pulled the door closed behind him. I started the shower and looked at myself in the mirror.

Now I was really embarrassed. The scratches on my face were just…ugly. The bruise under my eye was a deep shade of purple, and both eyes were puffy and red.

"Fright night," I muttered.

After my shower, I got dressed in my favorite jeans and a black pullover. I dried my hair straight, and attempted to cover the circles under my eyes with makeup. This was not easily done. After making my bed and picking up the bathroom, I clasped on my necklace.

When I came into the hallway, Michael was leaning against the wall by my door, smiling his crooked grin as he surveyed my appearance.

"Hmm," he said thoughtfully.

"What?" I smoothed my shirt nervously, his gaze causing my heart to pound.

"I just wonder if I'll ever look at you and not think you're the most beautiful thing I've ever seen."

I snorted a laugh, and he narrowed his eyes at me.

"I've thought that about you since the first time I saw you," I confessed. "I'm pretty sure I'll always think you're the most beautiful thing I've ever seen."

He raised an eyebrow quizzically. "Beautiful?"

"Sorry." I shrugged. "It's the only word that fits."

I didn't give him a chance to respond as I pulled him by the hand, and we joined the others in the kitchen area. Kate was cutting up strawberries, and Ava flipped pancakes at the stove. I made a cup of coffee for Michael and myself while he sat at the table with his brothers and Will.

I set the table for breakfast, listening to everyone chatter. When we were done eating, Michael helped me with the dishes, and we returned to the table to continue visiting. While we talked, the doorbell rang. I tensed, and Michael rubbed my shoulders soothingly while Garrett and Will went to the front door.

"I'm terribly sorry for disturbing you."

Michael and Miles seemed to recognize the voice as they pushed away from the table quickly. Kate, Ava and I followed them to the entryway. A very well dressed, silver-haired man stood at the door.

"I know I'm one of the last people you would like to see right now," the man said. "But I was hoping to speak with all of you. Just for a moment."

The tension emanating from the boys was palpable as they stood, expressions angry, glaring at the man in the doorway. Garrett's muscles were flexed, hands in fists, and jaw clenched tight. I couldn't understand why they were all so angry.

"There's nothing you have to say that we want to hear," Garrett said.

The man held his hands up in front of him in a defensive gesture.

"Please," he said calmly. "I can't blame you. But I really need to talk to you, just for a moment."

The boys all looked at Will, and he cleared his throat as he took a step toward the man.

"Mr. Sandler," Will began, and my stomach knotted as Kate stepped beside me, squeezing my hand in hers.

"Surely you understand our discomfort." Will spoke calmly. "Your daughter has been seen here in town."

"Yes," Mr. Sandler said. "That's why I've come to see you. Please, may I come in?"

The boys looked to Will, and he nodded to the man. Michael squeezed one of my hands, while Kate held the other, and we all followed Mr. Sandler and Will into the living room.

"Please, sit down." Will motioned to the sofa.

The man nodded and unbuttoned his thick wool coat before sitting down. The rest of us stood, almost in a single-file line, in front of him. He was clearly as uncomfortable as we were, but he kept eye contact with each of the boys as he spoke.

"I can't even begin to express how very sorry I am for what my daughter has done, and I know that there is nothing I can do to make amends."

Michael wound his arm around my waist, pulling me close to his side.

"Please understand, although I know there is nothing I can do to change what she's done, I felt I had to do whatever I could to help. That's why I'm here. Unfortunately, it's to caution you." He paused for a moment. "She won't stop."

The following silence was unsettling. Mr. Sandler cleared his throat nervously.

"I know my daughter, and she won't stop." His eyes roamed to where I stood, and I felt nauseous because I knew what he was going to say. "She won't stop until she finishes what she started."

Garrett and Michael both stepped in front of me, and Garrett muttered something unintelligible under his breath. Mr. Sandler continued, so much sadness in his voice.

"I knew something wasn't right. She's always been such a phenomenal businesswoman—a true asset to our company—but over the last two years, something changed." His voice began to shake. "I don't know what happened, but she became more aggressive, more violent."

"So why didn't you get her some kind of help?" Michael asked, his tone hard.

"We tried," he replied. "We sent her to a…place in California for eight weeks. When she came home everything seemed fine for a while, but then it started again."

Michael tightened his grip on my hand as I took a small step away from him. I wanted to see Mr. Sandler. His face was worn with deep lines around his eyes. I could tell that at one time, he was probably very handsome. Right now, though, he looked tired and grief-stricken.

"Please believe me," he pleaded. "If I ever thought for a moment she was capable of something so terrible, I would've put her away myself. I never thought she'd resort to anything like this."

When I looked at this man, I didn't see Nina Sandler's father. I just saw a father. A father heartbroken over choices his daughter made, choices out of his control. I didn't feel nauseous anymore. I only felt pity for the man sitting in front of us, devastated and broken.

I pushed my way between Michael and Garrett and sat next to Mr. Sandler, folding my hands in my lap. He was startled by my sudden appearance, but then his eyes became pained, and he pursed his lips tightly.

"I'm so very sorry," his bottom lip quivered as he spoke. "If there's anything I can do, for you or your family—"

"This isn't your fault, Mr. Sandler," I said quietly. "I don't blame you. None of us do."

Michael watched me worriedly as I tried to offer comfort to the stranger.

"I wanted to tell you," Mr. Sandler said to Will. "I don't believe she's been in town recently."

"The Denver P.D. called us—" Kate started to say, but he interrupted her.

"Yes, I know, but I received a call from Nina just yesterday. The police traced her call. She was somewhere in Mexico."

"Mexico?" Garrett said skeptically. "No offense, sir, but why should we believe you?"

"Garrett." I felt badly that Garrett was still so angry with this man, but Mr. Sandler patted my knee in a fatherly gesture.

"I understand. I don't expect you to trust me. I do know she'll be back. She will." He looked over at me. "You need to be careful. I don't know what she'll do, but I do know she won't stop." Remorse had taken over his voice as he turned to Michael. "That's all I wanted to tell you. To warn you to be careful."

Michael nodded, and Mr. Sandler turned to me, his face worn with grief.

"It's the strangest thing," tears glossed his eyes, "when I see her, I just see my little girl."

The sympathy I felt for him had taken over, and tears filled my eyes, too. "But she's not my little girl. Not anymore. I don't know who she is anymore."

I hesitantly placed my hand on his shoulder. "Mr. Sandler," I said quietly. "I'm so sorry."

His expression was puzzled, the pain on his face overwhelming. "After what she did to you, and you're trying to comfort me?"

I felt terrible for him, and I couldn't imagine what he must be going through.

"That just makes what my daughter did even worse. I'm the one who is sorry." He patted my knee again before standing. "I've hired several private investigators, and my wife and I are working very closely with the police. We want her found."

"But she has unlimited funds," Garrett said. "She could be anywhere."

"I've closed all of her accounts, cancelled her credit cards. She may have had a stash of cash, but that won't last forever." He put his hands into the pockets of the heavy coat he was wearing. "Her mother and I have accepted the likelihood of never seeing our daughter again. We'd try to help her if we could. She's our child, and we still love her. How can you stop loving your child?" He shook his head sadly. "But she must be held responsible for her actions." He took a business card from his pocket and handed it to Will. "Please. If there's anything I can do for any of you, anything at all, please don't hesitate to call."

"Thank you." Will nodded. "And you'll ask the police to keep us informed if you hear anything?"

"Of course," Mr. Sandler assured him. "Feel free to call anytime. My cell number is on there, as well."

We followed him to the front door, and he turned to face us before stepping outside.

"Thank you," he said. "I know I haven't been much help, but I felt I needed to do something. I don't want her to hurt anyone else."

I stepped to him, putting my hand out, and he shook it gently.

"Thank you, Mr. Sandler," I said. "We all know this can't be easy for you or your wife. Thank you for coming."

He patted my hand with a weak smile. "You stay safe," he said. "Please. Stay safe."

I nodded, and he turned to leave, Garrett closing the door behind him.

"I feel terrible for him," I said quietly.

Garrett draped his arm over my shoulder. "You're somethin' else, Gracie, you know that?" He kissed the top of my head. "Somethin' else."

Everyone retreated to the living room in silence. Kate sat beside me, her forehead creased with worry. "So what do we do now?"

Everyone looked at Will, including myself.

"There's really nothing we can do," Will replied. "Nothing's changed."

"Except Mr. Sandler just verified what we already knew," Miles' tone was somber. "Nina is crazy."

It was quiet for a moment, and then Garrett cleared his throat. "Gracie, do you still want to stay?"

"What do you mean?" I was confused by his question.

"Well, you heard him," he said. "Nina's not going to stop. Maybe we should rethink Michael's idea of New York."

I shook my head, and Michael sighed in frustration as he began to pace, but I ignored him. Mr. Sandler didn't tell me anything I didn't already know, and I had no intention of running.

"If we run away, she wins," I said. "And I don't want her to win."

Garrett nodded approvingly. "That's my girl."

Michael watched me with an unreadable expression on his face and then walked over to Will.

"So you think we should stay?" he asked. I'm sure he hoped Will would disagree, but Will put his hands on Michael's shoulders and nodded with surety.

"Okay." Michael sighed. "But we can't let our guard down. Things are going to stay the way they have been until Nina is caught. No going anywhere alone. Any of us."

Everyone nodded in agreement.

"Your mother and I have decided to stay for a while," Will told him. "It will be better if we're all together."

I smiled. If I had my way, Will and Ava would live with us. Michael hugged his dad, and I knew Will and Ava's presence was a comfort to everyone, not just me. I warred internally with what I'd wanted to tell them and decided now was as good a time as any.

"Um…may I say something?" my voice was quiet.

Michael eyed me cautiously—clearly uneasy about whatever I was going to say.

"What is it, Grace?" Miles asked with a smile.

I took a deep breath. "I want to go back to work. It's been weeks, and I'm ready to go back."

Everyone watched as I fidgeted in my seat, and Michael glared at me with what was either shock or anger, I couldn't tell which.

Garrett broke the silence. "I'm not sure that's a good idea."

"What's the difference in being here or being at the shop? I won't be alone. Kate and I will be together." Michael's expression hadn't changed when I looked at him. "And I know you'll be with me. Miles and Garrett, too. I don't think Nina will come to the shop again."

"She's insane, Grace," Michael argued. "She'll go anywhere she can get to you easily. I don't like it."

My stomach tightened into a sick knot. "If she wants me bad enough, it won't matter."

"Gracie," Kate shook her head sadly. "Please don't say that."

I squeezed her hand tightly. "I'm sorry, but it's true and you all know it."

Michael kneeled in front of me, the worry in his eyes almost painful.

"I'm scared. I really am," I said. "But, I might as well try to get on with my life the best way I can, instead of just sitting here waiting for her to decide when she's ready. I don't want her to have that power. She already has too much power as it is."

"Grace," Miles said sweetly. "We understand what you're saying, but you have to understand why we are worried about this."

“I understand.” I smiled at him. “I’m worried, too. But like I said, if she’s going to come for me, it’s not going to matter where I am.”

Michael stood and pulled me off the couch, wrapping his arms around me tightly. It was such a quick movement it took my breath away. I could feel the fear and worry rolling off of him as I wound my arms around him, resting my head on his chest.

“Did you hear what her own father said?” Michael asked. “He said she’s not going to stop.”

I’d always known she wouldn’t stop. Since the day I woke up in the hospital, and Michael told me Nina had gotten away. I knew then she wouldn’t stop and all this time I’d been afraid.

“I heard him, Michael,” I said quietly. “But I’m tired of being afraid.

Chapter Twenty-Seven

That night, I resisted the urge to beg Michael to stay with me as he kissed me good night on the front porch. I slept so much better when he was with me, but I just couldn't bring myself to ask, and he needed his sleep, too.

I got ready for bed slowly, brushing my teeth an extra-long time and doing the same with my hair. When I was done with things to do in the bathroom, I trudged to my bedroom and decided to alphabetize my CDs. While I worked on this project, I put on some music and hummed along with Norah Jones.

When I finished, I'd only killed an hour so I decided to watch a movie. Unsure of what to watch, I closed my eyes and ran my finger back and forth over the DVDs and stopped on one randomly. I snorted a laugh when I saw what I'd inadvertently chosen—"Fatal Attraction".

I dropped it into the trash. No matter how good Glenn Close's performance, the subject matter hit a little too close to home. I pulled another random case from the shelf—"Fiddler on the Roof". This movie always made me smile, especially since I watched it with Garrett, and he referred to the fiddler as the 'creepy dude with a violin'. I slid the movie into the player and started pulling pillows off my bed while I danced to the opening credits. My phone vibrated, and I snatched it from the bedside table quickly to read Michael's message:

Hey.

I glanced at the clock. It was after one. *Hey, why are you awake?*

Why are you awake?

I snorted a laugh as I typed. *I've decided sleep is overrated.*

You need to sleep.

So do you.

I pictured him raking his hand through his hair in frustration, and I smiled as I waited for his response.

What are you doing?

I just organized my CDs and now I'm watching "Fiddler on the Roof".

You organized your CDs?

I knew he'd have something to say about that. *Yes I did.*

And how did you organize them? Alphabetically?

I grimaced. How did he know? *Yes. What of it?*

Are you OCD?

I thought for a minute. Kate and I often laughed about the fact we probably were a little OCD. Before I could answer him, the phone vibrated with a message: *Are you trying to decide whether or not you're OCD?*

I laughed as I typed. *You think you're so smart. Are you laughing at me?*

Yes, you're adorable.

I rolled my eyes. *So are you just going to make fun of me? Or are you going to come over and watch the movie with me?*

Make fun of you.

Very funny.

Yes, you are.

Fine.

Sweetheart, please go to sleep.

I heaved a sigh. *I'll try.*

Promise?

I winced. I was tired, but I didn't want to sleep, and I definitely didn't want to make a promise I couldn't keep. My phone vibrated while I debated.

Are you still there?

No. I'm sleeping.

Oh, you're hilarious.

I actually thought that was pretty funny. Maybe Garrett's sense of humor was rubbing off on me.

Fine. I promise I'll try to sleep.

I love you, my Grace, good night.

I giggled as I typed the last message: *Night. And I love you. More.*

I set the phone on my night table, but it vibrated again and I grabbed it quickly, reading his signature response to that statement. *Hmm.*

I plugged the phone into the charger, climbing under the covers as I watched my movie. As usual, tears came during the "Chava Ballet Sequence", Tevye grieving because his daughter had turned her back on him.

I thought of Mr. Sandler.

That night I woke up twice. Not from nightmares, but from dreams.

In the first dream Mr. Sandler wandered around a children's playground. His silver hair reflected the sun in shimmers, his eyes were wide with panic, and his voice was devastatingly desperate as he called for his little girl.

His little girl was lost.

I wanted to help him find his little girl, but my voice wouldn't carry and my feet wouldn't move.

The second dream was much worse. This time Nina stood in front of her father as he called her name, over and over as if she were lost. He searched desperately but couldn't recognize her, as she stood there unseen, not answering and not moving. Tears fell as he called her name over and over. This time when I called his name, he seemed to hear me. His expression anguished as he turned to me.

"Grace," he pleaded. "Please stay safe. Please."

I cried silently and thought about Mr. Sandler, his broken heart and words of warning. The images were heartbreaking, difficult to dispel and kept me from sleep. By the time I got out of bed, I'd had less than two hours of sleep and my eyes were as puffy and red as usual.

Much too exhausted to put any effort into my clothing selection or my hair, I showered and dressed in yoga pants and pink Colorado sweatshirt, pulling my hair into a ponytail. My feet dragged as I straightened my bathroom and made my bed. When I came into the kitchen, Kate shook her head sadly as she took in my appearance.

"I think you should call Dr. Murphy. I'm not sure you should wait for an appointment. You need some serious sleep, your injury wasn't that long ago, and your body is going to shut down."

I heard what she was saying, knowing she was right, but I didn't want to sleep. I was afraid to sleep.

We decided to make breakfast for everyone. Blueberry muffins, bacon, poached eggs and potato heaven, which is leftover mashed potatoes made into small pancakes, dipped in flour and fried in butter. Not healthy, but oh-so-heavenly, hence the name.

Just as Kate was pulling the muffins from the oven, the Andersons filed in. I ran to Michael, I couldn't help myself.

"Hey." He hugged me tightly, but when he tried to set me down, I didn't loosen my hold on his neck. "Grace?"

His voice was worried, so I let go. He studied my face. With a sigh he pulled me to him, resting his head on mine. As he held me, my body relaxed, my mind cleared, and I felt safe.

"We made you breakfast," I said as I pulled him toward the kitchen, not giving him a chance to say anything. I knew we'd be discussing it later anyway. He kept his eyes on me as I poured him some coffee and led him to the table.

Everyone ate their breakfast, and as usual the chatter was non-stop, different conversations going on at once. Garrett draped his arm over my shoulder and hugged me to him.

"You look tired, Gracie," he said. "How'd you sleep?"

I just leaned my head against him and shrugged. It was quiet, and I flushed because everyone was watching me.

"She didn't sleep," Kate said.

"I'm fine," I said quietly.

"I think we should call Dr. Murphy," Kate said. "Her body's going to shut down if she doesn't get some sleep. I told her this, but she tends to be a little stubborn."

I felt a twinge of anger with her comment.

"I didn't argue with you, Kate!" I lashed out, defending myself, and not recognizing my own voice.

Kate's expression changed, confused by my reaction. As quickly as the anger came, it left even quicker, and I felt intense guilt because of my words. Garrett tightened his arm around me, and I looked down at my plate, which was still filled with food because I'd hardly eaten.

My throat tightened. I didn't mean to be ugly with her. She was just looking out for me and I knew that.

"Grace," Ava said softly. "Why don't you go lie down, you're exhausted."

Garrett kissed the top of my head, and I got up from the table slowly.

"I'm sorry, everyone." I walked around to Kate, and she stood from the table. The sadness on her face did it. I clung to her and bawled. I was exhausted and emotionally drained. She hugged me as I told her I was sorry again and again.

"It's okay," she whispered.

Michael took my hand, and I released Kate reluctantly and followed him to my room. Kate pulled the pillows from my bed, and I laid down. Kate covered me with a quilt and brushed the hair from my face.

"I'm so sorry, Kate," I cried. "I'm sorry for talking to you that way."

"It's okay." She tried to smile. "Can I get you anything?"

I shook my head, and she started to leave when Michael said something to her quietly. The door closed and he pulled the chair close to my bed. He kissed me and I breathed in a staggered breath trying to make myself relax. I wanted his arms around me, but I was too embarrassed to ask.

He stood up and I panicked.

"Don't go." I grabbed his hand, and he sat back down quickly.

"Grace, I was just going to turn on your music. I'm not going anywhere." His expression became anguished. "What happened last night? Was it a nightmare?"

I shook my head. "No. I think it was worse."

I wasn't really sure it was worse than the nightmares, and I considered maybe I was just over-exhausted. I pushed myself up so I was sitting, and Michael's expression didn't change as he kept his eyes on me. I told him about the disturbing dreams of Mr. Sandler. I hiccoughed as I tried to talk through my sobs, Michael's helpless expression making me feel even worse.

"Grace," his voice was quiet. "I wish you'd said something last night. I would've come and stayed with you."

"I wanted you to, but I can't expect you to be here just because I'm having bad dreams. I feel so ridiculously needy all the time."

"Never apologize for needing me." He held my hands tightly. "There's a difference in being needy and needing someone because you love them."

I was pretty sure there was no difference.

"You're strong, independent, intelligent," he said. "You have a degree, you own a business, you own a home—you don't *need* anything. Just because you feel the need to have me with you as much as possible because you love me makes *me* feel needed. And everyone wants to feel needed, Grace."

It never ceased to amaze me how he always knew the right thing to say, at the right time. Every time it happened, I felt like I needed to empty my heart of the love I had for him, to make room for more. My heart wasn't big enough. Maybe that's why it pounded and fluttered when I was with him. It had to adjust to make more room.

We watched TV together for a while, cuddling in the overstuffed chair. I was almost asleep when Kate poked her head inside my room.

"Evan's here to see you," she said.

I assumed Michael and Kate were the reason he was here, but I didn't mind. I always enjoyed seeing Evan. When we got to the living room, Evan was talking intently with Garrett. When he saw me, his forehead creased as he walked toward me.

"Hi." I smiled. "It's great to see you."

"Hey." He hugged me tightly, then stepped back, studying my face. "It's great to see you, too."

He was clearly focused on the fact that I looked like one of the walking dead from any chosen zombie movie. He greeted Michael and then took me by the hand, leading me to the sofa where I sat next to Kate. Evan got comfortable on the floor in front of me, while Michael stood behind him, folding his arms across his chest.

"Well," Evan shook his head, "I'm not gonna lie. You're looking rough."

I scowled at him as everyone chuckled.

"Talk to me." Evan's expression became serious as he folded his hands in his lap. "What's going on?"

"I can't sleep." I twisted my fingers nervously, and Evan raised an eyebrow skeptically.

"Can't sleep? Or won't sleep?"

He glanced at Garrett, and I surmised he already knew the answer. Kate wrapped her arm around my waist, and I felt like I was the focus of some kind of intervention. Everyone waiting for me to 'take the first step and admit I have a problem'.

"It's okay, Grace, Garrett already told me."

I nodded.

"Unfortunately, I can't write you a prescription," he said regretfully. "I could get into some serious trouble for that, because you're technically not under my care. I did put in a call to Doc Murphy, and he called something in for you as a favor to me. But he wants to see you this week."

"Thanks, Evan," I said. "Sorry you had to come here just for this."

I could see Michael rolling his eyes, but Evan smiled widely.

"I didn't come just for this." He smirked. "I came to ask Ava to feed me."

Garrett guffawed, and everyone laughed.

"Seriously," Evan said quietly. "Promise me you'll see Doc Murphy. This week. Promise?"

"I promise."

He patted my knee as he stood up.

"Come on, Evan," Ava smiled. "We just finished breakfast, but I'm sure I can find something for you."

He grinned. "If you insist."

I had to smile as I watched him. He winked at me and followed the others into the kitchen. Michael sat down next to me, and I rested my head against his shoulder.

"Are you okay?" He asked.

"I guess," I sighed. "I just wish this whole thing would be over. I wanted to go to work tomorrow, but I can't go like this."

"I know, but the shop isn't going anywhere. It will be there when you're ready."

I thought I was ready.

"Are you hungry?" he asked. "You hardly ate any breakfast."

"No." I shook my head. "Just tired."

Michael took my hand and pulled me from the couch, and everyone gave me a small wave, as Michael led me to my room. I lay down, and he covered me with my quilt, kissing my forehead softly.

"Do you want me to stay until you fall asleep?"

"I'll be okay." My eyes were heavy, and I knew I would be asleep soon.

"I'm just going to visit with Evan for a little while," he said. "I'll be right here when you wake up."He leaned down, kissing softly along my jaw until I could feel his breath on my ear, and I shivered. He chuckled. "I love you, my Grace."

I swore when I was more coherent, I was going to ask him why he always laughed when he kissed me.

* * *

When I opened my eyes, I could hear laughter coming from the kitchen. I rolled over, expecting to see Michael sitting in my chair, but it was empty. I doubted Evan was still out there. I'd slept too long.

I got out of bed, groggily making my way toward the kitchen. It was suddenly quiet. Eerily quiet. A knot formed in my stomach as I came around the corner, and the kitchen was empty, only the remnants of a meal remained. Dirty dishes were stacked in the sink, and coffee cups were lined around the table where everyone had been sitting. I walked slowly, surveying the mess I knew Kate, or Ava, would never have left. I shook my head in an attempt to clear the haze that seemed to be clouding my vision.

The sickening knot was now full-blown nausea, and my heart pounded as I accepted the fact I was having a nightmare.

Deciding I wasn't going to play the sick game my mind had in store for me, I turned quickly and returned to my room, closing the door and locking it behind me. My breathing was labored as I backed against the wall by the window and waited. Waited to wake up.

The doorknob turned, and I swallowed hard, knowing I'd locked it. It kept turning, and the door opened slowly. I closed my eyes tightly, knowing who I was going to see. Moisture formed on my forehead and neckline, my heart pounding like a jackhammer. I opened my eyes.

"You're all alone, Grace."

Nina stood in my doorway, wearing the same white ruffled dress she'd worn in my dream last night. Now it was smeared with blood. Her hands were empty, but she extended them toward me showing me the blood that stained her palms and fingers. I covered my mouth, feeling like I had to vomit.

"They're *all* gone." She smiled and shook her head in disdain. "You didn't deserve them anyway."

The bile rose in my throat, but I swallowed it down as anger stirred deep inside me. A hot, burning, fiery anger caused me physical pain. Tears escape my eyes as I stared at her, her face expressionless, her eyes emotionless.

"I'm not afraid of you," I growled between my clenched teeth.

She tilted her head slightly and continued to smile. "Oh," she said sweetly, "of course you are."

I didn't want her words to be true, but they rang in my ears, making me feel even weaker than I already felt. I looked around for something I could use to inflict pain on her. I spotted a large crystal vase on the shelf next to me, which was once full of pink roses from Michael.

Michael.

She'd hurt him if she had a chance. She would hurt everyone I loved if she had the chance. I wasn't going to give her the chance. I quickly pulled the vase from the shelf and smashed it hard against the shelf. The sound of shattering glass echoed in my ears as the vase splintered into a hundred pieces. I retrieved two large, ragged shards from the floor. They cut into my hands as I gripped them but ignored the pain. I didn't care about my pain.

I wanted her to feel pain.

"You aren't going to hurt me anymore," I told her. "I won't let you."

She tossed her head back as she laughed and pointed at my hands. I looked down at my hands, and my eyes blurred as blood dripped from my palms.

"You see?" she continued to point at my bleeding hands. "I *am* hurting you."

Her words became an echo in my head, over and over, and I knew they were true. Not because of the blood, but because of everything that had happened. Everything she caused.

The anger. The pain. The fear. She was hurting me.

I screamed in anger, dropping the pieces of glass to the floor. I closed my eyes and clamped my hands over my ears, trying to stop the sound of her voice from ringing in my ears. *I am hurting you…I am hurting you.* I slid down the wall, my body shuddering uncontrollably from sobs. I brought my knees to my chest, feeling the burn from the cuts in my hands I'd inflicted on myself.

There was a banging on my door. Someone was trying to get into my room, but I didn't move. I wondered if I was awake or asleep and kept my eyes still closed.

"Gracie!"

I heard Kate and was lifted from the floor.

"She's bleeding!"

Garrett's voice rang in my ear, and I realized I was in his arms, being carried.

"Get some towels."

Now Evan's voice. I wondered if I was in the hospital again.

"Gracie, wake up!" Garrett's voice was panicked. "Dammit, Gracie! Wake up, right now!"

I opened my eyes and saw Michael's face as he tried frantically to find where the blood was coming from. I was trembling, and Garrett was holding me to him tightly. I held out my hands to Michael, and his eyes widened.

"It's her hands," he said. "They're cut."

"Grace," Evan said sternly. "Look at me."

I didn't want to look away from Michael, and my eyes were heavy as I tried to find Evan. He took my face in his hands.

"Can you hear me?" Evan asked.

"I hear."

"Where are you hurt? Is it just your hands?"

"Yes. I broke the vase."

I heard Kate crying and felt remorse.

"Kate, please don't cry." I felt like I'd been drugged. My eyes didn't want to stay open. Garrett kept me in his arms as he sat down in one of the kitchen chairs.

"Grace." Evan was making me look at him again. "Why did you break the vase?"

I swallowed hard as tears came down my face. "I told her I wasn't going to let her hurt me anymore." I saw the blood on my hands. "But she did, and I let her."

Garrett muttered something and squeezed me to him again.

"Garrett, let me check her hands," Evan said calmly. "They may need stitches."

Panic came over me as I processed what was said.

"Evan, please don't make me go to the hospital," I pleaded. "They'll think I'm crazy. Please?"

"It's okay, Grace," he said soothingly. "Honey, you're not crazy. You're just exhausted. You're going to be fine, okay?" He looked to Garrett. "But I gotta say, I'd like to get my own hands on this Nina chick right about now."

Garrett said something to him, but I couldn't make it out.

Evan began cleaning the blood from my hands, and I winced with pain as the sting of antiseptic washed over my palms. Ava assisted Evan, as Garrett held me in his arms, my head tight against his chest. Will, Kate and Miles were huddled together, watching with pained expressions, as Kate wiped away tears. Michael seemed angry; his jaw clenched tight and his face red as he focused on Evan tending to my self-inflicted wounds.

"Michael?"

His eyes softened as he tried to brush away the hair that clung to my forehead from sweat.

"I saw her in my room. I'm sorry," I said. "Please don't be angry with me." My words sounded mushy, and my eyes wanted to close. His eyes glossed over, and he pressed his lips against my forehead intensely.

"Of course I'm not angry with you," he whispered against my forehead. He continued to stroke my hair as he looked at Garrett with an unreadable expression.

"Why does this keep happening?" Garrett asked, his voice vibrating in my ear. "I can't stand this—" Garrett's voice hitched, and once again, he tightened his hold on me, but I kept my eyes on Michael.

"There's a lot of blood," Evan said calmly. "But the cuts are clean, and they're not deep. Miles, will you go to the drugstore and get these things for me?"

Evan scratched something on a pad of paper, and Miles took it without saying a word, he and Will leaving quickly.

"I'm so sleepy," I murmured not sure anyone could even hear me.

"I know, Gracie," Garrett said. "But you have blood all over you—we have to get you cleaned and bandaged first, okay?"

Ava took two large dishtowels, wrapping one around each hand.

"Keep the towels wrapped around her hands, and she can get cleaned up," Evan told Kate. "When you're finished we'll dress the wounds. Miles will be back by then."

Garrett carried me out of the kitchen, following Kate. When we got to the bathroom, I could hear the shower running.

"I'm going to set you down," Garrett said softly.

I nodded, and my feet touched the floor. I was dizzy, but I leaned against the bathroom vanity. Garrett's white shirt was drenched with my blood, and I shook my head, ashamed.

"I ruined your shirt," my voice shook.

His eyes were sad as he leaned down so his face was close to mine.

"It's okay, Gracie." He kissed the top of my head and then turned to leave.

Michael stood in the doorway, his shirt had blood on it too, but not nearly as much as Garrett's.

"I'll be waiting out here." His expression made me feel even worse than I already did.

He closed the door, and Kate pulled the elastic band from my hair gently.

"You've got blood in your hair. We need to wash it, okay?"

I just nodded and climbed into the shower. Kate shampooed my hair while I leaned against the shower wall, the water turning a pale shade of red as the blood rinsed away. The towels wrapped around my hands made it difficult to move. I wasn't sure I wanted to move anyway. My body felt like gelatin. Kate took a washcloth and rubbed it gently over my face as she cried silently.

"Kate, please don't cry," I told her. "I'm okay."

She shook her head as she turned off the water. "No," she said sadly. "You're not okay."

I felt nauseous as her words hit me. I wasn't okay. I was a neurotic, pathetic mess. Kate wrapped a towel around me as I stepped out of the shower.

"You think I'm crazy." I wasn't asking. I wanted affirmation for what I knew was true.

"I don't think you're crazy. I just know you're not okay, and you won't be okay until Nina is caught. She's done this to you. You're not crazy."

When Kate opened the bathroom door, Michael was waiting for me, his expression anxious. I strode over to him, trying not to touch his now clean shirt with the damp towels still wrapped around my hands. He held me tightly and led me to the chair, pulling me onto his lap. I rested my head on his shoulder, barely able to keep my eyes open.

I hadn't noticed Evan standing there, unrolling gauze and cutting it into long strips. He looked over at me and tried to smile.

"How do you feel?"

"Sleepy."

He nodded, and Kate unwrapped the towels from my hands. The once white towels now stained red with my blood. I could see the singular cuts that ran along each of my palms diagonally. I closed my eyes while Kate and Evan dressed my wounds with more antiseptic and some kind of cream, and then wrapped my hands with gauze. After they finished, Evan patted my hands, and I opened my eyes.

He smiled. "How's that?"

I looked at the sterile white bandages that wound around my palms. Evan leaned down in front of Michael and me, patting my knee.

"I want you to sleep," he said.

I smiled and reached my bandaged hand to his. He squeezed it gently with a smile.

"Thank you, Evan."

He kissed my hand sweetly.

"You're welcome."Evan looked at Michael. "She needs to sleep."

"Thank you so much," he said. "I'm glad you were here."

"Me too," Evan smiled. "Do you think Ava will let me eat now?"

They both laughed, and I sat up straight in Michael's lap.

"What's wrong?" he asked.

I was confused by what Evan had said. "H-how long was I asleep?"

Michael's eyes shifted to Evan, and then to me again. "Grace, you weren't even asleep ten minutes," he said softly. "That's why I wasn't here. You'd just fallen asleep."

I swallowed hard and shook my head. It had seemed like hours.

"When your body is worn down," Evan said, "it doesn't take long for your mind to follow. You're exhausted, Grace. Physically, mentally and emotionally. I don't think you've really grasped what this whole thing has done to you. I know I'm just an E.R. doc," he said with a smirk, "but you need to listen to me."

I noticed then that everyone was standing at my door, listening to what Evan was saying.

"Miles picked up your prescription, but you look like you could sleep without it right now."

"Probably," I agreed.

"Well, don't take it unless you really need it," he cautioned. "It's some heavy stuff, okay?"

"Thanks, Evan."

He smiled as he turned to leave, and I laid my head against Michael's shoulder again, listening to Ava tell Evan she had a plate ready for him in the kitchen.

"Gracie?" I lifted my head, and Garrett was sitting on the ottoman, his brow knitted together. "You okay?"

That was a loaded question, but I assumed he was asking about my hands, so I nodded.

"Yes." I smiled. "Thanks."

He grinned, his dimples making me smile even wider.

"You owe me a shirt."

"Okay."

His smile left, and as he took my hands in his, his eyes became glossy. I didn't think I could take it.

"Garrett, don't." I wrapped my arms around his neck, squeezing him tightly, and he took a deep breath. "I'm sorry for scaring you. I really am."

"This isn't your fault," he said sternly. "I just want you to be okay again."

I wanted the same thing.

"You get some rest now." He patted my back softly.

I let go of him, and he kissed the top of my head before leaving, pulling the door closed behind him. Michael stood from the chair, pulling the blankets on my bed down so I could climb in. I slid under the covers and tried to make myself comfortable as he pulled the blankets over me, and then knelt on the floor beside the bed. He rested his head next to mine on my pillow, brushing the side of my face softly with his fingers.

"Please stay with me," I whispered.

He smiled weakly and sighed. "I'm not going anywhere."

My eyes started to close, but I fought to keep them open, not wanting to sleep. It seemed like days since I'd been with Michael, though I knew it had only been hours. I lifted my hand to his hair and combed through the soft strands with my fingers. He closed his eyes, released a soft hum, and opened them again, gazing intently at me.

"You scared me," he whispered. "You really scared me."

"I know."

He took my fingers, kissing each fingertip softly.

"I told her I wasn't afraid of her," I said quietly. "But she knew. She knew I was afraid, and she's right. I am afraid."

His eyes were pained, and he held my hand to the side of his face.

"Stay with me?"

Without hesitation, he climbed onto the bed, lying down behind me. His arms came around me, and I pressed myself into him, feeling like I couldn't get close enough. I felt his lips on the side of my neck, and my body relaxed almost instantly, my breathing slowing as I took a deep breath.

"You sleep," his breath was warm against my skin. "I'm not going to leave."

I nodded and pulled at his arms so they tightened around me, making me feel safe.

Chapter Twenty-Eight

When I woke up, the room was dark except for the glare of the television. I turned to see Michael, and he looked down at me with a slight smile.

"Did I wake you?"

I shook my head and rubbed my eyes. "What time is it?"

"It's after five," he said. "You've slept for over six hours, and I'm not sure that's enough."

I draped my arm over him and laid my head on his chest. I could feel his breath on my hair.

"How do you feel?" he murmured.

"Okay."

"How are the hands?"

"They don't hurt," I told him. "Did you sleep at all?"

"I don't need the sleep. Miles and Dad came in and watched a World War II documentary on the History channel. You slept right through it."

"And you didn't?"

He laughed. "No, it was interesting. Are you hungry?"

"Yeah."

"It's no wonder. You've hardly had anything all day."

I sat up, and he grazed his fingertips over the side of my face.

"Mom saved some dinner for us," he said. "I think she made lasagna."

On cue, my stomach rumbled.

Michael grinned. "That sounds pretty serious. We'd better feed you."

I pushed myself off the bed and walked to the bathroom. When I came into the kitchen, everyone was at the table, but Michael was the only one eating.

"Hey, Gracie!" Kate said cheerily. "How was your nap?"

"Good."

I took my seat between Michael and Garrett. Michael was already finished with his first helping by the time Ava gave me mine, and she piled his plate with seconds.

"Hungry?" I asked with a raised eyebrow.

He poked my ribs playfully making me squirm. When Michael and I finished eating our dinner, everyone congregated in the living room and talked about the plans for the week, which for me, consisted of staying home.

I didn't say anything, because even though everyone had agreed yesterday I could go back to work, I knew bringing it up now would be pointless. Michael would definitely not be giving the go-ahead to go back to work. I leaned against him and traced the back of his hand absent-mindedly with my finger, not really listening to the conversation.

"Gracie," Kate said. "Did you hear me?"

I shook my head. "No. Sorry," I told her. "What'd you say?"

"I asked if you're excited to go back to work tomorrow?" She smiled excitedly. "Kenny and Peggy are so excited they can hardly stand it, and you still haven't met Leslie."

She continued to chatter, but I tuned her out, confused by her question. After today, I assumed I'd be staying home.

"So," Kate asked me expectantly. "What do you think?"

"About what?"

She huffed impatiently, causing everyone to chuckle and repeated what I hadn't heard the first time.

"I said," she talked slowly. "The boys are going with us to work tomorrow. Fun, huh?"

"Um..." I stammered. "I don't think...I'm not sure..."

Michael nudged me with his elbow. "Don't you want to go back to work?"

"Yes," I said. "But I thought—"

"Then you should go." He was telling me I should go back to work. Tomorrow. But I wasn't completely convinced that's what he really wanted me to do.

Will, Ava and Garrett left for the night, and Miles and Kate were embracing by the front door. Michael took me by the hand and led me to my room. I climbed onto the middle of my bed while he leaned back comfortably, watching me.

I narrowed my eyes at him. "Okay. What gives?"

A grin touched the corner of his mouth, and he shrugged casually. "I don't know what you're talking about."

"Hmph," I snorted.

He chuckled and leaned forward in the chair, running his hand through his hair.

"Truthfully," he said with a sigh. "I'm not crazy about you going back. Especially tomorrow."

I waited for the 'but'.

"But," he said. "We all think you really need to go back. You love that place, and it makes you happy to be there."

I certainly wasn't going to argue. If we talked about it too much he might change his mind, or he might change my mind, so I just agreed. I was already in my pajamas, so I went into the bathroom to do my nightly routine to get ready for bed. When I came out, Michael was looking through my movie collection. I stood behind him and wrapped my arms around his waist while he browsed.

"Are we going to watch a movie?" I mumbled against his back.

"No. I'm going to watch a movie. You're going to take one of those pills and go to sleep."

I sighed while Michael slid his movie selection into the DVD player. As I climbed into bed, he opened the prescription bottle and shook out a pill and handed it to me with the bottle of water from my nightstand. I hesitated. Things I didn't want to see flashed through my mind.

Michael leaned down so he was eye-level with me. "It's going to be fine."

"Okay." I swallowed the small pill and Michael took the water and set it on my night table, he plugged in the twinkle lights above my bed and turned off the lamps.

"Do you want me to lie down with you until you fall asleep?" he asked.

I snorted a laugh and raised an eyebrow at him. As if he even needed to ask. He grinned and kicked off his shoes, as I slid under the blankets and he sat against the headboard. I rested my head against his chest, and he held me tightly. The medicine was taking effect and my eyelids became heavy as I watched the movie Michael had chosen.

"I love this movie," I murmured.

His lips brushed against my hair, and I closed my eyes.

"Are you going to stay all night?" My words were slurred, and I never heard his answer.

* * *

As expected, I woke feeling groggy and drugged. Evan told me the medicine was strong, and he wasn't kidding. I rolled out of bed and went to shower, eager to get back to the shop and into some kind of regular routine again.

I took the bandages off of my hand and studied the cuts. They weren't too bad. I decided to dress-up for my first day back. I wore a gray, pleated mini-skirt, black short sleeved v-neck sweater, shimmery gray opaque tights and black ballet flats with a silver buckle. I curled my hair, pulling half of it up into a barrette. I applied a minimum amount of makeup and lip gloss. I wrapped my hands with the fresh gauze Evan left me, and after making my bed I walked out to the hallway.

Kate came toward me, and chirped her 'good morning'. I had to smile. I'd missed our morning routine.

"How'd you sleep?" she asked.

"Like a rock." I shook my head. "Which is good, but that medicine is rough."

"Well, hopefully you won't have to take it for very long," she said. "I'm just glad you slept."

When we got to the front door Michael was there, waiting.

He was wearing jeans and black dress shirt, un-tucked, resembling a model from a magazine. As I walked toward him, his crook-ed smile appeared, and he pushed away from the wall. His gaze heated as I stood in front of him.

"Are you sure this is what you want to wear today?" he asked.

I felt self-conscious right away, rethinking my clothing decision.

"Don't you like it?" I asked. "I could change—"

He pulled me to him, leaning to my ear."I love it, that's the problem," he whispered. "You look absolutely beautiful. I'm not sure I'll be able to concentrate on anything else."

I wanted to roll my eyes at him, but his breath was warm against my ear, making my skin tingle and my heart pound through my chest.

"Well," I swallowed hard. "Maybe you could just help me in the bookstore. That doesn't require too much concentration."

He kissed the hollow beneath my ear tenderly and then studied me carefully. "How are you?"

I had to think a moment about his question, because I was still recovering from feeling his lips on my neck.

"Um, I'm good."

He smiled as he took my hands and looked them over. "How about the hands?"

"They're fine. The bandages are a little annoying."

He kissed each of my palms tenderly before helping me put my coat on, and then we made our way to Miles' car. The ride to the shop was fairly quiet, and Michael kept me pulled tightly to his side the whole way, not saying anything. He was trying not to show the tension I knew he felt. I just leaned against him and felt the comfort of having him close. Miles parked, and we all made our way into the shop, where I was instantly tackled by Kenny.

"Gracie!" He hugged me tightly, and I laughed.

"Hey, Kenny."

He looked me over, and smiled. "You look great," he said. "I've missed you."

"I've missed you, too. How are you?"

He nodded with a grin. "You want your usual?" I nodded and he turned to Michael. "Michael, the usual?"

Michael smiled. "Thanks, man."

Kenny turned to make his way to the coffee counter, and Peggy was standing there with her sweet smile, holding her arms out for a hug.

"Hey, Peg," I said. "It's great to see you."

"I'm glad you're back," she said quietly. "Things aren't the same when you're not here."

"Someone has to keep Kenny in line, right?"

She laughed.

"Hey! I heard that, Burke!" Kenny shouted without turning around.

Michael chuckled as he helped me take my coat off, and Kate took my purse.

"Gracie," she said. "I'll put your things away for you. Maybe you should have a look around."

I could tell she was anxious, Michael stayed close behind me as I walked over to the bookstore and flipped on the lights. The walls were a different color and the floor was different, too. A lump formed in my throat, and I swallowed it down as my mind tried to catch up with what I was seeing.

"You okay?"Michael asked.

"Yeah." My voice wasn't very convincing, and Michael picked up on that fact quickly.

"Honey, you know we had to pull up the carpet," he said softly.

"Kate said you've been wanting to put hardwood flooring in here. Do you like it?"

Of course they'd have to remove the carpet because of the blood. I hadn't really thought about it. I continued to look around, trying to recognize something. I didn't recognize my happy place anymore.

"If you don't like it," Michael sounded nervous. "Garrett will get a crew in here this weekend, and we can fix it any way you want."

The walls were a soft mocha color that coordinated with the coffee shop, and the darker shade of the hardwood complimented the walls perfectly. The look was very warm and very inviting. It was lovely.

I tried to smile. "It's beautiful. Really. You all did a wonderful job. It's just—"

Michael stepped in front of me so he could see my face. "It's just what?"

I sighed. "I don't recognize anything. It's all different."

He pursed his lips together as he watched me carefully. Kate put her arm over my shoulder.

"I know it's different, Gracie," she said sadly. "But you understand that we had to, right?"

"Of course," I said. "Really. It's beautiful. I just have to get used to it, that's all."

She smiled and brushed my hair off my shoulder. "Miles picked the flooring," she said proudly.

Miles smiled sweetly. "I did, but Garrett will try and take the credit." He winked. "You remember, Grace, we can change anything. Just like Michael said, all you have to do is say so."

I stepped over to him and kissed his cheek. "No," I told him. "I think it's wonderful just the way it is."

They really had done a beautiful job. The colors and woodwork were lovely. The shelves of books were organized perfectly, and I could tell Kenny had taken extra care of the place in my absence. I felt a surge of happiness as I slowly began to realize I was back. Back at the place I loved.

Michael smiled as he watched me. I stood on my toes to wrap my arms around his neck.

"Thank you," I whispered.

"For what?"

"For bringing me back here."I loosened my hold on his neck, but he didn't release me. His eyes sparkled, and I couldn't help myself, I pressed my lips to his and kissed him. Fervently and intensely. He responded with the same intensity, and I'd forgotten we weren't alone.

Kate cleared her throat delicately and tugged at the hem of my sweater.

"Gracie, really. Can't you control yourself?"

Miles chuckled and pulled her by the hand towards the coffee shop. I turned back to Michael who was still staring at me with the same intense gaze.

"I can't help it," I said.

He smirked. "We may have to discuss that issue sometime soon."

"What issue?"

He smiled his crooked smile and leaned slowly toward me, brushing his lips along my jaw and down the side of my neck, and I'm pretty sure my skin caught fire. My breath quickened, and he laughed softly by my ear.

"That issue." He pulled away quickly, his eyes dark and intense, and smiled widely at me as he took me by the hand. "Let's go have our coffee."

I couldn't seem to make my brain or my mouth work, so I just nodded. We walked to one of the tables where Kenny had our coffees and some muffins waiting. Miles and Kate were already seated. Kenny pulled up a chair and the five of us talked for a while. I realized as I sat there, that before the Andersons had come into our lives, this shop was my happy place, but now I knew.

Michael was my happy place.

Chapter Twenty-Nine

The day went quickly, as Michael and I unloaded several boxes of books that had been waiting on me. I enjoyed going through each box, and since Michael was with me, I enjoyed it even more. By the time four o'clock came, we'd coded and shelved five boxes. Admittedly, we probably would have had them done much sooner, but after each box Michael would pull me between the shelves of the storeroom and kiss me to death. I loved it.

As we were leaving for the day, I met Leslie Purcell, our new employee. She was about our age, with blonde hair—cropped short, and big blue eyes.

"It's nice to finally meet you, Grace." Leslie said with a friendly smile. "I feel like I know you already. Kenny has talked about you quite a bit."

Kenny waggled his eyebrows wickedly.

I grimaced at him. "We may have to talk about that later, Leslie, just to make sure Kenny got the facts straight."

She laughed and went to help a customer.

"You'd better behave yourself," I threatened Kenny. "I may be out of shape, but I can still kick your butt."

He laughed and patted my head. "I'd never doubt that for a second. See ya tomorrow."

Michael helped me put my coat on, and we started for the door.

"Hey, Gracie?" Kenny called, and I turned to face him. "I'm glad you're back."

"Me, too. Thanks for everything."

When we got home, Ava was busy preparing dinner. The aroma of rosemary and roasted chicken filled the house. Garrett greeted me with a huge bear hug and asked about my day. We all sat down to eat, and for the first time in a while, tension seemed to be at an all-time low. I was extremely tired, but it was a good tired, and I actually looked forward to going to bed just so I could get up and go back to work again.

Michael and I did the dishes together, while the others continued their conversation in the living room. I noticed Michael kept watching me, but when I looked at him he would just grin. Finally, I bumped him with my shoulder.

"What?" I asked.

He chuckled and shook his head.

"I'm just proud of you," he said, sliding a plate into the dishwasher.

"Why? Because I made it through an entire day without having an emotional meltdown?" My tone was derisive, but I knew that probably was his reason for being proud of me.

"Well, I guess that's part of it, although I don't fault you for having emotional meltdowns."

He put the last of the dishes in the dishwasher and then turned to face me.

"You had a lot to deal with today," he said. "And you handled it brilliantly. I'm proud of you."

"Brilliantly?" I raised an eyebrow. "That's the word you'd like to use?"

He seemed to contemplate my question and then nodded. "Yes, I believe that's the word I'd like to use."

I stepped closer to him and combed my fingers through his hair, and his eyes closed for a moment. "Thank you," I said. "Thank you for being with me."

"You don't have to thank me for being with you." He wound his arms around my waist. "I wouldn't have it any other way."

"I'm glad that's how you feel, especially with the way things have been lately."

"What do you mean?"

I shrugged. "I mean, I've been a neurotic, emotional mess for the last few weeks and sometimes I wonder why you don't just run. Far away."

"Why would you say that?" His voice was dejected and angry at the same time.

"I didn't mean anything by it," I replied quickly. "You've just been so patient and amazing."

His head tilted as I tried to explain my stupid insecurity to him.

"I feel…bad that you've had to deal with so much." I lowered my eyes, focusing on the buttons of his shirt. Once again, I'd said things when I should've kept my mouth shut.

I waited. I waited for him to say something. The tension grew until I looked up at him and tried to read his expression.

"With everything I've told you," his voice was stern, but his eyes were soft. "You think there's anything that could possibly make me want to leave?"

I swallowed hard as I thought about his question. The thought of him leaving made me sick at my stomach.

"Grace?" He was impatient as I tried to think of how to answer. "Are you going to answer me?"

"I know you love me, Michael," I said quietly. "I don't doubt that."

"But you doubt something, and I want to know what it is."

"I don't doubt anything," I told him. "I shouldn't have said that."

He narrowed his eyes at me, and I hoped he would just drop the whole thing, but I knew better. Without a word he walked into the living room. I kicked myself mentally over and over. It had been such a great day, and I managed to ruin it with my mouth.

There was no room on the sofa where Michael sat, so I made myself comfortable on the floor in front of Kate and listened half-heartedly to the conversation.

It was Garrett's turn to sleep on the sofa, but Will, Ava and Miles said good night. I waited to see if Michael was going to speak to me. He walked slowly toward me and kissed my forehead.

"Night, Grace," he said quietly and walked out the door.

I wanted to run after him, but I just stood there, feeling miserable.

"Night, Gracie," Kate made her way down the hall to her room.

I turned to see Garrett clumsily trying to shove sheets onto the sofa, which was going to be his bed for the night.

"Here," I said taking the sheets from him. "Let me do it."

I pulled the pillows from the sofa and tucked the sheets around the cushions tightly.

"Who makes your bed at home?" I asked him with a smirk.

He shrugged his massive shoulders. "No one. I kind of just lay on top of everything."

I shook my head, and he laughed as he watched me fix his makeshift bed.

"Here ya go, Goliath." I smirked. "Sleep well."

He bent down so I could kiss his cheek and then flopped onto the sofa making me laugh as I made my way to my room. I pulled pajamas from my dresser and turned on the stereo as I passed to the bathroom. I decided to leave the bandages off of my hands for the night. They weren't bleeding anymore, and I was tired of wearing the stupid things. As I brushed through my hair, the music cut off and I paused with the brush in my hand. After a moment, the familiar vocals of Steve Perry came through singing "Faithfully".

Michael was out there waiting for me.

Half relieved, half anxious, I put my things away quickly and emerged from the bathroom. The lights were all off, except for the twinkle lights, and he was in the chair with his feet crossed on the ottoman, his hands folded behind his head. He looked completely relaxed as his eyes met mine.

"Hi," I said quietly.

He didn't say anything, he just watched as I climbed onto the middle of my bed and sat down with my legs folded. I waited for him to say something, but he didn't, so I decided to do some damage control.

"I'm sorry for what I said," I told him. "I didn't mean anything by it, and I especially didn't mean to make you angry."

I fidgeted nervously, twisting a loose thread on the sleeve of my pajamas around my finger. I could feel his eyes on me. I glanced at him quickly, but he hadn't moved, so my eyes dropped to the thread on my sleeve again. I felt the bed move, and then he was sitting across from me, his legs folded like mine so our knees touched. The soft glow of the twinkle lights cast luminously over his face in a way that was breathtaking.

"You know," he said calmly, taking my hands in his. "You're still just as stubborn and frustrating as you were before I told you how much I loved you."

I wasn't sure what he was getting at, but so far I was a little irritated at being called stubborn, especially by him. But I held my tongue and waited for him to finish.

"I'm not sure why I thought that would change." He sighed. "Nor am I sure I'd want it to change, but—"

Always with the 'but'…

"Why it would ever enter your mind that I'd leave because of the way things have been," he shook his head, "that's what hurts."

I swallowed hard. I'd hurt him and the remorse I felt was painful.

"You've been through so much, and I've watched you. I've watched you go through the physical pain and the emotional distress." His eyes were pained as he spoke. "But through all of it, never once has it ever entered my mind to leave you."

He traced over the cuts on my palms softly with his finger, and I felt ashamed.

"This may surprise you," he said. "But as I've watched you go through this hell, my love for you has grown into something more."

His eyes were full of emotion.

"When I first saw you, I thought you were beautiful—physically beautiful—which, of course, you are." He smiled that crooked smile, and I flushed. "As a man, I was physically attracted to you. But, when I got to know you, I saw how beautiful you are on the inside. Your goodness, your sense of humor, your generosity and thoughtfulness. You are completely and in every sense of the word…beautiful.

"And now, I know your strength," he said shaking his head. "With all of this tragedy, I've witnessed your strength, and the love I had for you in the beginning is small in comparison to the love I have now. And that's the wonderful thing about love, Grace, it just grows and grows."

He chuckled softly. "I'm not sure how I could possibly love you more than I do, but I know I will and that makes me so happy." His brows creased together, and he put his hands on either side of my face. "That's why I never want you to even joke about me leaving you." His voice was full of intensity and made my heart pound. "The thought of leaving you," he closed his eyes, "I can't even think about it without my heart feeling like it will rip into pieces. Please don't ever say that again."

I threw my arms around him, and he pulled me close.

"You're right," I confessed, keeping my face burrowed against his neck. "I guess somewhere in my mind, I was afraid. Afraid all of this might be too much, and you would want to leave. Everything you said, I feel the same way. Please believe me."

He squeezed me tightly as I spoke.

"I do believe you," he said quietly. "But we're going to get through all of this, and I'm not going anywhere. I can't. I won't."

I looked at him then, and his eyes were soft.

"I forgive you." He smiled softly and wiped under my eyes with his thumbs. "And I love you more than you'll ever be able to understand."

"I love you, too."

He leaned closer to me and touched his lips to mine, his tongue lightly teasing my mouth until I thought my heart would explode. My fingers wound through his hair, and he whispered my name against my lips. The thundering in my chest increased as our kiss intensified, and we moved together until we were lying beside each other.

His hands moved to the small of my back and pressed me to him. A low moan escaped his throat as I kissed along his jaw.

"Grace," he murmured, and I knew what he was going to say. I brought my lips to his to prevent him from saying another word.

His hand grazed along my ribcage to my hip and back up again. The heat from his skin seemed to burn through my clothing straight to my insides. My hands explored his hair, lips, jaw, arms, hands, chest, stomach…when I reached the bare skin at the hem of his shirt he moaned, but this time he rolled to his back draping his arm over his eyes.

It was quiet except for our ragged breaths. Rejection flared inside me, and I rolled away from him and scooted off the bed. I could feel his eyes on me, as I walked to the shelf that displayed my DVD collection, pretending to search for something to watch.

"Grace?"

"Hmm?" I didn't look at him.

"Are you okay?"

I exhaled, and turned to face him, crossing my arms over my chest. "No. No, I'm not okay." It surprised me how angry I felt. "Why do you always push me away?"

He was now sitting on the edge of the bed, confusion etched in his features.

"Can I ask you something?" I asked.

He nodded warily.

"You told me you didn't love Allison," I began. "But you had sex with her."

His expression softened, but he didn't speak.

"You say you love me, but you push me away." I felt my face heat. "Don't you want to be with *me*…that way? Don't you…" my eyes found the floor, as I shifted my weight, "don't you want me?"

I was hesitant to look at him, but I did, and his eyebrows were furrowed together in an expression of pain. In one swift movement, I was on his lap with him holding me tightly.

"Grace," his voice was quiet. "How could you even think that?"

His arms tightened around me even more, his lips against my hair.

"You just walk into a room, and it takes all of my self-control not to carry you off somewhere," he said. "I want you all the time. I think about you and I want you, I smell your perfume on my clothes at the end of the day and I want you, I hear you laugh and I want you…don't you understand?"

He loosened his hold so I could look at him.

"You make me feel so different from anything I've ever felt before." He smiled softly. "I've already claimed your heart as mine, and one day, I want to claim the rest of you."

My insides tightened with the promise behind his words.

"I don't want just a part of you, Grace, I want all of you, and when that day comes there won't be any regrets or remorse. When I told you I caused Allison to be broken, it was true, but I was broken, too. Because it was wrong and there was nothing but guilt…and pain. I'm sorry I'm sending you mixed signals, it's just—I want you so much. But, I have to get it right with you."

I stroked the side of his face, and he leaned into my hand.

"I don't want you to be broken," I said.

"The day you told you loved me, I wasn't broken anymore."

He pulled me to him again, and I pressed my lips to his neck.

"So," I said quietly. "Are you still going to kiss me?"

"Every chance I get." He brushed his lips with mine before pulling away. "I think you'd better get some sleep."

Reluctantly, I moved from his hold and pulled the pillows off the bed. Michael picked up one of my prescription bottles and shook a pill into his hand.

"I don't want to take that tonight," I told him quickly.

He froze and his forehead creased. “Why not?”

“Because, it made me feel terrible this morning,” I said. “And I don’t think I need it anyway.”

“Why don’t you think you need it?” His tone was irritated.

I shrugged. “Because I’m tired enough, and I just don’t think I’ll need it.”

“Grace,” he said calmly. “Please don’t be stubborn about this. I can’t bear thinking about you having any more nightmares, or whatever they are, I don’t want you hurt anymore. Please just take it. For me.”

I pursed my lips together tightly, wanting to argue with him. But, again, one argument for the day was enough. I held out my hand, defeated, and he placed the pill in my palm and handed me a bottle of water. I swallowed it obediently, and he smirked the whole time, which made me want to smack him, or just really kiss him. I climbed into bed, and he covered me with my blankets, stroking my hair as he knelt by the side of my bed.

“Won’t you stay?” I asked.

“Just until you fall asleep.”

“You don’t have to stay if you don’t want,” I told him. “I’ll be asleep in about thirty seconds anyway.”

He rolled his eyes. “You have no idea.” He traced his fingers around my eyes and down the side of my face, my skin tingling every place he touched.

“No idea about what?”

“You have no idea how much I want to stay.”

“So stay.” It seemed simple enough to me, but his expression was telling me otherwise. My eyes began to get heavy as he leaned to my ear.

“Sleep well, my Grace,” his breath was hot against my skin, and I shivered.

“Night, Michael.” My words were garbled as I felt sleep taking over. “I love you…more.”

Chapter Thirty

The following two weeks were fairly uneventful, and it was wonderful. I was finally into my regular routine. Michael and I had even started running again, which I'd missed so much. It was slow, very slow at first, but I loved it. I'm pretty sure Michael enjoyed the fact he had to slow down for me instead of the way it used to be, but he'd never admit that. I didn't have to take sleep meds any more. Dr. Murphy said I was doing well, but I should keep the pills close just in case.

Miles and Michael accompanied Kate and I to work every day. Garrett, Will and Ava would come see us at the shop frequently, and it was just like at home—all of us together having a great time. Miles did quite a bit of work from home, and Garrett would take Will with him to check on the jobs in Denver. Michael didn't have much to do yet, but there were things coming up that he'd start working on soon.

As smoothly as things seemed to be going, we all knew Nina was still out there. Nobody ever mentioned her name, but I waited every day for some kind of word from the police department saying they had her in custody. So far, the call hadn't come.

* * *

My alarm woke me, and I got ready for my run. Garrett was snoring like a freight train when I came into the living room. I stifled a laugh at his huge body making the couch look like a piece of children's furniture. I'd feel sorry for him, except I knew he could sleep anywhere, through anything.

The sun was shining and the air was brisk, but it wasn't as cold as it had been. I inhaled the brisk air deeply and pulled on my shoes. The familiar crunching of gravel made me smile as Michael strode to the middle of the drive, zipping up his hoodie. I practically bounced over to him.

He smiled. "Good morning. How'd you sleep?"

"Good," I told him. "You?"

He nodded with a smile as he tucked a strand of my hair behind my ear, and we started our slow jog toward the main road.

As we ran, we talked about Miles and Garrett's upcoming birthday. Kate had found a fellow hummingbird in Ava as they planned for the party.

"Did you have big birthday parties when you were young?" I asked Michael as we turned around at our regular point on the main road.

"Not really," he said. "Our birthdays are so close together, and they always seemed to coincide with our family vacations. We always had cake and presents."

He smiled wistfully.

"One summer we drove our RV here. Well, to the Springs, and we went to Garden of the Gods. Garrett kept getting car sick, he threw up at least once a day. It was awful for him and for us. Mom had made the three of us a big birthday cake in the RV." He raised an eyebrow. "I don't know how she managed that, but she and Dad were singing happy birthday to the three of us and Garrett threw up everywhere. All over the cake."

He laughed, and I wrinkled my nose laughing, too.

"Ewww," I said.

"Yeah." He shook his head. "Poor mom. She put all that work into the cake, and Garrett puked all over it. Of course after that, Miles and I didn't really want any cake."

I laughed in a loud burst. "I'm surprised you still eat cake now."

"Miles and I didn't for a while, but you know Garrett. Nothing deters him from food. He asked mom to make another cake and she did, but it wasn't until we got home because the RV smelled like vomit."

I shook my head still laughing.

"Did you take any more RV trips after that?" I asked.

"Just one," he said. "To Florida. It was fun, so I suppose that made up for what we now affectionately refer to as the 'Vomit Vacation from Hell'."

We both laughed.

"I guess every family experiences some kind of vacation from hell," I told him. "It's nice to know your family is just as normal as everyone else's."

He grimaced at me and I laughed as we continued to run.

Suddenly, without warning, Michael had me in his arms for a split second, and then I was sliding across the shoulder of the road as if he'd tossed me. A sharp pain stung the side of my head, and a loud ringing echoed in my ears. There was a squeal of tires, and Michael's voice groaned in pain as I tried to push myself up, but I was too dizzy. After a moment, I realized what was happening, and bile rose in my throat.

The familiar red Porsche was only a few feet away, the front end facing me, engine still running with the driver's side door open. Nina stood with her back to me. Her arms were extended in front of her, and her hands were trembling uncontrollably as she held a gun.

Michael was lying on his side, blood on his face, grasping at his right leg.

"Why? Why, Michael?" Nina sobbed, her whole body convulsing and trembling. "Why couldn't you just love me? That's all I wanted…was for you to love me…like I love you!"

"Nina," Michael's voice was weak with the pain. "You don't love me. You don't even know me."

"Yes, I do!" She screeched. "And if it weren't for her, you would have loved me, too!"

She didn't take her eyes off of him. This was it. This was what she'd been waiting for. It wasn't just me she wanted to kill. It was Michael, too. She wanted both of us dead.

"Nina, please," Michael's voice was soothingly calm. "Please, just listen to me. You need help. Let me help you."

She shook her head. "You don't want to help me," she sobbed. "You just want her!"

"I do want to help you, Nina," Michael pleaded. "You don't have to do this. It doesn't have to be this way. We spoke to your father. He loves you, Nina. He wants to help you, too."

"You shut up about my father!" She screamed. "You don't know anything!"

Michael was trying to reason with her, but I knew she wasn't going to listen to reason. I was tired of her, and I'd had enough. I wasn't going to let her hurt him.

It was enough.

A warm stream of blood trailed down the side of my face as I looked around me, spotting a tree branch within my reach. It was several inches in diameter and about three feet long. It would do the job. I pushed to my feet and took the branch in both hands. I was dizzy, but steadied myself quickly.

Nina continued to screech at Michael, her hands trembling as she held the gun over him. Michael's eyes looked over at me inadvertently and grew wide in horror as Nina turned the gun on me.

She wasn't fast enough.

I was swinging the branch as if I were swinging a baseball bat. The gun flew out of her hands and hit the ground in front of Michael, and he scrambled across the gravel to pick it up.

Nina screamed. Whether it was pain or anger, I didn't know. I didn't care either. I swung again, hitting her shoulder and knocking her to the ground, then hurled myself on top of her. I thrust my fist against the side of her face, feeling a sting of pain in my knuckles as I made contact. Nina's eyes rolled in the back of her head for a moment, and she tried to grab hold of my hair, but I punched her again and then once more.

"Enough!" I shouted at her.

I grabbed her hair at the roots, slamming her head hard against the ground.

"Do you hear me, Nina? Enough! This is over!"

She released me, and her head lolled to the side. I was still on top of her and she let out a low moan.

"It's over!" Her eyes met mine as I screamed in her face. "It's over!"

As I looked in her eyes, I knew it was. It was over.

I rolled off of her and crawled dizzily to Michael. He embraced me, and I couldn't hold him tight enough. I felt sick and relieved and exhausted all at the same time.

"Are you okay?" I asked him.

"Pretty sure my leg is broken," he said. "What about you?"

I just nodded, keeping my eyes on his face.

"You're bleeding," he said with a wince, as he touched the side of my head.

I smirked. "So what else is new?"

He tried to smile as I kissed him tenderly. The door of Nina's car slammed, and we both jerked around. The engine revved, and Michael put his arms around me protectively as gravel spit from the back tires as she peeled onto the road. What happened next was like something from a movie being shown in slow motion.

As Nina fishtailed onto the main road, an eighteen-wheeler came barreling down at a high rate of speed. It collided with the rear end of the Porsche, causing it to spin out of control across the road and into a tree. The truck's brakes squealed loudly as the driver tried to bring it to a stop, but obviously, those trucks don't stop quickly. The right side of the Porsche was crumpled against the tree, and Nina's body was lifeless against the driver's side window. Michael already had his cell phone out of his pocket and was dialing, but I couldn't take my eyes off Nina.

Something stirred in me again as I watched her. It wasn't anger or hatred. It was pity.

I saw her father's face in my mind. The dream of Mr. Sandler looking for his little girl, and not being able to see her. Calling for her, but not being able to find her. His little girl was in that car.

A quick flash of fire ignited on the inside of Nina's car, and I saw her move.

She wasn't dead, and I couldn't let her die. Not like this. I scrambled to my feet.

"Grace!" Michael grasped at my hand, but it was too late.

I ran across the road and pulled at the driver's door, the smell of gasoline strong. My arms stung from the heat as I wrapped them around Nina's torso. I pulled with everything I had, trying to drag her from the car.

"GRACE!" Michael shouted.

She was dead weight, but I managed to free her. I continued to pull, dragging her as far away as I could from the car now completely engulfed in flames. There was a loud explosion, and I fell on top of her. I covered my ears attempting to block out the deafening noise. The smoke swirled around me, and I could feel the heat from the fire.

"Are you okay, Miss?"

An unrecognizable voice was at my ear. My head was spinning as I tried to focus my eyes. I made the assumption he was the truck driver.

"Yeah." I tried to catch my breath, and my throat felt raw. "I'm okay."

Michael was still shouting from across the road, his voice anguished. I checked Nina quickly, trying to see if she was still breathing. She was, though it was barely.

"The ambulance is coming," the man said.

"Stay with her please," I told him.

He nodded and I made my way back to Michael, my arms stinging and my head spinning. His eyes welled with tears as he reached for me.

"What were you thinking?" He squeezed me to him fiercely.

"Why? Why would you do that?" He held me so tight, I couldn't move. He didn't say anything, just buried his face in my neck.

Garrett's Hummer squealed to a stop in front of us. Miles, Will, Ava, Garrett, Kate—all of them, were at our sides in a moment. Embracing, crying and questioning all at once.

Two ambulances arrived, along with several police cars and a fire truck. Nina was loaded into the back of the first ambulance, and Michael was put into the second. Garrett argued with the driver of the ambulance until he relented and allowed Garrett to ride with his little brother.

A third ambulance arrived for me. I argued, but because of the blood on my head, and burns on my arms, I didn't have a choice. Kate rode with me while the others followed in the Hummer. On the ride to the hospital, I told Kate everything that happened, while the medic worked on me. I started to feel the cut on my head, and my arms stung with pain.

Kate squeezed me tightly and cried.

At the hospital, I was so relieved to see Evan's face. Of course, he was in full-doctor-mode as he checked Michael first, but Michael told him not to worry about him and to check on me.

He was the one with the broken leg, for crying out loud.

While Michael was having his leg x-rayed, Evan sutured my head. Kate stayed with me and held my hand. I had to have six stitches. He then took care of the burns on my arms. They weren't bad, just bad enough to sting.

"One thing's for sure, Grace," Evan said as he'd stitched up my head. "Since I've moved back to Fall Rivers, my life hasn't been boring. And most of the excitement has been because of you."

Kate giggled, and I rolled my eyes at him.

"Very funny."

He laughed, as he finished the sutures, kissed my forehead, and then wrinkled his nose. "You don't smell very good either," he added.

Kate really thought that was funny, and I punched him in the arm.

I cleared my throat, which was a little scratchy from the smoke. "Evan? How's Nina?"

He busied himself with the supplies on the tray in front of him.

"Not good," he replied. "She's in Intensive Care. Do you want me to find out what's going on?"

"Thanks," I told him. "Can I go see Michael now?"

"Sure."

Kate and I followed him to Michael's room. Will, Garrett, Ava and Miles all stood around his bed. When we walked inside, the nurse got huffy.

"There are too many people in here," she snapped.

"It's fine, Melinda," Evan said authoritatively. "I'll take responsibility for them."

Garrett stifled a laugh, and the nurse shot him a nasty look.

"It's okay," Evan assured her. "They aren't going to be any trouble. If they are, I'll take care of the big guy myself."

Garrett guffawed then, and the rest of us laughed as Melinda rolled her eyes and finished doing whatever she was doing before leaving the room.

"I'll go find out what's happening with Nina," Evan said. "You guys behave yourselves. Michael, you need anything?"

Michael didn't take his eyes from mine as he shook his head. Evan patted my shoulder as he walked out of the room, closing the door behind him. I strode to Michael's side quickly.

"How are you?" I asked, as he held my hands.

He nodded, and his eyes were so full of emotion it was difficult to look into them.

"What about you?" he asked.

I shrugged, and Kate sighed with irritation.

"She had to have six stitches," Kate informed him. "And she has burns on her arms."

Michael shook his head. "Garrett's right. You're something else."

Garrett snickered, and I scowled at him.

"Only you would save the person who has made your life miserable for so long," Garrett said. "Not just save her, but pull her from a burning car."

Everyone watched as my face turned red, and Michael squeezed my hand tightly.

"There's a difference in stubbornness and recklessness," he said.

"All I could think about was Nina's father. She's still his little girl. I just couldn't let her die, not like that."

I knew he understood, and I also knew if his leg hadn't been broken, he would've done the same exact thing. Everyone was still watching me, but I kept my eyes on Michael.

He winced in pain. "I think my medication must be wearing off." He closed his eyes and I ran my fingers through his hair, I hated seeing him in pain.

"I'll go tell the nurse." I started to leave, but he held my hand tight, not letting me move from my spot.

"I'll go," Miles said.

A few minutes later, a doctor came in and said that because of the type of break Michael had, he would require surgery for it to be set properly. They had it scheduled for two o'clock, and the nurse gave him some more medication to help the pain.

"I'm sorry," I told him.

He shook his head. "Yes," he said sardonically. "I know."

Garrett chortled a laugh, and when I glared at him, he pretended to cough.

"Why don't you go home and get a shower," Michael said. "I know you're dying for one."

He knew me well. The stench of gasoline and smoke was embedded in my nostrils. I figured my clothes and hair had the same stench.

"Well, I'm sure you're dying for me to have one," I told him. "But I'd rather not leave, thank you very much."

He rolled his eyes and turned to Ava. "Mom, would you please reason with her?"

I giggled. "Seriously? You're really telling your mom on me?"

Everyone laughed, including him. "Yes. She's the only one you won't argue with."

I rolled my eyes as everyone continued to laugh, and Ava winked at me.

"Come on, Grace Elizabeth," she said authoritatively. "Let's go get you cleaned up before he has to go into surgery."

"I'll go with you," Kate said and turned to Miles, giving him a kiss. "We'll be back soon."

"I'll be right back," I told Michael. "Don't be going anywhere."

He shook his head. "Very funny."

I started to walk away, but he held my hand tight, pulling me to him.

"What's wrong?" I asked.

"You're not going anywhere without giving me a kiss."

I bent down and kissed him, softly feeling the familiar heart-flutter as he smirked.

Garrett chuckled and patted my head. "You go ahead and shower, Gracie." He held his nose between his fingers and made a face. "Please. Go shower."

I punched his arm, and Ava pulled me from the room with Kate following. We all climbed into the Hummer, and Ava drove us home. I showered quickly, wincing when the shampoo stung the cut on my head, but I shampooed and shampooed again, making sure I was free of the stench of gasoline. I slathered Michael's favorite smelling lotion all over me and got dressed in jeans and a pink tee shirt with a black zip-up cardigan. I brushed my teeth and blew my hair only partially dry, twisting it up into a clip. I put on my shoes quickly, and once again, we were in the Hummer, driving back to the hospital.

When we got there, they'd moved Michael to a regular room. Will, Miles and Garrett were watching television, and Michael appeared to be sleeping. I went to the side of his bed quietly, and sat in the chair, wanting to touch him but not wanting to wake him.

"You smell good," he murmured without opening his eyes, a smile on his face.

I leaned to him and kissed his neck. His smile widened as I combed my fingers through his hair, and he opened his eyes.

"Hey," I said.

"Hey, yourself." He reached his hand to the side of my face, stroking my cheek gently. "You feel better?"

"I no longer smell like unleaded," I said. "How's the leg?"

"Broken."

I grimaced. As I watched him, something occurred to me.

"You saved me today. Nina was going to hit me with her car. That's why you got hurt instead of me."

"You got hurt anyway." He touched the stitches on the side of my head that were hidden under my hair.

I shook my head and held his hand to the side of my face. "I'm fine," I said. "Because of you, I'm fine."

Chapter Thirty-One

They took Michael into surgery, and all of us waited in the cafeteria. Ava insisted I eat something because I hadn't eaten all day. Will brought me a bagel and cream cheese with an apple and a bottle of water.

"I can't believe you're eating hospital food."

Evan stood next to our table with a smug grin on his face.

"Desperate times," I said with a smile. "Have a seat."

He pulled up a chair and folded his hands together on the table with a somber expression. I knew what he was going to say before he said it.

"Nina's dead. There was too much internal damage. They couldn't save her."

Everyone was silent. I looked down at my plate feeling a lump form in my throat, and Garrett pulled me to his side.

"I'm sorry, Grace," Evan said quietly. "They did everything they could."

"Was she alone?"

Garrett squeezed me tightly.

"Her parents were with her," Evan said. "They're still here, I think."

I started to stand up, but Garrett held me close.

"I should go see Mr. Sandler," I told Garrett. "He must be so heartbroken."

Tears were coming now, and Garrett shook his head sadly.

"I know you're worried, but it's probably best if they're alone right now."

I wiped my eyes and looked around the table, everyone watching me carefully.

"Grace," Will said. "Garrett's right. Now probably isn't the time."

"Poor Mr. Sandler." I leaned into Garrett again, and he rested his head on top of mine. Evan reached across the table and held my hand in his.

"I'm really sorry."

"Thanks, Evan." I smiled at him. "I appreciate you letting me know. I'm glad you were here."

He nodded as he stood up."I have to get back," he said. "Garrett, you guys stop by and see me before you leave okay?"

"You bet," Garrett said. "Thanks, man."

Evan waved as he walked out of the cafeteria.

"Gracie," Kate said. "You should eat."

I nodded and picked at the bagel, thinking about Michael. And about Mr. Sandler.

* * *

The Orthopedic surgeon came into the waiting room and informed us the surgery went well. We all sighed in relief as Kate squeezed my hand tightly.

"Michael is in recovery now," the doctor said. "I can take one of you back."

Reflexively I looked over at Ava. As much as I wanted to be with Michael at that moment, she was his mother, and I waited for her. She smiled sweetly as she touched the side of my face.

"I'll just see him for a minute, then I'll come and get you," she promised.

I nodded and watched as she followed the doctor to go see Michael. I sat down, nervously wringing my hands together, wanting to see him. Ava kept her promise and returned to the waiting room rather quickly. She took my hand and I followed her.

"He's asking for you." She smiled. "He's just beginning to come out of the anesthesia, so he's uncomfortable."

I nodded as we reached the recovery room. She pushed a large silver button, and the door swung open.

"I'll see you in the waiting room." She smiled and patted my hand as I walked through the door.

The long room was quiet except for the beeping of monitors and the low discussions of the nurses. Curtains separated at least ten beds, and I walked slowly toward the nurse's desk.

"Grace Burke?" I nodded at the red-haired nurse that stood at the end of one of the beds. "He's been asking for you."

She smiled kindly and motioned to the bed across from her, and I thanked her quietly before walking over to see Michael. He was asleep, his leg in a full cast, elevated on several pillows. I sat down next to him and took his hand in mine. He didn't move, but I kissed his fingers and stroked his hair. I didn't know if he knew I was there or not, but it felt good to touch him. His head rolled to the side, and he swallowed hard and winced in pain.

"Grace," his voice was rough.

"I'm here," I said quietly. "I'm here with you."

"I love you."

"I love you more," I whispered in his ear.

I kissed by his ear and then along the soft stubble of his jaw, until I met his lips, where I kissed him gently. The machines beeped loudly, and I flinched, worried about what was happening.

The nurse came in, pushed a button, and winked at me. That's when I realized, his heart reacted the same way mine always did, and I had to smile. All those times he would laugh at my reaction to his kiss. He was just better at hiding it, but now I knew. Maybe both of our hearts weren't big enough for the love we had for each other. I shrugged at the nurse, and she laughed as she walked to the patient next to us.

I leaned to his ear. "Can you hear me?" I asked him.

He nodded weakly and I kissed his neck tenderly.

"You're in big trouble, mister," I whispered. "You just think you're so smart."

A small smile touched his lips, and his voice was rough.

"I love you, my Grace."

* * *

Nina's funeral was in Denver at two o'clock, and I was going.

I felt like I had to, not for me, but for Nina's father. I had no hatred toward Nina. I felt sadness for her father, and though I'd never met her, Nina's mother. I didn't mention it to anyone. I didn't want them to do anything they didn't want to just because of me. If Michael asked, I would tell him, but I wouldn't ask him to go with me.

I got dressed in my black pencil skirt and black sweater, curled my hair and applied a small amount of makeup before putting Michael's necklace around my neck, smiling as I read the words on the small heart. I slipped into my black heels and made my way out of my room. The house was quiet, and when I came toward the living room, I froze in surprise.

Everyone was there.

Michael, Will, Ava, Kate, Miles and Garrett. All of them were dressed for the funeral, and they were waiting for me. Michael hobbled on his crutches to where I was standing.

"We knew you'd want to go, Grace," he said. "Do you really think we'd let you go by yourself?"

"You should know better than that, Gracie-Beth," Garrett said. "We're family. We're together."He kissed my head as he walked outside, and everyone filed out after him. I turned to look at Michael who watched me carefully.

"I just didn't want to make you feel like you had to go because of me," I explained. "I didn't want you to do something you didn't want to do."

He sighed and his eyes gazed into mine. “Don’t you understand? Everything I do now is for you. You’re everything, and I’m not going to waste a single moment.”

His words resonated in my mind as his lips met mine, warm and soft, and I knew with all my heart, I wouldn’t waste a single moment either.

About the Author

J. M. Hill is a wife, and a mother of five. She was born and raised in the beautiful state of Colorado, but now resides in the beautiful state of North Carolina.

She loves to write, but her family is her passion.

Other loves include an endless list of music and movies, an unhealthy obsession with Sylvester Stallone which she cannot explain, so don't ask, as well as a love for thunderstorms, snow, coffee, and cheesecake.

She is currently working on her second novel in *The Grace Series*. Lovers of Garrett Anderson take heart, his story is next in line.

21271518R00183

Made in the USA
Charleston, SC
12 August 2013